BLOOD
DIAMOND

C DEVLIN NOVEL

KEATING

HODDER

D0248694

First published in Great Britain in 2012 by Hodder & Stoughton
An Hachette UK company

This paperback edition first published in 2012

1

A CIP catalogue record for this title is available from the British Library

ISBN 978 1 444 72786 9

Typeset in Simoncini Garamond by Hewer Text UK Ltd, Edinburgh

Printed and bound by Clays Ltd, St Ives plc

Hodder & Stoughton policy is to use papers that are natural, renewable
and recyclable products and made from wood grown in sustainable
forests. The logging and manufacturing processes are expected to
conform to the environmental regulations of the country of origin.

Hodder & Stoughton Ltd
338 Euston Road
London NW1 3BH

www.hodder.co.uk

For my parents

But ships are but boards, sailors but men:
there be land-rats and water-rats,
water-thieves and land-thieves;
I mean pirates . . .

Shylock
The Merchant of Venice

Prologue

*T*he gentleman in the purple silk banyan and cap looked out over the ornamental gardens – not his gardens, only leased, along with the London mansion that had lately become his home.

January. An icy January. No wonder one could not enjoy fountains in this miserable city if even the Thames froze solid.

The gown hoisted itself as he set his hands on his hips, revealing bone-thin ankles and slipper-heels to the dark official sitting quietly several feet behind him.

The gentleman's back rose and fell as he took in the futility and desperation that now faced them. Faced the whole country.

He watched the peacocks on the lawn beyond and promised himself to shoot one after this tiresome meeting was adjourned. At last he spoke again.

'Well, how does one find a "pirate"? If that is our only choice.'

The official in black serge and Mechlin cravat shifted in his seat. He was senior in years to the gentleman at the window but lacked the capacity for indulgence that made the other seem the older man.

'Not our only choice, but for secrecy and immediate solution it has many avenues through which we may profit.'

The purple gown rustled downwards again as the gentleman turned to face the official. 'How so, profit?' Still a trace of accent remained in his vowels that years of cavorting in London had failed to erase.

A fidgeting emanated from the chair. 'If we engage a pirate for the task I believe we will more likely minimise future intrusions on our goodwill than if we choose a native party. Awarding a pirate a Mart will enable him to legalise his trade and grant him freedom from persecution by our navy, naturally. Then he will be gone. Back to the seas. A pirate will come with his own ship, his own men. We will leave no paper trail beyond these walls and the principals involved.' The official shifted again, leaning his chin into his hand. 'And, should he refuse our proposal, it would not seem untoward that such a fiend be destroyed, for that is our duty; and if he fails ... what mystery is there in a pirate attempting such an action?'

The gentleman nodded agreement. 'And of course he would want to be unknown? His life is discretion, no?' He pointed sharply. 'But he must be *good*. Perfect in fact. Already a success so he should not want to betray us. He should have no objective other than reward and pardon for his crimes to continue under sanction. Less than a base man would want.'

'Precisely.'

The gentleman picked up a burnished carapace paperweight from his escritoire and made it swim to and fro. 'But again, how does one find a such a man?'

'I have already taken the liberty of drafting a letter to accompany every packet that sails for the Americas and New Spain. I am sending a political advisor with the letter on every South Sea Company vessel. Any ship that is due to sail the pirate round will deliver such a letter until the appropriate party is found.'

'The "pirate round"? How so this?'

'The Caribbean, the Carolinas, the slave coast, New Spain,

Newfoundland, the Verdes. It will not be perfect. That is why I have given plenty of time for the task. We need only panic if September comes too soon.'

The gentleman put back the tortoiseshell. 'But who is to receive the letter? Who have you in mind that is neither too loathsome nor incapable?'

The other drummed his fingers on the arm of his chair and thought on the fact that the chosen man had been his decision alone, and his blame alone should all go wrong. But no matter; come September half the world would be ruined if he did not act.

'I have thought on a rogue known as Devlin. An Irishman, but no matter for all that. He has excelled beyond the curse of his birth.'

'How so? I have never heard of him?'

'It is pertinent that one only hears of "unsuccessful" pirates. Those of us in the polite world only know of them when they are . . . no more. This pirate Devlin has shown himself to be most able.'

'How so?'

The repetition of this question with its faint German inflection still caused subtle amusement in the official, although he had known the gentleman for years now and was sufficiently familiar to call him, in certain circles, a friend.

He cleared his throat, recalling the notes studied on the carriage journey to Leicester House.

'This is the same pirate that stole a considerable sum of gold from out of French pockets, and ours, some years back. Gold we had intended for our own use once we became aware of its existence. A year later he bought his freedom with the secret of the art of porcelain, which we gratefully profit from, as does all Europe, which shows he is a man not unaccustomed to

3

subterfuge and espionage while wishing scant profit for himself other than his ongoing freedom. You will know something of this in that he cost us one of our finest international agents. A man I had thought impossible to destroy and have found impossible to replace.'

The gentleman nodded at some memory of this, although the name escaped him. 'He killed him?'

'He killed him. And escaped from imprisonment on New Providence under the very roof of Governor Rogers. He has also collected enemies in our allies, all of whom have orders against him. Another reason why he may be willing to accept the sanctity of the crown. For a time at least. As we see fit.'

A small silence reigned as the gentleman tapped at his chin and lingered over the idea. 'Very well, Walpole. To your business, and bother me no further with the matter until the pirate is before me. I wish my father and my wife to hear none of this. Promise two thousand pounds to this pirate and my warrant. His head if he fails.'

Robert Walpole, Paymaster General, stood and bowed. From the door, already opened as if by some secret signal, a footman appeared holding his hat and cloak. Walpole, head still lowered, backed out of the room.

'Your servant, Your Highness. Our success is already written.'

Chapter One

London. August 1720

Seven months later.

*T*he gentleman in the black coat was Edwin Tinkerman's third fare of the Monday morning. He had just dropped off at Morris's causeway in Limehouse in the hope of having time for a pie, but the brown boots stomped into his wherry before he had time to decline. A shout from a neighbouring wherryman, however, halted his forming objection.

'Ho, governor, don't be sailing with young Edwin there! He'll bill you sixpence befores you sits down! I'll takes you for threepence anywheres you aim to. Step lively now, governor. Over here, now! Threepence to the city!'

Edwin motioned his passenger to sit as he yelled back. 'George Temple, you can busy yourself. When you gets your Doggett coat you can charge sixpence. Now, *off.*' He flicked a dismissive wave to his competition and hard eyes to the others who had begun to row towards the fare.

'Where to, Cap'n?' he enquired, for the man had the look of the sea about him, with his tanned skin and salt-bleached boots.

The gentleman tipped back his hat. 'How comes you get to charge sixpence, Edwin?' His voice sounded amused.

Edwin straightened himself proudly, still holding an oar,

and ran his free hand over his fine red wool coat. 'Ain't you seen me red Doggett, Cap'n?' He twisted his left arm to show his large silver badge, 'Or me silver horse? Hanover horse, no less. I wins the Doggett last month ain't I? Fastest wherryman on the Thames ain't I?' His passenger shook his head. Edwin winked. 'Ah, you been away ain't you, Cap'n? A man who don't know me Doggett, don't know London.' Edwin set to his pushing off, nodding that he was listening as the gentlemen replied.

'Aye, Edwin. I've been away ten years now,' he pointed a lazy hand vaguely north. 'Near the Pelican I used to be.'

'Ah, The Devil's Tavern, eh, Cap'n? You lived a rough one,' he said, and gave another wink to indicate that he meant no offence. 'I don't do those steps after midnight lest I don't sees me missus evermore.' But he had heard enough of his gentleman's past. 'Where to then, Cap'n? Mind I don't go near the bridge this time and tide for less than a shilling.'

They had moved off shore into the thoroughfare and the gentleman took pause as the magnitude of bodies and ships swamping the river burst onto his senses like a thunderclap.

From the streets on land one could hear the rhythm of mallets, the haul of chain and rope and the working shouts from the water: the background noise of the city. By looking up at the rooftops one could follow the meander of the Thames by the thicket of masts etching out every inch of her against the sky, but nothing had prepared him for the sight of the city's lifeblood pulsing along the current.

Amongst the fleet of ships that lined her wharves for miles toiled nearly five thousand watermen like Edwin, who sculled and rowed their hoys and wherries between the plying stairs of Surrey and the city, like beetles scuttling over pig slurry, whilst the giant barks towered over them; only St Paul's dwarfing them, dwarfing everything. The river seemed more wood than water and Edwin turned back to look as the thrill of it silenced his passenger – a man clearly used to wider, freer waters. 'Where to, Cap'n?'

Edwin's fare tore his gaze from the walls of oak now blotting out the lesser buildings, so that only the stone medieval city remained proud, hazy through a fog of coal-smoke.

'I'm to Leicester House. I have an appointment there.'

Edwin nodded and bit his lip. He appraised his fare differently now. A sailor of sorts but one of some note if the house of the Prince of Wales was his destination. Perhaps some great deed in the war was to be rewarded – or taxed, which was more likely.

'I'll take you to Execution stairs, Cap'n. Safe for a gentleman to get off at Execution.'

Edwin stalled expertly as a train of five passed before his bow and doffed their caps to his red coat. 'You can get a chair there or walk it. Only four mile from there, Cap'n.' He resumed the pace that had won him his jacket and rowed his way effortlessly upstream.

'It's all coal now, Cap'n.' Edwin nodded to the black ships lining the north shore, but still the cages of geese and other animals seemed to dominate. Or perhaps that was more from their vocalisation than their majority.

'Coal and paper. Tons of paper. We've daily sheets now, Cap'n. You can even buy daily prints of the Bailey's trials. I can find out what me father's been up to without asking me mam,' he winked yet again.

Silence now, just the plash of oar as rounding Rotherhithe the spectacle widened and demanded quiet respect. The whole of St Paul's lay before them, presiding over the jumble of smoking buildings below her still gleaming dome and columns built new from The Fire. In the distance, mired in a dark auburn cloud of yet more smoke, a small village seemed to float above the Thames.

The bridge.

Piled four-stories high with shops and dwellings and the doll's-house prettiness of Nonsuch House that stood over the Surrey entrance to the bridge, its four onion domes as tall as St Paul's.

The bridge. For six hundred years it had been the only walkway in and out south of the city, and the thousands of men like Edwin Tinkerman had enough sway to keep it so.

A quiet twenty minutes later, his fare not much one for talking, Edwin had reached the Execution stairs with its green walls and wet stone walk; sounds of revelry came wafting down from the casement windows of the Bell inn above.

Just visible, topping the water, stood the iron stake where at low tide the corpses of those tried and condemned for their wickedness at sea would sit on the shoal and wait for the solemn waters to wash over them three times before being pitched and gibbeted to hang as a warning, at Graves Point, to all those young men who might suppose that a life of piracy had more lure than honest sweat and sinew.

Edwin's fare alighted with easy balance, perfectly upright, well used to stepping from wood to shore, and slapped a shilling into his calloused palm in the same step.

Edwin protested honestly. 'I can'ts change a shilling, Governor. Not this early.'

The sailor turned back with a deep sniff of the rancidness of Wapping. 'I don't need change Edwin, but remember my face. If I need across in a hurry look out for me and I'll look out for your red coat. Could that be a deal?'

Edwin agreed and studied the sailor. Tall. Black hair, no

wig, no bow. Thirty, maybe, but the sea had made his eyes older. Good black twill coat and hat. Those ancient brown bucket-top boots.

'Aye, Cap'n, I'll remember you.' He tipped his hat. 'Good luck to you, Cap'n.' And he pushed off again into the rushing lanes.

Walking up the wet green steps still bubbling from the morning tide the sailor dodged past the shrunken corpse of a dead horse. Its tongue was missing, chewed out by rats, and two dogs ignored him as they growled at each other over the ownership of the animal's pizzle. He shook his head at the surprised look of the horse in its ignominy. London had changed very little.

A narrow alleyway ran straight off the steps. Tall stone walls blocked the light and funnelled the stench of Wapping straight into his face as the passage cambered upwards to the throng of people in the bright street ahead.

To his right he eyed a figure slumped against the black wall with lowered head and hat, drunk or pretending to be so, a smouldering clay pipe hanging from his lips. Early in the morning to be the worse for it, he thought, even for London.

The sailor raised himself as the traveller went by. The six foot and more of him would not be an easy mark. On his left, a few strides further, another wretch slumbered against a barrel, with bare chest and naked feet. To this one the sailor drew aside his coat to show the hilt of his sword, even though its presence was obvious by the rise of his left coat-tail. Still, a glimpse of steel would not hurt.

It was more his custom to wear his unfashionable cross-belt over his coat: all the swifter to draw. He had deferred to custom to seem more like a gentleman for the company that would follow at the end of his journey.

Twenty feet more to the street – moments away – but his shoulders sank as he heard the call behind him. He was sorry that they had not let him walk on.

'Ho, Governor!' came a friendly chirrup. 'I thinks you've dropped something. Wait up, Governor.'

He could carry on. Hurry to the breech of the alley with his back to them. But he knew them. Had known them all his life. They could run like rats and he would only be presenting them his kidneys. He could run though. He would make the street most definitely if he ran.

The chirrup continued, a scuffle of feet hurrying behind him. 'Dropped your purse, Governor: I has it here for you.'

But he never ran *from*. Towards, yes. Not from. Not any more.

Both sets of feet with him now, and still the voice, from his right, the one with the pipe, rasping from wood chip in his tobacco rotting him since childhood.

'Didn't you hear me! You dropped your *coin*!' The last word breathless as a knife drew back to pierce the twill coat and a hand reached for the collar.

The coat spun before the strike and the sailor's fist exploded with pistol and partridge shot into the bare chest of the footpad's partner. The footpad watched his mate fly back, red across his chest, and fall to the cobbles, dropping his small steel. The sound of shot still echoed around the passage as his mate choked on his lungs.

The footpad switched back to the sailor, his knife stayed by the grin that came with the sailor's voice as he holstered his smoking giant of a pistol.

'You dropped your friend.' His hanger glinted free, sweeping away the last of the pistol smoke as a beckoning hand invited the footpad closer. 'Come on. Show me my coin, then.'

The man stepped back, held his small gully blade loyally if

not courageously. His wide eyes were wedded to the wave of the sword. The sailor came on slowly, grinned wider. Then the shadows of others loomed from the mouth of the alley. His shot had brought curious eyes. No matter, this was by far his right. Still, he had hoped for a more innocuous entrance.

The footpad called out, his neck straining high, his voice higher.

'Jon! Jon! He's killed Arthur!'

The sailor did not look behind him but moved his free hand to the back of his belt where his dagger waited. He carried on but his ears pricked at the clump of wooden soles behind him.

The footpad aimed an accusing finger, lowered his knife. '*Him*, Jon,' then pointed the finger to his dying accomplice. 'Shot up Arthur he has!'

A bulk appeared beside the sailor, a gentle hand on his shoulder. 'Put up now, sir. Let's hear the tale of it.'

The sailor looked at the hand, then the body it belonged to. As tall as him, just over six feet. A gentleman, trying to be, but a farmer's quizzical scowl designated him a man doing better than he should by birth. He wore dirty lace and linen and a filigree sword more for ceremony than filleting. Only the heavy cudgel in his right hand signified that he worked at something – and that something distasteful.

The sailor looked at the crowd gathering and put away his sword. 'I defended myself, constable, if constable you be?'

'My name is Jonathan Wild, sir, if you do not know. I will be addressed by you in the next moment as Thief-Taker General, if you please. What be you called now, sir, so as I might settle this matter?'

The sailor checked once to the crowd, which seemed satisfied, and once to the footpad who had now put away his knife. It seemed that London had found some justice in his absence.

Patrick Devlin's name however was surely yellowing on the walls of the Bailey or on a magistrate's desk somewhere. Devlin tipped his hat to Jonathan Wild.

'My name is Captain John Coxon and—' His address was cut dead by the blow of the cudgel's oak head under his chin.

He flew to the cobbles, his head cracking on the stones, his pistol jumping free from his belt.

He rolled up and whipped out his ebony hilted dagger to the wavering form before him, shaking the shock from his head. He'd been hit before and he would be back to the fight when others howled or lay down. But Wild had been there before as well. He had already brought back his staff double-handed and the full back-swing of the oak across the sailor's temple could have taken a child's head off. Devlin stumbled with the impact and his blood painted the wall behind him like a brush thrown against it. He went down with his hand still gripping the dagger.

Jonathan Wild waved down the laughter of the crowd. 'Now, now, folks. Nothing here now. Go about your good business. Just an assault on two of my good men. Read all about it tomorrow, folks. Make a path, now, make a path.'

The crowd dispersed, persuaded by Wild's cudgel, whilst his fellow thief-taker rifled through Devlin's pockets and helped himself to the left-locked pistol which he stuffed into his string-cord belt. Wild returned to the prone body and looked down at the crumpled sleeping form of the pirate Devlin.

'We'll take him to Newgate for now. Before he gets his sense back.' He glanced up at the mouth of the alley, now empty. 'What's his tally, George?'

'He has a king's purse on him, Jon! Weighs more than me baby boy!'

Wild spied the pistol. 'I'll takes that snap, George. Help for his trial. What did he say his name was?'

George shrugged. 'Cap'n John Coxon or other. Sailor I reckons.'

'Aye? You don't say?' Wild mocked and stomped on the sleeping back. 'Welcome to London, Captain John.'

The two left the alley shouldering the dead-weight between them and dove into the quarrelsome fray of Wapping, leaving the bloodied body of their fellow dying alone against the cold stone.

He weakly raised his fingers to their backs, grasping forlornly as his friends walked away.

London had after all changed very little.

Chapter Two

*T*hree days earlier, before dawn, the *Shadow* had sailed up the Thames and settled at Deptford, the East Country dock near the Dog and Duck plying stairs. Most of the stairs were named after the mariners' public houses that lined the river, but the *Shadow*'s crew preferred dipping into the Plough alongside the dock itself for its darker air and less visited signage.

She had not come in under her own escutcheon. The peace of February had made friends of many nations but pirate ships were still unwelcome at any port that claimed to be civilised.

Instead she was warped in by her crew as the Dutch ship, *Ter Meer*, although a scrimption of consultation at the Navy Board in Whitehall would have revealed that the *Ter Meer* had been a fluyt and not a 24-gun frigate: the crew had spent a time boarding over her gunports and stowing her cannon to clip their bird's wings for prying eyes.

As a Dutch ship would make no claim to the Victualler or the West or East India Houses she was paid scant attention. Indeed, such was the mass of trade conducted that any vessel which did not shout for its wares was welcome to be ignored. Let her rest awhile. Let her men fill their boots as long as they stayed out of the city and demanded no attention of her officers and statutes.

The planned moonless night of her arrival saw two men

row the narrow distance to the Dog and Duck stairs, without lamp, without voice and avoiding the welcoming glow from the inn. They walked north, safe in a pair from the nightwalkers and gangs that prowled north and south of the river after dark, and where only lame and aged watchmen and drunken Charleys patrolled the snaking alleys that made up the veins of the metropolis.

One of the pair, the one in the yellow coat and hat, eventually shook hands and departed, leaving his companion to find lodgings at Limehouse while he made his way to the City to announce their arrival and find his own bed.

The ship arrived in the dark and in disguise; the mooring lay far from the churn of commerce. The midnight walk and the splitting of partnership all revealed aspects of suspicion and distrust. Distrust that perhaps a trap was being sprung despite the royal seal that had brought them to England under promise and protection.

But pirates lived longer by caution than trust. The black corpse swaying in the gibbet at Graves Point as they had entered the Thames attested quietly enough to this.

Two days on, Monday now, and the gentleman in yellow had spent the morning at Shudall's, the tailor's, a short stroll from where he had chosen to lay his head at the White Lion in Wych Street.

He had paid Mr Shudall in gold for a new dandelion-yellow silk justacorps, to be collected Friday, and although Mr Shudall had at first frowned at the weary and dissolute look of the young man, yet he had beamed like the sun at the fat bag of coin and gladly proffered directions to Mrs White's Chocolate House as requested. For Dandon was of the colonies; he had never known London.

Only a few hours before Dandon, still in his old frayed coat, had taken a seat at White's and a handful of cards at Lanterloo, the pirate Devlin's head had been stoved in by Mr Jonathan Wild and he dragged off to spend the day in Newgate gaol. He had thus missed his appointment with the Prince of Wales.

The afternoon went on. The game of Loo also. Dandon won a little, lost a little, enjoyed steaming coffee and gave a private smirk at the porcelain gleaming on every table and at the ignorance of the gentlemen sipping from the bone-white cups.

At six Dandon checked his watch against the long-case Harrison in White's rooms and ventured a concerned glance out to the street.

'Does something trouble you, sir?' asked one of his erudite partners at the game, friendly enough despite the reddening face and bulging eyes that hinted at some manner of madness boiling within.

Dandon smiled, his dull gold front teeth drawing curious looks. 'I am expecting a friend. He is a trifle late that is all.'

A bilious snort came back at him. 'We are all here expecting friends, sir! At least as far as our wives are concerned, eh, Gentlemen?' He slapped the arm of his chair and the table responded with knowing raps of knuckles and blue clouds of tobacco.

'Quite.' Dandon lay down his cards, went and watched the street from the bay window. He looked out onto Chesterfield.

Devlin was to join him here after his mysterious meeting with the prince. The audience was for two o'clock at Leicester House and yesterday, Sunday, Dandon had paid a trip there to confirm with a red-coated valet that the captain would indeed attend as ordered. He had left the address of the White Lion with the valet should any further matter require the captain's attention. That same night, Dandon was back at his inn, having agreed with Devlin to meet at White's after four. Two hours should suffice for whatever business the Prince of Wales sought with a pirate.

Dandon and Devlin had parted with a handshake at Limehouse, neither to know where the other slept in case of some snare being set. Their course for Monday was to meet at White's if all was well. Now Devlin was overdue and despite the carriages, the horses and the bustle and hawks of street vendors, Dandon's eyes cut straight to a man in black striding purposefully up Chesterfield. Dogged intent – or vengeance – was on his face. Always a man in black, Dandon thought, the colour of them their only similarity to holy orders.

He did not worry for his captain. He had seen Devlin perform and often enough had seen the usually merry face darken into something hard immediately preceding someone's death. It was more that for most of the few years he had known him, ever since Providence where Devlin had rescued him from that devil Blackbeard, Dandon had been with him, felt himself his lucky charm. Separation was bad for them both.

'Are you still in play, sir!' a stout beef-and-mustard voice warbled from behind him.

Dandon kept his eyes on the figure, growing larger, aiming directly for him, now puffing and holding onto his hat and wig, his pace increasing.

'I am always in play, sir,' he did not turn. 'In more than one game.'

The bell above the door rang, the man in black pushed past the fellow holding out his hand for his hat and made directly for Dandon at the window. Dandon held his breath. He did not know the man but his face had anxiety burning in it. He seemed to know Dandon, however, even unto some great familiarity judging by his brusqueness.

'Your man did not attend His Highness this afternoon, *sir*!' And at the word 'highness' the room shared raised looks and shoulder-to-shoulder murmurs. 'An explanation is most required!'

Dandon put his hand to the messenger's and brought him closer. 'Your discretion, my good man, is required more, would you not suppose?'

The messenger looked around him, lowering his voice, while the chime of cups and conversation resumed. He turned to the window. 'Quite,' his voice began to hiss. 'Where is the man? His Highness is most irate which bodes not well for you, sir, or for anyone within his sight!'

Dandon stroked the moustache he had been meaning to remove for some weeks but which served well for such conversations. 'I do not know where the captain is. Part of our personal conspiracy was to keep such matters hidden from each. And of such I take it that the landlord of the White Lion sent you hither, Mister . . . ?'

'Secretary Timms. The landlord sent me to Shudall's. They directed me here. Where is he, Dandon? My office must find him for all our sakes!'

Dandon had not removed his hand and stroked Timms's affectionately. 'The captain is resolute, Mister Timms. If he did not attend, he has good reason.' Dandon squeezed the hand and bit out his words. 'Perhaps he caught some wind of a trap? What is that option, Mister Timms?' Dandon's eyes searched the face, Timms close enough to taste the coffee on his breath. He looked at the hand pinching into his. To the room two men were speaking as close friends in front of the window, and Dandon's implied threat was invisible.

'There is no need for your master to fear, Dandon. The

prince, and his country I assure you, need his assistance immediately. If he wishes to test our intentions, however, it will not go well for any of you. I can perfectly assure you of that, *sir*.'

Dandon released his grip, resumed the smoothing of his beard. 'Assume we are not talking against each other, Mister Timms, and that you know nothing of my captain. That I know nothing of my captain. Why does a man disappear in London?' Dandon's friendlier face reappeared, the one that dropped petticoats and opened locked doors. Timms relaxed.

'I suppose he may be drunk?' Timms suggested. Dandon carefully shook his head. 'Lost then?' Dandon choked a little. Devlin had a compass in his head. '*Dead*?' Dandon hooked Timms's arm and began to leave, snapping for his hat and his winnings. He whispered into Timms's attentive ear.

'Mister Timms, would His Highness spend the time and a substantial sum of the South Sea Company's money to find a man who might turn up drunk, lost or dead? Would you suppose that might be the prince's best reasoning?'

Timms rubbed his nose and thought on. 'Perhaps not. But what am I to say on my return?'

Dandon took his hat and weighed his change in his fist and handed over a shilling. Outside the August evening was drawing in, the lamplighters in stately progress along Chesterfield.

'If my captain is absent it is not of his own designing I assure you, and it is certainly not with intention to displease the prince.' He led Timms outside and pulled on a pair of yellow gloves. 'Tell me Timms, do you have any power within this town?'

Timms tapped an inner pocket as he spoke. 'I have a royal seal and warrant to enter any place within the city. More than you I suspect, Mister Dandon.'

Dandon concentrated on his gloves and cuffs, thinking

about the hundred pirates and twenty-four guns at Deptford. 'I doubt that but never mind. It would however be wise to find the captain – if London would wish to avoid another fire, that is.'

He joined Timms on the street and plucked his sleeve. 'Oh, and to your earlier allusion, Mister Timms, the pirate Devlin is not my "master". He is my *friend*. And as such I will scour this city with a devotion beyond your loyalty to your prince.' He sniffed and meandered into Mayfair Row, without intelligence of where he might be heading. 'We should spy on the gaols of your town. That would be my first observance.'

Timms hurriedly matched Dandon's pace. 'The gaols?'

'Of course, Mister Timms. He is a pirate after all, and if he did not meet me, and he did not meet your prince, it is from no will of his own. Take me to them. Your gaols. Before he starts killing his way out of your city.'

Timms's voice wavered. 'Is that a genuine concern?' But Dandon did not hear, his attention snared by the white, white bosom and glowing youth of the orange-girl daintily blocking his path. He parted with two pennies and a golden smile for a paper pottle cone of cherries and received a coy backwards glance for his trade as she glided away, her basket swinging off her hip. Timms stepped into Dandon's lingering gaze as the first of the cherries popped in his mouth.

'We should try Marshalsea first. That is the seafarers' gaol.'

Dandon nodded as he chewed and resumed his walk. 'I would think that should be the place to start indeed. Is it far?' he offered the pottle to Timms, who declined.

'Not far enough. Filthy degenerate place. It is over the bridge I am afraid. Three miles by carriage it will have to be.'

'And there are other gaols?'

Timms gave a laughing snort. 'That is most certainly the

20

case. Most certainly and most notably Fleet and Newgate which are close to each other. At a good stride it would take us half an hour or more.'

Dandon raised his voice as he began to weave through the increasing bustle and traffic of pedestrians and pedlars, and as they approached more nearly the city wards. London was coming out for the night.

'Then perhaps we should cover those first, Mister Timms, rather than crossing the river only to come back on ourselves again.'

'Quite so. I would concur,' Timms gasped at a trot just as Dandon came disgustedly to the bundle of paper wedged into the bottom of his cone where the rest of the cherries should have been. He tossed it away. 'And they say *I'm* a pirate?' But the street was not listening and he dashed now, Timms struggling to keep up while trying to avoid being cut down by the flying rush of coaches and people.

East. At half a run. East into the city. To the very proscenium of cruelty.

Chapter Three

✗

'The Hellish noise, the roaring, swelling and clamour,
the stench and nastiness, an emblem of Hell itself.'

From *Moll Flanders*. Daniel Defoe.

*J*onathan Wild had his office, which was also his lodgings,
at the Cooper's Arms on Old Bailey itself, almost opposite
the sessions house. This gave weight to his authority and some
confirmation to those victims of theft and robbery in need of
his services that Wild, so literally close to justice, was the man
for them. Jon Wild was now a paragon of enterprise and
fortune. Long gone the pimp, house-breaker and debtor he
had once been.

Now he had the law on his side.

A few years past, the gentlemen of justice, so exhausted and
exasperated by the prolificness of crime in the city, had passed
a law to make the receiving and selling of stolen wares a crime
in itself.

This single enactment had ruined the daily trade of many a
housebreaker and pawnbroker in the narrows and districts
and it was in starvation that Wild had alighted on his plan.

Maybe if it had only been for his own good nothing may
have come of it; but he rallied his darkest minions around
him and gave out his scheme. Those whose bellies were
hollow and filled only with clay biscuits, who looked only

towards the compter for relief, saw their future again, Jon Wild their master.

If the buying and selling of stolen candelabras and watches were illegal then why not simply sell them back to the ones they had been liberated from?

'How?' his brothers cried.

'Simple, I tells you!' Jon Wild stood on the stage of an inn down Cock Alley at Cripplegate before a crowd of beggars.

'I set up shop that I can find anything for anybody. I tells it to the constables and marshals and magistrates, bold as brass, for ain't I a thief myself and knows them criminals all?'

For a price, dependent on the value of the items, Jon Wild appeals to the victim to give him a few days to scratch around. He swears he has a parade of rappers, quick-talking informants who will spill their guts for a penny. Something will turn up, he tells them. The trick is that Wild already knows the whereabouts of the article, for the man who'd taken it has shown the shiny thing to him, of course.

A split of the ransom means the gentleman has his precious articles returned, and Wild is smart enough to have no stolen goods on his premises as searches by more suspicious authorities are made. And if the thief demands more coin for his trouble?

'*Why, look sir, not only do I have your goods again but here is the man that took it. We'll hang him together. Of course he would say I was in on it with him, sir. He's trying to switch my neck for his.*'

And, as is reasonable, Wild would keep good records of those who came to him in their woe. Records that could be used to map London. A volunteered map of who had the choicest property.

Wild was shrewd. It had not gone unnoticed to him that

London had begun to put more stock in paper than weight and glitter and it was far easier to lift a gentleman's pocket-book than his furniture.

Pieces of paper could hold a man's entire fortune. Nowadays, when the quality turned up at his offices, they did not bemoan their wife's sobbing over some lost stones. Instead they sweated and begged and paid handsomely to get back their precious paper. The madness of the South Sea stock, where the fortune could change in hours, made his customers even more desperate. Jon Wild capitalised, and the fees for his services for finding certificates went far above that of a sedan chair or diamond necklace.

The genius of the man was to not deny his station or past. He had been there. He was one of them. He knew all the dregs and could wring them dry, and to keep them in his pocket he would occasionally take one of them before the beak and see him hung, and his children orphaned, just to show those who had elected him to his purpose the power he held over their very lives.

Puzzled by the sudden increase in highway robbery and house-breaking, the courts asked Wild what could be done. He motioned that the fee for finding the stolen goods needed to be increased as his rappers had gotten greedy now his enterprise was successful. They failed to connect that his success rate had increased along with the burglaries. They nodded and quadrupled his fees. After all, he did deliver them so many villains.

That very morning, for instance, he had brought into Newgate a thief and murderer no less. One John Coxon who had killed one of Wild's own assistants when they had tried to take him. Wild had already been to Paternoster to report it – the power of the press one of his most useful tools.

He sat at his table, in his doorway afore his stairs, his door always generously open to the street so his people could see him and doff their hats as they passed. There he counted the sailor's money in full view. He could leave his purse on the doorstep overnight if he wished.

The leather bag was a strange mixture of coin from every realm, cast in gold and silver, the waft of sand and rum on some of it, some broken into small change. He weighed it in his hand. This was either all a man possessed or a taste of what he promised.

He sat back and thought on the body now lying in the hold across the street in Newgate at the corner alongside the sessions house. He did not notice his assistant George Wattle bounding towards him.

'Jon! Jon!' He blocked Wild's sight of the grim prison stones. George had been at the taking of the sailor, had pulled a knife, seen his partner killed. They had not spoken of Arthur since.

While Wild divvied up their coin George had been sent to the sessions house to see if there were any warrants against their latest taking, or at least any that could fit. Nailed to a wooden board inside the entrance were the reward notices for highwaymen and those notorious pirates who had not taken the king's grace and therefore defied pardon. George waved one such black framed bill at Wild.

'It's him, Jon, look! That sailor!'

'What you rattling, George?' He took the page. On it was the visage of a young man with black hair and no beard. His height, known ships, known familiars and known crimes. A long list. 'Could be anyone.'

'See there though, Jon! Says he was the ungrateful boy of Cap'n John Coxon! He called himself Cap'n Coxon!'

That was there, sure enough. It would make sense that the pirate might assume a name and the description duly fitted better in Wild's eyes.

'Patrick Devlin, eh? The Pirate Devlin.' He jiggled the bag in his hand.

All a man possessed or a taste of what he promised.

'What's a pirate doing in my city, George?'

'I don't know about that but he has five hundred pounds on his head! Five hundred, John!'

Wild had not looked at the price.

'Bah! That's what makes you, you, George, and me, me. I say again. What's a pirate doing in my city? Lot of risk for him here. Take an awful deep purse to bring him in for something. And this here bag is nothing compared to what he might have. In mind or in box.'

'But five hundred, Jon!'

Wild leaned back and watched his street, passing an eye up to the prison. 'We'll go see him after dark, when it's quiet. See what he has to say. And if nothing else we still got five hundred on him.' He stretched out, saw a rosier future ahead. 'If he dies tonight or next week I'll still be a hero. Fetch us up a pie, George. And some beer. I got business to think on.'

To be belayed and hammered unconscious is not a perfect slumber by any measure. A few minutes at most of blackness and the rest, particularly if one is dragged along and has the noise and smells of Wapping as a background, is a grey watery world of dreaming and pain as reality forces itself back.

Voices jumble, sounds clang like bells, and all the victim feels is a sleep that promises to come but will not, and the gnawing of his toecaps and ankles dragging on cobblestones as the crowd filtering past takes sport in his sorrow.

It is even some comfort, then, to be dropped onto a bed of straw over oak planks, for some sleep must surely arrive now. But the pain galloping around the head like a dancing Pan pricks the tormented awake to enjoy his painful tune.

Devlin eased up on an elbow and surveyed the last corners of the damned.

A stone room laid with planks for a floor, studded with ringbolts to tether ankles. One barred window, high in the wall and narrow as a post-hole, lets in August and the fading twilight. The walls are made up of blocks of stone like the last room gladiators see before the arena; and perhaps in truth the chains that fastened men to the floor had been wrought by the same hands, for the gaol made up the last Roman remnant of the city's east wall. It was the bailey of old that once ringed Londinium and gave the street alongside the gaol its name. God had burnt it down once already but the Devil still had his need and Newgate rose again.

Charles II had the gaol rebuilt as a priority after plague and fire heralded the end of the world, when prisoners had lain like fat flies upon the carts.

Sir Richard Whittington and his cat saluted the inmates, with the pious figures of Liberty, Peace, Security and Plenty bowing to justice at his feet. The session house stood next door. Newgate, Old Bailey and Giltspur spread like the points of the cross, with Tyburn anchoring it three miles away to the west. Eight hundred turns of the cartwheel to the rural setting of the hangman's tree.

Devlin looked about. Grey, green and black, an etching of doom. A dark smell of the butcher's apron and effluence strange to a man now used to the brilliant vermillions and blues of the Caribbean and the wash of light, fresh-born every morning, that removed the stain of tobacco and rum from one's lungs. That air full of salt, boucan allspice smoke, fruit and promise.

This was grey. A grey sketched by the suicidal artist. This was stone and damp and death. This was London. He had left it once, the pores of its burnt walls reeking of gin and rotten oranges, fish and filth. He tugged at the manacles around his ankles. Fettered to the floor. This was not a London that Devlin wished to see. It was the London of his past, the one he had run from when he was skinny and poor with murder hanging over his head. No, not good for an Irishman to be found with a dead body. That had been old man Kennedy. Ten years ago. A long ten years but still remembered somewhere, for sure, somewhere an Irishman could still be hung just for his voice and of that he was certain. There was the son, Walter Kennedy, whom Devlin had shared lodgings with, alongside the father. Walter favoured house-robbing over the work that Devlin and the father shared at an anchorsmith's. The house had not been peaceful. Devlin returned one night to find the old man laid on the table with a dirk standing in his chest. He had only a few seconds to run with what he could gather. Just as bad to report a death as be caught with the knife in your hand. All that a world away now.

He lay in the Lodge, the area on the south side where prisoners were divided into debtors or felons and within those two groups again divided into who could pay for their stay and 'garnish' and who could not.

There were 150 prisons within the city, some of which could hold no more than a couple of prisoners at a time, and this number did not include the many sponging-houses where a gentleman debtor might lay his head for a time in more comfortable surroundings, usually the bailiff's own home.

Sponging-houses – so named because the Turks or Jews that lowered themselves to become bailiffs would sponge the debtor dry of everything but his name – at least kept his body out of the gaol.

One hundred and fifty prisons, just over 350 crimes settled by hempen rope, and still every gaol full; for the promise of death had never been a deterrent for the criminal as long as the noose awaited even for the burglary of a couple of silver spoons. Best to take the householder's life as well, then, to deprive the law of a witness.

Devlin patted himself down. Everything about him, everything that *was* him, had been taken save his clothes, and even of them he was short his hat and coat, and those small things mattered. Without them he was less. He was poor again, to the outsider's eye at least. Until he got his hands on pistol and sword. They would be welcome to judge him then.

He found he could stand and his manacles afforded him a wide circle of movement. He gingerly felt the tender swelling of his head. Thankfully the blow had been expertly administered and he was grateful to Jonathan Wild for that much. Just a little dried blood remained where the silver cap of the bludgeon had cracked into him.

He looked up to the only hole of light in the room. Night was settling. August night. The trundle of carriages and the cries of street hawkers still carried on, giving hope that life was not too far away. But he had missed his appointment with the prince, and perhaps that would be his ticket out.

Just to let someone know and hope that Dandon was not too drunk to not be missing him also. He thought of Dandon, who would be back to the *Shadow* and Peter Sam, and he thought of the ship whispering up the Thames, black flag fluttering and her guns ready to prey on the city like Drake at

Panama whilst someone tried to remember how to load the Tower's minions against a pirate.

Aye, there was confidence at the thought of his hundred men or so at Deptford and its assurance made him stride to the door and bang loudly to announce just who he was.

He hammered three times, shouting for some soul to come to the trap in the door. He waited, he listened, his anger growing. He could hear the sounds of a tavern nearby and guessed he was immured near the taproom where prisoners could purchase brandy, wine and tobacco with not too great a profit to the institution, as one might expect given the circumstances of the clientèle. Small beer also available courtesy of Mr Willcox, whose store was set up at the Newgate Street traders' entrance where prisoners could likewise purchase their chandler's wares, or 'garnish'.

Newgate may have been a gaol but like all gaols it was a private concern and even those with death at their shoulders held that an Englishman had the right to drink to his king if he so wished; and London still turned on the pull of a horse, a knife and a cork. The whole business dependent on the prisoner.

A dog barked at Devlin's hammering and was 'whist'd' with a kick. Prisoners had long been permitted to bring in their dogs, pigs, birds, even their wives and children. The families would hang around waiting for their men to pay their debts either to the king or 'Jack Ketch' – whoever came first to claim their due.

Devlin banged again and the weary bulk of Thomas Langley, sub-turnkey, scraped itself from its stool and tankard to waddle to the trap in the door of the hold.

Mrs Spurling, purveyor of watery brandy, called after him.

'Thomas! Be leaving him whoever he is. You be done for the day!'

He waved her down with a flap of his hand. 'No bones, woman. I'm sub-, day and night. I'll quiet him down anyways.'

Devlin heard and stepped back from the small wooden hatch lest a hardened bull's pizzle greet him with a stab to his eye. The door slid aside; Thomas Langley's slothful face filled the gap and squinted at the figure in white shirt, now almost blue in the evening light.

'Cease prisoner! What ails?'

Devlin could see nothing but the pale unshaven face and the small eyes shaded by the fur of eyebrows that even covered Thomas's eyelids.

'Where am I?'

'You are in Newgate's lodge, squire. Until such time as your disposition is assessed and your garnish paid.'

'*Garnish?*'

Thomas sighed deeply. 'Your garnish. Payment for candles, rent, food. Don't be thinking you're staying in Newgate without dues. But I gathers that Jon Wild brought you in with no coin so you best be hoping that some soul be trotting along tomorrow to garnish you himself.'

'That man, Wild, stole my coin.'

'Aye, maybe so, but what does that matter if you killed one of his? Reckon that's a poor purse for a man's life and I reckon the Justice tomorrow will see it the same, don't you?'

Devlin saw Thomas's eyes glint, and imagined that his unseen fist was tightening around his bludgeon.

'And what if I can't pay?'

Thomas shrugged. 'You ain't no debtor. Murder's for felons. So it's the Common Side for you. And if you can't pay no garnish for the Common Side . . . ain't no hope for you in Newgate, squire.' He began to close the partition then paused with a happier tone. 'You're lucky it's Monday. Hanging's already done. You've got a week to live at least. Though it be a long one!'

Devlin came close to the door, his hard eyes staying Thomas's hand to keep the small gap open a while longer.

'Who determines my ability to pay, Turnkey? Who rules this place?'

'That be Mister Rowse and Mister Perry. The principals. As I said, hangings is today and they ain't back yet. You'll see them tomorrow, afore the Justice.' Again he went to slam the wood back but Devlin came closer still and his hands pushed against the door so hard that Thomas saw the dust shake from the hinges. Thomas raised his weapon in his fist despite the wooden and iron door between them, which his malice penetrated as Devlin's voice blew hot on his face.

'I'm warning, Turnkey: no good will come from keeping me here. If your principals return tonight it will be best for you if you send them to me.' He repeated the crucial aspect.

'Best for you.'

He turned away and let the words hang in the air – appropriate for such surroundings.

'Bring me water, food, and some light, or I will let it be known I was neglected.' The panel began to slide shut, Devlin timing his last words to the movement. 'You may leave, Turnkey.' And then Devlin began to walk, a thinking, rattling circle around his cell that barely faded as Thomas went back to his beer, at first with a sneer and then thoughtful, pondering on the cut of the prisoner's damask waistcoat and Holland-tailored shirt.

But those brown bucket boots were old and worn. As old as a conquistador's. And that tanned face belonged to no sitting gentleman but a man of the sea or field. Thomas drank with a snort. '"You may leave, Turnkey!"' he mocked through his beer but thought on, slower, his eyes back to the door and his ears to the scraping of the chain as it dragged around the cell.

He lifted a finger to old Mrs Spurling. 'Fetch us some wine and broth, Missus. Stump of candle.'

Mrs Spurling gave him a disparaging glance and stopped pouring a half-quart of brandy for the Earl standing at the bar.

'I'm sure he'll be good for it,' he answered her look and went back to his beer. 'I've seen his kind before.'

The further east Dandon trotted the newer and tighter the city became. Here and there were memories of older buildings, the medieval heart of the city with ancient stone and Roman gods weeping down at the thoroughfares. Most of her churches were still miraculously standing, although with blackened marks where The Fire had bitten into them, curiously like a shark, before moving on to far more palatable wooden delicacies.

Here were no horses, the roads too narrow and dark for gentlemen after the broad thoroughfares and smooth, elegant stonework of St James's. These passages had been cut through London's veins for speed, for those unwilling to travel down to Holborn and civility to hail a cab.

The city had been rebuilt but had learnt little, as wooden and clay houses still towered high above, overshadowing the passageways. Some of the alleyways even now held shanties with little more than sheets for walls and timber frames like army billets where naked fires burnt within and hollow-eyed children stared as you passed.

Dandon, accustomed to the pastel freshness of the American colonial towns and the wide, sparse Caribbean hamlets, hurried through the city's smothering closeness like a man drowning, clawing for air.

And then at last he broke the surface as the wide expanse of Giltspur street, Newgate, Bailey, St Sepulchre, the taverns and shops, burst him back into civilisation.

He leant against a wall, gasping for breath. He and Timms had run and walked for two miles without a care for Dandon's thirst, and he wiped his face with his cuff. His lungs were bursting, his head aching.

He pushed himself away from the wall, looking up at it, its grim façade declaring that it could be nothing but a gaol.

'We are here, Mister Timms?'

Timms took his arm impatiently. 'This is the Giltspur compter. For gentlemen who have not caused grievous harm and owe very little, and for clergymen who disrobe where they should not. Hell is this way.' He pulled at Dandon, who gathered his wits and staggered on.

'Is there a hurry, Mister Timms? Do prisons close?'

'The hurry, sir, is in the concern that your pirate may have given word and used His Highness's name. The *concern* is that your captain is a notorious brigand that is overdue to hang, but, most of all, it is the *concern* that he may not be in there at all and but that you and I will be in there for breakfast tomorrow!'

They had crossed the street. The gatehouse of the old prison still stood across Newgate street, the last of the gates into the old city. Dandon took in the face of the gaol that stretched down Old Bailey.

Rebuilt after The Fire and Restoration it was now plain Tuscan in style. Four great arched windows rose either side of the 'keep', barred and glassless, and high enough for Dandon to presume their light covered the unfortunates' wards.

The keep made up the entrance of the prison, the glazed

windows above it and the circular window in the roof's pediment surely the chapel. Dandon looked around the street at the proliferation of blooms, now crushed and scattered, littering the road and pavement.

'The flowers!' His surprise halted Timms.

'It is Monday. Executions this morning. The crowds like to toss flowers at the felons. It is good luck to give a nosegay to the condemned.'

Dandon stooped to pluck up a bloom and explained himself to Timms's raised eyebrow.

'I may have need of luck.'

Left and right of the keep were the lodges and the residences of the principal turnkeys. Shallow steps led up to a simple alcoved door. Timms took the right one, whispering as he did so that the left-hand side was where the condemned came out for their free coach.

'Would be a bad omen I'm sure to walk up such which so many only ever come down.' He rapped on the door with his fist, regretting that he had no cane with him.

They stood awkwardly together in the cramped space waiting for answer and looked at the door or the street rather than each other, in case nerves betrayed their fears or their press-ganged partnership fell apart and one killed the other.

Timms rapped again, harder this time. He called through the wood, 'I hope someone will let us in at least!'

Dandon smirked. 'Not a sentiment one expects to hear outside a prison door. Its peculiarity I'm sure will bring someone. If only to direct us to Bethlem instead.'

Timms ceased in his reproach as a panel unlocked and the face of Thomas Langley peered at them, bored already. He looked up and down Timms's coachman-black perfection and then at Dandon's shabby coat and wilting hat.

'Dropping off?' he asked Timms.

'I need to see a list of prisoners you may have brought in perhaps today or Sunday, my man. Immediately and on royal warrant.'

Thomas audibly sucked out a sliver of pork from a back tooth and swallowed it. 'No principal in at the moment. Can't see any list without one.'

'I demand to see that list, Turnkey! My warrant grants me entry to any manor in this city! Now open up immediately!'

Langley shook his head, his eyes almost closing. 'No entry to the list without a principal's say. Come back tomorrow.'

Timms flashed his winning hand in Langley's face. The smudge of red seal and royal ribbon upon the paper. '*This*, sir, dismisses any power that you may suppose your principal supposes he may have in this foul place and I insist that you allow me entry!'

Langley gave a limp eye to the paper and then back to its bearer. He knew that the man in front of him was only one month's bad gambling away from being welcomed within his domain. He had seen enough viscounts and courtiers shitting in front of him to be unimpressed by fancy pieces of paper.

'Come back tomorrow,' he repeated and made to shut the gap.

Dandon touched Timms's arm before the king's man exploded.

His turn now.

Dandon carried no weapons. No papers. No titles. But he knew how the world turned.

'We should spend our *gold* at the Fleet instead, Mister Timms. Rules are rules after all. I believe we have been rightly told that their list is accessible day and night. Their turnkey shall warrant the *reward* instead.'

For the second time that evening, Langley stayed his hand. 'What reward?'

Dandon looked surprised at the question, believing the matter closed. 'No matter. We shall pay the Fleet the fee and reward the prize should his information be valuable and worth *two* guineas.' He took one step down with a baffled Timms and glanced up the street for a sedan or a cab.

'Hold!' Langley closed the smaller door and the sounds of locks and hasps rang out.

'I feel I should have just dropped you off, Dandon,' Timms murmured, quietly joyed.

'What prize?' Langley enquired from an open door.

Dandon turned back. 'You would be unaware that a dangerous Jacobite has coerced himself into one of the city's gaols in order to conspire with some fellows of his already so withheld. Secretary Timms and myself have been charged with weeding out the scoundrel.' Dandon produced his red silk purse like a lamb's heart lying in his palm.

'I can make it three guineas if you save me the walk to Fleet and supply a quartern of refreshment. What say you, Turnkey?'

Chapter Four

*P*eter Sam stood at the larboard quarter of the *Shadow*. The sun was gone now, the lights and chimneys of the Surrey side of the river giving life to this remoter part of the city, still holding on to being a countryside with hamlets and farmland. But the docks and the encroachment of industry over smallholdings were getting larger, an indolent bully slowly elbowing the rustic world aside.

Uneasy, he paced to the light by the mizzen and lit a pipe to calm him some. He was the *Shadow*'s quartermaster, second of a hundred men only to Devlin, and this was his third year with the Irishman as his captain.

This country had cooler air than he was used to, despite the month, so a long French coachman's coat hung down to his ankles and covered his normal goat-leather jerkin and breeches. Still no shirt beneath the coat; lace and cuffs were wasted on the big man. One cannot put hosiery on a bear, even a bald bear with a rough red beard.

His only formalities were leather bracers on his wrists and a sewing palm on his right hand. Less to protect him from the burn of rope and more to cover the scars that came from a chain that had choked the life out of one Hib Gow two years past. But that was indeed past.

Now the man, his captain, who had come to find him that day, saved him that day, was overdue to return. Much about

Devlin he still disfavoured. His rise to captaincy had ended the lives of some of those closest to Peter Sam. Devlin had been nothing when he had come to them. An Irish steward, a servant, to an English naval captain. His meagre lot in life was settled, and in an ill-fitting suit with a flat belly. His only use to them when they took him from his ship was his knowledge of the 'art', the skill to navigate learned from his master. So Devlin had found his place amongst them.

Peter Sam would call it luck, Devlin, fortitude and ability, but occasion and fate had made the Irishman their captain. Now they were richer than they had ever been under Seth Toombs, the unlucky patroon who had commanded before Devlin. Dead now. Dead twice – the second time by Devlin's shot to his face. And that had been one tale ended. Aye, richer than they had ever been, and the cost to be weighed by a better judge than Peter Sam.

Then there was his preference for the frigate which kept them out of the shallows and on the open sea. And that damned grin when he was right. Time for Peter Sam to leave perhaps. Settle with an inn on Jamaica. Six years from Newfoundland cod-man to pirate. Long odds for a pirate. A longer life than most. Then, to remind, the tide lapped up the *Shadow*'s freeboard.

Not old. Not yet. Always one more horizon.

Aye, a short life, and a merry one.

He chewed on his pipe and looked back into the city as if Devlin would any moment raise a flag to show him where he hid. He drew on the Brazilian tobacco like a bellows and Black Bill Vernon, named for his hair not his skin, emerged from the Great Cabin and stood close to the big man.

'Are you not to eat tonight, Peter Sam?' he asked, and watched the scowl come back at him.

'It's getting late. Cap'n should be back by now.'

Bill set about his own meerschaum. 'Aye. It's later than it was,' his sleepy Highland wit observed. 'The captain can handle himself. Would you not suppose that, Peter Sam?'

Bill was the *Shadow*'s sailing master, less violent than most of the crew, unless sheets were in the wind, and Peter Sam and he were the old standers. They had been on the *Cricket* and the *Lucy* with Seth Toombs, and other than old Will Magnes they were the last of the original crew. They were the corners of the ship.

Peter Sam looked back to the city again. 'He can handle himself. But it don't sit well – none of this.' He flashed a look at Bill. 'What if it be a trap? Likes I been saying all along?' Still he spoke with the Bristol burr despite all the world he had seen and bled over.

Bill joined him at the rail. 'The captain's no fool.' He patted the rail affectionately. 'And he has *her* behind him.'

'Even so. I says some of us should go in. Scout around. Sniff out if anything be up.'

'And what would be up, Peter Sam? And what would we do about finding it?'

'It couldn't hurt none.' Peter straightened up.

'It could hurt some; could hurt *plenty*. And the order was to stay south of the river. If anything were awry Dandon would be back.'

'Aye, and maybe they've done for him too.'

Bill thought on this, his placid dark face never changing its expression. Peter, and all the others, Devlin included, always looked to Bill for calm. If his fury leapt free then the world was surely on fire. He pulled on his pipe and ruminated. 'Order is to wait. The captain's mind is right. Why would these Germanium bloods go to all the trouble of finding him in such secret ways if all they wanted to do was kill the captain when half the bloody world is trying to do such anyways? Besides, as far as them who may do us harm are concerned we ain't even here. We came in at Falmouth and the captain took a coach to London. He'll keep us in his pocket for if he needs us. Stay your feet at least a day, Peter Sam. The captain's fine.'

Peter grunted and tapped out his tobacco over the gunwale. 'I'm waiting 'til midnight, Bill. Then I'm taking Hugh Harris across that bridge with me. Orders or no.' He started for the Great Cabin.

'I can't stop you, Peter Sam if that's what you aims to do,' his words to Peter's back.

'That's a damned fact!' The cabin door slammed behind him. A bottle or two was calling him to help raise his fire. Peter Sam had never been to London. He was thinking two bottles and two pistols each for himself and Hugh Harris, the bloodiest of them.

Aye, that should be enough for an English town.

Chapter Five

*T*he small candle on the floor did nothing to illuminate the face that appeared at the hatch in the cell door. The voice however set Devlin on his feet.

'Good evening, Captain,' Dandon's voice echoed around the room. 'I trust you are well?'

Devlin sprang to the door. 'Dandon! You have me found! Get me out of here!'

'In good time.' Dandon stood back and left Thomas Langley to his work, the three locks taking an age to unhasp while the shadows jumped across the walls from the lanterns now set for the evening. Timms and Dandon tried not to take in the moans and sobs all around, bewailing another night in the wards of Newgate.

At last the door gasped open. Devlin's chain rattled taut as he reached the limit of his freedom and Langley smirked and gripped his bull's leather.

Dandon and Timms tipped their hats to him and entered the gloom. Langley made to follow but Dandon placed a soft palm to his chest.

'Alone, if you please. Close the door behind and busy yourself at the taproom with my gold.' Langley sniffed and meandered away like an October bee.

Devlin stepped back, ashamed of his chain and surroundings and perhaps humiliated that he had grounded in the place he deserved; and there stood a fine courtier in Timms, judging him rightfully as such.

The two pirates embraced unashamedly, but just as a ruse: Dandon to check that Devlin still had his guineas sewed into his waistcoat and Devlin disappointedly to feel for hidden weapons about his friend.

'Captain Devlin,' Timms acknowledged as politely as he could.

'Or should we say, "John Coxon"?' Dandon chimed. 'Lucky I am humorous enough to spot such jest.' Dandon checked Devlin for injury. Sometimes, and certainly for friends, he took his position as ship's physician seriously.

'I figured my real name would not be welcome.'

Dandon raised his brows as he inspected the lump on Devlin's skull. 'I imagine that in here it would be most welcome, Patrick.'

Timms coughed. 'But it is most appropriate that you maintained your discretion. Well played, sir.'

Devlin turned to the man in black. The officious cut of him represented the sharp edge of everything Devlin despised. 'And, you are?'

Timms touched his hat. 'Secretary Timms. Attached to His Highness at Leicester House. Where you should have been at two o'clock this afternoon.'

'Tell His Highness that I have been delayed.' Devlin brushed Dandon aside. 'Now get me out of here and I'll see your poxy prince.'

Timms began to walk the room, watching his feet amid the straw, hands clasped behind. 'Nothing would be finer to me, Captain. But you have created an unfortunate chain of events that has clouded my position.'

Devlin's eyes did not follow the wandering Timms; his sight was locked on the door in front of him. 'I am sorry to have made matters "cloudy" for you.'

Timms stopped pacing. 'I do not think you appreciate the delicacy of your situation, Captain.'

Devlin faced him. 'I do not think you will appreciate the delicacy of your situation if I am not released.'

Timms threw a frustrated glance at Dandon.

'He always talks like that,' Dandon offered consolingly. Timms continued.

'You have killed a man this afternoon. Although this might seem a commonplace factor in your life, Captain, we take such matters quite seriously in London.'

Dandon agreed. 'It is true, Patrick. I have seen dozens of gibbets hanging above the very streets on my passage here.'

'I know,' Devlin said. 'I survived these streets once.'

Timms put a handkerchief to his mouth, remembering the gaols reputation for typhus – the 'gaol fever'. 'In my capacity I have the power of warrant to extract prisoners from gaol, but not felons held up for murder! And most certainly not ones who have killed one of the Thief-Taker General's assistants!'

'I was attacked. I defended myself and was robbed and placed here. It was no will of mine.'

'But doubtless another soul would have found an alternative to violence? Perhaps you could have run away? Your legs seem sound. That would have been a more prudent action for one whose main imperative today was to *bloody well meet the Prince of Wales*!'

Devlin said nothing but his teeth grated. He was not a boy, to explain himself to fops, but he knew Timms was right, and his anger abated. Dandon could understand his captain's annoyance but if they were not both to wind up in Newgate he assessed that Timms was a man to have on their side.

'What do you suggest, Mister Timms, to alleviate our situation and assist you?'

Timms sniffed and resumed his contemplative pacing. 'It is not as simple as it once was. I can return to the prince and inform him what has occurred.' He began to reel off notions as if no longer addressing either of them but instead picturing the days ahead.

'You will appear in the sessions house by ten tomorrow. Naturally not as the pirate Devlin but by this rather fortunate name you at least had the presence of mind to conjure. The Justice will set a trial, for this week, after which your punishment will be execution. Which gives us until Monday, by which time we can conduct our meeting with the prince. Thus there is no problem other than a lost week.'

'Save the problem of me being at Tyburn on Monday,' Devlin reminded him.

'Never mind that.'

Devlin and Dandon glanced at each other with the quick eyes of those used to conspiracy, which more innocent men barely notice and often mistake when they do – until they find a knife in their back. Timms went on. 'The most important matter is to get you through tomorrow, as this John Coxon, and get you back in here with justice seen to be done. Our real purpose must be kept secret.'

'And on that,' Devlin pointed at him and took a step closer, his voice low. 'One of yours finds me in Maracaibo in June. A letter dated January offers me two thousand pounds and a pardon for us all if I come to bow before your fat prince and accept his even fatter father's marque. The pardon for pirates expired two years ago, yet I am fine enough to be granted an extension?' Timms stepped back as Devlin advanced. 'And the full enmity of the Navy should I refuse. I noted *that*.'

Dandon belched and excused himself. 'For they have been so successful at finding you so far, Patrick.'

'Aye.' Devlin's eye was still on Timms. 'What goes on? Why am I here? I am constantly wondering what is so bloody *special* about me?'

'That is for discussion between yourself and His Highness. I only know that you being in Newgate – although I am sure it is where you belong – will be to the detriment of your country.'

Devlin showed Timms his back. 'Not my country. Not even my world.' He shouldered past Dandon. They shared the look again. Dandon took the hint and plucked his cuffs as he spoke.

'I wondered at the time that it must have taken some great powers and resources to search the pirate round. And not with mind to destroy, but to invite us to some ball or such. Most impressive.'

'Indeed,' Timms took out his watch. Now almost eight. 'There are many powers here. Do not flatter yourselves that this was merely some ploy to entrap a brigand and his fleas. This is to the highest order and, I stress, must not be public.'

Devlin turned. 'But I am to stay here? And return tomorrow? How then am I supposed to attend this dance of yours?'

Timms, fearing his own lateness, tidied himself to leave, for the prince would be half drunk by now.

'Not a difficulty I am sure. You will spend a week in the wards – I don't see how to avoid that without drawing speculation – and on Sunday be shifted to the execution corridor. We will remove you then. Come Mister Dandon, sir, time to go before we are kept here like as not.' He moved to the door to summon Langley. Devlin and Dandon both pondered Timms's complacent mention of 'removal'.

'And just how will you *remove* me?'

'Hmm?' Timms seemed mentally to have already left the room. 'Oh, we will swap you with some other fellow who is also due, with promise to fund his widow and children or some such. It has been done before you know.'

He called for Langley before nodding his last words. 'Then we smuggle you out of the tunnel. No need to make a scene in the sessions house. No need for the prince to intercede. We will make the best of *your* bad lot that has cost us time we can ill afford.' The door was opened.

Devlin edged close again, sure he had misheard. '*Tunnel*? What bloody tunnel?'

Dandon smiled and checked his fingernails again. Timms smiled blithely at some agreement lost on the other two.

'There is a tunnel that links to Sepulchre's church across the way there. It is most fortuitous that you were gaoled in Newgate for that matter. I believe some merchant bequeathed its construction. The warden comes down the tunnel on Sunday night and whispers some maudlin horrors through the keyholes of the cells. Must be ghastly.'

Langley turned to the door.

'One moment, Turnkey.' Devlin pulled the door shut again, his voice lowered to a whisper. 'Tell your prince, Timms, that we will repeat our appointment tomorrow. At two.'

'Captain, the prince will not attend here. His acknowledgement of you would be out of the question.'

But Devlin was no longer speaking to him. 'Back to the ship, Dandon. Tell where I am. Tell what to do. Tonight. I've had enough of this shit.'

Dandon took Devlin's arm. 'I wish I had come in sooner, Captain, and known of this. I would not have paid a guinea for a quartern of wine which I did drink before I saw you.' He shook his captain's hand. For luck. For sport yet to come.

Timms looked from one pirate to the other. 'Back to the *ship*?' His voice quivered. 'You were ordered to sail into

Falmouth. To come by coach to London. To come alone . . .' He pushed them both back into the centre of the cell, away from the door. 'By *God*! Do not tell me that you have brought a pirate ship into London, sir!' He swallowed, something awful in his throat. 'You cannot, nay must not, contemplate anything that will draw attention! You *must* wait for me to confer with His Highness. You must stand tomorrow and await until Sunday, I *beg* of you. This will all go to error if you do not.'

Devlin gave Timms his coldest look. 'Go to your prince, pup. I'm sure if all this matters so much he would not be pleased to wait another week for whatever task he beckons me with.' He shoved Timms to the door, where Dandon already stood. 'Go. It grieves me that the first words out of your mouth were not to tell a gaoled pirate that a tunnel was near.'

Timms shook himself free. 'You were *ordered* by His Highness not to bring any of your men to endanger this city, nor endanger such a crucial affair of state!'

Devlin dismissed him into the care of Thomas Langley just as the candle in his cell winked out behind him. 'Not my Highness. Not my city. Not my state. You trusted a pirate. Well done.'

He bid Langley lock him back in and slammed the door on them all, unconcerned by the snuffing out of his candle. Devlin planned that London would burn again soon enough to light his way.

Thomas Langley led a despondent Timms and a grinning Dandon back to the street of Bailey. Timms suffered in an effervescent panic but Dandon's face was glowing like a boy at his first fair.

'He is mad. One cannot break out of Newgate gaol and most certainly when His Highness requires the utmost of—' Dandon hushed him.

'Mister Timms,' he offered an effacing smile. 'I may have

underestimated your prince's ability to identify those of the world who can help him. I may not be the most worthy advocate of any such person myself but would I be wrong in the assumption that said prince is a gambling man, a sporting man?'

Timms tweaked his neck and pulled at his cravat with a finger.

'Then he would probably be most gratified in his choice of a man to undertake a dangerous and perilous adventure who would not willingly sit on his arse and wait to be gotten out of danger when he could fight, wrangle, deceive and conspire with friend and cohort, to effect his escape from the worst that any enemy in the world could conceive. Why, it would not surprise me that an intellect such as the prince must possess did not contrive these events just so, to test the mettle of the pirate Devlin.' He tapped his nose. 'What wisdom the prince must conceal beneath his wig! How fortunate that my captain finds himself in Newgate with a tunnel beneath the gaol. It is a test beyond the fathoming of common men.'

Timms looked into Dandon's red-rimmed eyes and detected the thrill of danger that hovered just above the love of wine. He bowed to a power he had avoided all his life since dodging around the prefects at Eton. This was not his world.

'I'm sure the prince will be most excited by the prospect,' he replied. 'As long as all is kept . . . *quiet*. We do not wish to end in the broadsheets of Paternoster on the morrow.'

Timms looked over to the church, and then back to the empty space where Dandon had been.

Open-mouthed he walked up the street, looking left and right for the yellow-clad figure that was by his side and had now been swallowed up by the night.

Defeated, he pulled up his collar and hurried on his way to Snow Hill and back to the real city, back to his prince.

This was not an evening to be abroad.

Chapter Six

All you that in the condemned hole do lie,
Prepare you, for tomorrow you shall die.
Watch all and pray: the hour is drawing near
That you before the Almighty must appear.
Examine well yourselves, in time repent,
That you may not to eternal flames be sent.
And when St Sepulchre's Bell in the morning tolls
The Lord above have mercy on your souls.

The bellman of St Sepulchre's poem.
Sunday midnight in the tunnel connecting the gaol to
the church.
Paid for in testament from 1605. Ended in 1744.
The last two lines to be whispered through the keyholes
of the cells.

*T*en o'clock. The *Shadow*, with her sidelights glinting like a chandelier in a bagnio house, was mostly asleep for the night. Only two men on her deck passed for a watch; pirates never followed the naval convention of the larbolins and starbolins. The bell in the belfry just below the quarterdeck was kept solely for Devlin in his perversity to maintain a watch at sea for his reckoning and traverse. But to the pirates the bell was anathema – a memory of the life of an indentured man of the sea. An alarm to tell him when to eat, when to sleep, when to work or, so help him, be flogged for ignoring it. The bell and the trickle of the sand. Not their life. The first rule of the pirate captain when wooing men to the trade: Take away that which they hate, and men will follow.

The *Shadow* herself was a small light-frigate, ably suited to the narrow channels of the Mediterranean but too weak for a ship-of-the-line and thus classed according to the Fighting Instructions of 1653 as a fifth-rater.

French by birth, she had been commissioned in 1715 by the late governor of the small Verdes island of Sao Nicolau, Valentim Mendes, and she began her pirate life two years later when Devlin plucked her from the pocket of said Valentim, and the *Sombra* became the *Shadow*.

Nine nine-pounders stood on the weatherdeck, the final three beneath the quarterdeck and part of the Great Cabin. Two more were on the quarterdeck and one at the fo'c'sle. Two more were set to chase in the bow – a distinction of a Mediterranean ship where the low winds hindered turning to broadside. Her final complement was two more niners at the stern waiting to poke out of the Great Cabin, and two breech-loading half-pound swivels along the quarterdeck rail; but the pirates had added yokes to mount more when called upon.

A fine ship, chipped here and there, with new strakes over old where she had been holed once or twice, some furniture missing along her rails and gunwales where misguided fools had attempted to defend themselves with shot and grape. And to be fair, although the Atlantic treated her narrow beam unkindly she was still here, and the pirates, whose normal way had been to trade up or even down when a ship became worn or in need of repair, had kept her well and careened and caulked her fresh every summer. They painted that which needed painting and took from others whatever fresh sail or rigging she had need of.

Perhaps if she had not been so young when they had found her, perhaps if she had known other crews and seas years before, she would not have sat so well for so long. Aye, perhaps.

Peter Sam and Hugh Harris sat at the long table on the only two chairs in the cabin. The sparse cabin. The Great Cabin. On any ship it was the *sanctum sanctorum* of officers, but on a pirate it belonged to the ship, to the crew one and all.

It was a dry room to make plans, to drink, cooler than below deck or warmer than on the open one. And sparse indeed. Away over the side with the vain bulkheads and lockers, the oddments and baubles of naval crews. It had taken Devlin's hardiest insisting that the doors to the coach and cabin should be saved; for the captain, for all his democracy, had won the concession that he could sleep in the cabin if he so wished. And to Devlin, in some childish fancy, it had been the only place he had known all his life that sported a door that was his to close. Now two pirates, two near-empty bottles between them, sat at the table and checked their guns.

Peter Sam replaced the pyrite flint on the Sibley maple and brass blunderbuss that had no right being on the Dutch merchant he had rescued it from. He loaded it with swan shot over grain and rammed cartridge paper on top to prevent the deadly charge from slipping out, then slid the fearsome weapon back into its holster upon the table. 'I'm done,' he announced to Hugh.

'Just that little hog's leg?' Hugh smirked. Peter Sam said nothing and went about loading his *gargoussier*, his belly box of cartridges, the small hardened leather pouch and a wooden insert in the base with ten holes for the prepared shot wrapped in paper: five for the blunderbuss, five for the Bohemian cavalry pistol with the belt hanger he had favoured of late.

Hugh lifted his pistols in the air with glee. 'Me? I'm ready as I ever was!' He admired his weapons with a loving look to each. Once he had worn Post-Captain John Coxon's matched pair but that devil had taken them back on New Providence two years past when Devlin and he met up with Devlin's former master. Now, he would have almost paid for the handsome turnover Doleps he brandished.

Each pistol had two barrels, one atop the other, with a frizzen and pan for each and one lock to fire. Two shots for every normal man's one. Hugh had further specialised them by loading one barrel with ball, the other with partridge shot, depending on the damage and distance required for the unfortunate standing in front of him.

'Pity ain't the word when I walks out tonight!' he crowed, the pistols above his head. The door to the cabin clicked open behind them and instinctively Hugh flashed a pistol to the body coming through, the pistol's swift cocking and the two staring barrels freezing the face of Bill Vernon. Hugh laughed and lowered his weapon.

Black Bill cursed, his voice still calm, and came to the table and looked down at the mass of knives and guns. They would take no cutlasses to the streets. Better a knife for close quarters, and easier to prise free information when you had a steel fist at someone's throat.

'You still planning on going out, Peter Sam?'

'Aye. Soon enough.' He stood to fetch another bottle from the rack in the coach, the personal cabin space where a captain could keep his effects. 'After a time.' He stared in challenge back at Bill as he pulled the cork, the amber light from the swaying lantern moving him through shadow and back again, adding to his grave look.

Hugh giggled nervously between the two large men, himself

a scrawny fellow with long hair and a dirty aspect, unkempt even for a pirate. He had been born for the life and after years of starving on merchant ships could never put meat on his bones, but he was a natural killer and a loyal soul to have behind you. A look from Bill and he went back to tamping and tending his guns.

'If you must be for going ashore, Peter Sam, I suggest you take someone who can help find the captain.' Bill cocked his head to the door and Dandon swanned in, breathless and red from his row out to the ship.

'Salutations, Peter!' Dandon swept off his hat. 'I have word from Patrick.' He spied the bottle in Peter's hands and stepped forward uninvited. 'And I thirst like a desert.'

Peter held the bottle to his chest. 'What word?' Peter had little time for Dandon, in his opinion a failed drunken coxcomb who hid behind Devlin's coat and purse. Dandon took no share from the pirate's accounts for he took no share in the gaining of it. He held no position on the ship other than Devlin's association and a loose inkling of medicine that the others admired in their stupor. But the yellow-coated fool carried no arms. It would be unfair ever to kill him but he would have none of Peter's wine.

Dandon pulled back his hand when the bottle did not come and looked to Bill for security. 'I have come from Newgate gaol, gentlemen, where our gallant captain is now dwelling.' Dandon cast around the room for another drink. With a grin Hugh offered his own green bottle up. He at least liked Dandon.

Dandon tipped a bow and wiped the mouth with a filthy cuff. 'Thank you, sir!'

Peter Sam growled behind him. 'He is in gaol? Speak man!'

Dandon paused with the bottle to his lips. 'It has taken me almost two hours to get back here, Peter. Two *dry* hours. And as we will leave immediately allow me some ability to slake my thirst, if you please.'

Too smart. Too smart for his own good. 'Talk, damn you! Leave for where?'

Dandon looked surprised. 'Why, for Newgate, naturally.'

The others shared a look. The whole world knew of Newgate and criminals could reel off the names and ins and outs of prisons as other men could the fields and factors of their trades. Dandon noted the look. 'Aye. Newgate. I met him there for he murdered a man this morning.' Dandon finally drank.

Hugh laughed. Bill rummaged for his pipe. Peter Sam's red beard lifted as he looked upward. He walked back to the table, put down the bottle and picked up the holstered hand-cannon. 'To it then. It is a trap as I feared,' he glowered at Bill. 'As I ever said it were.'

'No,' Dandon corrected. 'Not a trap. An accident I assure you, Peter. I have met with the prince's man and all is in order. It is the captain who has made a mess of things.'

Peter shouldered the leather holster. Built for a saddle, it fitted his back fine, the gun slung behind his massive hide. 'His fault or no I'll not stand by while he waits.'

Dandon emptied his bottle. 'My sentiments exactly, Peter. He has already rearranged his agenda with the prince for tomorrow. I hope you have all eaten, Gentlemen, for it will be a long night.' He reached for Peter's discarded wine. 'He needs our hand.'

'Hold,' Bill stopped loading his pipe. 'You intend to break him free? From Newgate? Is it not wiser to buy him out? He must have a price.'

'You're getting old, Bill.' Peter hung his pistol to his belt and a pair of knife sheaths vanished around his waist. 'Stay and help Dog-Leg wash the pots.' He picked up his long coat and belly-box. 'Hugh. Up now.' Hugh scrambled for his pistols and a bag of grenadoes at his feet.

'Dandon,' Peter slapped Dandon's chest. 'Tell me where this gaol be.'

Dandon turned to Bill. 'Peter is accurate to a degree, Bill. The captain has asked for this matter to be settled tonight. He was most insistent. I gather time is an issue to the prince. Also, bargaining would bring unwarranted attention and as yet his gaolers know not his real name. He called himself Captain John Coxon, no less.' He drank quickly as they laughed at the name familiar to them all.

'The man has something about him to be sure, even in his current straits.' He watched the weapons being buried about the two men. 'But a frontal assault would also be an errant choice. We must be prudent.' Hugh and Peter glared at him.

'First we need to know more about this fortress. I suspect that there would be one amongst us who is familiar with this gaol? The crew are abroad in the inns I take it, Bill?'

'Aye. Gaming and whoring for the most. The Dog and Duck stairs and the Plough. Three days drunk for the lot of 'em.'

Peter Sam pulled Dandon's shoulder. 'But you've seen him! You know where he lies!'

Dandon winced under the bruising grip. 'And I'm sure Morgan knew where Portobelo lay, Peter, but a map or two no doubt assisted.' He tugged himself free. Peter Sam's dark look returned.

'Am I to be sure that you don't just want more of us to follow you into this gaol, Dandon? Where maybe you've taken a pretty coin or two to betray us all, perhaps? Are you sure there is not a squadron of men waiting for us at the inn? How would that sound to your mind, jackal?'

Dandon went back to his bottle. 'It is this suspicious mind, Peter, that keeps you lonely in your old age. Come and see for yourself.'

'Oh, I will, popinjay, I will. But mark that you'll be the first to fall if I smell a trap!' He stared into Dandon's face. 'The first to fall!' he spat. Dandon reeled away.

'If you can smell anything above you own maleficence, I would be most surprised.'

Peter's hand went for some steel at his belt, Black Bill seeing it in time. 'Enough, Peter! Away with you both! Is this what the captain would want whilst he sits and waits for you! Fight over a shawl in your own time! To the boat, to the inn and find one of us who knows Newgate!'

Peter Sam glared. Hugh went for the door, taking his sniggering to the deck. Dandon brushed the creases from his coat and followed.

Bill's pipe glowed, his voice peaceful again. 'Go easy, Peter. And bring the captain home.'

Peter Sam adjusted his baldric beneath the long coat and checked the apostles of powder strung across his chest. He strode out without a word.

Adam Cowrie was their man. He was in the Plough with at least a dozen of the others who all became humble when Peter Sam ducked under the door.

The Plough's regular patrons had all kept to their own corners when the young men in fine but tattered waistcoats and hats had bowled in hours before and slammed their gold onto the counter. The eye of the barkeep held none of their looks and he kept his attention on the coins and the pouring of drinks.

The old salts of the inn knew well the sort of young men

who carried more than a gully blade, and who rattled with coin and steel, and so they stayed less rowdy than usual.

They knew most pirates were young, most as little as twenty-six when they finally hanged. They were youths who willingly leapt away, while their spirit still remained, from the lash and drudgery of the merchant or slaver that their father had sold them into.

Why work hard for shillings when you could live easy for gold? The worst of it was just an aversion to choking. And that fear had never filled anyone's belly.

Adam Cowrie, twenty-three himself, had been with Devlin on Providence when they had escaped from the fort's old Spanish gaol, two years ago now.

He was not a bold one, not a Hugh Harris or a Dan Teague, the finest cut-throats Devlin had. Cowrie, with still enough of the bible worked into him, needed to be madly drunk when a boarding came, so he shrunk more than the others when Peter Sam loomed over their small round table, peculiar in a coat, so used were they to his powerful bare arms.

'So you knows Newgate, Cowrie?'

Cowrie whispered over his drink. 'Aye, I knows it. Knows it too well I fears.' He opened his palm to show the round scar where he had been burnt in the hand for stealing a pair of clogs.

Dandon appeared behind Peter's back, pencil and paper in hand. He made himself room at the table. 'Tell me about your time there, Adam.'

The notion of escape did not cause any horrific reaction from Adam Cowrie. He had been there in December 1715 when Charles Radcliffe, one of the principals of the Northumberland Jacobites, simply walked out of the door after a party with the departing guests. Eight others had done the same in May. Their escapes made the broadsheets, the whole of London being mad for Jacobite blood, but others, dozens of others, had gone out of Newgate without any hue and cry. At Dandon's request, Cowrie described that which he knew.

The gaol was divided up into three distinct parts: the Master side, for debtors that could pay, and the Common side for those who could not. The third part, the Press Yard, was for criminals of state and those others who could pay whatever price the benevolent owner believed you could afford. There one could enjoy its open air and have the freedom to walk within the Yard's grey enclosure, handsomely paved with Purbeck stone.

The Master's Side and the Common Side were each again divided up into three separate wards, although the Master's Side had several apartments still in the old gateway itself, again – as long as the price was right, of course.

These wards were all on the ground floor, Cowrie informed Dandon. If Devlin was in the hold near the lodge, he was in the right-hand side, south corner. Cowrie took the paper and sketched the ground floor, loosely shading in the location of the hold. Dandon looked up at Peter Sam and nodded once. The boy knew what he was talking about, for that had been the very corner he had visited.

'Would they have moved him by now, Adam?' Dandon asked.

'The doors inside are all locked after nine. If he was in the hold then, he's staying there. As a felon anyways he'd be in the Common Side with the poor souls that can't pay. His garnish would just be for a bed and drink. He's in one or the other for sure. But,' his voice became solemnly slow, 'if he can't pay as a felon he's in hell for sure. You see, the Common Side is divvied up for those wretches. Five more wards. Worse than graves.' Adam crossed himself for probably the first time since his youth.

Dandon watched him sketch the whereabouts of these other wards and shrank back when Adam added two words above them.

Below ground.

'The curse of the Lord is in the house of the wicked.' Dandon's voice was almost inaudible.

Peter Sam leaned over the paper. 'What about constables within? How many?'

Cowrie laughed. 'There's only four turnkeys in Newgate, mate! *Four*! They don't want to have to pay for any more. The gaol looks after itself!'

'How is that?' Dandon asked.

Cowrie began almost to whisper, relishing the feeling of his peers hanging on his words. 'If you can't pay for your food and lodgings they makes you a steward. If you're the last man in you do the scullery and the slopping and the fires, and the man who did it before you gets put up to something better. That can go on for years.' He paused and his face dropped at some memory. 'There's some bastards in there who've been at it so long they run the wards now. They keep the order. They have to, else someone might remember they should've been hung years ago. Perfect bloody world in there, so it is.'

Peter Sam scowled. 'Would they resist?'

Cowrie shrugged. Answer enough. Dandon thought on the tunnel and the bellman from St Sepulchre tolling his poem down the final cells. 'Where are the cells for those awaiting execution?'

Adam went back to his sketch. 'Along the north side, here, below the streets. The way leads to the sessions house next door to take the condemned straight down. But don't think you can break into the sessions to get to the captain. You can get out of Newgate eventually. Easy enough. There ain't no legal way to get in.'

Dandon folded up the sketch. 'We do not intend to break into the gaol or the sessions house, young Adam. The Lord will provide our entrance.' He stood, dwarfed by Peter Sam. Cowrie, sensing his audience was at an end, waved his brothers in closer.

'But listen, lads. I ain't told you of the worst of it.' He leered at the faces drawing closer, some of the patrons of the Plough forgetting their manners and edging in also. 'Debtor's Hall is on the first floor of the Common Side, near the chapel, a ward without beds, which don't mean much in itself but next to it is a kitchen.' He paused again and took a drink from his leather mug of buttered ale. 'Now there's lots of kitchens in Newgate but this one has a couple more fires and more grates besides. Grates for the draining of *fat*. This be called "Jack Ketch's Kitchen" to be sure.' He drank again, swallowed hard. The others passed looks around at the traditional title of the man who held the axe or tied the hemp knot.

'What goes on there, Adam?' a voice piped up at his side. He smiled again but there was pity in the limp attempt. 'Well, Old Jack there, that be his galley, see? That's where he boils the quarters of those been had away for treason, see?' He swivelled his head to the cold faces waiting on him. 'It costs you sixpence a day for supper in Newgate . . . But thems that can't pay has to eats as well.'

Dandon, Peter Sam and Hugh had not heard him. They were already on their way. To the river. To their captain. London just another horizon to cross.

Chapter Seven

✖

At Newgate another knock came on Langley's door. This time he lit up at the sight of the face at the hatch and hurried to unlock the bolts and hasps.

'Jon Wild! General!' He opened the door wide and Wild stepped in, George following at his heels loyally. Wild sniffed the air, rubbed down his red wool coat and plucked out his cuffs, his silver-capped cudgel under his arm. 'Good to see you again, Thomas,' he said. 'I was wondering if you could afford me some time with that prisoner I brung in this morning. That John Coxon.'

Langley locked back the door. 'He's a popular fellow that one. You be the second to see him tonight.'

'The second? Who else?'

Langley saw no harm in telling. Wild after all was a court's man. 'A secretary from Leicester House so he says. And a dirty fellow in yellow with him.' He walked past, carrying his keys, towards the hold.

Wild and George followed, Wild's face screwed up in thought at the revelation of a man from the Prince of Wales come to see a prisoner of Newgate. There was coin here somewhere.

Langley spoke on. 'What is your business with him, General? It's late now. I could be hung for this.'

'He killed one of mine did he not? Left a widow and four

children.' A lie. 'I believe our Arthur deserves some instant justice. His wife has beseeched me so.'

Langley stopped. 'I can't have any killing or word against me.'

Wild patted Langley's shoulder. 'No, no. Just want to know if he has anything more to confess, that's all. That might take a bruise or two, Thomas. You wouldn't begrudge a widow that.'

Langley nodded. Right was right. 'He's still in the hold. Everywhere else is locked up at nine. Come.'

Devlin still sat in the dark. He hadn't bothered to pick up the flint striker bestowed upon him by Thomas Langley to light his lump of candle. It was after eleven now, as rang out by the Charley in the street outside, and despite the imminent arrival of his men there was a gloom within him that the atmosphere of the Lodge made even more seductive to indulge in. He sat against the cold wall, listening to the unsettling mixture of laughter and sobs coming from above and, peculiarly, from below. Perhaps it was just a symptomatic echo from the old stone all about. This was not a quiet place for introspection yet his disposition could not help itself.

A prison, Devlin thought, was a far more lucrative investment than farm or house or hospital. The disadvantages of piracy loomed larger the more time he spent in the company of ordinary men. The prospects and profit of misery seemed to be its only coin.

The gloom crept in again. The loneliest man is the prisoner; a man's self-judgement in the damp darkness is far worse than anything others can tax him with.

He was a pirate. To his recollection he had killed fewer than ten men. Although he reasoned it was in defence of his own life, he had no desire to form their faces in front of him.

Half his life ago he held no violence against any man. Butcher's boy, poacher, servant, fisherman, sailor. Now a pirate. Now murderer and thief.

But perhaps it had been there all along. Waiting. Waiting for the trigger to release the lock. The primer already in the pan. Only a small spark needed.

Maybe this was it now. The end. No pirates would come. They had chosen another captain and sailed on. None of them had wanted to answer the call, the promise of pardon, the legitimacy of a Mart to make them privateers. He was where he belonged. Where he would end. He had killed a man that very morning. Aye, Devlin was where he deserved to be. This is what happens to little boys whose mothers leave them. This is what they get.

He sniffed the thoughts away. It is only the gaol, he agreed with himself. It is the dark and the sorrow of ten thousand souls engraved into the walls and the moans of the poor and guilty. I am only *in* here, he thought, and reached for the flint and striker. I am not *of* here.

He lit the candle and sat back. The light settled like a spell over his mood. And what would I be if not pirate? Still Coxon's servant? Breaking my back on a merchant ship – or worse, a slaver, and begging for scraps of food from what the slaves did not eat? Or back in some trade befitting my birth and tipping my hat to every silk and master wearing a father's purse.

He smiled, softer than his normal rakish grin that preceded someone's death. A prince has called for my assistance, he thought. Little Patrick Devlin from Kilkenny who never knew his mother or a full belly and whose father sold him for four guineas to be a butcher's boy. Summoned by the Prince of Wales, by name.

He looked around the walls glistening in the glow from the faint candle. These walls were fragile now. Transient. Aye. In an hour, maybe less, they would tremble. The candle winked out. He remembered how Blackbeard had cut a similar-sized candle in front of him when Devlin had stared him down. Blackbeard promised to light it when by his own hand he had snuffed out his life, to mark the end of Devlin's days. Devlin smiled in the dark. He had at least outlived that one. The great and terrible Teach was gone as well, the world getting thinner all the time.

The lock sounded again. The door swung, the light stretched to Devlin's boots, and Wild and George bent under the lintel. He knew the rough, wide face of Wild at once and then recognised the other also. The other had been shitting himself when Devlin had last seen him, but his face was different now. Devlin swallowed his instinct to strike. This might mean something.

'Leave us, Thomas,' Wild watched Devlin as he spoke. 'Lock us in. I'll call for you when I'm done.'

Thomas handed George a lantern from the passage, gave a black-toothed sneer and closed the door.

George put the lantern to the stone floor between them. Its light crept up their bodies and under their chins, ghoulishly illuminating their faces and casting their shadows on the ceiling so it seemed that giants looked down on them.

'Well, well,' Wild clapped his cudgel to his palm. 'Captain John Coxon ain't it, George?'

'Reckon it is, General Wild, sir. Aye, Cap'n John Coxon.' George brought out a small turn-off Queen Anne pistol, a gun for shooting under tables or to surprise a man beside you in a carriage who had kissed your mistress. Up close, if you were a step away – in a cell, perhaps – it would be enough.

'What do you want?' Devlin asked. Nothing in his voice.

Wild pointed his cudgel at the man. 'I want you to tell me your name. I want you to tell it and think why I'm here before you say it.' He rested the weapon on his shoulder and waited.

Devlin was still. It had been hours now. His doubts were gone. They were coming and right soon.

'It wouldn't be best to be around me right now, lads.' He touched his head. 'I still owe you for this.'

Wild took a step. 'Your name. I asked it.' Wild was used to men going back when he came on. This one stayed. No mind. He had all the power here. And he had been in Newgate before. He bent down quickly, blurred in the light, and whipped up Devlin's chain and pulled it high. Devlin slipped to his back as Wild put it over his shoulder and held it there, got comfortable under it. Devlin writhed on the floor; he was nothing more than Wild's hooked fish now. George was laughing and Wild grimaced, keeping the chain taut, as Devlin struggled, his fettered leg above him. Wild jerked his head and grunted at George and George went to work.

Peter Sam strode down the centre of Old Bailey, keeping apart from Hugh and Dandon who stuck to the walls and alleys like rats since crossing the canal at Fleet bridge. He did not follow Dandon's reasoning that the tunnel was their best action. To him, if you wanted anything, if you wanted a town even, you went up to the largest door and shot the man who opened it and it was yours.

But Dandon had warned of watchmen and riots and guards so that, softly, softly, they would enter and softly, softly, they would leave. Peter Sam thought Dandon did not understand the world. His was linen and silk, Peter's steel and lead, and Dandon would be grateful for that when the time came. He had walked through London for the first time in his life and seen ten swinging cages above the streets and three scaffolds. Nothing in those sights persuaded him that his world was wrong. Even so, the edifice of the gaol slowed him a little.

'Where is this church?' he called to Dandon, who put a quietening finger to his lips. The streets were empty, the shops long closed, but the taverns glowing and full.

'It is there,' he pointed north and joined Peter who then saw the impressive tower framed against the sky, the tallest church tower in London since being rebuilt from the ashes of The Fire. 'The road widens some at the crossroads here. We should stay to the shadows. The patrons of the inn opposite may become curious of those abroad at such an hour.'

Peter went on. 'I won't question thems that don't question me.'

Dandon and a giggling Hugh followed.

Peter gave a nod to the gaol on his right, noting the two small doors either side of the large one. 'I still say we should just blow that and be done.'

'Aye,' Dandon dashed ahead. 'We are all aware of what you say.'

They crossed Newgate Street to the left, the gaol at their backs, the church railings ahead where Snow Hill began, and heard from some way ahead the strangely discomfiting sounds of song and company from the Saracen's Head.

No gate to the porch, only a low wall and railings around the churchyard, a light from the bay window above. They sprang up the wide steps and Dandon lifted the great ring knocker and cracked it on the oak. He straightened himself, shadowed by his companions, and waited.

Hugh nudged him. 'Do we not try the door ourselves, Dandon?'

Dandon closed his eyes. 'That would imply, Mister Harris, that we were attempting to enter in secret and stealth, would it not?' Hugh began to argue but the sliding back of the bolt behind the door snapped shut his mouth.

Dandon began to contort his face into a pleasing mask as an inch of light opened; but Peter's patience was at an end.

'Enough of this!' The opportunity of an opening door with someone stood directly behind it was too good to pass up. His boot kicked against the wood as he charged between Dandon and Hugh.

There was a startled cry and something fell and rattled and cried again, then held its bloody nose as it looked up at the black form stood feet wide apart in its porch, with blazing eyes and terrible red beard.

Two others followed, one of them pulling pistols and closing the door with a backwards kick.

Richard Maynard, for that was the warden's name, began to slide away from the intruders, his magnificent porch now turned fearsome. He kicked along the flagstones, away into the church, hand held out for mercy toward the giant slowly bearing down upon him.

Blood from his nose soaked his shirt and chilled his chest. There was something clumsy and childish about such a wound; Richard Maynard almost apologised for the drip of his blood onto the fist that pulled him up, as he felt the hot drunken breath in his face.

'The tunnel to the gaol. Where?' The beast dragged him to his sandalled feet with one heave and Richard was thankful that he had at least the answer to the question.

His hand trembled to the right-hand aisle and the steps leading down between two tombs that ended at a low door. Peter threw away Richard Maynard and unhooked a lantern from a pillar. 'Bring him, Dandon,' he ordered, and Dandon took the terrified warden softly by the hand.

'Perhaps a key, Peter?' Dandon suggested to the back already at the steps. Hugh Harris's wicked chuckle filled the church as again Peter applied a powerful boot to its lock and the mortice ripped from the masonry, his lamp already glowing against the white stone beyond as his body vanished below.

'Peter don't do keys, Dandon,' Hugh advised, as he followed Peter's shadow, Dandon pulling a protesting Richard along with them.

'Come, now,' Dandon coaxed the warden. 'Better to be witness than victim, sire.'

A stone stair wound downwards three turns, then an arched coffin of a passage revealed itself, where Peter had to bend some, his lamp the only source of light and even that guttering in the diminished air.

One hundred and twenty feet long, stretching beneath the street – as long as the *Shadow* bow to sternpost, though a longer, narrower walk with the damp walls scraping at their clothes, cobwebs pasting them with dust and flakes of stone.

Squealed alerts ran ahead of them and twisted away from their feet, Hugh stamping and cursing at the sleek, fat bodies that tried to ride on his shoe buckles.

Then a smaller space emerged as the men who carved out the hole lost interest in its finale. Dandon wondered if it was even possible to turn around as his head went into his neck and they sidestepped along.

Peter Sam's grunts echoed his discomfort from the van, while his weapon across his back chipped at the stone overhead. Maybe the final drag had been so designed to force the bellman to carry on, his only option to move forward to the gaol and the condemned, to recite his grisly words outside the cells and recall them to their doom.

Just as every breath became dust the lantern's light shrank to a square. It went no further; a wooden door stood before them. Peter passed the light back to Hugh. He reached for the ringbolt handle but he had no room to force this one – his great strength was reduced to useless nothing in the suffocating confines.

But the iron turned and the door opened like a sea-chest before him, darkness beyond. Richard Maynard's voice rang out behind Dandon. 'One presumes the dead have no need for locks, Gentlemen. May I enquire as to what you fellows intend now you have reached the gaol?'

Dandon was impressed by the man. He had been assaulted and mildly kidnapped, but had piped up like a constable once it was clear that these men had no designs upon his church.

No light within, the lamp pushed away the dark to reveal another passage. No windows. Still very much below ground. An iron latticed door slowly grew discernible some twenty feet ahead, and four similar doors stretched towards it along their right. The condemned cells were now empty after the day's events. They awaited Tuesday and fresh company.

Dandon recalled the plan Adam Cowrie had mapped for them. This passage and its iron door led to another which passed two stairs, one to the wards above, the other to the sessions house beside the gaol. Its principal purpose was that prisoners need not be taken out into the street when summoned, where escape or rescue might occur. Similarly, when condemned, they could be taken directly to the last rooms of Newgate without passing any of their fellow inmates or even a ray of daylight to warm them before their final journey. He took out the crude drawing but cursed as Peter carried away the lantern to scowl at the iron door that mocked him. This one would not move aside so easily.

'Hugh,' he called behind him, not deigning to whisper. 'Bag. To me.' And Hugh shouldered off his satchel with a grin.

George kicked about the ribs and kidneys as Devlin tried vainly to roll away. George giggled and sweated with every blow.

Wild yelled above all the moans from the rooms and cellars about them. 'Your name! Tell me your bloody name!'

Devlin had heard the giggle before. There had been a giant Scotsman once, a real giant. He had giggled and had wide white eyes as he beat on Devlin in a garden in Charles Town in the Carolinas. Devlin feared nothing now and had taken beatings all his life. And once there had been a giant Scotsman. Once. No more.

George took a breath and a wipe of spittle and Devlin grabbed the planted foot and then the back of the leg and then George was flying. Wild watched him slap to the wall and floor and pulled Devlin tighter.

'Bastard!' But he kept back. '*George!*'

George was up and went for the head, away from the reach. A soft noise, again and again. Devlin covered his head and coiled up as best he could with the chain dragging him round. The cell filled with gasps and blows like a bullring and Devlin began to fade.

Soon. Be here soon.

The inmates of Newgate, be their internment short or long, felt the sounds of the night deeper than most. A prison set in a city, rather than excluding those inside from the world, only magnifies the life outside denied.

The thrum of the music of the streets during the day, the laughter and the curses sifting through the open windows, served more justice than the most boiling and fuming judge could ever pen. But it is at night when the dread most comes and for those of the common and felon wards the withdrawing of the day leaves a loneliness like an ossuary upon men's hearts, and sounds that no man should hear are commonplace:

Throats choking on linen, swallowed to end the guilt. Sobs of children hushed by women lamenting their hunger. The drip of blood from necks and wrists of those not wanting to see the dawn.

Now came a new sound, the clap of an explosion from beneath their feet. Those capable sprang upright from their wooden benches or straw-strewn floors, eyes scouting the dark for some account of its origin. Only the large hall of the Felon and Common ward, arched and cloistered like a church, was privy to the dusty cloud pushing up from the staircase below, heralding two dark shapes cut out from the smoke. These were two men with weapons for hands, outstretched and seeking for heads straining through the smoke. The largest of them was silhouetted with the bulbous bulk of a blunderbuss held out from his hip.

The constables of the ward were those prisoners chosen for their ability to keep order. Often they were the most violent men whose price for not being hung was to make sure that their ward was kept clean and peaceful. They had their garnish lifted, their punishments forgotten. And they knew there was always someone straining to take their place, so they protected their corners like wolves.

Bill Dunn owned this hall. He slipped out of his bed, halfway down the wall of the ward, his hardened bull's pizzle dropping out of his sleeve and into one hand, his gully blade from under his pillow held fast in the other. Dunn felt his stewards and the other prisoners look to him as his eyes locked on the big man with the other smaller one now at his back, pistols swinging left and right as they approached together. Two more came behind them, coughing away the sulphurous smoke.

Dunn raised himself out of the dark and into their path. Boldly. Drunkenly. This was his ward by right and scars. The devil to those who entered it. He had raped, robbed and cut his way through London for years, but slept peaceful and deeply despite it all. He had a lot to lose and damn any bastard who dared enter his realm.

'Who the fuck are you?' he asked, his weapons dipping. He had too much gin in his head to fear the lead against him. And he was too used to men backing down from his bullying to expect any different.

Peter Sam was ignorant of Bill Dunn's power. His weapon bellowed and lit the room as much with its noise as its flash – enough muzzle flare to show Dunn's insides painting those too close with a red mist. His body landed with a wet slap upon the stone floor, twenty years of evil deeds finally paid for.

Peter Sam stroked his hot barrel as Hugh Harris at his back ran his pistols around the room to belay the curious. Peter Sam quietened them all with a command to stay in their beds.

'*That's* who the fuck *I* am!' He glanced behind him. 'Dandon! Where away?'

Dandon pushed aside Richard Maynard, who was clinging to his yellow coat. The warden realised his ordeal was over and sank onto a bench in relief.

'I think out of here, Peter, to be the best course.' He held out Adam Cowrie's map and walked toward the only other door in the hall, far to their left under coffered arches and past dozens of beds. Pale faces from the walls watched their weapons as the pirates strode along. Dandon pointed upwards and right to the large arched windows. 'That is the street. Our captain is near the street . . . if he has not been moved, that is.'

Peter Sam opened one of his apostles of powder, lifted a cartridge from his belly-box and reloaded. Hugh covered him as they followed Dandon's steps to the door. This one was iron also. Locked also, after nine o'clock, as Adam Cowrie had warned them. The three rescuers were now prisoners by choice.

Behind them, miscreants who had murdered men, women and children, who had viciously stolen what no man from their streets could afford to buy honestly, lay still in their beds and held their breath until the intruders moved on. Only then did hands in the darkness scurry over Bill Dunn's body like crabs, to strip his corpse naked.

Richard Maynard watched the defilement, the bloodied corpse worse now unclothed. He felt his stomach rise into his mouth as he crept away back to his tunnel.

Peter Sam holstered his weapon on his back and studied the door. It was locked from the outside and another grenadoe was the only way. He went again for the bag but Dandon tapped his shoulder.

'You have had too much of your own way, Peter.'

Peter scowled. 'If I had my way this would be done by now, popinjay.'

Dandon soothed him with a smile. 'This is not a place I wish to be, amongst this walking dead. Beyond this door is a corridor that will lead to the lodge. A fat turnkey named Thomas Langley has heard an explosion. He has heard the boom of your weapon. He is near and clutching his pitiful club and wondering what goes on. We need only to let him know.'

Peter Sam's expression demanded more from Dandon, who merely stepped past him to the door. 'I believe that the fire that last befell this place is still ingrained in the memory.'

He banged his fist against the door fast enough and hard enough for the sound to run down the corridor beyond and echo to the floors above and below, bringing others to hurl themselves against their doors as they heard his cries.

'*Fire!*' Dandon screamed and hammered. 'Fire within! Thomas! We *burn!*'

Dandon charged the door harder and Hugh joined him until it sounded like a hundred desperate fists pounding the stout iron.

Five floors of the gaol took up the cry, for although the burning of the gaol was not of their living horror its rebuilding was very much so. They had seen the charred bones carried out in buckets, the skulls locked in screams later sketched for the broadsheets as stone by stone the Newgate hell was raised again.

Men condemned to die but still fearing judgement and an earlier dispatch by fire, too close to judgement, howled for release. Thomas Langley sped from his lodge to the nearest door. The Common Felons ward. That was where the horrendous clamour that had broken his sleep was coming from.

He soon had the right key rattling off his apron leathers, his pizzle in his fist. Buckets of sand along the walls stood ready and prisoners to aid him, for they would help to save themselves. The governor would be pleased that he had averted tragedy. With a few of the constables from the wards to assist, the fire would be quelled. There would be no fire on his watch. Why was he so heavy? Damn his feet.

Shouts for mercy ricocheted about as he scurried along the corridor. He heard his name called again and again from above and below, yet something was not quite right. Certainly there was the smell of smoke but the stench of the sea-coal was always present and screams were nothing new. Whatever niggled him was forgotten as Langley reached the ward. The key turned soundly even though his hand trembled and the faces beyond the open door seemed right – but only for a moment.

It was the black turnover pistol emptied into his face that told Thomas of his error.

No fire without smoke.

Hugh Harris stepped over the body and switched the double barrel to its second load as calmly as winding a watch. Peter Sam and Dandon studied the map.

Another corridor ran to the left and right of them, this one lit at least. Old lanterns hung from the ceiling, polished horn instead of glass lending a waxy hue to the stone of the walls. The stifled cries above them were merely irritating.

'There is a taphouse soon. The captain is lodged beyond.' Dandon folded away the map. 'Then, Peter, we shall leave as you wished to come in. Onto the street.' He relieved the late Thomas of his loop of bridge ward-keys, almost all of which would open any of the doors of the gaol; the ward-lock was simple and common throughout.

Dandon locked the door behind them. 'I don't think we need any more distractions. Prisoners finding their way out through the church by the tunnel may cover our escape.' He pocketed the keys. 'And with these we need not add more violence to our exit.' He pointed them all southwards and they hurried on, for the cries echoing from all floors would bring query from the streets outside soon enough, and their endeavour would be discovered.

'Hold, George!' Wild needed a breath himself. The pirate had taken enough. 'I thinks your name's Patrick Devlin. I thinks you're a pirate. A wanted man. Five hundred pounds to me, dead. This can't go much further. You tell me what the prince wants with scum like you. How much coin to keep you alive? What you got, pirate? Where is it?' He nodded to George for a final kick but Devlin held up his palm.

Wild was satisfied. All men break. All of them. 'Let him be, George. Pirate?' He gave him enough slack to sit up. George clicked his snap at the pirate and stood back.

Wild purred. 'What'll it be? Dead or alive?'

Devlin looked up and grinned through his blood.

'Can you hear that? That's your end.' He wiped his face on his sleeve and tutted at the claret. A Holland shirt wasted. Wild dropped the chain. The two men listened to the walls and heard the cries, faint but growing louder, and Devlin looked at their faces which moments ago had been hard and thoughtless. Devlin would remember the effect of the word '*Fire!*' on the world.

Chapter Eight

*T*he sounds of terror had not been lost on Patrick Devlin. But unlike Wild and George he calmly stood and straightened his clothes.

Wild sprang to the door, the cries louder there, his ear to the hatch he could not open from his side.

'Fire, Jon?' George held a nervous pistol on Devlin.

'Langley!' Wild hammered the door with his wood. '*Langley!*'

'He can't hear you,' Devlin said. 'He's busy.'

'What'll we do, Jon?' George wiped his forehead, already imagining the sweat of a fire.

'Keep him back against the wall. Langley will come for us.' He banged again, called again, but only the cries of woe responded.

'Justice has found you, Wild. And me.' Devlin looked at George, the face he had worn that morning back again.

'Shoot him, Jon?' George hissed.

Wild backed away from the door. 'No. We may need that shot.'

'You may need me.' Devlin shrugged. Then they all heard the key rattling in the lock and Wild grinned back to the pirate. 'Langley knows where his bread is buttered, scum.'

The door opened again, as it had many times that day, far more than usual. Three men filled the frame, sharing different heights and aspects but just one expression for all. George grabbed Devlin and put his little gun to his head.

'Keep away! I'll—'

Hugh Harris shot him in the eye. George's other eye rolled up and he fell away like a dropped broom. Devlin stepped away and nodded to Hugh.

Peter Sam was now inside the cell and Wild drew back his stick. Brave man: Peter Sam towered above most, but no-one could question that Wild had sand.

Peter Sam crashed the stock of his blunderbuss into Wild's thick chin and he went back like a hurled sack. His legs held, though, and he staggered up again, only to have the butt repeatedly driven into his face until he stayed down in the corner with his eyes closed.

Dandon came in last and looked to the fallen. 'You have grown company since last I saw you, Patrick.'

'You took your time,' was all Devlin said, as Dandon rifled through the keys on the ring to one that looked suitable to free the chain above his boots.

'Forgive our tardiness, Captain.' He grimaced at Devlin's bloodied face. 'Although you seem to have been entertained.' He went to work on the manacle.

'My gun. My hat, coat and sword,' Devlin ordered as he shook the iron free.

Peter Sam kicked the lump that was the Thief-Taker General. 'And him? You want him dead?'

Devlin touched Peter's shoulder and looked down at Wild's unconscious form. 'I think this one's time will come soon enough. I reckon he owes the whole city justice. We'll get my things.'

Dandon sympathised but sensed danger. 'We have a hundred guns and twice as many swords, Captain, on the

Shadow. We should leave with the greatest expedience, for London is probably gathering outside as we speak and—' Devlin placed a hand on his shoulder to quiet him.

'My gun. My hat. My coat and sword. And dagger. They took them from me.' He stepped out of the cell.

'He don't understand, Cap'n.' Peter Sam held out his hand for the keys and Dandon passed them over with a shake of his head. Hugh Harris jigged an elbow into Dandon's side. 'You be wise, Dandon. But you ain't a pirate.' Then they followed Devlin and Peter Sam to the hold, Thomas Langley's guard-house afore the Lodge where prisoners' goods were kept. The cell and the bodies within were now just another bottle-neck tale to drink to.

Dandon rued another five minutes in the dank cavern, away from the front door and the freedom of the night; it was another five minutes for Charleys, constables and watchmen to gather in the street outside and wonder at the strange lack of flames.

Outside in Old Bailey and Newgate Street a crowd was indeed gathering. Richard Maynard, the church-warden, had returned to St Sepulchre, too weary to ring the bells but able enough to shout for help in the streets. He was sobbing through his cries. The good book had not prepared him for the actual touch of devils.

Thomas Langley was not the only turnkey that night. Two others regularly attended on the Master Debtor's side, the gatehouse of old that bestrode Newgate Street and retained its original Roman wall, though hidden now beneath the sprawl of the city.

The turnkeys had joined the throng in the street. At first

they had fled from the cries of fire, but were now trying to calm the people who had stumbled out of the nearby inns, informing them there was no fire and to return to their holes. Private firemen appeared, pushing their engines up Bailey and Sepulchre-Without, and checked whose buildings displayed their brass insurance plaques. It was those that had paid for the service that would be watered down first.

The Watch and Ward, their lanterns aloft, their cudgels keeping back the mostly drunken crowd, prayed that the absence of fire would settle the maddened horde. But still from the edifice of the stone gaol the prisoners howled for release and rescue, and the crowd began to push towards the massive double-doors, the aged watchmen unable to reason with or hold back the human tide. The mob was about to break; a riot crouched just a smashed window away.

Then gunshots rang out from the gaol. A collective gasp rushed through the crowd and ceased the cries from the windows of the gaol. The street fell into silence.

One report after another as a world of guns blasted into the great wooden doors and lamplight pierced like arrows through the shot holes. Then nothing. More silence. Behind the doors calm men reloaded for whatever waited outside.

The oak doors crashed open.

Women put their hands to their mouths and ragged children peered excitedly between their fathers' legs as four unholy figures, framed for a moment in the light from behind them, stepped slowly from Newgate and into Old Bailey. The figures wallowed in the breathless hush that met them; terror their meal.

The firemen pulled back their carts and the watchmen shrank into the crowd as three of the men swept weapons across the circle of eyes frozen upon them.

One spoke. Pointed his sword to his left and the populace covering the street.

'Clear a way,' he ordered, and the crowd opened for him as if a tree were toppling down on them. Now their eyes followed his bloodied face as he strode through them.

The others came with him, walking backwards as if well practised in being outnumbered. No uncertainty was on display; their weapons were held steady as stone and just as quiet. All save one, that was, a fellow unarmed, wearing an elaborate yellow justacorps, who tossed to the street a ring of keys and whisked off his flamboyant hat in farewell as his comrades disappeared into the shadows.

'I am sorry for the gunplay! I could not find the correct key! Goodnight, London!' He bowed. 'Regrettably your hospitality is not to our taste!' Then he too was gone, swallowed up by the narrows of the honeycombed streets. They had appeared for seconds only but would remain in the crowd's memory forever.

The mob closed together, huddled now, with guesses and rumours shivering around the cross of streets where justice and punishment proudly stood. Whispers and then even laughter arose from those who realised what they had witnessed.

One of the turnkeys picked up the key-ring and tried to lock back the doors to general disapproval from the assembly. He gave up, faced them with a grimace, waved away their catcalls and went inside to bar the door.

Whatever had happened this night, no matter how small his part, the turnkey was certain that a fire could have been no worse. Tomorrow was already regretted.

Chapter Nine

Tuesday

*T*wice a day the booksellers of Paternoster Row would churn out their broadsheets. London groups of quality, so impatient to learn of what had occurred in the hours just gone by, would gather in the nearby 'ordinaries' and were affectionately labelled the 'Wet Paper Club'.

The narrow street off St Paul's, almost too narrow for even the most demure *caroche* carriage, had since medieval times been the centre of the printers' world, although then of a more ecclesiastical nature. The publishing of religious doctrine had long been replaced by the no less important regurgitation of scandal and political fervour.

Street signs had long been banned in London – so severely did the over-hanging signs interfere with the traverse of carriages – and consequently, ingeniously, the traders alighted on the idea of models and wood-carved figurines to announce their trade and compete against the hawking of the street vendor.

With no street numbers and with so many of the common populace illiterate, these symbols and statues were signposts as clear to the Londoner as milestones to the rural bumpkin. The pawnbrokers in Cheapside, sir? Certainly, that be Mr Mainwaring where the three golden balls hang. The hosiery in

Whitechapel? The golden leg of Joseph Barnes will be your destination. And so Paternoster Row adopted the same.

To your right the Black Boy, no sir, not a tobacco purveyor, but the premises of Mr Taylor where you may still purchase that most famed work of Mr Defoe's, *Robinson Crusoe*, published last year. And here be The Ship to your left and The Globe and all manner of colourful filigree – so that the whole street glistened and shone like a toyshop with its tiny dolls and models.

Prince George knew none of this and cared less. Secretary Timms had sent a boy out early, as he did every morning, to purchase the morning editions for His Highness. He dried the sheets personally in front of the kitchen fire at Leicester House and presented them, pristine, on the prince's reading table at his breakfast; his ten o'clock breakfast of ham and beef joints and not the earlier awakening of bread, milk and honey that he took in his rooms.

The prince, still in his night-robes and cap, chewed determinedly as he glanced over the morning sheets. He nodded his dismissal to Timms but called him back with a spluttering of beef as he choked on the morning headline.

'Your Highness?' Timms returned to his master's side as George wiped his mouth and aided his recovery with a sip of brandy and water. Then Timms's eyes fell to the crisp sheet of print upon the desk. The prince coughed through his linen. The servants in the room studied the prince's exasperation from the doors and corners but would never move without being summoned.

The headline Timms saw was typically garish. 'MURDER'. A murder in Wapping, he read. A timely apprehension by the brave and competent Thief-Taker General, Mr Jonathan Wild. But alas to no avail as the villain's accomplices had aided the escape of the murderer identified as one John Coxon of unknown origin. Escape from Newgate no less. Murder of the unfortunate Mr Thomas Langley and another of Mr Wild's assistants added to the villain's toll as did the suspected murder of one of the inmates also.

Timms shivered at the repetition of 'murder'. Four deaths in less than a day. Four killings that could all be marked by one man's hand. Walpole was insane to bring such a man to aid them.

Last night the prince had been assuaged by Timms's inference that if Devlin could escape from Newgate it would bode well for their far more dangerous intentions for the pirate. But this? An inconceivable disaster. The prince's anger was most certainly justified.

Timms lowered his eyes. 'My apologies, Your Highness. I will inform Walpole immediately that we should consider an alternative arrangement.'

Timms was not expecting the riotous laugh.

The prince slapped his thigh, his face redder than usual. 'No, no, Timms! This is perfect! Stupendous! *Capriccio!*' He re-read the broadsheet, his head shaking in disbelief and joy. 'I look forward to meeting this fellow for myself, Timms! I am envious that you have been so privileged before me!' He forked some more of the beef. 'If anything he has no other recourse than to assist us!' Again he almost choked on his humour. 'He has probably made himself the most wanted man in London, by God!'

Timms forced a smile. He kept sheltered his own distaste at considering the services of a murderer to be beneficial. Walpole's insanity, he decided, was clearly infectious. The afternoon would settle it. The pirate had still yet to appear, after all.

* * *

Leicester House sat on the north end of a public landscaped square in what had once been St Martin's field. The public gardens, now known since the building of the house as Leicester Field, were a left-over from the old 'common-lammas' where cattle-men could graze their stock freely and without reproach. Now it served for Sunday strolls and coy 'meetings'.

At one time the house had stood almost alone, with a southerly slope of fields cascading all the way down to Charing Cross. Now it was surrounded by shops and taverns as much as any part of the city. Still, the house was one of the grandest in all of London and had proved a suitable dwelling for the Prince of Wales for the last two years, since he had fallen out of favour with his father. And since then it had also become the unofficial hub of the King's opposing government. The prince could think of no better circumstance to annoy than to patronise the politicians that his father distrusted the most. This afternoon, however, it was Whigs that ate and drank their way through his stores.

Devlin approached. The wide thoroughfare that edged the square was divided by bollards the shape of sugar-loaves with pyramid tops, to separate the pedestrians from the carriages, and he used the throng of people as cover to snake towards the open gate of the mansion.

He stopped by the Standard Inn, built almost connecting to the front wall of the house, and loaded his pipe to study the palace – for palace it surely was.

He counted from basement to attic four floors, and glass that outdid every other house in the square. Five hundred pounds a year was the prince's rent, and it showed.

There were two entrances. One for trade and servants with a single wooden gate and one of iron with Tuscany square pillars, lanterns atop, almost as tall as a man, which would not have looked out of place on the stern of a Spanish hundred-gunner. Devlin halted a passer-by for a light he did not need just to spy over the fellow's shoulder on the two manned sentry-boxes athwart the gate. Shako-wearing lobsters stood scratching themselves. He thanked the Samaritan for his tinder box. The man tipped his hat at the clean shaven young man who, although he did not wear wig or queue to keep his black hair from about his shoulders, had some manner to him judging by his silken black coat, damask waistcoat and fifty-guinea sword – chosen by Devlin as more elegant than the face-cutter he normally wore. The man's brown leather boots had seen better days, however, and his face was bruised in a way that only comes from drunken fighting; thus observed, the gentleman sniffed hautily and went on his way.

Almost two o'clock now. Devlin rapped out his pipe against the wall of the inn. He had agreed to come alone and so took off his hat, fanning his face in the August sun. His three watchful companions, Peter Sam, Hugh Harris and Dan Teague, keeping their distance, saw the signal and manned their posts at every other entrance of the square, watching Devlin approach the sentries.

The lobsters' buckles and brass rattled as he came towards them but they relaxed when they saw no pistol hanging from the tall man's belt. They gave him the dead eye as Devlin passed his letter to the one who at least looked like he might be able to read. Their manner changed at the sight of the royal seal and they let him through immediately.

Patrick Devlin. Butcher's boy, poacher, sailor, servant and pirate, declined to hand over his hat and was escorted to the staterooms on the first floor. He had to pull down with one hand his spreading smirk and entered looking as serious as he could manage.

Chapter Ten

The prince and the pirate.

*O*f everything in the room the first thing Devlin noticed was the gigantic fireplace in black and white marble. Large enough for four men to stand in its hearth, it dominated the spacious first-floor hall. Four ceiling-high casement windows drew down the afternoon sun as if those needed it to bask like reptiles, and its heat was such that Devlin could not help but remove his hat, required or not. The circular oak dining table in the centre of the room, and the five men seated around it who turned their heads to him, stopped his reckoning of the room. Cards in hand, their game froze as if posing for a portrait, while they took in the figure of the pirate.

One was corpulent and flushed, even beneath his white-powdered cheeks. His colourful clothes accentuated his shoulders, padded to give him a warrior's profile, but his drawn-in doublet could not hide his paunch. His hair, without a wig, was grey and tufted like a squirrel's brush. Still, Devlin put him at under forty. That man, Devlin thought, is the prince.

Two others were as corpulent but wore subtle natural wigs and more muted clothes. They weighed Devlin with their eyes. A brief wince at his freshly beaten face was noticed by the pirate. The last two, were lean and handsome, their clothes as neat as pins. One Devlin knew, but did not betray his recognition. The man hid his own expression behind a thoughtful palm and studied the new arrival.

Devlin waited for an introduction but the servant who had led him upstairs had already backed, bowing, out of the room, and locked the door behind him.

Five pairs of eyes held him rooted to the spot where he stood. The opening duel was important and Devlin would not feel awkward. He knew this was how these men ran their lives in houses of servants and slaves. It was how they commanded ships and serfs, how one percent of the population controlled ninety-five percent of the nation's wealth. Their sneering arrogance was really all they had. Every drawn lip and disdainful eye he had ever seen was seated in that room before him.

Devlin did not run his hat through his hands. He did not scrape his forehead or shift his feet. He gave his rakish sneer and made for a bowl of grapes on a pedestal set near the round of men. He slung his hat on a chair against a wall and plucked several of the grapes, rolling them like dice in his hand as he motioned to the cards.

'A game of Ombre is it, gentlemen? Full table, so I make it is a five-hand game.' There was no sixth place, nor any chair, available for their guest.

A friendly voice came from behind the hand of the familiar face. 'It is Primero, Captain. And I am not doing well at it I am sorry to say.'

Devlin chewed on a grape without looking in the direction of the voice. A cough from one of the black-clothed men at last opened proceedings. 'Forgive our manners, Captain Devlin. Would you allow me to introduce our company, grateful as I am that you have afforded to join us.' This was Walpole, in charge of the room.

Devlin spat his pip to the floor. 'If you would. I've come a long way.'

Walpole drew a breath, and began to gesture toward the first of the men around the table, but the prince waved him down.

'Wait, wait, Robert,' George turned his chair square to the pirate; put down his cards. 'This man's insolence beguiles me!' Devlin was genuinely surprised by the English from the Hanoverian-born prince. Unlike his father, who ruled Britain with barely a word of it, the son sounded as if he spoke it well enough for the worst whore's bedroom instructions. The prince pointed to the elegant sword at Devlin's waist. 'Whereabouts did you acquire that gold-hilted blade, sir? I'll wager it at least a hundred guineas by its shine yet you appear to wear quite possibly the dirtiest waistcoat I have ever seen and boots that not even a hangman would put on.'

Devlin looked down at his boots, the same boots he had taken off a dying Frenchman three years previously. These were the boots that had bequeathed him the map that had set his destiny. There was luck in their soles.

'These boots are Cordova leather. A cordwainer's master-piece. Older than you or I, easy to suppose. The stitching is entwined with animal skin; it shrinks tight when wet. The heels are elm and the sole is buffalo hide. I'd be buried in them. As for my sword—' He scraped it free, prompting a moment of epilepsy around the table save for the prince and the man still smirking behind his hand. 'I wore it for your company and for the street. Fine for a parade but not much else. You can rest easy on that score.' He ran it back; cracked more grapes in his mouth. 'And, if you want to hear the word, I stole it from another man.' His gaze roamed over all their eyes. 'That's what I'm doing here is it not?'

George grinned and slapped the table. 'Just so! And I suppose the arrogance of a thief is exactly what we do so indeed require!' Devlin briefly detected a trace of accent behind the 'so's and the 'r's.

Walpole riffled through his papers and hemmed. The prince's amusement could never be subdued but to allow Devlin too much brevity at this time, in all probability the only conversation they would ever have on the matter, was not his plan. This would be it. Tomorrow Devlin would be gone to his task. This would be ten minutes that would affect the fate of the world and, if he had to, Walpole would speak over his prince.

'Captain Devlin, if I may, my name is Robert Walpole. The gentleman you have availed yourself to be so familiar with is His Highness the Prince of Wales, heir to the throne of the United Kingdom of Great Britain and the dominion of the Americas.' Walpole paused to watch Devlin pick a grape pip from his teeth. Walpole carried on.

'To my right, Earl Stanhope, to my left Viscount Townshend. We three represent His Majesty's Government in this matter.' Walpole noticed Devlin stiffening as the final member of their party readied himself to be introduced. 'This is Mister Albany Holmes. He represents certain business interests along with the patronage of George Lee, currently at Christchurch.' Walpole waited for some recognition from Devlin. None came. Albany Holmes took the opportunity to reacquaint himself.

'Surely you remember me, pirate? Surely you remember myself and George? Or has the rum finally rotted your brain?'

Devlin took a step closer, his manner threateningly personal. 'Remind me.'

The prince slapped the table again and laughed. 'Ho, this fellow is priceless! Forgive Albany, my boy. His own mind is too addled by his own vices, just so! Methinks he frequents his Sunday club at The Greyhound with far too much involvement!'

Albany bowed to the prince. 'Your Highness,' he acknowledged. 'If the good Captain cannot recall then I shall remind him it was almost a full two years ago now that myself and George were his "guests" on one of his delightful cruises.' He watched Devlin for a reaction but the pirate offered up nothing. 'Where he abandoned us – or rather I believe they call it "marooned" – on an uninhabited island when we had no further use to him.'

'That is not wholly true,' Devlin raised a finger. 'I never had any use for you at all.'

Walpole refused to countenance any retort from Albany. '*Gentlemen*! Now that we have reminisced and dried our sentimental tears may we proceed? Before the rug is pulled from underneath us all.'

Townshend and Stanhope had said nothing. They untied the leather folders that lay before them. They would speak when necessary. Between them they were two of the most powerful men in the land. Their speech mattered too much to waste.

Walpole continued once the prince had waved him on; the prince's amused eyes never left the figure of the pirate.

'Captain Devlin, my intelligence informs me that you are not a stupid man. Also that you are very capable and accomplished in your . . . *field*. Certainly if your actions last night are to be considered, that would seem to be a reasonable assumption at the very least.' Intentionally, Walpole had maintained a standing presence, he and the pirate the only ones. The conversation was just for them. 'Do you perchance have any designs on what we may have in mind for you?'

Devlin checked to the prince, whose grin had not abated. 'A letter found me. You offer me two thousand pounds to attend. Letters of Marque and a pardon for my men – most generous, especially the part in which, if I refuse, your Navy would hound me to the ends of the earth.'

Walpole huffed away Devlin's final statement. 'An over-zealous description, Captain. We merely wished for you to understand that you were not simply being invited to supper.'

'Then I take it that my task – as it is a pirate you wish to engage – has an element of bible tearing attached to it?'

Walpole hemmed again. 'Something like that, Captain. Certainly it is not one that His Majesty's government can be seen to be embroiled in.'

Devlin leaned in, his fists on the table. 'Then I name my own terms.' The quintet leaned away from his glare. 'You assume that a free man would want nothing more than to be chained by your Marque! I don't need your pardon either.'

Walpole took his seat. 'Then what do you want?'

Devlin straightened, now the only man standing. 'I want an amnesty. For my whole ship. All our crimes forgotten. I'll be measured for my new ones only. My past removed.'

Walpole feigned confusion. 'Did you not just say you did not want a pardon, Captain?'

'Not as you give it. A pardon means regret. A pardon means I'll toe the line from now on, means I'm sorry to have picked your pockets in the past. I ain't sorry. I don't need your forgiveness. Just wipe my slate clean and I'll go on and be hung for my future, not my past. Now tell me what shit you need stealing and I'll be on my way.'

Prince George's laughter burst the indignity like a champagne cork. The rest of the table sat aghast. Albany's left hand was resting on his sword pommel.

The prince jumped from his chair and pumped Devlin's hand. 'Good God, sir, you shall have it! I wonder if I could not ask you for the moon and damn you if you would not bring it just so!'

Devlin felt awkward now. Despite his swaggering vigour there was still something uncomfortable about being so close and familiar with a man who would be king. He felt his head involuntarily nod a bow as George thumped his back. In other circumstances he was sure his outburst would condemn him, for these were men who would hang him as soon as think of him; but here he was a fool at court, able to say and do anything so long as it provoked laughter in the prince.

'Show him, Stanhope!' George commanded, and Stanhope obliged. His turn to speak was a rare event, for when he decided to speak his mind nations could fall. He paused for one more second before he slammed onto the middle of the table the largest diamond Devlin had ever seen. Stanhope waited to allow the pirate's eyes to enlarge, transfix themselves and then melt into the gem's infinite whiteness before he spoke again.

'You should get to know it. That is if you are to *steal* it.'

Stanhope spun the diamond on its table, the flat part, its point, almost two inches high, danced a torrent of light as dazzling as the first sunrise across the rapt faces of its audience.

It was small enough to fit softly in the folds of one's hand, gentle as a star and almost as ancient, and in its sparkle and its evocation of eternity even Devlin's cynicism paled.

Stanhope sat back and smiled at the wonder on Devlin's face. But not yet greed – there was no greed in the pirate's eyes. That would need to change if they were to succeed.

Chapter Eleven

The First Diamond

*I*t was the largest diamond in the world at its time of finding and like all great and valuable things that man lusts after its facets were tainted with blood. Even in its earliest age it had become legendary, its gathering of myth greatly enlarging its value.

It would be generations before Africa became the bearer of the world's greatest diamonds; for now that honour was bestowed upon the Indian continent, and even then the term 'blood diamond' referred as much to the diamond mines' use of slavery as to the colour of some of the gems. The diamond that would become 'the Pitt' and finally 'the Regent' had its own share in that blood.

The slave who scraped it from the earth saw in the diamond's immensity the opportunity to buy his freedom from the mines of Parteal. His desperation was so great that he gouged out a hole in his own calf to hide the enormous rough stone. Once buried in his flesh he wrapped his leg in a bandage torn from his clothes and thus hid his crime when his masters searched him at the end of the day. His injury was none of their concern. But the diamond had tasted its first tang of human blood. The nameless slave limped from the mouth of the mine into the light bearing infinite wealth.

He saw in the diamond not beauty or eternity but the price of saving his petty life.

The mines were on the great Kistna river in Bengal on India's east coast, and it was not far for the suffering slave to make his way to the merchant captains. The diamond which would become part of the crown jewels of France and be valued at 480,000 eighteenth-century pounds meant nothing more to the slave than a passage to Madras and liberty.

The captain of the ship also saw the promise of the young man's burden but unfortunately saw no future in the slave's knowledge of its origin. Once at sea, assured by the sea's forgetfulness and drawing the veil of greed over his conscience, he slit the young man's throat and tipped his body overboard – and the diamond had supped its second draught of blood.

Continuing to Madras, the treacherous captain sought out a diamond merchant of quality, the most famous in the East. He sold the diamond to Jamchund for one thousand pounds, a handsome price for a slave's life.

The captain did not barter but sold on the diamond no more than a day after disembarking, ridding himself of the accusing stone as fast as he could before the taint of its acquisition bred regret in him. But it was for naught.

He had already spent too much time with the gem.

Drunk and remorseful he placed a noose around his neck, slung a rope over the roof-beams of a squalid hired room and kicked away a stool: a third meal for the white stone.

When word reached Jamchund that the captain had hung himself the night after he had released the diamond into his hands, the merchant too became uneasy about its future in his house and sought in turn to pass it on.

The governor and appointed president of Madras, Thomas Pitt, had already let it be known that he would entertain any merchant who had interesting diamonds for sale and Jamchund, having fruitfully dealt with Pitt before, made his way to Fort St George, the East India Company's stronghold that protected their interests in the Malaccan straits.

Thus the diamond found its way into Thomas Pitt's possession, and his destiny, but not as profitably as Jamchund would have liked. Pitt sensed an urgency in Jamchund to be relieved of the gem and refused to pay the original finder's fee of eighty-five thousand pounds. Two months of bargaining later, Jamchund was almost begging for the largest diamond on earth – four hundred and ten carats in its uncut state – to be taken off his hands for twenty thousand pounds. Thus its path to the West, and to royalty and empires, began.

The diamond was cut in London to its present one hundred and thirty-six and three-quarter carats, the cleavage and dust of which alone netted Pitt almost eight thousand pounds. And thereafter London wits delighted in Pitt's anxiety concerning his precious stone.

It may have been the diamond's blood-red history or simply the fear of robbery, but when Pitt returned to London to sell the gem he took to disguising himself and developed the nervous habit of never sleeping twice under the same roof. No inn-keeper or hotelier knew of his destination in the evening until a surreptitious knocking on their door announced Pitt's arrival. It was most ironic that the most exquisite gem on earth was hidden from the sun that it craved and that its owner was reduced to a skulking hermit, guarding the stone against the eyes of the world.

'Diamond' Pitt, for so he was mocked throughout the broadsheets, had found his own curse, but nonetheless one that would lay the foundations of his fortune and begin the ascent of his family to greatness.

'Quite a story would you not say, pirate?' Stanhope was watching for Devlin's reaction to the tale.

Devlin came closer. 'You want me to steal this diamond? That is it? That is all?' He put out his hand to the stone. 'Close your eyes.'

Stanhope covered the glittering gem with his palm, stealing its great light from the pirate's eyes. 'Not so simple, Captain. This is but a replica – a substantial one worth a small fortune on its own, but a replica only. It took Pitt two years to have it made. It is an "Irish diamond". Paste. But do not mock it for all that. Its artistry is valued at five thousand pounds on its own. There is not a Jew in the world who could distinguish it I assure you. This is how much we trust in you, Captain.'

Devlin began to sniff the plot; a stagnant stench. 'And where does the real one lie?'

Walpole and the others shared looks, mirth gone from the prince's face. Walpole bid Stanhope to take back his stone. 'The replica was used to enable Pitt to negotiate a somewhat "clandestine" sale to the Duke of Orleans, the regent Philippe, the representative of the French King on earth. Although apparently almost bankrupt after the war, Philippe managed to offer Pitt a king's ransom over several payments. Something I'm sure his starving people very much appreciated.'

Devlin interrupted, fortune ever his abiding interest. 'How much?'

Walpole ignored the vulgar query. 'The regent had made acquaintance with the disgraced financier, John Law, and it was Law who introduced the replica to him, along with Pitt's son who has managed his affairs since Pitt has gone abroad for *seasoning*.' This was the word for acclimatising one's bowels to the Caribbean. Pitt was now governor of Jamaica.

'Philippe intends the jewel to be set into a crown for the

young king at his coronation.' Walpole paused and swallowed. 'We would like it before that.'

'And you want me to go and get it.' He looked at them all. 'Am I permitted to know why?'

Viscount Townshend, Secretary of State, cleared his throat. His turn to speak. 'My brother-in-law has quite a verbose turn of phrase, Captain. We shall be here all day if we are to rely on him to give you your orders.'

Devlin's manner shifted. Orders. The wrong word, spoken softly enough to be missed by powdered ears. He let it lie but would remember its utterance.

'Do you know anything about "business", boy?' Townshend had perhaps fifteen years on Devlin, hardly enough to warrant the form of address. Again, these would be the things that Devlin would keep in his pocket for when the time came.

'I know my own business,' he said.

'No doubt. However, in the earnest world, it is trade that feeds the people. And trade is the order of companies. And British companies rule the world.' There was pride in his tone that did not match the worry in his eyes.

'The design is a simple one. In a company no one man has the power. The responsibilities, and the profits, are spread to all those who have invested so. And, in order to maintain that companies operate appropriately, ministers are "invited" to accept shares, to have an interest in the company pursuing the King's best interests and so on and so forth.' He waved away the last statement as if it were superfluous to all.

'You are aware of the South Sea Company, are you not Captain? I'm sure at some time – how is the phrase? – they have chanced across your bow?' He did not wait for an answer. 'Situations in Europe, for which the aforementioned Mister John Law is not wholly without blame, and developments in the

Americas and Indies, have led to a collapse of several companies, and consequently the financial institutions that depended upon them. We are facing a similar problem in England.'

Walpole snorted under his breath. 'Rather more than a *problem*, Charles!' He assigned a smirk with Stanhope.

Townshend affected not to hear. 'You see, Captain, when one forms a company, the aim is to sell shares in said company in order to support its actions,' he leaned back in his chair, patting his belly in concentration, wondering how far he would need to dilute his intelligence for the simple sailor. 'The object being of course to return a profit for those who partook in such shares. Do you see, man?'

Devlin shifted his feet again but said nothing.

Townshend continued. 'Now, we shall suppose that the company will do well, in fact it cannot fail, sir. The consequence of such confidence elevates the value of the shares to fantastical proportions. A man's very estate can be paid for in the exchanging of his shares in the company. The success is so fully guaranteed that the company even buys the country's war debts, so supreme is it in its confidence that its profits will be sufficiently gargantuan in the years to come.' He raised his arms in mock salutation.

'Hallelujah! The nation puts its faith in a single consortium! "*A company has bought our national debt!*" they cry. "*We are free! And we are rich to boot! Let us invest more into these great things!*"' He slammed his hands on the table. 'And then it bursts!' Townshend slapped the table again. 'All around us! The ships do not exist and no-one is planting any crop! *Parturient montes, nascetur ridiculus mus.* The mountain will be in labour. And a ridiculous mouse will be brought forth.

'The companies sell stocks that can never be returned on. The stocks are oversold. But as long as people believe the

100

shares have value they are traded. First the Dutch companies begin to collapse. Then the French. All allies of the war, expecting great things to come. But alas, the Americas are not delivering the bounty they promised; Spain is still holding the cards she promised to throw! Then panic! Distrust! Disaffection . . .' Townshend's voice trailed off like a poor actor in a poorer tragedy.

'The South Sea Company is the most heavily speculated. It is the cornerstone. It cannot possibly return on its investment. There is not enough coin in the whole of Europe for it to do so.'

Devlin was unmoved. 'And none of you foresaw this would happen? Did you not profit? So a few rich men lose some guineas. What matter? That may teach the dogs a thing or two.'

Townshend's eyes boiled. 'No, no, sir! You do not understand the world!'

Another insult to pocket.

'Whom you perceive to be a rich man loses some of his backing. No matter, you say. But then he cannot afford to pay his tailor's bill. What then, sir, what then? The tailor cannot pay the merchant trader for his cloth. The merchant cannot pay his sailors for their lading. The sailors cannot buy food for their children's mouths. And so it goes on, sir. The companies do not have the money to pay back their loans to the banks that helped them form; the banks then do not have the money to lend to new companies or pay back that which they borrow from each other, until the whole kingdom falters under a mountain of debt and dishonour! A mountain of promise has given birth to only a tiny mouse!'

'Hold, Townshend!' The prince snapped. He had heard enough. He had heard it all for months now, since first Walpole had brought the matter to his happy rooms and suggested the pirate to their cause. This was a time of action not discourse. Townshend bowed his head.

The prince stood and everyone stood with him as always.

'This fellow has been courteous enough to travel half the world at our request. He escaped from gaol mere hours ago only to come here so and listen to you trouts! He holds a sword, not a pen, for us! You wish him to save you all and yet you treat him like a schoolboy!' He came and stood next to Devlin; placed a white hand upon the pirate's shoulder. 'I will tell him what he needs to know. Enough of your paper and wash!'

He took Devlin by his arm like a bride and led the awkward pirate away to his private rooms beyond the table. Devlin looked at Albany Holmes, the gentleman he had marooned two years ago and had never expected to see again. The hate-filled look he returned suggested that Albany had long hoped their first encounter was not their last.

The next room was as large as the first, with a simpler fireplace but the same grand windows from floor to ceiling with black velvet curtains beneath gilt pelmets. Stools, loungers, cushions and small tables suggested some kind of drawing room. Doors in every corner suggested yet further rooms. The only occupant was the skinny black form of Timms, seated at a small desk in the centre. At the door's closing, secretary Timms stood to attention, carefully lifting his chair rather than pushing it back over the enormous Asian rug. After the chamber of strangers the familiar if hostile sight of Timms lifted Devlin's spirits.

The prince moved towards the light of the windows and signalled with a hand for Devlin to follow. 'That is better.' His tone was relieved. 'Such bores these politicians are. Not fighting men like you or I. Save for Stanhope of course. He has blood. As you and I. The Spanish war. The Jacobite problem.' No further word was necessary. George had led the Allied cavalry at the battle of Oudenarde during the Spanish wars. His horse was shot from under him but still he fought on. He was twenty-five years old then. Twenty-three years later he would be the last British king to lead his army into battle.

Devlin joined him by the window, for the purpose it seemed of George showing him a porcelain vase of red and blue tulips sitting in the light. George cradled and weighed the bowl of one in his hand. 'Perfect, Captain! An allusion straight from God.'

Devlin watched the prince caress the flower. This day was quickly becoming one of Devlin's more memorable experiences. He felt no threat or animosity from the Whigs or the royalty smiling amiably at him. But the splendour, the remoteness from his world – he felt the tethers binding him to his men growing thinner with each piece of gilt and opulence, so far removed from his wooden sparsity of ship and tools, mire and blood. He was a servant again, quiet and respectful. As shy as when the butcher appraised him up and down and bartered with his father for his price.

The prince's attention stayed focussed on his flower. 'These are expensive decorations, Captain. Two guineas' worth. Yet one can buy a nosegay for a penny that smells sweeter. Last century, Captain, the price for one bulb could fetch two hundred and twenty-five pounds. The Dutch did little else but trade in tulips. They stopped making things or growing anything else for their people. Tulips became everything.' He peeled a petal and popped it into his mouth. 'I could even be imprisoned for such an act as that.' He placed the flower back with a ridiculous chortle. 'Yet it is just a flower. But if one man – the right man – says one thing is valuable, it becomes so. And men go mad for it.' He moved away and Devlin followed a step behind. 'The diamond has the same power. In the world they are often found at one's feet; washed up in rivers, picked like potatoes.' He spun to Devlin with a raised finger. 'But they are not found *here*. As the tulip, they are exotic, absent. That makes them rare. They are on the other side of the world. And one man tells another man that they are valuable and they become so.'

Devlin had a piece to add, and scaled his voice as politely as he could. 'I have some experience of porcelain along those lines.' He could not bring himself, even deliberately, to inject any title in his address to his companion. The prince did not appear to notice but Timms flashed a violent eye at Devlin.

'Exactly!' George beamed. 'Once the myth is broken it is like a fairy tale outgrown.' He picked out the remainder of the petal from his teeth and dropped it to the floor. 'But it is just a flower after all.'

The prince puffed out his chest. A hand on Devlin's shoulder. He patted him like a favoured dog; almost a tear in his eye.

'My father is the appointed head of the South Sea Company. Half his government sits on its board. Almost all of them have interests in its success. But it is finished. It will break.' He moved to the table where Timms stood. 'Come September, when the Company must pay its dividends, the pot will be empty. As much as I would enjoy my father experiencing such public embarrassment I do not wish it on his people.' He gestured to Timms, his first acknowledgement of the black-coated presence. 'Timms will explain. I ask, personally, for you to aid us. To aid me. Far beyond any monetary reward. A royal hand will be at your command.' A tear truly welled in his eye now, as if emotion could move Devlin to action more than coin.

Timms cleared his throat. 'The plan, Captain, is that you will secure the "Regent" diamond – as the Duke of Orleans has christened it – secretly and without arousing suspicion. You will exchange it for the replica so its absence is never missed. Once returned the diamond will be cut into smaller stones, the object of which is that the smaller gems will be enough security to keep the South Sea Company from collapsing. The diamonds will underwrite the debts. All will be well. The Company secured. Your reward given.' He paused, swallowed, the final words given almost apologetically.

'You have two weeks to turn the tide of fortune.'

Devlin burst back into the main room, flinging wide the doors, and the men at the table started and ducked at the wild entrance. The prince and Timms stood behind.

'*Two* weeks!' He began to circle the table, a panther's creep, stalking around the wigs and paunches, their heads following him like dogs watching their master's plates. 'Last night you were willing to have me rot in Newgate for a week if I had not taken matters into my own! What then? Would you have given me a week to snatch your gem?'

Walpole stood. 'Just so, Captain. Your resourcefulness has given us a wealth of time and we are honoured to you. The Company is to hold a general meeting on September 8th. We need the diamond – that is the new "diamonds" – to give a positive to that meeting; to claim that those diamonds represent merely a promise of the Company's future. Of course if you had come to us sooner our time would not be so limited.'

Devlin stopped. 'I had guessed at some point the blame would fall at my feet. Though I hadn't judged so soon.'

Walpole, his statesmanship his mark, was unruffled. 'Time is our enemy. The Company's reports are due next month. Our intelligence informs that the diamond is to be sent for setting in a new crown in a matter of days. We are committed to not allowing that to happen.'

'And why me!' Devlin raised his arms. 'You must have hundreds of agents more willing than I. More *worthy* than I.'

'And more trustful,' Walpole resumed his seat. 'Do not presume in particular that we flatter you, Captain. Our task must be vouchsafed to as few souls as possible. To include our own agencies in this matter would be suffering to the end of it. You have your own ship, your own men and a talent for theft.'

'But why me? You could lift a thousand pirates who might bow more. Why my head to risk?'

Albany Holmes snarled from the back of his hand. '*Parlez-vous français, Capitaine?*'

Devlin understood. That was it then. Not his competence or fortitude, although his history had no doubt played a part: his selection was due to his other life, his life before this one.

Before becoming Coxon's servant, before being whisked into this pirate life, he had lived for two years along the French coast in Brittany. He existed as a poor fisherman, hiding from injustice in London, whence he fled to avoid a murder charge but where he had originally run to, dodging a noose in his native Kilkenny – some shot had cracked the teeth of a magistrate's wife as she bit into his poached game.

It had been a good few months in London at an anchorsmith's with a man named Kennedy, almost learning a trade until the old man's murder, most likely by his dog of a son, took him to his feet again. Devlin was innocent, but an Irishman was wise to fear English justice.

He had even spent some time in the Marine Royale, the French navy. Had been to Paris and seen the great privateer René Duguay-Trouin, now chef d'escardre of the Marine Royale.

Devlin spoke French. Spoke it well. That was it then, nothing more.

A conspiring chortle lifted around the table at Albany's words. Walpole raised his voice above it. 'Your knowledge of the language and the coast will be invaluable Captain, I am sure, but more important is your secrecy and subtlety.'

Devlin turned away from the table and went to the window to look over the square.

'I take it, Captain,' Walpole pitched over to the window, 'that you accept our proposal?'

The prince and Timms crossed the threshold of the room, the others rising as they did so. All waited for the answer.

Devlin, his eyes still on the square below, spoke slowly. 'And what would happen if I did not? Now that I have heard all this, I wonder.'

Walpole sighed. 'Then I'm afraid I shouldn't wonder – especially after your activities last night – that you may not get out of this city alive, sir.'

Devlin turned. The evil on his face was the least of their expectations. Walpole especially shrank from it, while Albany again touched his sword.

Devlin looked beyond the men at the table straight at Timms. 'You've not told them?'

Timms found himself blushing as all eyes fell upon him. He survived the stares by addressing himself only to his prince.

'I'm afraid, Your Highness, that I have neglected to inform that the captain did not arrive at Falmouth as instructed. Nor come to London with just one other.'

George's smile vanished. The noble prince returned, his glare for Timms alone. 'Go on.'

'The captain informed me, last night in the gaol . . .' the words stuck in his gullet and Timms looked at a point above his prince's head, not wishing to meet his eye. 'He has brought his ship with him. His whole crew apparent.'

The table exploded with flung papers and cries of outrage and disgust. Devlin shattered the tableau, more suited to the hustings, with a shrill whistle.

He crooked a finger at the prince and beckoned him to the window. Amused again both by the pirate's flavour and the splutter of the Whigs, the prince went so and Devlin gave him room; showed him the game in the square.

Devlin leant in close to the prince's ear and pointed out those he had posted to watch the house. Obediently each seemed to turn and look up at the house. Each had a sword at his side, a brace of pistols hanging from his belt. Devlin tapped the glass with a dirty nail to draw the prince's eye down to the front of the house. The two sentries were sharing a pipe with a big man in a long black coat, distinguished against the smarter set of the square by his bald head and red beard.

'At my signal,' Devlin whispered. 'They come.'

George backed away from the window. 'What signal?' he asked, but already his eyes had fallen to the small turn-off pistol, smaller than the hand it now sat in, which was pointed at his belly. The weapon had been hidden somewhere in the folds of the pirate's clothes but was now revealed.

For a moment Devlin enjoyed George's revulsion then shifted the pistol harmlessly to the window. 'I shoot the glass, perhaps.'

The prince straightened and turned back to the table of shocked, frozen faces that had glimpsed the now-vanished pistol. He did not move away from the pirate.

'It appears, Walpole, that perhaps it would be ourselves who would not leave alive. The pirate has men all about.'

Walpole stood, his voice unperturbed, weary of the drama. 'In that case, Your Highness, may you permit me to escort captain Devlin further. Set him on his task and meet the men he needs to know.' He lowered his chin to Devlin. 'That is if you will permit me safe passage, Captain?'

Devlin nodded. 'But they will follow.'

Chapter Twelve

Some in clandestine companies combine;
Erect new stocks to trade beyond the line;
With air and empty names beguile the town,
And raise new credits first, then cry 'em down;
Divide the empty nothing into shares,
And set the crowd together by the ears.

Daniel Defoe.

*T*he value of a diamond falls to but two points: its weight, which can be estimated in the rough by even the most common hand; and its water. The water is the diamond's clarity, its *caelestis* property, the heavenly clarity and depth that beguiles and tempts even the gods to possess it.

In the ancient world the diamond was revered for its supernatural aspects, its eerie nature, almost forgotten in modern times. Rubbed upon flesh a diamond will glow in a darkened room as well as when exposed for hours to the sun and then removed to the dark. The lapidaries, the artisans of precious stones for us simpler Europeans, examine their gems in the light; in India it is done at night.

Steeped in hot water a diamond will also glow, and brushed with silk the same occurs – magic in a world where the new science was pushing back the old mysteries. And where the diamond is, there too is gold. It was no coincidence that the hunt for alluvial gold in the South Americas and the Indies first brought diamonds to the surface, the two linked forever with wealth and avarice, sharing the same properties of portable wealth and the same power to make even the most sordid hand beautiful.

The Pitt Diamond held a water quality of the highest level, a true transparency. After cutting, it weighed just over one-hundred and thirty-six carats and when tossed in the hand, no greater description befits the magnificence of the most valuable diamond in the world than that it shared the size and weight of a small plum.

It was supposed that Pitt had settled for a third of the diamond's true worth, perhaps in the same sweat of dread that persuaded the merchant Jamchund to lower his price to be rid of it.

Between the murdered slave who gouged a hole in his own leg to hide the stone and the captain who murdered him before taking his own life in remorse, one can suppose in a more fanciful age that it was more than the diamond's eternal beauty that haunted its owner's dreams.

So Pitt accepted a sale for a third of its value to the ruler of France. To be rid perhaps. After expenses he still came away with at least one hundred thousand pounds, four times the yearly income of the King. The cutting of the diamond into smaller stones might make ten times that – enough to warrant enlisting a pirate to steal it back.

First, Change Alley in Cornhill then on to Jonathan's Coffee house, an area of London unfamiliar to Devlin although the narrowness of the ways and the shadow from the crowd of buildings was very much recalled. The London streets of his memory had looked much the same, but their trading of purse for the flash of a knife perhaps had more honesty than the financial chimeras lurking in this quarter.

A two mile walk meant nothing to Devlin's boots, but the thinness of Walpole's soles meant his black coach was called. Devlin had never been in a coach. Alighting, he took the step down daintily, as if afraid to fall, and hoped that his men, shadowing them, did not see.

He had almost sailed the world, met almost every foreigner in it and was knowledgeable in all its coin and politics that ended at the point of a sword. But he stepped down gingerly like a child before Walpole's smirk.

'Have you ever had tea, Captain?' Walpole pointed his cane to the alley.

'Daily, Minister. Coffee too. Never paid a penny for it.'

'That's my boy!' He slapped Devlin's back. 'If they ever bill me I'll be broke!'

Small-paned windows made up the frontage, revealing the crowd within. A single door opened into a large hall that reason insisted should not have been inside such a narrow alley.

The room was full. Fawn and white coats under black hats and candle chandeliers. The high ceiling echoed with laughter and clouds of blue tobacco hovered. A pendulum clock hung on one wall, its face as big as a table, and oil paintings covered every other.

Devlin spoke quietly, hushed by the atmosphere of power and possibility. 'What goes on here?'

Walpole breathed the room in, nodding greeting to certain coats. 'Everything, Captain. Everything. I have a back room for us.' He pulled Devlin closer. 'London always has a back room.'

They climbed a cramped stair to a simple door and a wood-panelled windowless room. More faces and cards met them, two men this time, and there were more disparaging looks as Devlin came in with his hat on. Walpole wasted no time shaking hands. 'Gentlemen. I give you our saviour. Captain Patrick Devlin. Our pirate.'

Only one stood and offered his hand. Almost fifty Devlin guessed, tall and handsome but a closer look under the sanguineous light of the chandelier showed a pock-marked face, souvenir of a sickly youth.

'Captain,' a deep Edinburgh timbre rolled forth. 'John Law. You are welcome at our table, sir. A drink?' And he went to the wine without answer. Devlin liked him at once. Walpole and the prince had not offered a drink.

The other had the same appointed look of Albany Holmes: thirty years of privilege in waistcoat and silk hose, an unpleasant smell under his nose always. His importance was measured in how much his arse remained seated. Walpole took the honours.

'May I introduce Lord Londonderry – although do not suppose that he has ever been there – Thomas Pitt the younger. It was his brother, Robert, who smuggled the diamond from India to England in the heel of his boot.'

The Lord spoke from his chair. 'Well met, pirate. Or ill met. Depending.' He flashed an eight of diamonds at Devlin. 'Law is teaching me how to cheat at cards,' he was already half-drunk despite the clock. 'He owes me money, I am glad to say. Or more money, rather.'

The diamond had been paid for in instalments. Although reduced in price France had still found it beyond the means of easy purchase.

Law turned his head back to the table. 'We will settle that, Thomas. That is why we are here.'

Pitt went for his glass. 'I am only observing on my father's behalf, John.' He saluted Devlin. 'He is governor of Jamaica don't you know.'

'Morgan was governor of Jamaica,' Devlin said. 'He was a pirate.'

Pitt put down his glass and corrected grimly. 'Ah. I think you'll find that should be: "He was a pirate, *Sir.*" Lord Londonderry, if you please.'

Devlin moved to the edge of the table. 'Where is Londonderry? *Sir*?'

Pitt looked to a frowning Walpole and went back to his glass without looking at the pirate at his quarter.

'Buggered if I know!' He waved his glass around the table. 'Sit down all of you. Let's get this over.' He kicked a chair out for the pirate. Devlin pulled it away and sat with his back to the wall, all of them in front of him, none beside him. Law passed him a glass of wine and took his seat with Walpole.

Devlin gulped and wiped his lip. A mouldy tasting wine, black and strong like coffee and chocolate. These men could drink. 'Tell me what I need to know.'

The world had gone mad. After the war, the Spanish war, when the Americas had come to be divided, companies had become a feverish commodity. Most feverish of all were those investing in the colonies, for America was a golden teat. The New World had made Spain great and now it was defeated everyone could suckle; its sweetest milk was the *asiento*, the settlement that granted England the right to buy and transport slaves to the Spanish colonies and their own. Thus the Royal African and South Sea companies became the new gods of the New World.

In a few short years London, Amsterdam and Paris had become the triad of a world written down and noted, no longer drawn on paper by the hard experiences of explorers and adventurers. They had already found all they needed.

Iron and cloth, dyes, spices and wood. That was the Old World. Now it was coffee, tea, sugar, gold and diamonds. And flesh was needed to work it all. Flesh most of all.

Gresham had built the Royal Exchange for Queen Elizabeth on the model of the Amsterdam *beurs* but it was in Garraway's and Jonathan's coffee houses that the financial floor really moved.

Thomas Pitt the younger and John Law exemplified this revolving floor. Gamblers by nature, their thumb-prints almost worn away by cards, their methods were built on the invisibility of paper and the cards that a man didn't see.

'Captain Devlin,' Walpole's voice was grave. 'His Majesty's government needs the diamond returned to England. It will save lives if you would but believe it, and even if you do not care for that sentiment then understand that I do. But I will not lie.'

'Meaning?' Devlin leaned back.

'The Company will collapse without security, without bond, for its paper is worthless. I sold my shares, as did Lord Londonderry, as did Law, and I removed the prince from their board. We took advantage of those who did not know better. But this is for the greater good. I hope Stanhope made that clear.'

Pitt raised his glass, 'My brother-in-law!'

'As Townshend is your brother-in-law, Minister?' Devlin noted.

Walpole's face never moved. 'No doubt you believe us all incestuous, Captain. But do not consider that I would save my own hide to see my country fall.'

'If you say so,' Devlin said, half believing. 'Spell this out for me.'

Walpole addressed John Law. 'Mister Law? I will speak candidly. Do not take offence.'

Law waved away the instruction. 'Let this man hear. It is all written. The smut on my face is long known.'

'Very well,' Walpole pulled himself closer to the table, the edge of it pressing into his paunch. Law and Pitt went to their wine.

'The South Sea owns the exclusivity of transporting slaves and goods to the Spanish colonies. The Royal African maintains the forts and the factors. The South has no such overheads. It has the royal warrant yet is barely a decade old. It has purchased the nation's war debts.' He splayed his fingers like a firework exploding. 'But it has nothing. Nothing but the paper. It is all an illusion. And if that becomes known the stock will plummet, the millions will want to salvage what they have invested and the Company cannot pay. It is an unstoppable beast.' He put his palms to the table. 'Judge as you will – if you carry such sentiment – but this place is where fortunes are made on intelligence and the future. And often in whispers.' He took Devlin's arm. 'Come. Let me show you.'

Walpole led him to a wall. He slid aside a narrow panel just wide enough for both their faces and looked down through a latticed grill to the throng downstairs.

'When you came in you saw gentlemen at leisure. An afternoon of coffee and tobacco, horses and hearths. Look closer.' He reeled away from the smell of caked blood and ship that came from Devlin's hair and gave him room.

Below, Devlin saw the same scene as when he entered, only from this vantage he could appreciate its intricacies, as ballets are enjoyed more from the gallery than the stalls.

It was not a crowd but groups of hats in small parties whirling between each other with paper and pens, sealing wax and newspapers. Devlin saw players at the few tables writing on playing cards, tearing them in half or clipping their corners. He looked at Walpole.

'Yes. Even gaming cards. Some for hundreds of pounds for companies that do not even have names or a business to trade. To protect their secrets of course. In just the few moments you have been watching you have witnessed tens of thousands changing hands. It is doubly encouraged because they have seen Londonderry enter and myself later. If they knew Law was here they would tear down the walls. This vent I had constructed to keep an eye on the worst. We used to buy and sell real things. Now we sell the future. We deal in promises.'

'This is madness.' Yet Devlin could not turn away. The room seemed to revolve faster and faster, for the white coats and black hats all looked the same – like a field of black-faced sheep – and it seemed a giant was turning a handle some-where on this carousel.

John Law called over, snapping Devlin back to reality. 'It is worse in Paris, Captain. You will see it soon. Are you not going to tell him of my shame, Walpole?'

Pitt grinned over his glass. 'Pride, surely, John?'

Some Scottish mumble was drowned by wine.

Walpole shut the vent. 'Mister Law is a financier and gambler, Captain. He is head of the Bank of France. That fact seems more incredible to me each time I say it.' They rejoined the table although Devlin chose to stand. Walpole did not mind. 'He is here in secret like yourself.'

Pitt began to sway. 'He is pretending to bring wine for my father's cellars after his final instalment for the diamond carried no weight.'

Law mumbled some more. 'Ten thousand pounds of wine is no pretence.'

Devlin understood nothing. There was the sense of strained friendship across the table between the Englishman and the Scotsman. They had clearly known each other for years. Their mockery and flippancy appeared just banter. Devlin lived on a ship. He spent his whole life cramped with others. It was easier to hide a horse on a ship than animus.

Walpole explained his wish to offer no offence to John Law.

Law was a wanted man. A quarter of a century earlier he had duelled and killed a love-rival and the family of the victim had demanded his neck. Law escaped before sentence and fled to France, as Devlin had done, only Law did not settle amongst the fishermen of St Malo like Patrick Devlin. Gamblers and drinkers make friends easily, but sober success-ful gamblers make the right friends.

He had met Philippe, the regent of France, ten years before, over the gaming tables of Venice and when Philippe was only a duke. Now after Louis's death, Philippe ruled France until the boy king reached majority. Then John Law came looking for a job.

Devlin now shared wine with one of the most powerful men in Europe but one who still had a noose waiting for him in London. That made him Walpole's whore as much as Devlin and Devlin appraised him as such.

Law, or *Monsieur Lass* as the populace had graced him – unable to wrap their tongues around his name – had become a Midas of his own making.

Like the South Sea Company's speculation in Change Alley, the hurricane of paper blowing in the Rue de Quincampoix in Paris flayed men's senses like a whip.

When the regent granted the *Compagnie des Indes*, Law's Mississippi company, all trade from China, the south seas and their American lands, the flurry of arms waving their money above their heads or climbing over duchesses' backs to grab a piece almost brought Paris to its knees: it seemed that nobody did anything but trade paper.

It was said that when the streets and offices were filled with writing desks a hunchback made a lively trade renting out his back for people to sign their shares.

Law had caught the tide at the flood and convinced the regent to allow him to open a bank and issue paper money to parry alongside the ridiculous coinage that had almost become valueless. It had worked for England and Holland and it would work for France. The scheme was as brilliant and flawless as the diamond that now ruled his future, the diamond that he had brokered for Pitt and the duke. Plutus would have been proud.

Law swirled his wine. 'I had hopes, drunken arguments with Londonderry, that I could break the East India Company, that France was the ruler of the world. If I could break the East India, bring down the South Sea Company, mine would be the most powerful on earth.'

Devlin poured his own wine, still standing. 'Then you have succeeded.' He looked to Walpole for confidence. 'Or do I not understand?'

Law laughed. 'It is done. My company falls as well. The *Banque Royale* will fall also. I need to run.' He chimed his glass against Devlin's. 'I am your partner. You are working for your freedom and so am I. If I betray my adopted country for this diamond, England will grant me a pardon.' He drank like it was the last glass in the world. 'I have destroyed France and France has destroyed itself.'

Walpole coughed for Devlin's attention. 'There is too much invested in these things. Too much of our money in promise.

Too much greed for short gain by men has built a house of cards. But if the South Sea Company could stand – just past this year – we could make it better. If it falls, faith will fall. The companies are all knots in the same rope. The diamond would stem the tide. Show that the Company has promise. No-one will see the empty ships. They will be dazzled as you were. Hold your faith in diamonds and gold, Captain, the fruits of the earth, as the world always has when houses fall.'

Devlin began to pace. He felt the game rising within him.

'You wish me to exchange your replica for the real. How did you acquire it?'

'Stanhope is married to my lovely sister Lucy,' Pitt drawled. 'It was a wedding gift.'

'Fair enough. You believe it valid? It will fool?'

Law now. 'I only ever saw the replica when Londonderry brought it to France, as did the regent. We are not fools but knew no better.'

'But the jeweller will know?'

'Tested it would fail. But the lapidary will be handed the greatest diamond in the world by his ruler. What would you question?'

'Everything. That's why I'm still alive. What is your plan?'

Walpole took a breath. 'Law has concluded his business on the regent's behalf. The wine for the instalment that did not clear was an effective ruse. He is the one who knows Paris, where you will attend.' He wiped his face with his hand. 'Your map, Law.'

The map came out from a leather-bound packet, a grey linen masterpiece. It cracked as Law unfolded it, a beautiful gentle sound like the stretching of a bird's wing. France was drawn across it. Law placed his finger to Calais and dragged down an inch and Devlin finally sat to take in the map. Maps were his world. Whatever riddles these men spoke the map at least was his work.

'This is Sangatte, Captain. I have procured a fisherman's cottage there. The regent knows I am here to furnish wine for Pitt's cellars, after which I am to spend some time at my home in Peuplingue. We cannot travel together. Both of us do not exist past this night. You will meet me at Sangatte and travel back with me to Paris as my aide. *Je comprends votre Français est bon?*'

They all looked at him expectantly. Devlin could not resist a playful pause. '*Oui*,' he said at last. 'But I do not look like an aide.'

'No,' Law agreed. He took in the lithe form, the dark skin accustomed to the sun, the mess of hair and bruised face. 'No, you do not. You look as much like an aide as a lamp looks like lightning. But perhaps that is only your dress and you could change your manner I'm sure.'

Walpole jumped in. 'This is important, Captain. Law can get you into the palace but they have no need for scarecrows.'

Pitt rapped the table. 'You may make a good valet. You are Irish are you not? I am starting my own company in the Bahamas now Woodes Rogers has scraped you from it. Perhaps you could help. I'm sure you remember how to use a shovel.' He laughed into his glass.

He stopped laughing at the small click under the table and Devlin's grin.

A tapping of metal upon the table's underside from Devlin's arm and Pitt knew what was pointing at his groin; could almost see it. He put down his glass.

Devlin dropped his smile. 'I know all sorts of tools. And I don't think I need to know you to get this deed done.'

Pitt's lips went white. 'You cannot threaten me, sir. I am a peer of His Majesty. You would not live another day.'

Walpole lay a hand on each of their arms. 'Captain, put away your pistol. Lord Londonderry, Devlin pointed his pistol at His Highness less than an hour ago so I would be quiet if I were you. Let Law carry on.'

Devlin stood, his chair flying back. 'No. *I'll* carry on. Where is this stone kept?'

The lower half of the map had stitched pockets hiding detailed, smaller ones. Law pulled the one for Paris and laid it across the other.

'I reside at the Palais Royale with the regent. The boy king is at the Tuileries. Philippe, the duke, keeps the diamond either about his person or hidden. I have seen it when I am in company with him but have never seen it placed or removed anywhere. It could be in his breeches for all I know, and I am his friend.'

'This is the Tuileries palace,' he indicated an enormous building at the head of a long garden along the west bank of the Seine. 'If you follow north you will see that it connects to the Louvre palace.' His finger drew their eyes along then swiftly he dragged it to another grand square. 'This is the Palais Royale. Where the duke is, where I am, and where the diamond hides. If you keep this triangle of buildings in your mind you can navigate between them with ease, run between them in minutes,' he traced the triangle for them. 'Keep in mind that a hundred soldiers can do the same and close them off in minutes.' He looked at Devlin carefully. There was only focus on the pirate's face; no flinching at the word of soldiers. Law took a breath.

'As I do not know where the duke keeps the diamond it will be impossible to steal it from the Palais Royale

– notwithstanding the fact that it is one of the most heavily guarded buildings in Paris – which is why we shall make the exchange when the diamond reaches Ronde, the lapidary who will work on the crown. His place is on the Rue du Richelieu here,' his finger stabbed the map west of the Palais Royale. 'That will be our mark for the exchange.'

He held out the map to Devlin. 'We shall go to the Palais Royale and wait for the diamond to be taken to Ronde. Then we will break into the lapidary before work on the diamond begins and exchange it for the replica.' Law drained his glass. 'And that will be *all* we will have to do.'

Devlin took the smaller map, scrutinised it as he began to pace again. He tapped at his sword as he took in the streets between the palaces. He stopped and turned.

'And the duke would not suspect me being brought into the palace with you?'

Law considered this. 'I have many aides and stewards. I'm sure it would not matter.'

Devlin resumed his walk around the room, then slapped the map back to the table. He had memorised what he needed.

Law carried on. 'Without knowing where Philippe hides the gem I do not see any other recourse than to take it once it leaves the safety of the palace. At least then we would know when it leaves and where it is. I am privy to that much, I'm sure. It would certainly be safer than robbing one of the most guarded places on earth, Captain.'

Devlin picked up his glass and swallowed the dregs before holding it out for more. Law obliged as Pitt checked the measure, concerned he would be left short.

Devlin waited for his glass to brim, his eyes lost in thought. He drank for one moment. Then he began.

'The diamond is in the Palais Royale under the regent's

protection,' his voice rang out as if reading a purser's list of victuals and recounting them to his own. 'You tell me the only chance to take it is when it is removed to the jeweller. That is a fair enough assumption. But not wise. It is more probable that once it is removed it will be more protected. At present only the duke knows where it is,' he laid down his glass.

'That is only one man to trick it from. If this jeweller sees the gem and then the replica he will know it's been cuckolded. This is his craft. But if he is given the replica and only the replica he will know no different. I agree that he would not check that which was handed to him by his master. I believed it real myself and I've used diamonds for coin.'

Law began to protest but the tone that controlled a hundred men brushed him aside.

'You wish to take me into Paris as your aide. Wait for the diamond to be taken to the jeweller. Replace it. And then take it back to England. What of you, Law? Are you to come also?'

'No. I will wait until my bank and company fall – as surely as they will – and then flee to Belgium, where I am granted passage to England.'

'So your position will be to remain after the theft. And do you suppose nobody will question that your trusted aide has suddenly disappeared? Would it not raise some suspicion?'

Walpole began to hide a smile with his hand and leaned back, confident now that he had chosen well. In a different life, one in which he had been better born, this lean young man could have been an asset. He had outlived most of his kind and had bested the finest set against him, as every report that Walpole had studied in several languages attested. It would be a crime if he had to die. He stood in front of the head of the Bank of France, the First Minister and a lord, had pulled a pistol on the Prince of Wales and had only removed his hat to wipe his brow. Terrible indeed if he had to die.

Devlin finished wiping his brow. 'It occurs to me that you gentlemen have never stolen anything in your lives. Nothing that Law has said will happen: I'll be dead else. I'll meet you in Paris, Mister Law. That'll take three days. Take the diamond from the regent himself and make the change there.' He touched his hat to Walpole. 'Then I'm after bringing it back to you. Eight days and I can get back to the sea. With all my crimes forgotten.'

Walpole closed his eyes and nodded.

Law found his voice. 'No, Captain! I have stressed that I do not know where the regent keeps the diamond and—'

Devlin cut him with a look. '*You* do not know where he keeps the diamond. Don't judge me by your own ignorance. I'll not put my life into the hands of men I don't know and who don't know theft from gaming. I'll find you when I'm in Paris.'

Law jumped up. 'The diamond cannot be taken from the palace!' He gestured to the map, rapped his finger upon the trio of buildings. 'Look at it! Look! That map is true! Fifty guards patrol day and night! More than three hundred servants and twice more in ministers! It is not a ship upon open waters, it is a fortress!' He went to grab Devlin's coat then lowered his hand wisely. 'The plan is good, Captain. Come with me to Paris and follow it and we will all live to tell the tale. I beg of you.'

Devlin patted Law's shoulder. 'Don't beg of me. Paris. Three days. Wait for my word.' He turned to Walpole. 'Minister, I'm going. Come and tell me what else I need to know.' He was already at the door.

Pitt expected no farewell and got none. The door closed leaving himself and Law alone.

'Bloody bogtrotter,' he scoffed. 'You'll be lucky if he even makes it to Paris, Law.'

Law sat and folded away his map. 'I feel, Londonderry, that I shall be most unlucky if he does.'

Riding in the coach back to Leicester House, Walpole had given up trying to spot Devlin's escorts during their slow progress. He brought his head back inside. 'They hide well, if they followed us at all.'

'You may have want of such skill,' Devlin said.

'You more so, Captain. I chose you because you seemed discreet of your kind. Our lives almost touched when you dealt with that gentleman in Charles Town two summers ago. I had tried to kill him several times myself. That is how I knew I had found my man.'

'Don't call me that. That won't help you. How am I to France?'

'There is a plague in Marseille, come from Cyprus. Naturally northern France and Paris would not appreciate this plague reaching them. My design is that you portray yourself to be a plague ship. That should deter any curious patrols. The problem will be that since you refuse to accompany Law, how will you get to Paris?'

'That'll be my problem.'

'I would not propose that you conduct yourself as you have done in London. You cannot sail a pirate up the Seine.'

'I know that. What happens when I bring the diamond back?'

'You will go to Falmouth. Where you should have come to London. I will set a fellow to meet you there as of next week. No names. He will spot you. There is an inn on the quay, a shipwrights' inn, alongside the customs house and prison

– make of that what you will. You must be there by September fourth. My man will leave on the fifth. We must present some promise of the diamonds by the eighth or all is lost. However, we will insist on a party to attend you. To attend that our interests are being adhered to, naturally.'

'A chaperone! Aye, for why trust me else.'

'A logical precaution. No personal discrimination. Our man shall be in charge of the replica until the exchange is made and you return with the diamond. This is not a mark of distrust against you, Captain. Your men may have other plans for the diamond. They may question your loyalties if they know it is in your hands.' Walpole lowered his voice.

'And you will not bring your ship of brigands back into this city. Your reward will be waiting for just *you*. Am I clear?'

'As diamond, Minister. So who's to wet-nurse me through my voyage?'

Albany Holmes was a good choice. Devlin may have been able to sway or intimidate someone else. Someone who had no bones against him. As Walpole had put it: 'He has no interest in befriending you and more than enough interest in ensuring the success of your task, without having any attachment to the government.'

Devlin had abandoned Albany at Ascension Island, after taking the ship he was on. That had been on the adventure of the porcelain letters when the man Ignatius had taken Peter Sam. Devlin had taken a brig, the *Talefan*, from Madagascar, and Albany and his companion had been his ruse. The manner of his marooning, together with the disrespect and stealing of his goods would grate with Albany; maybe even a little revenge was heating him. There would be some sport ahead, no doubt, with Albany at his side.

Devlin waited outside the trade entrance of Leicester House. His men would be catching up somewhere about. He needed to get back to them, back to his ship. All these people moved too fast, talked too much. He was used to being the one who walked against the crowd but this was just a lost feeling, like a wild animal cowering not from the hunter but from his shouts and spear rattling.

The carriage wheels, the clomp of horses and rushing feet, the hawkers, the handcarts, the blur of faces. For what? What truly was the rush? Had these people not seen the sea? He looked up at the towering stone all around. No. Perhaps not. They could not even see the sun.

Albany Holmes rounded a corner of the house. Boat-cloak almost to the floor, leather portmanteau slowing him down, the solemn face of the man did little to remove the mirth from Devlin's face. Aye, there would be sport enough to be had with Albany Holmes.

His wig had gone and there was just short brown hair beneath a simple tricorne, a sword at his side, silk hose and buckled shoes. He looked like a young man now, without his wig, but just as arrogant as the day Devlin had met him in a filthy tavern in the hills of Madagascar.

'You do not carry your sword-cane any more then, Albany?' Devlin asked as the man fell in beside him.

Albany ignored the remark. The cane had been thieved when he had fallen in with the pirates. 'Am I to take it, pirate, that you are to address me informally during our companionship?'

'Want to challenge my tone, Albany?'

Albany walked on.

Entering the square, Albany sought a carriage from the few that always loitered around the entrance to the house. He spied a large bald man with red beard and greatcoat striding towards them and took the approach as an offer. He held up his bag to push it into the man's chest.

'Here, fellow. Careful with it now.'

The giant elbowed him aside as he passed and Albany stumbled backwards, struggling to regain his balance like a newborn foal. He saw the pumping of hands between Devlin and the brute.

'Cap'n,' was all the giant said.

Albany had never seen Peter Sam. At the time of his passage with Devlin the big man had been taken from the pirates, held hostage in the Americas and ransomed for the price of a porcelain cup. Devlin had sailed across the ocean to bring his quartermaster back into the fold. In the handshake Albany saw nothing but crude men attempting manners. He did not see the past where one man had tried to kill the other, where both had wiped blood from their mouths. Devlin's pistol was forever scarred with the stripe of Peter Sam's cutlass. They had rescued each other in two long adventures that had cost both of them many friends.

Albany saw none of this in the touch of hands and slapping of shoulders. The two pirates saw everything but in a moment it was gone and the hard faces returned.

'Who be this streak of piss, Cap'n?' Peter Sam judged Albany up and down.

'He is back to the ship with us, Peter. Now, Albany,' Devlin bid Albany to walk with them. 'This be Peter Sam, my quartermaster and second, but you'd be wise to listen to what he tells you more than me.'

The black look from Peter Sam confirmed the advice. Albany adjusted his bag and walked on. As they moved silently up the left side of the square, Albany became aware that others had joined them as if they had sprung out of the ground beside him. They were now five abreast and London stepped aside to let them through. To his shame Albany found the power of the street parting before them stirred his blood easily as much as any hunt.

He found his voice again. 'So . . . Captain . . . We are to all be squeezed together again on that little brig of yours. The *Talefan* was it not?'

Devlin laughed. 'Ho, Albany! That would explain how little you think of me to be sure! Wait 'til you see what I have to show you, then measure me so!'

From the casement windows above, the prince and Walpole watched the ragged party leave the square. Stanhope and Townshend were still at the table, nodding at each other's affirmations of undoubted success, pulling their watches at the same time, late for their clubs.

'You are sure the diamond will be enough, Walpole?' the prince asked as he watched Devlin's back turn the corner and disappear.

'Just enough for the tide, Your Highness. Law has worked it out to the utmost. He has a head for figures that is almost uncanny. Uncut the stone is worth almost half a million. Cleaved, its children can be insured for company assets three times that. The company will become great diamond merchants overnight. The stock will rise. France will fall thanks to Law's paper money that he has convinced the regent to back. The South Sea Company will be second only to The East India Company and shall gain time to rebuild. The Americas will come good. We are at least not running out of slaves.'

'But if he fails? How so us then, Walpole?'

'Then you may well become king sooner than you had

hoped, Your Highness. Only you will be king atop of the largest dunghill in Europe.'

The prince sighed. 'I trust in a pirate.'

Walpole gave half a smile to his prince. 'We have all become pirates now, Your Highness.'

Chapter Thirteen

Wednesday

*S*ail the English channel on an easterly tack; take no word to another course. The wind, the white-capped waves, as fat as plague corpses rolling off a cart, loll constantly towards you, breaking against your keel like glass and stinging into eyes just the same. Lose abaft every foot you gain abeam. These are cold waters where fishermen earn their keep, a churner of ships. And cold; so cold as tides collide, and hundreds of ships lying dead below, still moving across the seabed as summers pass without calm and the small creatures of the deep make homes in eyeless skulls.

The master of the sloop *Vendeen*, Jean Minot, studied the ship lying off his larboard quarter. An afternoon of damp and mist, the slab of the sky low and heavy, meeting the sea in a dour curtain of grey that would discourage even the most devoted sailor from his work.

He spied a three-masted ship through his cracked smoky glass, moving slowly under courses. No pennant at her backstay. He followed its line up to her mainmast where a large yellow flag whipped back and forth through a veil of cloud.

The yellow flag. Quarantine.

He held the scope tighter as the channel pushed against his bow and he swept the sharkskin tube up and down across the ship. Surely not a plague ship this far north? Far out to sea the ghoulish sight of skeletal ships bucking and drifting, empty of men at their ropes and sails, had become almost a common sight in the last few months. The yellow flag fluttered on some of them but not all.

This ship was at least alive. A dark figure waved slowly at him from the gunwale. Jean Minot brought down his scope and did not wave back.

The horror of the outbreak at Marseille in the south had almost destroyed one of the largest ports in the world. Since May and the first few cases the disease had spread through the surrounding towns and villages like the wind. Now at the height of August almost a thousand souls a day were dropping in the streets or ending themselves rather than fall to the disease; some even placidly walked into the sea until the waves washed over their heads or laid down in the streets amongst the piles of corpses and simply waited. Whole families sat propped up against the dead.

The regent had sent his own doctors from Montpelier to confirm the disease and, shortly after, the army began work on a two metre-high wall across Provence with guard posts erected all along, and had been ordered to shoot any of the pitiful shuffling creatures trying to leave – and even the healthy who might seek sanctuary.

Marseille was doomed.

Ships from the Levant were ordered into port at the islands off Marseilles and flew the yellow flag until inspected. If clean they could raise a white signal and continue on to trade with the rest of France. If not, either wait and die, or return from where you came.

This black and red ship flew a yellow flag. She was large too. Almost a ship of war, if not a powerful merchant.

And she was coming about.

Figures now ducked beneath the courses fore and aft. The sprit sails began to unfurl, the spanker dropped free and still the figure waved calmly back and forth to Jean Minot as the ship crawled into his lee.

Minot would take no chances. He snapped to his bosun a dozen quick commands and paced along the gangway shouting to his lazy crew and keeping one eye on the black ship and the waving, friendly hand.

His own spanker and jibs came out. With her size and laying in his lee he would steal her wind and race ahead. Perhaps she just closed for news. Perhaps she wanted help. No matter. She would understand and as the *Vendeen* charged away from the closing bow the hand stopped its morose wave. The dark figure retreated from the gunwale like a shadow.

Dandon saluted Devlin with a tip of his bottle as he came back from the gunwale. 'That worked admirably. That yellow flag is almost as effective as our black.'

The wind prevented Devlin from hearing and he cupped his hands to his mouth to order the bosun, Lawson, to carry on, to take them into shore. The day had brought them into the north sea and south around Folkestone. They crossed the trade lanes that went to Dunkerque, where other ships had avoided them hurriedly, and now crossed the Calais lanes, the long flat coastline of France stretching to infinity off their larboard side. Now the tide was with them. They could come about and sail along the coast to Le Havre.

Peter Sam took Devlin's arm, bringing him close so the wind would not steal his voice.

'He summons you.' He motioned with his head aft to the cabin where Devlin had permitted Albany Holmes to sleep and eat, away from the rabble. Devlin pushed his way through the busy men amidships, fondly slapping the shoulders of some, damning coarsely the slower of them.

He ducked into the outer coach where the first of the *Shadow*'s guns lay beneath the quarter-deck and where Albany slept in a foldaway cot that would double as a coffin.

For the most part Devlin took pleasure in entering the Great Cabin. His cabin. It was the first place on earth he had known where he could close a door that belonged to him. The cabin was for all, but somehow when he slept in his cot or sat on the lockers beneath the stern windows and read alone with a good pipe, a childish warmth came over him that his past life never gave even when his work was done, or even when he was a child and such warmth should have been part of every day. Now he came into the cabin to see Albany sprawled across the wooden locker seat at the windows and leafing through one of Devlin's books.

'You called for me, Albany?' Devlin put his hat on the table and found himself waiting for attention. Albany held up a finger, his eye to his page, finishing his sentence. With a pleased nod of his head he slammed the book shut and swung his legs to the oak floor.

'Yes, Captain,' his tone was inflected up as if questioning Devlin's entrance and title. 'I could not help but notice that there is some air of animosity about my presence on this ship, although it has only been a night and a morn since I have become company.'

'What about it?'

'I gather there was some talk below deck that I was not a party to last night. I wondered if this meeting could explain such.' He sat back easily. 'If we are to be partners I would hope that your men would accord me equal respect.'

'I'm sure it is not your presence that vexes. More this fool path we are on. And as for us being partners, Albany, I wouldn't swear to that if I were you. Get in my way or my men's and it'll only come hard for you.' He picked up his hat and turned to leave but jumped on Albany's final words that he sensed were coming. 'Don't think I gave you this cabin out of respect or for your privilege. It is for your safety only.' He squared his hat and went toward the coach, his words spinning back over his shoulder. 'They might not kill you if they think I like you.'

Outside, the deck ran with water to the scuppers with every pitch and Devlin's boots were splashing now as Peter Sam loomed over him.

'Tonight then?' he asked.

Devlin looked back to the closed cabin door. 'Aye. If that's what the men want. After supper. I'll not have him lord it over me.' He slapped Peter Sam on his shoulder. 'Watch our head in these crosswinds.'

Devlin gripped a manrope and swayed with his ship. He watched the grey coast to their larboard creep along with them. The last time he had seen it he had been a Frenchman in white tunic, starved into the Marine Royale. 'The world turns and revolves us back,' he thought, and then thought of the darkness ahead.

From across the ship Dandon watched his friend frown at the spray and stare out over the waves as if he could see beyond the horizon and tomorrow. He caught his eye and waved as best he could without losing his balance. Devlin, his mind elsewhere, looked through him and went below.

That evening the *Shadow* sailed with the blue and white stripes of a French merchant from her backstay, and a white flag on the mizzen to indicate freedom from plague. The weather stayed with them, damp and ugly, which was for the good, as every ship would keep to themselves around such an iron-bound coast.

Bacon and eggs for those who wanted to help themselves; for the rest, patience and the wait for Dog-Leg Harry's pots and skillets to be served up. Dog-Leg was the old ship's cook, formerly of the late Seth Toombs when Devlin had first turned pirate. In the navy old Dog-Leg would have been turned ashore with the wound that had cost him his hand, but here, with the pirate's rules that made up their narrow view of democracy, he would be compensated in pieces of eight, each limb its own set price, and given an easier day's work. He was still paid – only a half-share like that of the few black Spanish slaves that had begged to come aboard a year ago, but better than what the rest of the civilised world offered any of them.

So boiled shark, pressed dry, then stewed with peppers and vinegar, with fresh cobbles of bread and olive oil for all the men; for Devlin too, for the captain would eat no better than his men. It was a tradition that the gentler stomach of Albany Holmes had yet to become accustomed to and Devlin and Peter Sam found him knelt on the lockers leaning out of the stern windows of the cabin. His blue face turned weakly to the crash of the cabin door that slammed behind the pirates as they entered the room.

'What do you want?' Albany slurred, wiping his chin. He paid no attention to the two-foot long belaying pin in Peter Sam's hand, the furniture of ships a dull enough topic to Albany's refined mind.

'We've been a-talking, Albany,' Devlin said. 'Close my window: that's how accidents happen.'

Albany pulled the casement to. He was not bothered about

anything except keeping his supper down. 'Talking about what?'

Devlin stepped from Peter's side. 'We want the diamond. No sense in you holding it.'

'*We*? Oh, yes of course, you all decide "together" don't you. I take it you refer to the replica, not the prospect of you keeping the real gem for yourself . . . ah, sorry, for *yourselves* I should say.' He straightened up painfully. 'I am to hold the diamond until the exchange is made. It is in my keeping. And it is also I who will hold the actual diamond until we return it to London. That is Walpole's instruction.'

Peter Sam slammed the wooden club against the bulkhead, the crack of the wood enough to make Albany's bones jump. He twisted the wood in his hands and came closer. 'We wants the diamond!' He repeated for his captain.

Devlin put a hand to Peter's shoulder. 'There ain't a choice in the matter, Albany.'

Albany rose unperturbed. 'I have been entrusted on my country's and the Company's oaths, Captain, to safeguard both the diamond and its replica and ensure no deviance from the plan as given. I see no reason for you to possess the replica until the moment of exchange.'

Devlin went to the rack that held his drink. His hands pushed back his coat-tails to rest on his belt and show the massive left-locked pistol at his right hip. Then he turned his back and spoke as he poured.

'I know that your trust is greater than mine, Albany. But I want the diamond. I want to show it to my men, who will help me take the real one,' he held out a glass of watery rum. 'And as you'll not be coming to Paris with me I see no sense in you holding it.'

He watched Albany's face pale even further and nodded to

him to take the drink offered. Albany found an exigent need to wet his suddenly dry throat. 'I am not to come to Paris? We are partners, Captain. Where you go, where the gem goes, there go I.' He drank before continuing, the odd compulsion to both know his fate and shrink from the answer overwhelming. 'Unless you have some other plans for me that is? Aware as you are that I will be obliged to inform Walpole of your actions?'

Devlin raised his own glass and passed the bottle to Peter Sam. 'I don't want to cause you harm, Albany.'

He waved them all to the table. Peter Sam tucked his club in his belt, his cold eye set to Albany.

'Give up the replica to the table, and I'll tell you what goes on.'

Albany stood his ground. 'And if I refuse?'

'*Don't.*' Devlin's voice was level enough to be no more threatening than as if written in a letter. He pulled from inside his shirt his own map of Paris, drawn from the memory of Law's, and placed it open on the table. It only showed the triangle of the three palaces and the river alongside. The other acres of the city were meaningless. This would be his small world now.

'The stone. If you please,' Devlin said and waited.

Albany went to his effects, took out a small black velvet bag and conceded it to Devlin's open palm which rested on the conference table. 'On your honour,' he demanded.

Devlin coaxed the soft velvet and the stone slipped into his hand like running water; his fingers at once alight with its brilliance as if a star had fallen into his grasp. Even the stoic and mighty Peter Sam softened, gazing into its deep mystery, sure that every violent act of his life would be wiped clean from his soul as long as he stared upon it. And this the replica, he thought. What heaven could make the real thing if this is but its mirror?

Devlin placed the stone on its flat side, its table, where it danced in its release. The stone sucked the light from the lantern overhead to coruscate between all their faces.

'Good man. For both of us.' Devlin directed Albany and Peter's eyes back to the map.

'For your own mind, and so you can tell Walpole that I kept nothing from you, Law's intention was for me alone to travel with him to Paris,' he touched the map where the Palais Royale stood. 'The regent has the diamond here. Law would have us steal it when it reaches the royal lapidary. I intend to take it from the palace itself.'

Albany looked down at the pirate's dirty finger tapping on the square of the building. 'Why? Surely that is a greater risk? Why deviate from the plan suggested by wiser men?'

Devlin let the insult pass. 'Because time has some essence here. And neither Law nor Walpole have any notion of when the jewel is to be sent to the lapidary, only that it is to be set into a crown for the boy king any day. That could be tomorrow or it could be a month from now, and who's to feed my men while we wait, or while your bubbles burst all around you? Easier for me to take it where I know it is now.'

Albany sneered, 'I also take it that it does you no favour to sail a pirate ship around these waters for too long.'

Devlin could only agree. The Channel – La Manche, as the French knew it – was one of the busiest trading lanes in the world. The *Shadow*'s disguise would not last, for she would be less a cat amongst pigeons than a pigeon measuredly becoming encircled by tigers. 'I have been given two weeks. I intend to be back in England in six days and then on my way back to the Indies.'

'*Six* days! Are you mad? Have you ever been to Paris, sir? It will take us half that time just to get there!'

Devlin put away his map. 'I have been there. Up the Seine it will take me two days. That gives me one day to meet Law and plan and three to get back to Walpole.'

'Oh, that's *it*, is it? One whole day to plan and steal the most famous diamond in the world from the pocket of the man who rules France! How I have underestimated your genius, sir!'

Peter Sam rushed forward to get at Albany's throat. Devlin held him back with just his palm across Peter's leather-wrapped chest.

'Six days,' he said. 'And I'll be on my way.' He picked up the fake gem. 'Watch me.' He turned to leave, Albany's voice holding him back.

'In which case I insist on accompanying. I'll not wait on this ship with your men in fear of my throat being cut every night.'

Devlin looked Albany up and down. A fine strong gentleman. A few years younger but with that born-and-bred confidence of his kind that was as ageless as it was sickening to men like Devlin. And for that he probably would not live too long without Devlin's protection amongst a ship of men who shaved others' necks more than their own beards.

'All right, Albany. You may come. But you'll do as I say. And pack for the dawn. We'll take a fishing boat on the tide.'

'*Take* a boat?' Albany queried.

Peter Sam grinned through his red beard and followed Devlin to the cabin door.

'You're about to become a pirate, Albany. Look lively now.'

Chapter Fourteen

Thursday

*J*ean Minot, captain of the *Vendeen*, had convinced his crew that to report the presence of a plague ship could only go in their favour, and that it would certainly go against them if it was discovered they had spied the ship of death and ignored its potential threat. The reality, however, of sitting deep inside the Citadel of Calais awaiting an audience with the chef d'escardre, the commodore of the Marine Royale, had produced a black ring of sweat that stained his steinkerk.

Minot wiped his forehead constantly, pointlessly, as rivulets of perspiration ran out of his hair and down his cheeks. Merchant traders and the austere navy rarely liked to mix. To deliberately approach now seemed ludicrous when at any time a white uniform could requisition your ship just because it looked pretty.

He began to look to the door and think of escape, and his mind was almost made up when the loneliness of the ante-room was cracked by the opening of another door and well-polished shoes rang across the stone floor.

'Captain Minot? The commodore will see you now.'

Minot shambled up, humbly thanked the man, put his hat on his head and then quickly removed it again as he followed the officer in white.

For the sake of his courage he tried not to think of the man he was meeting as he was led through one stone room after another. His heart still banged against his chest when his journey ended abruptly before a table at which the great René Duguay-Trouin, in shirt and tucked cuffs, busily masticated his way through a boiled hen. A brief, disinterested look rose over the leg of the bird working through his hands. Minot visibly shivered at the glance.

To a Frenchman, any Frenchman, not just those Malouines from his Brittany homeland, Trouin was a god amongst men.

He had begun as a young corsair of St Malo, the proud sea-wolves who answered to no king yet served their country in every war in defence of their beloved Brittany. Hundreds of British, Spanish, Portuguese and Dutch ships had fallen to his guns over the decades. Now, at forty-seven, the peace of February and the honour of chef d'escardre drowned him in paper and audits. The only resemblance to the Lion of Breton of old was the wig that curled and tumbled over his shoulders.

'Who have you brought me, Fossart?' he asked his clerk with his mouth full, as if Minot were dessert.

'A Captain Minot, Commodore. He wishes to report that he has seen a quarantined ship nearby.'

Trouin wiped his hands and chin as he spoke. 'Ah, good, good.' He reached for a glass of wine. 'When did you see this vessel, Captain? What was its course?' He indicated his clerk for paper and pen and pushed away his charger.

Minot held his hat close to him like a shield, twisting it through his sweaty hands. 'Yesterday, Your Grace. I thought it prudent to report such an incident, Your Grace.'

'Indeed,' Trouin began to ink in the details, feigning gratitude. Just more useless paper to be filed and ignored, but it would not hurt to show the gallant captain that he valued his sagacity. 'Describe the ship for me if you would be so kind, Captain.'

Here Minot grew braver, for he was sure that the ship had some significance out of the ordinary and he was proud of this assertion.

'That is the thing, Your Grace,' he took a step closer. 'It was a large ship. Square rigged. Three masts. And even in the fog I could see she carried many guns.'

Trouin looked up. '*Guns?*'

'Yes. More than a merchant, Your Grace. Many swivels too. Perhaps twenty or more guns altogether.'

'You could see that? Or a guess?'

Minot shook his head. 'It was easy: her wood was red, blood red and black. I could make out the gunports clearly.'

Trouin put down his quill. 'A name? A flag?' The old feeling crept over him like a teasing caress. Instinct and a thousand experiences suddenly filled him more than his simple dinner. The light that sparked in his eyes was not missed by Minot and he courted it lavishly.

'None but the yellow. But she was as a frigate. A fighting ship I am sure. Or trying to be, Your Grace.'

'Or trying not to be,' Trouin spoke only to himself. He sat back, his eye to the window thoughtfully. 'Black and red you say? You are sure of this, Minot?' He graced the captain with his name. Jean Minot would tell his grandchildren of this moment.

'Yes. With grey sails, Your Grace. A dark ship. I gave five Hail Marys when I left her.'

Trouin nodded, scratched his quill across the paper. A black-and-red frigate. Armed to the gunwales according to the sweating merchant in front of him. Some memory of a black-and-red ship drifted in and out of fog in his mind. Some crime against the crown. He bit his lip in thought – the fog was lifting, the memory almost there. Minot shuffled his feet and coughed politely. Trouin looked up from his reverie.

'You have done well, Captain Minot. Return to your work. We will keep watch for this plague ship. Good day to you, Captain.'

Minot bowed. His head was no longer sweating but glowing gloriously. 'My honour, Your Grace.' He left the room beaming like a butcher's dog.

Fossart closed the door and waited for his commodore to speak. He knew the look on his commander's face from long ago. Trouin did not make him wait long. He jolted up, his words firing out of him like a flowing broadside.

'Records, Fossart! Bring me the commandant records for 1717.' He quaffed his wine like water, a satisfied gleam across his face.

'Commodore?'

Trouin laughed, a sound rarer in these days of slumber than a swallow's walk. He poured more wine, a salute to himself. 'I recall three years ago, Fossart, a black-and-red frigate with grey sails assaulted one of our islands in the Caribbean. Men – our brothers – killed, a fortune in gold stolen. Twice, I recall, orders have been signed against such a ship. Confirm that with the orders you will bring me. I need to remind myself of her captain and crimes.'

'Crimes, Commodore? She was not a ship of war, an enemy?'

Trouin looked hurriedly around his chambers searching for his coat and his red sash of office. He needed to ready himself. Here was an opportunity for action. 'No Fossart, better! A *pirate*! I am sure of it – if memory serves – but we will confirm. Go, man! She will not hold long in these waters.'

Fossart backed from the room leaving Trouin to his tiger's pacing. For thirty years he had been a warrior of the sea. A privateer captain at twenty, son of the great Luc Trouin, he had joined a vessel at sixteen and had fought almost every day of his life with the smut and stench of cannon all around and a cutlass forever in his fist.

The wars were his playground and he had trumped the blue-bloods who would have him remain beneath them with successes that could not be ignored. But at long last they had won. He had captured Rio de Janeiro and made his king rich again, but with the monarch's death, five long, long, years now, his patronage had ended. And now the Breton boy was put back in his place, his glories forgotten by all but the people and those captains who served him.

His rank was honorary, perhaps, but still a rank, still with ships to command and none could say that he would be in error to chase a pirate from his coast, his citadel.

Others may have found such retirement welcoming. Bask in the sun by all means but do so from a lounge chair. Put away your sword in a box and lock your past shut.

His eyes locked on his own cutlass resting above his mantle. Not in a box. Not put away. He lifted it tenderly from its place, its gleam reflecting more than light across his face.

He had dozens of ceremonial swords presented to him by the king, the best his king could do next to granting him a captaincy when he had dragged home dozens of English ships. He had been a titan with a hawser chain over his shoulders pulling them into Brest and barely grunting with the effort.

'It cannot be, Your Majesty,' the men in red robes or cloaks and blue sashes insisted. 'We cannot make a captain of a corsair, of a *despicable*.' Even the heroic Forbin, who Trouin had rescued from the English, could not see beyond his aristocratic blinkers.

'He is not of the blood. He is a lucky merchant sailing under his father's purse.' A pension instead. A thousand livres. But stay from our court. No uniform.

But Trouin did not falter, did not bow. His king knew merit but although he commanded gentlemen in white, had squadrons of ships, still they kept closed their court until it could be kept closed no more – his triumphs, his name written in more English captains' log books than any other Frenchman. When he petitioned to lead a force to capture Rio de Janeiro from the Portuguese, the Minister of Marine withheld sanction. Privateers did not capture cities despite what English pirates had achieved. The English did not understand nobility. They knighted farmers who had turned pirate.

Trouin backed the mission himself with funds from merchants in Brittany and went himself to Versailles. Eventually, reluctantly, the Minister of Marine gave unique sanction to a commoner.

Rio fell as all fell before Trouin and he filled the king's pockets to overflowing. And finally he was ennobled. No more pretty swords: uniform and title. But it would take until the king's dying breaths to bestow it permanently.

But this sword was his. Not a decoration. He balanced it at the full length of his arm, feeling a small ache along his forearm that had not been there years ago – but no mind. He slashed it once, twice, three times through the air back and forth as boys in the streets of St Malo still did with wooden epées, pretending to be him. The ache had soon gone.

The breath came from him in satisfied gasps and he ran the cutlass to his sash. Forget the filigree limpness of his commodore's sword and frog. This is how a corsair fights.

He stood in his window looking over the sea, his fists planted on his hips. A pirate. Yes, that would do, that would serve for the end of summer. He pictured the pirate, a toothless drunkard in beard and rags preying on witless merchants; a bully with a hundred men drowning weaker numbers. If he could remember the name he would speak it now, and then speak it once more when the pirate was dead. And then no soul would whisper it again, except when recounting the glorious deeds of René Duguay-Trouin and the manner in which the pirate had met his end.

Chapter Fifteen

✖

'So, this is it?' Dandon held the stone between finger and thumb, turning it curiously. 'So much hanging on such a small object. It is a strange world we find ourselves in, Patrick.'

They sat out on deck on a Persian arabesque-patterned carpet to keep the damp wood from their clothes. The gem had travelled around the ship, as promised, for each man to have a sight of the thing that had brought them to shiver in these rolling waters rather than their glorious Caribbean. Devlin had spared them the tale of the diamond's grim history – pirates being as superstitious as any other sailor – for they would not care that this stone was only its twin.

'An incredible replica, I agree, Captain,' said Dandon as he plopped it back into Devlin's hand and filled his own with a bottle instead.

'Took two years to make it and five thousand pounds, I'm told. It should be good enough.'

Dandon flinched at the value of the object that he had briefly held. 'How can such chicanery afford so much?'

Devlin looked deep within, helplessly drawn to it, like all of them. Somewhere, twisting inside its facets, his father's spade-like hands blurred, swinging him along the road to Kilkenny town to be left at a butcher's for four guineas.

His father had sung all the way. Tried to carry him on his shoulders. But the boy – skinny as he was – had been too heavy and he had laughed at his father's attempt, and they went hand in hand instead.

To Kilkenny for a toy, for his father had told him it was his birthday and the boy had faith that such days existed. Another turn of the gem and flash of light and his mother's voice seemed to rise from its surface, swiftly blazed away by the melodic tones of his aunt's singing – one person at least whose features he could still recall. The beauty of the stone reminded him of how far he had travelled to have outrun the bad little boy he must have been to be left so.

Devlin shrugged. 'The water of the diamond is the same. No white one exists of such parallel.'

'But you believe that this lapidary will know the difference if it is switched after it reaches him?'

Devlin held the diamond up into the dying twilight sky, scrying some future from it. 'I don't care. I only wish this matter done. It's not safe in these waters.'

The *Shadow* suddenly dipped. Deeper water beneath her keel off the ironbound coast. A call from the tops lifted their heads.

'*Deck there! Sail ho!*' The speaking trumpet dropped by its lanyard and the hand shot out. 'Three points off larboard bow!'

Devlin stood and followed the hand from above. A tartane bobbed lazily on the horizon, naught but a splinter of wood against the grey sea and sky and Devlin's shoulders soon became crowded by Peter Sam and Black Bill as if from nowhere. Dandon was pushed back from the gunwale. This was not his place.

'That's her,' Devlin said almost beneath his breath.

'Aye,' Peter Sam growled and went to his work, dragging Bill away with him.

Dandon pressed forward, straining a view to the little craft. 'That's who? That's what?'

Devlin spun back, brushing past his yellow-coated friend – there was no time for friendship now.

'*Ours!*' Devlin's solitary answer.

The game was upon him, and Dandon recognised the old brusqueness as a way to protect him, not to give offence.

Devlin swept aft to the cabin for weapons and to drop his manner to the depths that were necessary for the acts yet to come.

Dandon was left alone now, despite the dozen-or-so pirates milling around him and shifting sails to meet the tartane. He was alone and thinking on his friend.

The early evening had descended, a good time for ships to exchange news or trade goods. The *Shadow* would close, fall into the other ship's lee, away from her wind to not slow her, the correct approach for a friendly vessel, though the normal path was for the weaker vessel to take the lee. The curious courtesy of the larger ship volunteering so would hopefully have the desired effect on the *Junot*'s master: that he might suspect that the ship was in distress or had some serious news to impart.

Then the rest of it, Dandon thought.

He hoped for no blood.

He had known Patrick Devlin for three years now, longer than anybody in his life, but the man the rest of the world knew as The Pirate Devlin had changed in that time.

No, not changed; but he differed now from the young man with the rakish grin who had saved Dandon's life when they first met, saved him from Blackbeard's enmity in a tavern on Providence. He had joined Devlin as ship's doctor after that. There was adventure, food, drink and a notion that Dandon had found his place in the world. Then had come the agent and the porcelain conspiracy and Devlin had ascended to another plane. Now governments watched them, governments used them, and this pursuit would either spiral down to the depths or Devlin would have his portrait on a wall someday and a governorship like some of his kind.

But Devlin was also less now the man jumping from the peg-hole he was born in. Now he was relishing his freedom upon the sea and growing more the bloody pirate, inevitably falling deeper and darker in deed.

He had seen him in Charles Town, two years ago now, kill two guttersnipes like brushing dust from his shoulders, and more since then; each killing was easier and easier to do, but each was taking more and more drink to swallow away.

Something had changed that same year, after the death in Charles Town of Valentim Mendes, the Porto governor of St Nicolas who had travelled across the Atlantic to exact revenge against the pirate who had taken more than just his hand and ship. That had been the last adventure that had taken them from out of their pirate round. The hunt for the secret of the 'white gold', the porcelain mystery that the world craved and they had given. They had been beckoned by powerful men on pain of death to fill their pockets, not his. And now it was happening again. Devlin's smiling days of drinking and gaming and 'honest' pirating had been torn away from him by more black-suited men in wigs who seemed to spawn like frogs in an ever more degenerate world.

Dandon smoothed his moustache, tutting to himself that he had forgotten to remove it yet again. Devlin's mood, he was sure, had slunk back to the days after Valentim's death when Dandon saw more of his friend's face through the bottom of a wine glass lifted high than from promenading on deck. There was a guilt perhaps, some chipping of his soul that the man he had wronged had died, that Valentim had been slaughtered not in the noble pursuit of vengeance but in actually fighting at Devlin's side. What man could splice the two ends of such a rope?

At their late table, or on nights on deck, the drunken laughter of his mates and crew were lost on the sullen face of their captain who sat with a bottle and his dagger, whittling away at the table or deck of the ship of the man he had stolen it from; the same man who had stood in a garden in Charles Town by Devlin's shoulder and had bled his noble life away in the grass.

Dandon hoped still for his friend. Hoped still to see that Irish grin return when he trumped everyone. And hoped, as the tartane grew broader in his sight, there would not be too much blood to come.

Romantic novellas would have English schoolboys and swooning virgins believe that the raucous bloody days of pirates were filled with gold and jewels, swinging cutlasses and roaring broadsides, and the sacking of great colonial cities full of fat Spaniards quaking in their boots and sweating like pigs before the English buccaneers.

In truth pirates lived mostly by trade. A merchant ship would be spied, closed upon under friendly guise and then a single salvo of powder from a gun would sound and a black or red flag run up.

Surrender.

A boat sent across.

Two captains meet and exchange that which one needs with that which one does not.

To be fair, the pirate would gain the most under the wave of his pistols: two barrels of molasses for all your sail and brandy – but the principle was there.

To sell their surplus the pirates would sail to a welcoming shore, of which the Americas afforded many, willing as the colonials were to buy goods for which they did not have to pay a British tax.

Only wealthy vessels would suffer the worst. Then the officers would be robbed of all their wares, the ship of all its charts and medicines, the passengers of their fine clothes and portable valuables. These occasions often led to comical reports of pirates dressed in motley as harlequins, with several years of fashionable silk and velvet on their back, gold and diamond necklaces about their necks but barefoot and black as a hearth.

To most merchants the prospect of being pirated was an inevitable consequence of being at sea and putting up a fight was pointless. The insurance against the same was as old as pirating itself.

The worst came, however, if it was your ship the pirate wanted. Then you could find yourself on a sinking vessel with no food or water and watch your own fine ship sail off into the distance. If you were lucky you might live to make your report, which would lie with the thousands of others browning in some file. If you were unlucky the crabs and lobsters would be the only ones to know your fate.

But pirates in the Channel were rare. The waters heaved with trade but also with the naval might of the world. The Dutch, the British and the French sailed the 'sleeve' daily. There were no pirates here. That would be madness.

So why not allow the flush frigate flying a French merchant flag to sail in close? Why not lower sail, call over and hear a French voice call back for news? La Manche is a friendly sea. Here we are all brothers under sail.

The tartane was a swift, single-masted ship able to lift both a lateen sail to catch all and a foresail from the same mast, as well as rig jibs along her bowsprit. From a distance, the landsman's vantage, the *Junot* was a giant lateen sail coursing along as if pulled through the water, more cloth than wood. A small boat, and like all small boats she needed big men upon her; but big men with families still shrink from black pistols waved at their chests by grinning rogues.

There should be no need for weapons other than personal arms, for who would harry a harmless fishing boat eking a living along the coast?

Even so, Devlin had sent Hugh Harris and Dan Teague to head the boarding party to the little boat. Men he might have set against Panama herself for their expertise in killing. Their morals were as slim and contrary as the faces and backs of cards, and with as much space between to judge who should die and who not.

Dandon had noted the choice. 'What will you do, Patrick?' he asked quietly, half fearing the answer. Devlin stood by his side at the gunwale.

'We'll keep our distance. She can see our guns. Knows it's over. If we board we'll pull too much attention.' Now both had anchored only a hundred feet or less lay between their freeboards. It was a normal shouting distance and row towards that should not draw suspicion from any passing observer.

'And for her crew?' Dandon asked. 'What for them?'

Devlin walked away, his eyes keen all along the ship over the way, watching the black shapes for any sudden action. 'I'll leave that to them.'

Dandon noted then that Devlin had sent Englishmen to a French ship. He had not requested a French speaker, had not gone himself or sent Dandon, who could speak the better French of the two. No, he had sent Hugh Harris and Dan Teague, the bloodiest of them all, and now Devlin was ordering the lowering of the second boat from its home between the masts. A chill came over Dandon that had nothing to do with the flick of the wind at his face.

He sprinted to Devlin, stood with Peter Sam in close debate. 'Patrick!' he very nearly yelled the name. 'I will go across with the boat. I will mediate between our different souls. With Hugh and Dan, these fishermen may have short prospects.' He swallowed at Peter Sam's scowl. 'Unless that is you wish them to have short prospects?'

Devlin put his arm across Dandon's shoulders. 'What are you thinking of me, Dandon?' He walked them away from the boat swinging over their heads. 'You think me a monster now, is it?' His voice was laden with charm.

'No, my friend, not a monster. Colossus perhaps. I thought I may help with any misunderstandings, Patrick, that is all.'

Devlin nodded toward the far ship. 'They will know the game. If I send English pirates they will not attempt to reason. No point in arguing with a man who does not understand you. And Hugh knows enough French curses to let them know how he feels. I intend to bring the men over to us. Let their master know that we mean them no harm.'

Dandon was relieved. So fifteen men would join them for a spell, their only loss to be their ship to Devlin's cause. But what of after?

'And when you return from your task, Captain? What then for them?'

Devlin slapped Dandon's back. 'I shouldn't worry. You and I may be dead ourselves by then, *mon frère*!'

Dandon's body leaned away in surprise. 'I am coming with to Paris? This is a danger I did not account for, Patrick. It should be considered judiciously. Particularly by myself.'

Devlin reeled him back in. 'I don't think I could succeed without you.' Then he pushed Dandon away, laughing. 'I think that will always be the way I'll have it.'

A boat came across. Just six men, the captain of the *Junot* observed. Six to share news. He had no concern with his stout fourteen men behind him. A rope from below, belayed by pin and closer now, looking down into the boat, just ragged fishermen, no swords or even knives, and bringing a bundled up black cloth with them, a gift perhaps.

Hugh Harris and Dan Teague scampered up the Jacob's ladder flung down to them. They swung over the gunwale as they had done dozens of times before on dozens of ships: all smiles and empty hands, just the black cloth thrown to the deck where it rolled out as the others clambered up behind.

The cloth spread. A white grinning skull rolled free, two crossed pistols beneath, and the *Junot*'s crew stared down riveted to it, missing the pistols being pulled from behind the backs of their guests.

Hugh Harris grinned like the death's head at his feet. 'Hold now, lads!' he warned. 'You be pirated! *Forban*! Drop any steel to the flag for your forgiveness!' The rest of his words were English swearing, his pistols bolstering his skinny frame against the big Frenchmen.

Dan Teague echoed him. No violence, Devlin had said. These men should report nothing against them except the taking of their little ship. But this stepping on a foreign deck was a pirate's breakfast. There had to be some sport or why get up at all?

Pistol followed pistol and pistols were rare for the common. If these pirates carried them it would be right to assume they had taken them from resisting gentlemen. So raise your hands and smile and bow.

'Stand easy now,' Hugh snarled, and they used their pistols as shepherds use their crooks and waved their sheep to one quarter where a dozen pistols could cover every head.

'Hugh?' Dan asked. 'Is this all we're to do?' Dan Teague was of the old standers with Hugh. From before Devlin, when Seth Toombs had been their captain. But unlike Hugh, who had been scraped from London walls, Dan was a Norfolk man and broad and big. He could have tilled as much as sailed and lived a quiet life arm-wrestling on a Saturday night in any inn five miles from where he was born. But the Spanish war had bought him for a shilling and he had been taught to furl and pull, splice and haul, where he would have hoed and picked all his life. He had fired a musketoon into a Spaniard and had liked the sound and the red again and again. He had split a Frenchman's skull with a mallet and seen his pink brains. Then the navy had signed papers with those they had paid him to kill and no-one had thanked him for his talent. He had come into a world of iron and hoped to live in a world of gold as his queen had promised. It was inevitable that he would meet Hugh, meet Peter Sam, meet others betrayed the same. Pirates do not write invites. The world draws them together. And on this deck, men shivering before him, two stolen pistols in his fists drawing their eyes, this was indeed his breakfast; and the only fear was that one dawn, somewhere, his head would become a stranger to his neck.

But there was Devlin. And though he fed them with blood when he needed it of them, he went a different way when he would.

'Hugh? Is this all we're to do?' he repeated, itching to cock his pistols.

'Aye,' he said, a lament in his voice. 'Cap'n's orders. We don't rob 'em.' He smiled at the fat captain, who grinned back nervously. 'You'd think one of 'em would have a go,' he sighed to Dan.

Hugh understood that this adventure needed a softer

touch, that their presence in these waters should go without incident but still . . . Maybe Paris would give them blood.

'How you weigh her, Bill? What's her burthen?'

Bill pulled his fingers through his beard, and looked at the ship with calculating eyes. 'Reckon she be sixty feet stern to stem. Seventeen feet beam to beam at a guess. That'd make her ninety-two tons thereabouts, Cap'n.'

Deane's *Doctrine of Naval Architecture* still remained the bible of the day for sizing up a ship and the waters she could travel. Not for the weight of the ship herself, but to judge her size by the burden she could carry. View a ship and multiply her length by her breadth and then by half her breadth again and divide the lot by ninety-four. Simple enough, but Devlin was still impressed by the old mariner's quick thinking. Numbers had always been Bill's world. Devlin could navigate well, taught by his master John Coxon long ago, but Bill's skill was near magical. He had no love of numbers, he just needed them to survive. Even so, Devlin remembered him winking proudly at him when he had told his captain that forty-eight tons of rope would stretch thirty miles and that the *Shadow* had seventeen tons that would stretch ten.

'Good,' Devlin said. 'That'll do. She's not too big to make the river. I'll need you Bill, to take the *Shadow* while I'm gone. Keep away from these lanes. Make to sail for the Verdes, then come back here in four days and find me.'

'Four days?'

'To Paris and back here again.'

'Would anyone be wise to know how you aims to devil this rock so easily from this frog duke's pockets, Cap'n?'

Devlin shook his head. 'Best not. A light heart lives long,' he slapped Bill's back. 'That's Shakespeare, Bill!' he grinned.

Chapter Sixteen

Friday

Letter from René Duguay-Trouin
to Joseph Jean Baptiste Fleuriau d'Armenonville
Secrétaire d'État de la Marine
Rue Royale. Paris.
August 1720.

Secretary, herein accept my most obedient salute and salvation.

It has come to my understanding that the ship Vendeen, Captain Jean Minot master, has come across a large vessel of some twenty-four and more guns these two days past, west of Calais. I do not believe this vessel to be allied. It is reported directly to myself that the vessel displayed the flag of plague and merchant rank. However, I respectfully note that, having had its descript confirmed, this vessel relates pertinently to a known pirate and enemy of France since the year 1717 and I encourage the secretary to confirm this also through the same record.

A pirate would be unwise to reach further than Calais or Dunkerque, so ably defended, but may have some desire to hinder transport in La Manche.

As Brest is of a distance to lie within the circuit of this pirate's intent it is my resigned object to investigate this ship personally. Please accept this letter as Your Obedient Chef d'Escardre's design to report La Françoise, 24, and La Patient, 18, to patrol for this vessel known to records and captained by a former Irish patriot of the Royale known as Patrick Devlin, who served His Majesty in the great Spanish war before desertion to the English.

I hope that along with myself The Secretary considers this as the action of a traitor to the crown and The Secretary will appreciate my urgency to apprehend this villain without hesitation. I will therefore accept this mission without the need for reply of consent.
Your Obedient Servant.
René Duguay-Tourin.
Chef d'Escardre Marine Du Roi.
Citadel Calais.

'How is it that you speak French, Captain?' Albany slouched against the gunwale of the tartane. They all wore simpler clothes, loose petticoat breeches and undyed wool coats and caps that thus still retained some of the water-resistant lanolin of the original fleece. But Albany kept his London sword at his side.

Devlin turned to him from where he crouched beneath the sail, gauging the weather helm for Peter Sam at the tiller to keep a straight course into Le Havre.

'I was once a fisherman of these waters. Before all this. I learnt roughly but learnt enough.' He stood and joined Albany who gave him space. 'I was in their navy for a time and learnt quicker there.'

'*Their* navy? When?'

'When you were shivering in your bed when the war echoed all around you.'

'In the war? You were in the French navy against your country?'

Devlin smirked. 'Not my country. War's a great place for hungry men, Albany. Flags are just for wiping gravy off your chin. I was on English ships as well. Although they took me as an Irishman so I shined their shoes.'

Albany said no more, gave Devlin room and contemplated the enormous mouth of the river at their bow.

Le Havre, the shallow face of the Seine and the river into the heart of France, far wider at its mouth than the Thames. Thousands of ships traversed it daily; the *Junot* was just a small single mast amongst the throng and who would pay attention to the delicate ship with but five honest fishermen aboard?

Only Peter Sam, for strength if need be, Hugh Harris for incredible blood when it comes, Dandon for his French, Devlin for all, and Albany because Walpole willed it.

Dandon weaved his way beam to beam, ridiculous in his new clothes, and grabbed Devlin for anchorage. 'Little ships, Patrick, do not suit my legs I fear. I may have to rethink your choice of myself.'

'Too late, patroon. You'll do better in Paris.' He brushed him off and forced himself to speak to Albany again, for he still had questions to ask.

The tartane was a coastal ship, used by men who returned to their homes at night. This dictated that there was no berthing, just a low cabin below aft and a boat trailing behind for her catch. Men would have to be mates around such a small table and Devlin willed Albany no quarter.

The size of the ship was not lost even on Albany. His own head tonight would lay on deck or he would be cramped below with the spare canvas and cordage. 'Will not the families of the men we have supplanted miss them, Captain?' he queried as Devlin came on.

Devlin shrugged. 'They may. May not. It's not unlikely for fishermen to sail to St Malo for the night. And when I fished I had no family to return to. A small matter anyways to what troubles me.'

Intrigue turned Albany's face. 'And what is that, dear Captain?'

'You, Albany,' Devlin rounded to face him. '*You* trouble me.'

Albany seemed happily bemused. 'Why? You have no fear of me.'

Devlin turned his back from the wind to be heard clearer; side by side with Albany.

'Why are you here? What hold does Walpole have over you that you swap silk for wool? Why put up with my gall, for one?'

Albany crossed his arms and looked to Peter Sam at the tiller, who always seemed to be glowering at him. 'I am here to protect the diamond. Myself and George Lee have interest in its safe passage.'

'You mean its theft. Say it as it is. This is a dangerous path. This could be your end.'

Albany snorted. 'I am no fop, Captain, as much as you would like to paint me so. I have duels to my credit. I boxed and fenced for Eton. You will not find fear an attribute in a gentleman.'

Devlin tacked harder. 'Do you know what life is, Albany? What real life is? It is waiting for suffering. Days of life but always waiting for the sword to fall. If you're lucky it is only small things, the inevitable things, the death of loved ones, disease and pain. But it can be more.'

'Do you always talk with such profoundness, Captain? I thought pirates such jolly souls?'

'Everybody owes someone, Albany. Kings, princes, dukes and drunkards. As soon as a man feels his first coin he owes another. Only the dead and children owe nothing. I want to know what it is that you owe that you stand with us.'

Albany stiffened. 'Yes I owe. Debt is being a man, a gentleman, a rich man. But I understand more than you. A rich man can owe millions and it matters nothing for there are millions of the ordinary folk keeping us afloat. But if *they* should collapse all is lost. The top is supported by the ballast beneath. If the ballast cannot pay . . .' he shook his head. 'And that is the circumstance we face. *We*, the better of the world, have land and houses, companies and titles. But if the common man cannot pay his taxes or borrow from our banks because he has no work or the bank has no coin . . . it all goes away. A page of paper crushed into a fist.' He demonstrated, holding his palm out and clenching it dramatically. 'And thrown away.' He tossed his imaginary paper to the sea. 'But we can unravel it. We can spread it out and return it to itself. With only the creases still remaining.

Devlin listened. He knew the 'we' did not refer to him.

'And what is it that you owe, Captain? Why are you here?'

Devlin held his voice in thought and provoked a sneer from Albany.

'I owe my men. I do this and they can be free. I could be free.'

'And would you take it?'

Devlin pulled off his wool cap that itched like fleas and probably was. He shivered a hand through his black hair then studied the poor cap, the symbol of a working man made and worn by peasants. It was utterly unlike the beaver lap and silken tricornes that milled around the fine streets of the world. He had many hats but none made for him and this woollen one fitted too well.

Albany repeated his question. 'Would you take it? The chance to join the regular? What will you do if we succeed?'

Devlin wedged the cap back on and gave Albany his finest face. 'I don't know: I'm making this up as I go along. I'm a new whore.'

He twisted away, pulled himself along the ship, hand to halyard, to rail and wood, to the fore of the ship. To the fore to savour the slow pleasure of meeting a river after the rolling of the keel over the fervent birthing of the Atlantic that was in the Channel, that was La Manche.

All was quiet now as night came. They ate cod mash and drank brandy courtesy of the poor men they took the ship from, who themselves were no doubt wolfing their way through salt-horse and port wine from the *Shadow*'s stores. Devlin's instruction had been to feed them like the king's dogs.

Paris soon. Paris and the diamond. No sea to run to, no ship to protect them; literally a handful of men relying on him to bring them back. And he had only one plan and that worried him; and its foolishness made him keep it to himself, trusting not even Dandon to it.

Maybe this was it. Maybe this was where he failed. The guilt of Valentim Mendes' death and the dozens of others over the scant years, spiralling into a deserved end.

He knew that murderers and thieves often thanked their captors with the relief that it was finally over, and that a thief steals more and more until it is impossible that he is not caught. He had spared Jon Wild in Newgate so that eventually he might meet better justice. But in that scoundrel crumpled on the floor of Newgate's hold Devlin had looked down at himself. And had not the last years seen hundreds of pirates meet their end? Even Blackbeard was gone now, two years gone, dead a mere month after they had stood together, his head cut from his body and paraded into harbour on a bowsprit, the skull boiled clean, silvered and used as a drinking cup. He had known too much to live.

What was it John Coxon, his former master, had said on The Island years past when Devlin had bested them all? In his first days as a pirate when the world seemed huge?

'They are coming. This age is at an end.'

He looked back to Albany still steadying himself against the gunwale. This world belonged to them.

But if *they* found Patrick Devlin, if *they* found The Pirate Devlin, cornered and breathless, alone and desperate . . . it would only be written down by one who was not there, for no-one present would live to tell the tale. A second-hand, whispered story only.

He would make sure of that.

Chapter Seventeen

*U*nder Louis XIV, France had enjoyed peace for just seventeen years of his astounding seventy-two-year reign. For two generations of Frenchmen that averaged one year in four free of international warfare over the duration of the Sun King's time.

And so no more.

Blessed with genius, the giants of French engineering and warfare – men who had cut their teeth in conflict with the enemy constantly at their gates – had fortified their coast and political boundaries to make the entire kingdom a castle.

Men such as Sebastien La Preste de Vauban, infamous enough to be recalled only as Vauban, built, or helped build, hundreds of citadels and fortresses across the land. France's principal points of defence becoming walled cities forming a 'hexagon' of battlements that even the greatest siege could not demolish.

Like a constellation of stars the hexagon stretched from Dunkerque down through Brest to Bayonne, on to Perpignan and Nice, then back north even to Strasbourg. And between these 'citadels' dozens of further fortresses were strung like beads around and against the necks of the enemy which, to the French, was now nothing less than the whole world.

The citadels were an engine of defence that changed warfare, designed as much for offence as holding out against an invader. And Vauban, not content with changing the art of war for sieges, left another legacy that would forever change the field of battle.

He invented the bayonet, and war got dirty fast.

For René Duguay-Trouin, Calais was not one of the great citadels. Even Vauban, who had merely restored its medieval defences rather than build new ones, described its fort Risban as simply 'a home for owls and a place to spend the Sabbath'.

A lesser man would have been insulted that for all his prowess and achievement he was not given the magnificence of Brest – the shipbuilding port and gateway for the French trade to the Americas – to defend. But at least he had something.

This new regime had a hatred for any man of power who was not born to it, who had succeeded and progressed through ability and not privilege; and if that man were a Breton then so much more so, for those proud peasants believed themselves nobles.

Trouin fortunately had been summoned by the king on his deathbed and in gratitude had his position secured. An official nobility had been bestowed. All the same they could bury him in the provinces where he could do no harm. But now? Now after a few days' sport and he would bring to their bigoted court an enemy of France, undeterred by their allies and boldly pirating under their haughty noses. That would be a feat worth a trip to Paris.

So *La Françoise* and *La Patiente*, forty-two nine-pounders between them, sailed out from Calais. They were more than a match for a rag-tag *forban*. A real pirate who had abandoned the Caribbean.

Trouin hoped they had not fled. Please let them still be near, he prayed.

He had launched at dawn. His frigates had been warped out of the harbour by their sailors in their boats like mice pulling a carriage. Then they had unfolded like swans, white canvas spreading across the cross-trees as the whistles blew, the wind at their backs, a rare portent that nature was with them.

Trouin paraded the quarterdeck, not as commodore but a captain to one hundred and sixty men who would give up every limb they had just to say they stood near him once, as crippled beggars in St Malo still declared on their placards.

Already, at the sight of his standard, merchants and navy patrols began to raise sail to slow themselves and be demure in his presence.

He breathed in the future that the waves brought into his lungs. The promise. The fury. Two ships, but the real weapon the coast itself. For decades success had come from the rocks and reefs that ran from England's Lizard to Brittany and Trouin knew them like the knuckles on his hands. This Caribbean pirate would not. He would drown him. He would crush him. And the regent would give him Brest as just reward, closer to his beloved Brittany home.

He ordered music to cheer his men and the morning this late day in August, the sun lightening his deck, his captains huddling close to him like hens. They were young and knew of him only from instructions he had written. Rumours of a Spanish war only months away had invigorated them and if he, Trouin, were to return to the flagships of his youth this would be a fine test to choose those worthy to be with him.

There was scant pity for the pirate.

Deep in the mouth of Le Havre Devlin and Dandon puzzled over the wealth of cutters seemingly crammed with men, women and children making their way to the galleys waiting along the shore. It fell to Albany to come between them and explain.

'Colonists, Captain.' He nodded at their curiosity. 'The regent has a city now. *La Nouvelle Orleans*. He names the diamond after himself so why not his lands in Louisiana? They do not volunteer of course. They are crimped from the people. The vagrants, the peasants. They are married *en masse* to comply with the king's doctrine that only Christian families are to enrich his Americas.'

'They marry strangers to each other?'

'If they had wives before they have new ones now and a brass ring to prove it. They even abduct children to send with them. They use toys to lure them off the streets!' Albany found this detail entertaining and slapped their backs as he meandered away.

Dandon shuddered. 'I wish me back to the Caribbean, *mon frère*. I was born in the colonies. This is a colder world and not just its inclemency,' he brushed his jacket hatefully, 'or for what passes as fashion.'

Devlin watched the boats. 'Nothing has changed, Dandon. Over ten years I've been out of this. I hope the New World will really be such. Else we are the last free men.' He backed away to the sack by the mast. 'I need a drink.'

Dandon tugged him back. 'And yet you will take *their* freedom as offered. Is this what you want? Their definition is as mysterious as their religion.'

Devlin leaned down to pull a bottle. 'There's a reason the Lord turned water into wine.' He plucked the brandy cork with his teeth. 'I'll wait 'til I have the diamond, then decide.'

'Let's hope it doesn't decide for us. Now if you excuse me; I think I am going to be sick.' Dandon weaved away leaving Devlin to gaze over the bow.

Paris lay a full day away; thirteen bridges had to be passed along the meandering vein of France; the *Junot*'s tabernacle mast would need to be lowered on its pivot to whisper under them. The bridges were the reason they had to leave the *Shadow*, leave their strength behind. The tartane's mast could lower like a yacht's, and then raise again, so they might sail right into Paris. Instead of lines of latitude, bridge after bridge marked the miles. Devlin had done the journey before as a fisherman but had not expected to do so again, and this time for a prince and a government that would have hung him on any other day. To the regent, get the diamond, carry it back to London. Freedom from persecution his reward. But if he failed he would surely die and those who had come with him also.

He turned to look over them. His little band. Even Albany was risking himself. At least if they fell the *Shadow* would go on – he had preserved that much. He had no children, no legacy save that ship and a hundred men to tell who he had been.

'Dandon!' he called and Dandon pulled himself from the gunwale to look back. 'Have you ever thought that we should write down all of this. Leave something behind.'

Dandon tapped his head. 'It is all in here, Patrick. I am noting it all.'

'You should start. Before you get killed.'

'I cannot die, Patrick.'

'Why is that?'

Dandon was surprised at the question. 'I always stand behind *you*.'

John Law's coach bowled south to meet them, his spine jolting with every rut in the road. Tomorrow he would be in Paris.

His first duty as director of the bank of France was to report to the regent Philippe at the Palais Royal and hope that on his face could not be read the wiles and anxieties of a conspirator. He rapped his cane on the ceiling of the coach, to urge his faithful driver onward, then shook his head at the irony of desiring to hurry to his fate.

He had known many long weeks in his life. He had killed a young man once, shot him in a duel, and after such an act, so quick and passionate at the time, a man's perspective on time changes.

He goes one way or the other. Either he squanders time and smashes the hour glass to watch the sand filter through the floorboards like the spilt blood, or else he wields it triumphantly like a sword and cuts a path of his own, knowing that his death is only ever a moment away and that the moment is at his shoulder if he pauses and looks behind him.

Law had begun his life several times over and was a polymath of infinite talent, its pinnacle the merging of his bank with the Bank of France and the creation of paper money instead of coin so that people would trade via the banks and not with each other. But the riotous trading in New World companies had ruined it all, broken it all, shattered his hour glass.

It could have all been controlled of course; charters and governments could have prevented the release of yet more shares if it wasn't for the fact that it was those who should have controlled the frenzy were becoming most enriched.

'*Quis custodiet ipsos custodes*. Who guards the guards?' he scoffed aloud. And after that who checks the coffers, who is to account for those who only account for each other? And he as guilty as any of them. He was running from a fire with stolen gold bundled in his arms. And a pirate was trusted to save one company and England itself, with Law hanging on his coat-tails to flee when the mountain fell.

He looked past the curtain to the rushing countryside. At this moment, this hour, only his driver knew where he was in the world. He could run north now to Belgium, to Amsterdam, places where his name still carried weight. He closed the curtain. No. There was his family to consider and still the hope that if they could save the South Sea others would also be saved. And the world would learn from its errors with men like Law to teach them.

It was the pirate he felt sorry for.

The naïveté of peasants to trust fine coats and carriages with their future was still obviously ingrained within him. But after meeting Devlin he wondered how it would be done, how they would kill him. Not face to face, that would not work. It would have to be devious and dark or done from afar. Or perhaps just simply with a rope and a hood as befitted his role in life, and no-one listening to his speech from the gallows. Law pulled his cloak tighter, swaddling himself against the shiver of his own trust in those same coats. A man's final moment always just over his shoulder. It would be a long week for those who knew too much.

Chapter Eighteen

Paris. The Palais Royale. The regent's rooms.
Saturday

'The door, *Lass*, the door! Shut out the light!' Philippe's voice boomed from the near darkness. 'Dubois here surely has his man out and I do not wish to see it!'

John Law closed the study door, sending the room back into its eerie gloaming as the light projected from the 'Laterna Magica' shone onto the white sheet against the wall and its returning light silhouetted like caricatures the two seated figures before it.

Law could just make out a valet slotting in and out of a large cuboid contraption the canvas and glass plates of grotesque erotica. Each new plate prompted guttural approval from the two men in the dark.

He moved delicately into the room, seeking a chair away from the projector's light. By Philippe's remark he surmised that the hateful, ageing archbishop, Guillame Dubois, was also in the room.

Dubois had been Philippe's tutor and was now his first minister, the second most powerful man in France and therefore one of the most powerful men in the world. Just this year he had become archbishop, and already he sought to be cardinal. He had achieved such status without ever being able to recite a mass, for Philippe's rise to power had also been Dubois's. Each knew enough about the other's past to cement a lasting bond. Their companionship was balanced like a scale and as long as it had equal coin in both bowls it would stay that way.

Law found his seat and the noise of it scraping on the floor reminded Philippe that he had duties to perform before the real pleasure of the night began.

'*Light*!' he called to the valet, a click of his fingers ending the laterna show. Dubois's gruff mumbling and fiddling of his robes announced his displeasure at its cessation.

'I do not wish to disturb, Milord,' Law declared honestly as candles were lit and the two men sat revealed.

'Not at all, Lass,' Philippe waved away the apology. 'You remind me that I still have work to do.'

Nevertheless he slumped back in his chair, his royal blue banyan gown and shirt almost open to his waist, and he scruffed his close-cropped hair as if trying to rouse the blood to his head and away from other extremities. 'You return from your country sojourn and have settled your business with Pitt? I trust this has served you well, Lass?'

'Not as much as I had hoped, Milord,' Law confessed, averting his eyes from Dubois. 'I take it that the company's future has not improved?'

Philippe shrugged with the same weary brevity of every Frenchman. 'I have made you the head of the Indian and American companies and merged your bank with the Bank of France, but even your genius for trade, Lass, cannot save us if there *is* no trade, and so no monies in the bank. It is doomed. France is doomed. My France.'

Law leaned forward. 'But surely there is money, Milord? The banknotes? The securities are guaranteed?'

Philippe shrugged again, pushed away some papers from his sight and reached for his champagne glass. Dubois scratched his red nose with the gold cross that rested on his chest, showing that there was at least one use for it.

'Politics is an expensive mistress, Lass,' Philippe continued. 'I have policies that would never have been born if it were not for the support of nobility. And I in turn must support them in their follies and furbelows. And they in turn take the money that they did not have in the first place and push it to Switzerland. And do not think that the people have not seen the cartloads of gold being robbed from the bank. I would sell that accursed diamond if I thought that there was a kingdom who could buy it now. What would Spain say about Philippe if he sold the crown jewels? I would be the laughing stock of Europe.'

The words from the regent that all was lost gave some relief to Law that his actions were not betrayal but only survival.

Dubois raised a velvet-gloved finger. 'Perhaps another conspiracy? Enough to gain public support at least.'

Philippe gave his finest Gallic guffaw. 'Have you not quelled enough *mistouflet* armies, Dubois! Besides, I do not think we have enemies that are not already in their graves. No, we shall ride it out, that is all.'

Dubois went on unperturbed. 'A few heretic Catholic deaths always strengthens well our allegiance with the English. Stanhope wishes us to be great friends. And England has much the same troubles. If we make it seem that we are all suffering because of some heretic conspiracy – no fraud or greed – just religion rearing its ugliest head.'

Dubois caught Law's raised eyebrow at the flippant comments about death from a man of God. He sniffed and rubbed his nose with the cold metal cross once more. 'Money has no religion, Monsieur Lass. The people forget their poverty if they believe they have a common enemy.'

Philippe smashed his hand down on the desk, rattling more than just glasses and wine. 'There will be no more conspiracies, Dubois! I have had enough of breaking backs on the wheel! You are as bloody as a real bishop, *dog*!'

Dubois chortled into his chest at the outburst. Philippe's ministry had crushed two 'conspiracies' since coming to the throne, both conveniently engineered to remove those nobles set against him and those who felt that the king of Spain, the late king's grandson, had more right to the throne than the great-grandson who was but a child. Philippe himself had been fourth in line to the throne when he was born. In the years he was at court, death had whittled that list down to all but the boy. And suspicion amongst the boy's tutors just sufficient that the child's handkerchiefs and even his butter were kept from Philippe's reach, for smallpox travels well.

Six days before his death, after a late and private audience with the man who had now become second in line, Louis XIV added a codicil to his will. Philippe would rule until his great-grandson had reached majority.

Three years remained now, for the boy would reach majority at thirteen. That was three years to fleece as much as possible from France before he would hand back the keys to an empty vault. But there had been so many deaths, necessary perhaps, but what a cost.

His daughter, his favourite daughter, the Duchesse de Berry. The scent of her, her caress, the absence of her was to him like the loss of taste. She had been four months pregnant when the parties and scandal had finally taken their toll. Whispers had circulated around the court that Philippe was too attentive even for a father – especially one who lived separate from his wife.

'Let joy commence!' he slammed his hand down again to snap himself out of his melancholy. 'You will come to my supper tonight, Lass! Eat and drink ourselves out of this misery!'

Law shook his head. 'I have been away, Milord. I must work. If I can help us it will be from my company.' Law knew that Devlin might contact him at any moment and, besides, he had already been to one of the regent's champagne suppers. One was enough for a lifetime.

Philippe had removed the court from Versailles as part of the official policy of making the city of sinners royal once more. In truth it was to be closer to the sinners.

Louis XIV had spent a month on his deathbed legitimising his numerous bastard sons. Philippe would need two months at least. There was no need for whores when there were plenty of ladies vying for a place at court through their offspring or plenty of cousins begging you to be godfather to their fourteen-year-old daughters for the same.

'Very well, Lass. You are a good man.' Philippe stood, energised again by his draught of champagne and the delicious prospect of the night ahead with its tresses and flesh. 'Come, you old sod, Dubois. We will dine on breast-milk tonight!'

The bishop dragged himself up. He was in his sixties now and a bladder complaint affected his own participation in the revels, but the sights and sounds of the orgy were like a *carnivale* to him still.

Philippe straightened his dress and moved around his desk to Law's shoulder. He was shorter than the tall Scot but a broad strong man. 'Lass, you are a great gamer but we must teach you how to love. Life is joy, Lass. Sadness is a sickness.

That is why the poor die so young. They cannot afford to be happy!'

The ruler of France held open the door for Law to exit, even bid his valet through but left the archbishop to his own devices. The whole palace was set in a square and they walked down the window-lined corridor that looked out onto the gardens. Philippe stopped at the man with the two pails who stood like a statue against the wall. He undid himself and resumed speaking to Law, who joined the servant with the pail in staring out at the garden as Philippe urinated noisily into the tin bucket.

'In the morning I have called Ronde, the jeweller, to attend to discuss the setting of the diamond.'

Law's heart jumped. The piss-boy glanced at Law's flushed face then switched his gaze back to the window.

'Tomorrow, Milord?'

'At eleven. And I wish you to be there. I have little time for the man. He is such . . .' he paused, and emitted a grunt of satisfaction as the weight of his stream became quite pleasurable '. . . a bore, you know.'

Dubois brushed past Law to take advantage of the piss-boy's second pail, the sound of the regent's relief too much of a temptation for his nervous bladder.

'But I will tolerate him. I feel the longer I hold onto that stone the worse everything becomes around me.' He grunted through the last three forced squirts and shook himself off. 'At least it cannot get any more deplorable.'

Law thought quickly. Tomorrow morning was too soon. The diamond would be on its way to join the crown and the pirate was not yet at his door. 'The crown is ready for the stone?'

The duke wiped his hand down his banyan and tugged at

his nose. 'No. The fool says it will take almost two years to complete. I wish to survey his design. Concur that it matches my own desires for the Regent.' Philippe had christened the diamond after himself and his court had grown accustomed to the gem's third-person title.

He fixed Law with an eye. 'I want the Regent set in the foremost of the crown. So all that see it will know that it is *I* above the king's head, and *I* am watching them all.'

Law could not afford to seem agitated but he could allow himself to appear as disgusted at the prospect of Ronde as the duke, or by Dubois's hissing imprecations toward the man holding the bucket.

'We will need an armed escort if the diamond is to leave tomorrow. It would be unsuitable for Ronde to walk out with such a fortune in just his pocket. It will take time to choose appropriately discreet men.'

The duke walked on in silence. Law could feel his blood pounding in his veins and wondered if the duke could also feel it.

'No,' he said at last. 'I only wish to force my hand in his design. He will not have the Regent.' He smiled up at his Scottish friend, the sound of Dubois's stream behind them making tension impossible. 'You must miss the glory of the diamond, Lass, there is such a tremor in your voice!'

Law dipped his head. 'I am anxious for it, Milord. I was responsible for its acquisition from Pitt. There is relation there. But I wonder if we could delay until the afternoon, Milord? I am tired after my journey and have much to catch up on.' Maybe that would give Devlin time to appear. They walked on, leaving Dubois to painfully shake out his final syrupy brown drops.

The Parisian shrug surfaced again. 'Very well, no matter. At three then, yes? Now, good evening, Lass. Get your rest, old man!' He slapped Law's back and spun off toward one of the smaller cloistered dining rooms above that deliberately did not have windows. Law's chambers were near the regent's in the western side of the palace, far away from the debauchery to come, and he wandered there slowly.

Time had shortened now, like a candle burning down, its wick a fuse.

The pirate had to come tomorrow – and early – or all was lost. Law halted. But then perhaps tomorrow would force the pirate to follow Walpole's original plan, to take the diamond from the lapidary instead? Aye, that might be the safer path. The pirate could not design a scheme to overcome the walls of the palace. When he saw the palace tomorrow he would surely understand and swallow his pride.

Law would make his way to his offices in the Rue Quincampoix, a fifteen-minute stroll, and wait for the pirate to meet him there or not at all. The man was no doubt drunk beyond diligence. He laughed and clapped his hand to his mouth, his gallows merriment resonating all along the corridor as he ascended to his rooms. Devlin would fit perfectly in such a Paris as this.

Dubois heard the faraway laugh. Perhaps it was some joke he had missed between the regent and the financier. No matter. He tucked himself away while looking at the man with the pails, daring him to meet his eye or at least look down to his steaming buckets. Nothing. Just tight-jawed and staring straight ahead.

Dubois stroked the man's cheek with his purple velvet. 'Are you perchance from Mirebalais, young man?'

Unaware of any address that did not earn punishment the man stayed silent.

'The ladies upstairs do so love a man from Mirebalais. Still I suppose carrying buckets of piss has purpose in life. Perhaps the police is your destiny?' The waxwork before him was irresistible now that the regent had ignored him.

'You know, the English, they did wrong when they removed their king the last time.' He moved closer with his hot breath. 'They killed the revolutionary principals but they sent the smaller ones to their colonies as slaves. That was a mistake. Revolution is carried in the blood. I have urged often the death of dissenters. And I am proved right. If they breed, the children will carry the thought in their blood. The English king will lose the colonies because he sends his haters away to breed. And we do the same by filling Louisiana with hate.'

The nostrils of the bucket bearer widened; his arms were beginning to tremble, his buckets filled with hours of waste by every wanderer within the walls.

'I, boy, have condemned hundreds. Those Bretons seeking republic. Foreign Catholics seeking home. If you do not kill them their children's children will return.' He patted the man's cheek with emerald- and ruby-banded fingers. '*You* will punish us if we allow you to breed . . . *malheureusement.*'

He wheeled away, scuffing his shoulder against the wall as he spun back to face the unmoving sentinel. 'I did not break *conspiracies*! I cut blood for the sake of the divine!' Then, his finger waggling foolishly, 'I can hear *you*! I can hear you *all*!' He moved away to seek the drink and the flesh, his voice heavy. 'I am glad that I will be too long dead to meet you when you come.'

Chapter Nineteen

Sunday morning

'*T*hey're still coming,' Dan Teague said, and passed the glass to Bill. They stood on the *Shadow*'s shallow quarterdeck watching the square towers of sail roll over the horizon. No deck was visible so the ships were still a ways off yet.

Two ships. The dawn had brought them, the sun presenting them to the *Shadow*'s anchored stern, the working day of the pirate some hours off yet. Dan Teague and Bill were late in greeting the sails.

Bill spoke his mind aloud. 'She'd turned by now if making for Malo or the coast. They ain't in too much of a hurry least-ways: they have royals if they would but use them.'

The *Shadow* had cruised under her French merchant flag almost out of the Channel and into the wide welcoming arms of the Atlantic, her passage marked by the *Îles d'la Manche* to larboard and the Lizard to their starboard bow. Then came the Scilly archipelago and at last they left the rough white-capped waters between France and England. Now, though, two ships of the line from the east seemingly dogged them, matching them knot for knot. It was more like a drag than a hunt.

Bill lowered the glass. 'We should raise English colours. If they're Frogs we ain't the heads to fool them, not with the captain and Dandon gone.'

'We could make closed waters. Round to Bristol,' Dan suggested.

'Aye,' Bill agreed. If the ships were French they had no business within the three miles of Mare Clausum, that territory around England's coast that had been hard fought for and whose measure was defined by the range of a cliff-top cannon – or an Englishman's hate. 'But we're to make for the Verdes and back again for the captain. Back in three days. Can't leave him lolling in that tartane. Besides, Dan, it ain't a chase yet.'

Others had joined them, shielding their eyes from the morning sun to watch the white pillars suddenly grow taller and wider still as the royals fell and studding sails struck out like wings. The course of the twin ships stayed as faithful as if the *Shadow* had laid them a towing hawser.

Dan did not need the scope to see it, and made sure Bill had. 'Ain't it a chase, Bill? Looks one to me now. Time to hauls it, I says!'

Bill showed nothing, not with the crowd around him. His was the rule now, as Devlin had passed it, for whatever it was worth. He made a slow swallow beneath his beard which none could see. 'Know your scripture, Dan,' he whispered, then moved round for them all to hear.

'*Be not afraid*. Three hundred and sixty-six times the Bible says that! That's a blessing for every day of the year, and one for the leap!'

Already he had begun to think of powder, but not out loud to them, not yet. 'I'll have mine today, lads! Be not afraid now. Sunday after all. Who fights on a Sunday, save for us!

* * *

Trouin left the scoping of the horizon to his officer pups brimming over the fo'c'sle. No need for him to lay sight of his fox. A black and red frigate rigged to the gallants, not intelligent enough to change her grey sails from those as described years past. The faint plume that detailed a hearth on the weather-deck where men ate above rather than below – a sure mark of a pirate biting against convention. Closer and he would know; see her French-built strakes that overlapped, clinker-built for outer hull strength. If so that would confirm she was the *Shadow*, '*a Sombra*', as surely as the wax seal from the governor of the Verdes that bought her, whatever masked escutcheon she was sailing under.

It was *him*. The pirate that had two royal warrants against him and more from every ally. Too far for his eager officers to perceive a flag but close enough for Trouin to feel, the hair rising on his skin, that this was the ship that the merchant had told him of three days ago.

He had given no margin for error or ingenuity from the pirate. Like fool's chess the brigand would sail into his trap. *La Françoise* would stand to the pirate's forefoot, feinting to lure her to the treacherous Scilly rocks of the aptly named Hell Mouth – a sailor's graveyard. The weaker *La Patiente*, Trouin's command, would give her leeway, allow her a gap to run, and when she took it . . .

There was no need for signals or orders shouted through trumpets. Captain Cassard on *La Françoise* had his orders to follow like calculus. One only needed to mark time until the distance between them closed. A fine Sunday morning in August that some artist would soon immortalise in oil. Trouin would choose the artist himself, not out of vanity – no vanity in glory – but to ensure that the painter had the right sanguinary spirit for the task.

The sea pulled. The bow dipped. Everything ran in his favour just as it always had. Pity those against him on the sea. His sea.

The *Shadow* unfurled her sail slowly in the distance and moved on. The game was afoot. His game.

'*La chasse est ouverte!*' he cried out over the sea rather than to the horde behind him who cheered raucously in response. He presented no expression of pride, made no flourish with his hat. Already, coolly, thoughts of his chicken supper seemed more important: René Duguay-Trouin at his table. But he had told none of them of his innermost thoughts, the pricking at his skin and instinct.

A pirate had come into his waters, famous and bold, but had ignored the fat merchant ships in his sight, and instead had veiled himself as a plague ship. Why?

There was more game here than just a *forban* rat.

John Law sat at his desk in his company's offices in the Rue de Quincampoix, a small white-panelled upstairs room with one shuttered window and the yellow light of candles dwindling away the hours. At least Sunday provided peace from the maniacs selling and buying stocks in the streets below. Even those fools needed mass or bread eventually.

He mused over the papers that had been waiting for his return. He was a formidable mathematician, perhaps greater than the finest astronomers of Greenwich, and if he had turned his skill to the Longitude instead of the gaming tables of Europe, Halley and Flamsteed may have slept more. Now he lifted each page as if it were ballast, despairing over his figures as if they counted plague victims.

Still, his Scotsman's optimism – or obstinacy – led him to feel that something could be done other than flee to the Netherlands or back to England if the pirate should succeed.

But the more the abyssal figures trailed away before his eyes the more difficulty he had in ceasing the trembling of his hands.

The banknotes had been a sound notion. Perfectly sound. When England almost a quarter of a century before had needed to rebuild its navy it had started its own bank, offering notes promising an eight-percent return. So successful was the scheme that England now challenged France for European supremacy, her defeat at Beachy Head forgotten, her navy ruling the waves.

In France the scheme to offer notes for gold and silver had won even greater popularity. The people had embraced the notion that their notes could not be devalued by a king's whims and the fact that paper was more portable and practical than coin in so vast a realm – particularly so when the ferocity of speculation in the New World companies, of which Law was now head, hit Paris like a hurricane and littered the streets with chits and credit notes as if it were exactly just such a cataclysm.

But John Law, *Monsieur Lass*, had not counted on the lust that sight of such vast profit could create in the regent's eye and in that of the blue-bloods who had promised to support his ascension in return for livres rather than policies. Somehow, Philippe still carried the people's admiration but not so for *Lass*. Over the summer, as the price of shares in his companies fell and fell, the people who had once labelled him a genius now sought his hide. He had sent his wife and children to his country estate for safety and for the health of his youngest son who had developed the first signs of the dreaded small-pox, the illness that had plagued Law in his youth. Bravely he had stayed in Paris, albeit under the protection of the regent. Perhaps indeed his only chance of safety was to run, Walpole's plan his avenue of escape.

How could this terror have gripped France? America should have been fat, a goose with layers and layers of grease and pregnant with golden eggs to boot. The kingdom of France should have been her master. But America was not the whore of plenty they had banked on.

Swamps, hostile natives, pirates – especially the pirates – stopping a third of the trade like a tax collector wandering up and down the pews of a church with cudgel and sack. And there was no gold.

It was hoped that the northern plains would have the same alluvial abundance as the wealth of New Spain, but that had not transpired. Spain still held civilisation's pursestrings and laughed at them from its treasure fleets sailing still from Potosi.

Law trembled more with every statement from each department that landed on his desk; they provoked a rising nausea that could only be temporarily quelled with whisky, or permanently by some miracle.

'There is a baker here to see you, Monsieur Lass.' He was pulled from his pit by his administrator's soft voice at his open door. He wearily lifted his head.

'Hmm?'

'A baker.'

'A baker?'

The man pushed his pince-nez back to the bridge of his nose. 'He says he has the pie you ordered. A "tarte rat" it would seem? He says it is a Scottish dish for yourself.' The administrator had some knowledge of the vulgar stomach of Scotsmen. Why not a rat pie to add to their repellent list of delicacies?

Law however struggled to recall any such request, and his bemusement did not go unnoticed.

'He says it is the "backwards" pie of your homeland? That you eat it back to front or some such nonsense?' Law simply stared at him. 'I will send him away, Milord,' said the administrator with a nod.

Law pursed his lips. A rat pie. Eaten backwards. A slap of realisation hit him in the face. He shouted at the back of the man at his door, his hands suddenly no longer trembling.

'Show him up, Henri! I remember perfectly! It was before my trip – yes, yes, show him up at once! My rat pie! Splendid, man!'

Henri pushed his pince-nez once more back onto his nose and bowed, exiting with French expressions of disgust under his breath.

Law admired the new steadiness of his fingers, his corpse-pile of numbers instantly forgotten. A moment later, hope sauntered into the room, although in a more surprising manner than to Law than when he had first laid eyes on the pirate Devlin.

Devlin wore no cocked hat this time, just a leather sailor's cap, long on one side, a woollen shirt, a common eighteen-button waistcoat and slop hose. Finishing off his much-changed appearance were wooden shoes that clacked on the bare floor as he came into the room and closed the door behind him.

'Well met, John,' Devlin said, not minding his English and sure they were alone. He pulled over his head the thick leather strap by which means the tray of his baked wares was held out before him.

Law watched him place the tray down, unable to stop grinning at the transformation of pirate to pie-man. He sprang to his feet, scampering around his desk and warmly pumped the pirate's hand.

'Well met indeed, Captain! Good to see that discretion is your loudest virtue! A rat pie indeed! To eat backwards! *Pie-rat*! Ho, *pirate*! Splendid! But what if I had not known?'

Devlin took away his hand. 'Then I'd have guessed you wrong,' he said.

He looked around the plain room. A blackboard on one wall, books lining every other. The blackboard, Devlin assumed, was a symptom of Law's obsession with mathematics. He took a chair, uninvited, and pulled it to face the desk. Law took his cue and sat back at his place; the pirate was clearly not one for small talk.

Devlin removed his cap, scratched through his hair and checked his nails for whatever stowaways his borrowed fisherman slops carried. 'What goes on, John, since we parted? What of the diamond?'

Law squared his papers nervously. 'I'm afraid the pace has run far ahead of our plans.' He caught then the smell of ammonia and smoke, the pure lanolin waft from the raw wool. It was not an atmosphere that any man should have to grow used to. But the pirate had disguised himself in Law's aid and he was grateful for the sacrifice. 'A drink, Captain?' It was the best sympathy he could offer.

Law sprang from his desk, using the enchanting melody of glasses and pouring liquor to soften his words. 'It may occasion you to reconsider following Walpole's original design.' He passed an eye over the baker's tray of pies and pastries. Devlin had admirably gone to a lot of effort in his disguise. He stood over the pirate and handed Devlin a glass. 'That is, I mean, Walpole's plan to take the diamond from the lapidary Ronde. Surely now our best course?'

Devlin thanked him for the whisky that covered the stench of his outfit.

'What's changed?'

Law explained that the regent was to see Ronde at the palace that very afternoon. 'It is not of my doing. I am as surprised as you.' Devlin's face showed none of the surprise Law expected. 'It hurries things along, Captain, which is all to the good, but now with time against us we shall wait until the diamond is removed.'

Devlin swallowed his glass. 'Good. Then we will know where the diamond is hidden today. That means we can take it today. I thought we might have to wait for tomorrow. What time?'

Law's heart staggered. 'Three o'clock. I will attend, but—'

'And the duke's offices are where?' He pulled out his rough map. Law looked down and indicated the east wing. 'And that is where you'll be at three?' Devlin asked. Law nodded as firmly as he could.

Devlin looked for a clock. 'Almost three hours.' As if Law were no longer in the room he placed his glass back on the table, picked up his tray of wares and began to put it back on as he headed for the door.

Law followed him like a toddling infant. 'You misunderstand. What could you possibly do? I cannot take you in to meet the regent. You cannot manufacture a robbery under the eyes of a castle! It may be Sunday but the palace does not sleep! Captain? There is nothing you can do! How can you be so obtuse?'

Devlin stopped slipping on his baker's tray and put it down slowly but hard enough that the crack of it on the table made Law flinch.

A silence ensued, the pirate stock still, his head down, some offence clearly riling him. Law rapidly unpicked his thoughts to recall what offence he had uttered.

The head of France's national bank, one of the most

auspicious men in one of the most powerful countries on earth, stammered and wilted at the motionless form. 'That is . . . I mean to say . . . that it will be impossible to—'

Devlin spun round. He appeared at the blackboard opposite as swiftly as if he had always been standing there. Ridiculous as his clothing was, his voice came as powerfully and exact as if he were draped in ermine and gold.

'Right. Obtuse.' He picked up a chalk and began to draw a crude map complete with waves and two ships, each stroke on the slate, in his anger, like a stabbing knife. Law, his pupil now, awaited his lesson.

'This is an island,' he drew a smattering of trees and hills across it. 'Cliffs from which you can see thirty miles all around. Impossible to approach unseen.' His voice was hurried, impatient with his companion's ignorance. 'Here is a fort protected by a barracks. A barracks of French marines.' His angry strokes chipped pieces of chalk to the floor; his knuckles were just as white.

'On this island, inside the fort no less, is a chest of gold that weighs the same as four men. *This*,' he slapped one of the ships, 'is an English Man of War sent to protect the island.' He half-turned to let his representation sink in, then rapidly crossed out the ship under a flurry of white.

'*Beaten*!' He crossed out the fort, 'Beaten! Dead! All of them *dead*!' – an inflection in the last word like a bad taste. 'Me and Dandon did that and sailed away like kings.'

He did not wait for a response but merely rubbed the story away with his sleeve and immediately began another island.

'*This* is New Providence. A pirate island, now English. Another fort. *Two* hundred soldiers. *Two* men of war this time,' he drew the ships vaguely, their presence smaller, his patience at an end.

'In the fort, Governor Woodes Rogers and *all* the soldiers and a letter that I was sent to fetch – fetch for men like you.' He scratched out the image with cutlass strokes of white and threw the chalk at Law's feet.

'*All* beaten! Done! Dead! Me and Dandon!' He stood still only to let his stature climb to the ceiling; stood before the tall Scottish man second only to the regent in the kingdom of France. 'Don't strive to be a sanctimonious shit like the rest of them, John. Mark me: if you are – if you plan to be – I'm usually the only one that walks away.'

He strode back to his tray, cradling it to his hip and opening the door in the same movement like a skilled waiter. 'Meet the regent. Keep him there. Stay with him. Then you can tell me where the diamond is . . . so pay attention. Oh—' his parting shot. 'And the day before we met I escaped from Newgate. My memory's still a bit hazy on that one so forgive me if I don't draw you a picture.'

The door slammed. Law was left staring dumbly at the portal the pirate had flown through. Eventually he turned to the blackboard smeared with thunderclouds of white, the pirate's past etched beneath them.

'But . . . I don't know where . . . ?' Pointless. Pointless to talk to an empty room. The clock ticked. Weeks of secret correspondence and mad schemes had been reduced to hours. He had pawned his future. Aye, and only a pirate held the redeeming ticket.

Chapter Twenty

A glass of Oporto for Dandon and Albany at the *cabaret*, 'Image Notre Dame'. The inn was in the sandy Place de Grève beside the Seine, almost right on the river where the square was lapped by its shallow tide. Here they waited, outside, for the inn bulged with bodies. Albany waited impatiently, Dandon ecstatically, mesmerised by the city's grandeur.

Dandon was a child of the New World. He had known the simplicity of the French forts of Louisiana, little more than log cabins and mud, and the burgeoning replication of English towns that were Charles Town and Bath Town.

London had been a disappointment. A city of kings but made of daub and smoke where abandoned children died in the streets while gold carriages trundled by.

But here *was* a city. It had its cruelty and brutality – the pillory and gibbet in the wide square said enough – but the magnificence, the pride . . . It was enough for Dandon to be convinced that this was Europe's jewel. No great fire had eaten its soul and with its wide streets, squares and gardens, Dandon doubted that one ever could.

He turned to every side, looking upward to take in the gabled towers of the shops and houses, his admiration inevitably always ending at the palatial Hôtel de Ville, its golden stone and blue slate rooftops more welcoming fairytale castle than the dusty bureaus of the city's civil administrators, the cold heart of Paris.

Dandon raised his glass to Albany as the young noble lingered on the steps of the inn, toying with the elaborate sword hilt that clashed with his peasant's clothing. Dandon swayed over. He had removed his coat, setting it over his own tray of baker's fare near the steps of the inn where the occasional half-starved dog sniffed and wagged its tale entreatingly before being dispatched by Albany's boot.

Dandon, in a white blouse, slop-hose swinging with his gait, wineglass safe to his chest, still carried a handsome confidence that brought fans to the blushing cheeks of amenable women sauntering along the strand. He met all of them with a flash of gold-capped teeth and a pinching of the moustache he had still yet to preen. Albany hated the very bones of him.

In fact, Albany belonged to the set that dropped coin for women in the bagnio-lined streets or had to pursue with his purse those of better breed, casting dresses and deerskin gloves before them until they showed their petticoats.

Dandon belonged to a school of libertine that did not need a purse or a father's estate to grease his pole and the pirate showed he knew it with every delivery of his raised eyebrow and jaunty bow. Albany's schoolboy envy was that of one pupil's for another's bigger bag of marbles. He anticipated the yellow popinjay's address with his own.

'We have spent our morning purchasing trays of pastries. Do you think our gallant "leader" will return to enlighten us as to their purpose?'

Dandon said nothing, his eyes smiling over his glass's rim. That morning they had rowed into the Seine and past its islands, Louvier and Saint-Louis, the former for farmland and livestock – Paris's own larder – the latter a city of its own with grand houses for the elite, linked to both the left and right banks by bridge.

The tartane had earlier slipped under Pont Marie, a smaller double of London Bridge, with its dingy houses and smut-faced children leaning perilously out of the windows either to wave them through or drop pebbles and carrot-tops on the cursing wherrymen. Then, rising from the mist, almost floating out of the sky towards them, approached the monstrous presence of Pont Notre Dame, her arches littered with boats and wherries duelling for trade. Houses and shops towered five storeys tall all across, their chimney-smoke blackening the sky, linked with wooden walkways on the outside above the water, and the people bustling in their business all about her like maggots writhing through a corpse. The water, and those that worked it between the two bridges, lay almost black in shadow.

Here they left Peter Sam and Hugh Harris and walked into the Place de Grève, Devlin planting them at the inn. He knew the working alleyways of the quarter, and it was better to go alone.

After half an hour of waiting for the *cabaretier* to serve them – their peasant attire hardly hastening him – Devlin returned with two muslin-covered trays and two small pepper pots.

'I am gone to see Law. Don't touch anything,' he said, and pointed. 'Especially the pepper. Wait for me.' He took up one of the trays and vanished into the smart Sunday crowds. And now here they were, awaiting his return. Albany, bruised by Devlin's secrecy, nagged at the only source of information that he had. Dandon's ears were soon bruised.

'If he believes he is protecting us by leaving us in ignorance he would do better to let me in on his intentions at least. I am not some brainless sot with no thoughts of my own. He has estimated me too much with his usual company.'

'In that case,' Dandon leaned into his ear, 'would not a wiser gentleman lower his very English voice?'

He leaned away again before Albany could send a riposte.

He looked over the water to the exquisite prettiness of the red wooden bridge that crossed from Saint-Louis to Île de la Cité where the Gothic might of the Notre Dame cathedral preached over the whole city.

How could anyone leave such a place for the sweat and rusticality of the Americas? He had to restrain himself from exclaiming such a mystery to the nearest passer-by, then remembered from the day before the impressed colonists being herded onto barges.

A hand on his shoulder jerked him from his deliberations on the marvellous canvas before him.

'You look like you're in love, Dandon,' Devlin smirked.

Dandon, too overjoyed to see his captain to blush, excused himself and almost paraded him over to Albany on the inn's steps. Albany tugged his cap, pleased at least that Devlin had returned. He indicated the tray that Devlin still carried about his chest.

'So are these pâtissier's fancies part of your master plan? Or is this simply a more honest trade you are taking up?'

Devlin came to the railings below Albany's step. The square was noisy enough to cover any intimate talk. 'We have a couple of hours to spare. But no drinking. Some food and small beer.' He moved in closer. 'Law is meeting the regent today. That's our chance. I can feel it. I thought tomorrow but perhaps Sunday may be better – quieter, I'm sure.'

Albany descended to him. 'Today? But how?'

'Consider yourself lucky that you don't speak enough French to be of use to me.' He pushed them both up the steps then picked up Dandon's tray with the pepper pots and whispered to the sky.

'At least one of us alive. Someone to tell Walpole how I died anyways.'

Chapter Twenty-One

*B*lack Bill had thrown the *Shadow* into a 'cocked hat'. He knew this by the latitude of the Lizard, now disappearing off their starboard quarter in a grey mist, by the longitude of London an hour away across his chart, and by telescope, comparing where Jupiter should be and the daymoon was. The resulting pencil lines intersecting on his chart and the small triangle where they differed was the so-called cocked hat. A tricorne margin of error into which mariners tossed their luck, and possible defeat, and coined a phrase for even landlubbers to adopt. By dead reckoning and maintaining a speed, a good captain could, without the mythical good longitude, plot a course as safe as able. Steady as she goes and I'll be here in the world tomorrow without needing to see land.

But, now, this morning, to maintain a speed while being chased for battle was out of the question.

A splat of sweat from his brow fell to the linen paper and marked at least one of the ships closing to their bow. He looked up and tried to imagine the spirit of Devlin across the table. Like his own trigonometry Devlin's was learnt in practice, for survival, not at school. Maybe if students were told, 'Learn this well, or you'll die,' fewer ships would go down with half-learnt schoolboys fumbling their way.

Devlin's ghost was dumb before him. If he had but one member of the *Shadow*'s crew that could bolster his confidence. No. Not his to think like that.

Devlin's spectre melted away. He had no need of the Irishman through all the years sailing from Trepassey to New Spain and no need of him now to navigate this pond. His brain had grown flabby with Devlin's ability to hand, but he was still Black Bill, still the sailing master who had followed sea-birds and clouds above as much as the waves.

From Devlin he had learnt the skill of quadrants, backstaff, traverse board and walking dividers stepping over the leagues. Devlin had gleaned his own art from his master, John Coxon, and that skill had won him the role of Seth Toombs's artist-navigator. But Bill had learnt his runes in an aversion to hunger and thirst.

He drew a line along his rule from his cocked hat to the Verdes and threw down his pencil. There I am. There I be, and damn him that says otherwise.

He swept out onto the deck past all the expectant eyes upon him, past all the wood and rope, and there was the sight of the white squares of top gallants encroaching over the stern. He felt a strong reluctance to climb to the quarterdeck and see their decks.

The pirates had raised English colours but that had done nothing to slow the two French frigates. Two, by God. What could even Devlin do against two? No, don't think like that. That's counting down the end to be sure.

The one to starboard, the twenty-four gunner, had come up when they had changed course to the Scilly rocks, cutting them clean, and Bill had lost leagues turning away only for the other to slow and open a door for him to sail west and away, inviting him to escape or meet.

Bill chose to run – a red rag to a bull that the *Shadow* was hiding something. Satisfied now by her show of clean heels, René Duguay-Trouin laid on sail and an hour had brought him here.

The *Shadow* was still running, and two men of war closed on her like sand falling in an hourglass.

'Bill?' A quiet voice escaped out of the crowd. Other echoes followed. Orders were needed.

Run to the Verdes and back again, the captain had ordered, but he could not have foreseen this hour, when two warships lay intent on breaking the *Shadow*'s guise, to see if she buckled, waiting for her to slow or run.

Bill loped to the starboard gunwale to where the larger ship filled their quarter, her rigging and white sail now visible, passing through the cobwebs of the *Shadow*'s rigging.

He could see men now. White coats running to and fro, shadowy shapes in the rigging. He could hear her breathing. The chinking of iron, the strain of cordage and the chatter of French voices as if just from another room. White water rushing between them, petrels and gulls screeching over the ships' cross-trees, waiting for fish to be churned to the surface.

An honest ship would have slowed long ago. An honest ship would have waited for a speaking trumpet to share news. But when she had cut them the *Shadow* had turned, edged away, only to have her follow. An honest ship does not turn from an ally. Bill looked down to the gun by his thigh then moved away to watch the bowsprit and foresail of the smaller ship now coming off the opposite quarter. Coming fast.

And then it came. The slow creak of chain again and again, hauled by dozens of hands as gunports flew open from both ships. He spun behind to the larger ship again, twelve black eyes patiently staring back along her, water running off the open ports.

'Bill?' Again the soft voices all around him, feet above his head coming down the rigging knowing they had a better use now than being aloft.

'Bill?'

He walked amidships, shoulders all around him. Nothing else to do now. Without calling, Robert Hartley, Gunner Captain, loomed in front of him. Nothing else to do now. But one thing first. The proper thing. Their finest weapon.

From his fo'c'sle René Duguay-Trouin lifted his hand for his officers to observe the lowering of the United Kingdom flag. 'Here they come.' His young men looked at each other on hearing the strange announcement and missed the first sight of the other, darker, flag rising. 'Here they come,' Trouin repeated, this time with a tighter lip.

A black and calico-white cloth. A grinning skull set in a compass rose. A pair of crossed pistols beneath. It whipped as it rose, as if the eyes of the skull were looking at first one and then the other of its foes, its billowing mouth snarling as the cloth flapped in the wind. The design was exactly as the orders of 1717 described. Trouin stood on his heels, satisfied with his instinct.

Behind him bustled the urgency of gun crews, the solid calls of their captains, the rapid hoisting away of the boats to be cast over the side – for their wood could kill when shattered by shot.

Calmly he detailed their time and position to the boy at his elbow and watched the lad's shaking hand badly scratch the words. Trouin patted his head and sent him to join the other boys at the magazine carrying up the serge canisters of powder. He held out and studied his own steady hand.

It had been three years since a pirate staked out ten dead Frenchmen to dry in the fort they had sworn to protect and had stolen a chest of the late king's gold, embarrassing the nation before her allies. All that shame was ended now, and it had been as easy as pulling at a loose thread. How had Devlin eluded justice for so long?

Two hours, maybe less, and he would look into the eyes of the pirate and tell him who he was: René Duguay-Trouin. The one who had finally brought him to heel, his end long overdue.

'Patrick?' Dandon had felt the body slow beside him then stop dead in the narrow alleyway some feet behind him. '*Tout va bien?*' French only now as they got closer to the palace.

Devlin stalled, a clockwork automaton unwound. Dandon moved back to him. 'Patrick?' he repeated. 'What ails?'

'I don't know,' he said. 'Nothing.' He looked down at the goose-flesh on the back of his hand. 'A miasma of the street. It felt like someone had walked over my grave. Come on.' He elbowed Dandon along and they joined the Sunday afternoon amblers once more.

Almost three now. The Rue Saint-Honoré was an easier walk, the street wide and sided, it seemed to Dandon, with buildings that were palaces in their own right. Rising storeys of glass and great stones, lined with shops and taverns as much as London, but at almost every corner and *place* the trickling sound of running water. Paris, he had decided, was a city of fountains; not just for decoration and beauty but to bless the people with drinking water that had not come from the river but been carried via aqueduct from the countryside. More than once they had to back to a wall to allow passage to a mass of water-porters who earned their living selling water around the quarter.

Londoners drank from the Thames and left their water to sit for a day until the filth sank; or they settled for gin and beer that at least was purer.

On. Past the imposing beauty of the pillared front of the Palais Royale. That would not be their entrance. Minutes later they turned into the Rue de Richelieu and the first meeting with white-jacketed soldiers. Here, at the corner, was the trade and civilian entrance to the palace. Just two soldiers stood guard over the tempting sunshine of the courtyard just beyond.

If nerves trembled the two men did not show it. They had no weapons, and no other hope if they did not make it through this first barrier. But having nothing to lose was part of their daily life. Let other men fear consequences: this was the work they drank to.

Neither of the soldiers straightened at the approach of the two peasants, although their eyes widened expectantly at the trays.

Three years ago Devlin had approached an island fortress that had orders to accept no ship at its shores. He sailed in with a ship of whores and was welcomed with open arms. The world over, common soldiers – who took naturally to the career, being too indolent or drunk for anything else – had only three appetites: lust, thirst and hunger.

Devlin and Dandon, common as any of them, knew how to carve cogs that could turn the world.

'Well met, soldier!' Devlin greeted them with a slur in his voice that only faintly alluded to wine. His French, like Dandon's, who had learnt the tongue at the Mobile fort from the heavy hand of his surgeon master, was of the curt gutter. It would not have carried them into any court but it fitted their current cloth seamlessly. The soldiers eyed them lazily and sucked on empty clay pipes.

'Gentlemen,' Devlin continued merrily. 'My daughter this day has married a good soldier from the Faubourg quarter.

In celebration I bring some fine remnants from my *pâtisserie* in Les Halles. Free of charge for you and your gallant watch.' He shrugged then, as if doing them no real favour. 'I will only throw them away or sell them for dust tomorrow. Help yourself.'

They pored over the trays. Fruit pastries, small meat pies, some glazed tarts. The greedier of the two spied the largest and poked its crust. 'What is that one? Duck?'

Devlin shook his head. 'Strange tastes from my new son-in-law's family. I should not have brought it, but you never know,' another of the shrugs that passed for a hundred comments. 'Perhaps you have a friend inside you should like to jape, eh?'

'Why?' the soldier picked up an apricot pastry. 'What is it?'

'Rat. Would you credit that for a Faubourg?'

The four of them laughed, the second soldier blowing pastry crumbs from his cheeks as he sampled Dandon's delicacies.

'*Rat?*' the soldier pushed it away to a corner of the tray. 'Those Faubourgs are dogs to be sure! No offence to your daughter for taking one, Monsieur!' He put down the pastry on his stone seat and picked up and crunched through a tart, the pleasure of its cold sweetness wetting his mouth.

Devlin and Dandon stood shoulder to shoulder with the soldiers, their backs edging past the pillars and under the cover of the passage.

The soldiers shared an ear. If Devlin had not missed his guess there was always a captain who deserved a rat pie. The soldiers filled their pockets with crumbly delights.

'You should go through,' the solder waved Devlin on. 'The courtyard only. Find a Captain Droussard. I am sure he would enjoy your pie!' More laughter. 'Tell him it is goose! And good luck to your daughter, Monsieur, and her rat-loving husband!'

Devlin and Dandon bowed their way past and into the sun and Dandon tried not to gasp as his eyes squinted through the glare.

A palace indeed. The building that framed the dazzling garden was the same they had seen from the outside, tall arched windows with blue roofs housing smaller, oval windows – the servant's quarters – and around the edge a walkway of doric and ionic columns and glass doors as grand as an image of Rome that Dandon had seen as a child, when he had leafed through a book and imagined the gods that walked there.

Devlin snapped him out of his awestruck trance. He cocked his eye to the almost separate building to their right, a low wall shielding a smaller garden.

'That is the real palace. This is just a garden for fops and mistresses. That is where we need to be. We have the name of a captain: that might help.' His voice expressed nothing but ease, as if this were simply any Sunday in any garden. 'And Law is here. It's three. He should be hungry for some rat pie by now.'

One more guard to go. Devlin leaned into Dandon. 'This passageway runs around the palace. We get in here and we're done.'

'Done what?' Dandon slowed his captain. I have no idea what we're doing. Am I about to die?'

'The pepper pot,' Devlin shook his tray. 'It is filled with priming powder. We're going to make a fire.' They walked on toward the broad soldier.

'A fire. Of course. Why should I have not known. I *am* going to die.' He grinned at the guard and followed Devlin's lead.

The guard agreed with his colleagues at the gate that Captain Droussard would indeed enjoy a rat pie and he waved them through. Devlin had become sick of simpering, sick of wearing rags. In minutes he could end it. He could burn it.

They clacked down the corridor in their wooden clogs. Diamond-shaped black-and-white tiles graced the floor, silk curtains in gold and pink the tall windows. They stalled at the first corner.

'Law is with the regent down there,' Devlin pointed his tray to the adjacent corridor. 'Get me a candle.'

Dandon went to the walls and plucked one free. They were unlit but Devlin had striker and flint already in his hand and then snatched his fist closed as a tall, white-moustached officer rounded the corner on them.

'What is this?' he glowered at them both, taking in the baker's trays and the candle in Dandon's hand. 'Who are you? What is your business?' He was in his white uniform and red sash but wore no hat and his buttons were open; it was Sunday after all. Devlin and Dandon edged together like schoolboys caught with a frog behind their backs.

Devlin chanced his arm. 'Capitaine Droussard?'

'I am,' replied the officer, surprised.

Devlin offered up his tray. 'Your men suggested you may like a goose pie for Sunday. I am giving away my last trade for the day.'

Droussard's face grew lighter as Devlin placed one of the two larger pies in his hand. But he became stern again at the candle in Dandon's hand. 'What are you about with that?'

'Forgive me, Captain,' Dandon gave the officer his fawn-eyed look that usually persuaded maidens to show him their pale thighs. 'I like to read at night. The regent has so many. I meant no offence. I shall return it.'

Droussard bit into his rich pie and smiled deep. 'No harm. Payment for your meat. Keep it, my friend. Read to your children by its light. But both of you will be gone now. Thank you for your delicacy.' He raised his hand and turned away.

They listened for the squeak of his leather boots to fade. Alone again, Devlin swung his tray to his side and went back to his striker. One moment later the candle was lit. Dandon could not resist one question amid their dreamlike circumstances.

'The pie, Patrick? Was it really rat?'

'I saw no geese or ducks where I bought it.' He unscrewed the pepper pot and poured it at a curtain's hem. 'It was fortunate I gave him the right one. The diamond is in the other.' He flung the candle to the powder but did not expect such a roar of flame, and they both jumped back.

Within seconds the fire had crept to the crown of the wall, and the primer powder billowed out a cloud of smoke like a bonfire – smoke that would panic people better than the flames. They stood mesmerised for too long and followed the flames until they reached the ceiling above their heads, which shook Devlin from his fascination.

'Maybe better than I hoped! We should go.' He slapped Dandon and off they trotted.

'Hmm? I'm sorry, Milord?' John Law sat in the regent's office with him and Claude Ronde, the lapidary commissioned to make the crown. He had spent most of the last quarter hour looking absently between the door and the window. His distraction was not missed by Philippe.

'Your opinion on the crown, Lass? I think there are too many gems. It is not as elegant as it should be. The king would be disappointed I'm sure, no?'

Law managed both to bow and rise at the same time. He walked over to the brass replica of the crown and stole a glance at one of the trio of clocks in the room. Quarter past three. His heart matched the ticking that sounded deafening to his over-alert ears. He casually picked up the crown from its red velvet cushion.

'These are paste gems I take it, Monsieur Ronde?'

Simpering, Ronde humbled himself to his feet. Although only a replica he forbade his fingers to touch the crown and instead pointed out its detail with a gold retractable pencil. 'Yes, Monsieur Lass. Two hundred and eighty-two diamonds.' He touched each arch in turn, his voice clicking out the numbers like a rosary. '*Sixteen* sapphires, *sixteen* rubies and *sixteen* emeralds. Two hundred and thirty-seven pearls! A crown truly for the king of kings!'

Philippe beamed. 'Or a mad pope!'

Ronde could not help his glare which the duke matched effortlessly. Law carried on to distract them.

'And the Regent? Where is it placed?'

Ronde's teeth shone. 'Here,' he tapped the empty front-flower setting. 'In pride over all. Even the Sancy diamond will sit humbly at the base of the silver acanthus with the Mazarin stones,' he touched his pencil against the wooden fleur-de-lis on top of the crown.

Law nodded his approval. 'I think it will be splendid, Milord.' He put down the crown reverently and idly pulled his cuffs from his sleeves. 'Would it suit, Milord, to honour Monsieur Ronde with a glance at the Regent? So he may know what he is to work with?'

Ronde clapped his hands. 'Oh, yes, Milord! That would be delightful!'

Law went back to his seat and watched as Philippe thought.

'No need,' he said at last, and saw Ronde's shoulders sink. 'The crown will be made under the supervision of Duflos. He will set the gemstones. I could not risk the Regent and the Mazarin diamonds to leave the palaces.'

Law held in the reeling of his stomach. It was over.

He had only ever heard Claude Ronde's name mentioned in relation to the crown. Augustin Duflos was the young royal jeweller, resident at the Louvre Palace. Naturally Augustin would look over and approve the work – as befitted his appointment – but it was to be the master, Ronde, who crafted it. Law had always presumed that would be at his own workshops. That was Law's understanding, that was the tinder that had fuelled Walpole's plans. But it seemed that Philippe had kept close to his chest the idea that it would be only under the heavy protection of the palaces that the diamond would find its setting. It would not go to Ronde's workshop in the Rue de Richelieu. It was never going to the Rue de Richelieu. It would never leave the court at all.

Something Devlin had said in London fluttered through Law's memory. Something about Walpole and himself never having stolen anything. Maybe Devlin had known. A thief's wisdom. He had known that Philippe would never let the diamond leave his pocket.

John Law was a gambler through and through; but the pirate, surely, was reckless. Yet he had been right. He knew all along that the diamond would have to be stolen from the palace. But where was it? If the regent would not even show Ronde, what were they to do?

'*Lass*!' Philippe barked. 'What is with you today? You sit there like you have lost a bride!'

'I'm sorry, Milord. Have I missed something?' Law even managed a smile. There was some surprising small relief in failure after all.

Philippe began to reply but his bellow could not compete with the cries now rising outside the door.

In the centuries when flame and wick ruled the night, and kings and emperors studied siege warfare as keenly as dancing, two phrases filled their palaces with dread.

'*The enemy is at the gates!*' was the first, understandable enough.

The second could change your world even more.

'*Fire!*'

The shout went down the corridors and up the marble stairways.

'*Fire!*'

Law tensed. A look at the clock again. But surely not? Not even a pirate could be so bold?

Guards and footmen ran from door to door with the cry, smoke at their backs, horror greeting them at every open door as lords, viscounts and clerks ran from their offices with linen at their mouths and valuables clutched about them. They made for the garden, for the courtyard. There were certainly enough glass-doors for easy escape, to be flung wide, allowing in oxygen enough to stoke the flames.

In the garden, they coughed and dried their eyes and watched the smoke billowing out of the open doors and climbing up over the blue roofs where servants hung from their windows and screamed futilely for help to the lords and ladies below.

Skinny, aproned men and women, dusted with flour, filled the courtyard from the kitchens below and pointed and yelled at the smoke engulfing the east wing. Their senses returned, some of the more regal witnesses sent their servants scurrying back into the smoke to fetch more of their goods, lowly protests impatiently slapped away with bejewelled fists.

Philippe stayed at his desk, his eyes on the door. Ronde cradled his brass and wood crown to his chest. Law watched the regent measure the threat by the rush of footsteps in the hall and the screams of women far off; but then they would shriek at a cold wind, so that was hardly a gauge. Philippe's eyes flashed to the foot of the door as the first trickle of smoke began to puff and spread.

'*Lass*!' he shouted. 'See what goes on!'

Law sprang up, his hand at the door just as it was thrust open, catching his wrist painfully. A white wig appeared and a spluttering footman with streaming eyes and powder running off his face begged them to leave, as a black cloud formed behind him. Ronde ducked beneath his arms and was gone before he had finished his plea.

Philippe held to his desk, clutched the sides like a pitching deck. 'Firemen to their sand! Where is the fire? *Report*!'

The footman wiped his brow. Somehow a fire had broken out in the east wing. A curtain set ablaze by a fallen candle had then spread. A quick thinking piss-boy had dashed to the area with his pails but some accident with another fellow, a collision with an arm to his throat, had sent him and his waste spilling along the floor. Now there were pastries and piss everywhere and fire all about.

'*Pastries*?' Philippe's exclamation provoked some coughing fit from Law, or perhaps it was only the smoke.

'No matter, Milord. Please, hurry! Come now!'

Law gathered himself.

'*Pay attention*,' Devlin had said.

'We should retreat to the garden, Milord. Let the firemen to their work.' His request was suitably punctuated by a sudden black belch from the corridor.

Philippe's instincts were not without their reward in Law's

eyes. At first, disappointment, as the regent grabbed a miniature oval watercolour of his late daughter and pushed it into
the highest pocket, closest to his heart; then, as his footman
could no longer wait and fled, the duke's hands were beneath
his chair. An instant later Law glimpsed a small green silk bag
slip into another pocket. Philippe's head rose in a snap,
cautious in case Law's eyes were upon him; but he only saw
the Scotsman peering anxiously down the corridor, and heard
his voice calling back.

'We should leave, Milord.'

Philippe was already at his shoulder, hearing more than
seeing the panic of a fire. 'To the garden, Lass,' he said, and
closed the door behind them.

Priming powder alone makes for good smoke. Primer poured.
A candle dropped. A curtain suddenly engulfed. Two men
running, shouting down the corridors, alerting the denizens
of the palace to their impending doom. Others take up the
call without seeing the sight; the word is enough.

Minutes later, the corridors cleared, the firemen with
their sand victoriously extinguish the small blaze and
puzzle over the vast clouds of smoke that one curtain had
managed to create.

In the garden the fortunate saved begin to return to their
offices, the smoke still hanging above their heads, and the
higher-appointed order a change of clothes to be brought to
their apartments. Philippe, crowded by ministers and clerks,
nods at every apology and explanation and walks calmly back
to his rooms. He dismisses with a wave those that irritated
him, his only concern being that he had secured the diamond
in one pocket and his late daughter's only miniature in another.

John Law surveyed the rooftops, the chaos diminishing into nothing but a smart anecdote for the evening's supper before the commencement of Philippe's other feast of flesh that crowned every evening.

'Monsieur Lass,' came not a question but a whisper at his shoulder. He turned to see Devlin admiring his work rather than meeting his eye, as if the two were not talking at all, Devlin's tray empty save for the one large pie.

'You did this?' They were the only horrified words Law could shape. Once he had stood on Primrose Hill and shot dead a man who had dared to kiss his darling's hand. That is what gentlemen do. They do not set fire to royal palaces. 'People could have *died*!'

Devlin, growing into his French demeanour, shrunk his neck into his shoulders. 'People die every day. You paid attention like I said?'

Law, aware of those lingering around them, picked up the pie on Devlin's tray as if it were his only interest. 'Indeed. I know where the regent keeps the Regent.'

'Then we're done. He did not see that you watched him?'

Law put back the pie. 'I thought you did not take me for a fool?' Here, in Law's very place of position, Devlin's brusque tone would at least be matched.

Devlin looked about for Dandon and found him offering the last of his tarts to a giggling pair of kitchen maids. He pushed his tray back to Law. 'Take the pie: the replica is inside.'

Law paled, looked down at the crust with new light. 'Could you not have given it to me this morning? Was the drama so necessary?'

'And you'd have spent the afternoon trembling in front of the duke if you'd have known. I said before that you gentlemen are not thieves. Besides, you'll be the one taking the diamond for the other tonight. I figured that would be enough for your nerves.'

'*Me?*'

'Who else? You belong here. I'll see you tomorrow in your office. My part is played. I showed you where it was. Take the pie. Don't worry, John. It's only beef.'

'I cannot,' he said as, still, his hand took hold of it. 'I will be killed if caught!'

'We'll all be dead if you do not play. Tomorrow morning, Monsieur Lass.'

Law watched him walk away to summon Dandon, who had at least earned two kisses for the afternoon. Law dragged himself back to the palace, mulling the weight of the pie between his hands. His failure weighed more so. The dreams of his greatest venture, his dream to raise France above all others, reduced to a crust.

From the tall doors of the passage, through the mullioned panes, Philippe watched the lank form of his finance minister trudge away from the tall peasant. Philippe ducked, as if he could hide behind glass, and watched the dour face of Law study the pie in his hands, clearly not pleased with his gift.

Philippe followed the backs of the two others as they went to join the crowd leaving the grounds. His thumb rested in the coat pocket where the green silk bag lay.

He straightened and switched his gaze back to Law, now entering under the pillars far to his right and disappearing.

He sniffed the smoky air, the thumb now stroking the hard lump inside the bag. He ignored the trio of ministers with raised fingers and flapping papers vying for his eye and spun back to his rooms, slamming the doors against their indignant white faces.

Chapter Twenty-Two

A good pirate ship possessed an enviable selection of marksmen. Often pirates took to the sweet trade from an impoverished hunting background – those that had not sprung from a decade of service as soldier or seaman.

Such men were accustomed to sleeping with a gun; they were men with powder forever lined or pocked in their faces. The buccaneer of the old Tortuga ways was marked by his long French musket. His clothes might be little more than rags of goatskin, his features indistinguishable under the filth, but his gun was waxed, oiled, cleaned and screwed to watchmaker precision.

The pirates upheld this tradition, valuing their arms as their most prized possessions. Twenty men with muskets was worth more than a six-pound cannon.

At fifty yards the musket's value would fall off, its usefulness almost as great as a thrown stone; but when ships collided in a brawl, bruising against each other like cattle through a gate, fifty yards is the end of the earth. At fifty yards you could see the red eyes of the faces you shot into, hear the curses and squeals as men instinctively patted their wound and looked at the blood on their palm.

The *Shadow* had at least sixty men that suited, and had the added lot of knowing how to triple their 'sticks' threat by double-shotting or loading with swan-shot over ball and scraping faces from bone like a carpenter's plane.

Half an hour after the first cannon spoke, Trouin was appreciating the skill his foe possessed to this end. They fired fast, these pirates, and he even elbowed his officers to stand up and admire their ferocity rather than duck the hail of shots from the opposing rigging and the gunwale nettings. He admired them as much as the beauty of a pheasant's futile escape before his gun or the struggle of the fish upon his hook before it gives up on the bank. Noble but pointless.

His two ships flanked the *Shadow*, providing a blazing *rencontre* that punched back and forth. The fire-fight was watched from miles away by curious ships who could make out nothing but a dark cloud of snapping cracks and flashes on the horizon. They were as far removed from the drama as if looking at a painting on a wall.

The swell of the Atlantic and the pace of the pirates' musket fire slowed their cannon's report. Hard to run home a gun when thirty men are plucking your gun-crew like feathers off dead game. Not all good shots mind, the yawl of the decks put paid to that, but try to get your job done with eighty or ninety whistling balls a minute chipping the wood around you and ringing off your iron.

Half an hour of sharing shot and ball. The men aloft wearing black masks for faces, their eyes raw with powder. The deck littered with splinters. The last of the *Shadow*'s elegant furniture had been whittled away from her rails, white wood visible under split oak and a heaving of lungs under the dust and smoke.

The weaker of the ships, *La Patiente* on their larboard, began to heel away. A cheer erupted on the *Shadow* as the bow began to slowly turn. They were running. They were running from the black flag. Now Bill only had to worry about the twenty-four gunner, the stronger ship off their starboard. The time had arrived to hurl caltrops from the rigging, crows feet of iron spikes to cut the bare feet of the gun-crews. Time for grenadoes to be flung from the deck, clay pots filled with shrapnel and brimstone. And time, too, to play them a tune to welcome them to St Peter. The drum and the fiddle or fife worth ten thousand men when your enemy heard that you deemed their efforts limp enough that you could jig while they sweated and fell. He ordered it now, musicians being as favoured on a pirate as any other man.

'Bill!' A shout at his back turned him from the heeling ship. 'She's raising fights!' Bill pushed through the crowd amidships to see for himself, wiping the sweat and smut from his eyes.

Behind the gunwale, rigged long in advance, now hauling up from the yards, *La Françoise* on their starboard was bringing up fighting-cloths – great blankets designed to shelter the men working at the guns. They stretched like tents over their heads, tight from the gunwale, closing at the masts. It was now impossible for the men in the rigging to mark their quarry. Their skill was nullified; they were reduced to punching holes in cloth and trusting to their luck. The grenadoes and caltrops would just roll down, to fall into the thrashing white waves between the vessels. The gulls, oblivious to the madness of men, hovered and snatched up the fish swept to the surface between the closing wood, dodging the flying lead and iron with a wheel of their wings before flying away, grateful for the folly that fed them, their screeches mocking them all.

Something cold went through Bill. The smooth running of the arming cloths, readily prepared, as if this was how they had wanted it to play, as if they had expected the pirates' close quarters. This was no panicked captain's final order hastily rigged: the arming cloths rolled up as calmly as Roman blinds and Bill imagined the gun-crews working on the nine-pounders beneath their cover.

Another shout of victory from his weary men above as the marines opposite began to descend.

What now?

He shouted at his own gunner crews to stop gawking and load. Were they not beam to beam? Shatter their cannon in their faces.

Behind the arming cloths the descending French marines passed their muskets to the sailors who would mount the quarter and fo'c'sle decks, there to hinder the pirates at the swivel guns which the *Shadow* relied upon when it came to scraping wood.

The marines picked up the crossbows which Trouin had prepared for the moment when they saw *La Patiente* turn and the moment when *La Françoise*'s captain raised his arming cloths. The music on the *Shadow* fell as the cloths came up. Bill, watching them rise, did not press his men to play on.

'And wet the arming cloths,' Trouin insisted. 'The final thing you will wish is to set fire to your own ship.'

One bucket of oil for the marines to dip their bolts.

'The pirates will manage at least one more broadside. Then,' Trouin commanded, 'the quarrels, the bolts for your bows, to have a tow of oakum. Light and fire them into the sails. The crossbow at thirty yards or less is perfect. It does not need the skill of a bow and windage affects it less. If you can hit a barn you can hit a mainsail. It will not be spectacular – unless you are very lucky – but the impact will dishearten them, I assure you, and if the flaming arrows find some target, and if they have powder around . . .'

The arrows flew, lit by linstock match, *La Françoise*'s deck loosely sanded to cover any accidents and to snuff any grenadoe that made it through from the pirates.

In the *Shadow*'s rigging, the marksmen stilled at the dozen bolts of fire streaking towards them. Instinctively they ducked amidst their ropes and yards and followed the smoking trails as they stabbed at the canvas or twisted through the ropes and span off wood to sail to the deck.

Bill watched them thud to the oak head first to stand like candles about him. Robert Hartley clutched his bags of powder to him like a scared child as the bolts fell about, the flames already licking at sheets and lanyards.

Bill barked for his guns to fire at the higher ship. His cannon could lay only at the wood below her guns but holes were holes and wood as good as iron at splitting bone.

He left the gun-crew at his back to deal their cards to the other ship and their broadside rocked the *Shadow* closer to *La Françoise*; then, on the uproll, his own row of starboard cannon punched them back again, hammer blow after hammer blow, sending the *Shadow*'s men to a crouch; their arms shielding their faces as French splinters showered back at them.

Bill slapped his ears and opened his mouth to try and shift the clogging in his head that two broadsides had created. The swivel guns' report cleared his hearing and he looked up at the good men at the upper rails who paid no mind to the rest of the world and went about reloading their falconets. He dodged to larboard to see the other assault, stamping on flaming bolts with a curse as he ran.

La Patiente had finished her turn, her guns fully raised to his canvas. She had sucked up the *Shadow*'s barrage painfully: good black holes gaped where gilded blue and yellow had decorated her quarter but now she had enough distance to eat the pirate's masts and sails.

Bill looked above. The sails were already scorched and were now catching with playful flame, burning like paper, fizzing as salt and wet cloth met the flame; and then the French bowmen fired their second strike and he watched the slow course of rockets flapping into the canvas again and again, like black fingernails scratching down their grey faces.

The same effect came again: those arrows that did not stick spiralled to the deck, to eat at his wood and rope or sniff the dribbling powder. He felt time left alive was narrowing to a knife point. Then he saw it.

Between the stern of *La Patiente* and his *Shadow*'s bow was the Atlantic, the door of an ocean. A horizon. The oncoming assault cleared his mind and his decision.

La Françoise fired and the *Shadow*'s weatherboard snapped like gingerbread. Three guns flew from their shackles and men rolled up against the flying iron and wood, yet, without respite, once the noise fell away, they dragged themselves back to their places, as purposeful as ants, back to their guns, coughing through the dust. But Bill had seen his window. The dash of a cornered rat to the kitchen door ajar, mindless of the foot poised to slam the door against its skull.

'Then,' Trouin roughly sketched his earlier prediction in his mind, 'the weaker *Patiente* will turn away, leaving the pirate an escape. He will take it or wait to die as both of us give him fire and deny him a chance to board. One ship too far away, one too strong. He will run for he has no land or ally but the sea. There is nothing for him to surrender to, or for, but death. It has been ever his only motive. And that is how you split his loyal crew, split his forces, for some will wish surrender, some will wish to run. The best will wish death.' He had thrown down his pen. 'And we win. And we bring him into Brest and glory. And then we hang them all.'

Black Bill took the opportunity that the ships had given him to make for the Atlantic. He had mapped his course to the Verdes but now, with two warships shaving his wake, he would have to cut. No time for maps, just run and trust.

Against fatter ships with Atlantic beams and keels, the slavers and caravels, the *Shadow* was like a shark and preyed on them just so, but against these Mediterranean frigates with the same bluff lines the *Shadow*'s speed counted for naught.

Only an eye on Île d'Ouessant would guide him, and the heeling of the ship as she heaved to windward, the helm pushed right over.

He could not spare a man aloft who did not hold a gun, their cracking of muskets and the echoes back a constant refrain of the attack wearing them down. Damn Devlin for holding to a frigate. Pirates survived with smaller ships. Their doom had always been to trade up: to lose the safety of the shallows. Their arrogance bought them only a noose or shipwreck. He would have words with Devlin if they survived.

The *Shadow* had two stern guns on the lower deck, ninepounders, but the two French ships kept their bows angled away. Two falconets swivelled on the taffrail, single-pounders, and at least these could strafe both enemy vessels, and immediately the pirates set to almost melting them with shot. But still the ships came on.

The sea was white between the three ships, close enough to

throw insults now, but Trouin had no wish to close and board. Not while the pirates still had courage.

'Shorten sail,' Trouin ordered from *La Patiente*'s quarter-deck. 'To larboard.' He held his hand out for a speaking trumpet and gave back the spyglass in return. No need for that now.

From over the water, Cassard on *La Françoise* watched the gallants begin to haul and the yards turn and mirror the action, according to his orders.

Events move quickly on a ship. For every seemingly endless hour of nothing but rolling waves it can take barely minutes for the rug to be pulled from under you and your semblance of control dashed. A slipped rope, a moving reef, a misheard order, a clumsy lamp and all can become panic. Death leaps aboard your bow.

From the sight of the petrels above, the black-and-red ship arrowed ahead and the two others at her stern began to turn outwards and away, their wakes in the water like a flower opening, their guns effortlessly turning to bear on the fleeing ship's quarters.

The pirate's marksmen stopped their firing and looked down to Bill at the helm. Those in the tops at the foremast saw too late that which Bill could not. Ribbons of white water before their bow and the Celtic wind behind them pushing them forward like a giant's palm.

They cried below but already Bill could feel the judder through the helm in his fists as the white water became their water and the keel began to shiver on the rocks that only Trouin knew of.

Events move fast on a ship.

The *Shadow* lurched and screamed. Men were thrown to the deck and limbs and heads smashed against cannon and wood. Bill held fast, could feel the hidden rocks biting beneath his feet, the eerie sensation of the rocks travelling from fore to aft and the deck rippling. The earth was reminding him that she only ever let them exist out of kindness.

The sails above cracked and billowed, the tiller ropes buckled at the lack of strain and Bill let go the helm before it took his arms and the wheel spun in relief as the stern began to heel round. The *Shadow* sailed no further. The bosun and his mates hurried to furl the sails that could drag them further into the grinder.

Bill turned to the ship's guns set to them, his men gathering at his back. The French ships had stalled as much as the *Shadow*, but deliberately. He walked to the taffrail, the sea quiet, no more gunplay, only the cruel laughter of the birds circling above.

Trouin raised his speaking trumpet.

'Capitaine Enemy, of the *Shadow*! I petition for your surrender. I am Commodore Duguay-Trouin of the Marine Royale. Your lives will be spared if you desist and lay down your arms.'

The good English words hurt more. Bill lowered his head. He had been taken by one who had not chanced upon them but knew who they were. How much more did they know? Was Devlin dead even now?

It seemed the trumpet had read his mind.

'Captain Devlin! I offer only mercy. Lower your flag and I will accompany a boat for your surrender.'

So they did not know, and Bill felt better, but not those around him. Dan Teague squeezed his shoulder.

'No surrender, Bill. We don't lower our flag, do we? Let them come I say!'

Bill pushed the hand away and looked up at the black flag still grinning in the breeze. 'You heard him call for the captain.

That means he knows less than us. What good us to Devlin and Peter Sam if we are dead and our girl blown to pieces.'

Dan thought on. Bill faced them all. The bloodied, the ragged, the drunk. The beaten. The never beaten. Not under Devlin.

'I've lost this day. But I'll not let you die for my wrong.' He moved through them, pulling their eyes to his back. 'They haven't got him. We can get him and Peter Sam back by living, lads. If we don't talk they can't win.'

'But the flag, Bill!' Dan Teague spoke for them all. 'That's *us*!'

Bill wiped his face. 'Put the pistols to the lockers. Don't let them take them from you. I'll be the one to take it down.'

Trouin watched the flag fall. He passed on the trumpet and ordered the linstocks to be doused. 'Pull in the boats,' he said demurely. 'I am going across.'

Chapter Twenty-Three

'Any trouble?' Devlin's greeting to Peter Sam came from the stone steps that descended from the street to the water. The dory rocked unsteadily as Peter Sam held a hand to his captain; Dandon was left to his own luck.

'No trouble, Cap'n,' Peter Sam replied, but their eyes were on the languishing form of Albany Holmes at the stern of the boat. 'We slept for the most. It's warm down here.' They had rowed to the steps that morning in the *Junot*'s dory, the palpable stench of fish polished into her wood. The tartane was left moored with dozens of others beneath the shadow of Pont Notre Dame.

'Hey now, Captain!' Albany waved. 'How goes your day? Sold your cakes I see.' Devlin and Dandon had ditched their empty trays in the first alley they had run through.

Devlin did not answer. His confidences were for Peter Sam only and Peter bent his head to listen.

Peter Sam did not spend much of his time with his captain. He did not play cards well or enjoy wine as much, and as for books, which Devlin and Dandon shared like bread, to Peter they were only fit for ripping cartridge paper from. And, without shame to remember it, he had tried to kill Devlin more than once when they first met.

But Patrick Devlin had sailed across the world to find him when he had even thought himself dead.

He would listen intently to every syllable that ever fell from his captain's mouth until the trumpets of Judgement Day blew, and Sam would be standing at Devlin's shoulder when they did.

Albany at least could find some talk in Dandon. 'Went the day well, sir?'

Dandon looked at him kindly. 'Well enough. We are still alive at least. I hope we did not cause you too much concern, Albany.'

'Not at all. Your other companion, the filthier one, has absconded somewhere. No doubt for drink. I found *this* bald fool,' he jerked his head toward Peter Sam, 'rather dull for company.'

Dandon watched Peter Sam's ears burn red, the dory too small for much privacy. 'He has his uses, Albany. And when I figure out yours I'll let you know. Besides, you should be grateful that our Peter Sam does not find you to his own . . . *taste*.'

Albany seemed to rejoice in this revelation. 'Is that so? Well, they say you can never tell, eh?' And Dandon winked in his wickedness.

Devlin turned to them both. 'Hugh has gone to the inn. That wouldn't be a bad plan for some supper and wine anyways. We should reward ourselves something at least.'

'Agreed,' Dandon pulled off his woollen cap. 'As long as I don't have to wear *that* any more.'

Devlin tugged his own cap from his head. 'What say you, lads? What do you reckon four men can do with a Paris evening?'

Albany curled a lip at the prospect of what pirates might consider entertainment. 'I'm sure we will do well,' he flapped a limp hand at Peter Sam. 'And I'm sure we could find a Molly house to distract this ape.'

The small boat rocked with Peter's clamber to get at the grinning head of Albany, with Devlin dragged across the boat as he held on to him.

But Albany was the only one of them armed and his blade cut short Peter's path.

'Come on then, fool!' He stepped back for Peter to consider his steel, his eyes wide and laughing. 'You'll not find me with my back to you!'

The rocking boat drew looks from the others all around and from the Sunday strollers on the street above. Devlin hissed for them to calm, aware that lapses in discretion tied nooses; but the gun had been cocked. Peter Sam came on, the sword only maddening him more.

Albany drew a circle at Peter's chest, daring him forward and Peter obliged, his hand protected by a leather sewing palm as he grabbed the point and closed it in his fist.

Albany tried to tug back the blade only to find he had struck carelessly into an oak tree. Peter Sam twisted the blade and Albany's wrist, committed in his grip, was wrenched painfully.

In a fight if you own a man's wrist you own his entire body; you can angle him to his knees as easily as tumbling a kitten. Albany yelled out in pain as his arm, shoulder and torso bent him to the bottom of the boat as if his spine had left him.

He looked up at his master holding him at a leash, his twisted, entangled hand unable to let go of his sword's grip. An enormous fist rose above his head.

'*Peter*!'

Devlin's shout broke Peter's rage like a spell and he dropped the sword. Albany whined at the bones in his wrist, hated his arm and let his sword fall as the giant stepped over him out of the boat and to the stone walkway. Dandon danced behind him and laughter came from the other boats all around.

Devlin stood on Albany's sword and leant down to him. 'Are you *mad*? That man will kill you as easily as throwing a rat against a wall and with less thought.'

Albany looked up hatefully, his good hand holding his wrist. 'I am not mad! But I begin to suspect the affection you "matelots" have for each other. I think Walpole would be very interested to know what den I have found myself in! In England we still find such acts punishable by death, whatever your colonial instincts, Captain!'

Devlin ruefully shook his head. 'I'm for a drink. We are hours away from our aims and you pull this shite.' He stepped out of the boat to join his men. 'You can come if you want. You need to drink with Peter at least. That's how it goes on a ship. No room for grudges. He's hit me enough times.'

'I will come! If only because I am dressed like a pig and could probably find no other company!'

'Do what you will.' He went up the steps and trawled through his pockets for his pipe and tobacco. He tapped a stranger for a light. As he sought the flame's relief with cupped hand he considered his small band wearing the tension of their days like tight boots. How did his *Shadow* fare? How were a hundred men coping without him to rule them? He had but five to carry and yet dogs would work closer.

He had to get back. Back to the wood. London, now Paris. A mass of stone and crowds all moving faster than him. No control. No ropes to pull to change things. The endless sea felt small in comparison.

There was no order in this order. The straight streets, the houses on top of each other, the rush of carriage wheels always rolling somewhere. He understood then that his men had not ended up on the sea. He had not ended up on the sea.

They had escaped to it.

Get back to the *Shadow*, hold it together for one more day. John Law to do his duty and then back to Walpole and the prince. Take his amnesty for the past and then back to the real world.

He swallowed deeply his Brazilian smoke. His head light-ened and his eyes turned misty, and he soon caught up with the others heading to the cabaret, the Image Notre Dame. Tomorrow he would be free again. One more day. And if Law failed, what had he lost? They would be on the sea again and no more hated than the day before.

The night came too soon for John Law. He dreaded it like the jilted lover looking mournfully out over the city and knowing that somewhere the woman that had been his heart was pulling the chemise from her shoulders for someone else now that the day was done, with every light in every window a reminder of your loneliness.

Only a warm bottle for company. He resided in a palace that had now become a cell. His cuffs brushed over the glass, a blackness at their ends, his laundry overdue. A whiff arose from his blue velvet waistcoat. Candle smoke and damp. He had neglected being a gentleman, perhaps deliberately, as a small punishment to himself. He drank deep until his throat burned.

Did he have to wait until the palace was asleep? He looked to his clock. Two porcelain cherubs pointing their arrows to the white face. After ten. The regent and his court were fed and drunk by now. There would be midgets cavorting beneath the table passing their tongues between the ladies and gentle-men; one of them, trussed like a pig, would be laid out naked on the table, an apple in his mouth.

Law counted Philippe as a friend, as fellow gamblers count themselves, the same as drinking partners measure their alle-giance. He knew him as a painter, a sculptor, a composer of operas and did not understand how the debauchery fitted in with these accomplishments. To Philippe there was no division. His power was simply a means to enjoy and develop these better things. Politics just a means to this end. He had created some of the finest art galleries in the world for his people, made public the royal library and funded the Sorbonne university for all who were too poor to attend elsewhere. His desires were only fuel to the notion that life was joy without limits.

What Law missed, what Law misunderstood, was that these men of royal blood tied themselves to the gods. They were above morals and despised the church built by men. They could trace their line back to heaven. The world needed their breeding or it would cease to be. They were forestalling judgement with their lusts, for if not then the meek would surely inherit the earth. It was a warning to carry on indulging, not a prediction. Every seed sown increased their line, each one a noble angel. Everyone below them was allowed only to till the earth to fill the gods' bellies.

Law had not been born to be a king so he did not understand. Philippe admired his genius for numbers and balance that had temporarily restored France to greatness but for all his formulae the Scotsman was still only a broken dog shivering with raised paw for approval. Philippe had raped his paper bank of its coin but even he had been dismayed at the number of nobles now plundering the vaults and making for Switzerland and Belgium. The dismal end lay only a few suppers away.

Law threw another brown glass of liquor down his neck. So I owe him nothing, he confirmed to himself. He has ruined my schemes with orgies and diamonds.

He put down his glass. Enough courage. He looked again at the clock and threw his wig to his bed, then shoved his hand through the crust of the pie that Devlin had given him, his probing hand as urgent as the Indian slave's who had first plucked the real stone from the walls of the Parteal mine. And with the same slave's hope he gazed upon it as it sucked free from the rancid meat and gravy. He gave it a wipe of linen and spit. It had been years since he had first seen and brokered it to the duke for Pitt, and this replica looked just as magnificent. Clear and hard. Sitting heavy in his palm like a stone. Just a stone.

Amused he watched his beating heart make his waistcoat tremble. Might it fail before he had a chance to complete his task? Then his door was open and with a shuttered lantern in his hand he crept into the corridor without another thought.

He could not remember the long walk to the regent's study. The dark passages still held lingering smoke. The piss-boys had disappeared and he heard only distant laughter and violins' notes falling from high above, the musicians wearing blindfolds so they could not report who or what they had seen. He could be caught at any moment, but only by a man dressed as a satyr chasing a giggling maiden down the stairs. Such was the night in the Palais Royale, the guards as dumb as the musicians were blind.

He padded on, respectfully quiet for the hour but with the confidence of one who belonged in these halls. And then the doors, and the gold handle softly turned. He stepped into a darker world, unaware of the eyes that had followed him and still observed him surreptitiously. Then the watcher moved away, on to the rooms upstairs to report what he had seen.

Law opened the shutters on his lantern, but still the shadows outweighed the dim light. He placed it down and sought a stronger source.

Above, Philippe had gathered twelve of the prettiest girls from the opera, all now enjoying the attentions of his *libertins de bonne compagnie.* Tokay and champagne, a course of the feast in themselves, poured directly from bottles into the faces of the naked young ladies, who laughed and spluttered and pretended to struggle as the dwarves dressed in grapes and laurels tied their wrists and ankles to their chairs under his guests' slavering gaze.

Philippe, distracted, uninterested in the sights around his table, tapped a finger against his cheek. His conversation had been melancholy this supper, his appetite subdued, his eye glassy and resting on the empty chair beside him – the chair that no-one spoke of any more.

He had taken his usual cup of chocolate for luncheon, its energy rewarding and luxurious but light enough that he could indulge in his suppers that his mother chided him for again and again: three animals every evening and two hundred bottles of wine a week for his guests, enough to bury Bacchus and she cried and begged him to be bled more to purge his vices.

But tonight his attention flitted between the chair and the door behind which the blindfolded musicians played in their anteroom. His heart fell when the man he had sent to spy on John Law covered his eyes as he bowed into the room and leant to Philippe's ear.

Philippe excused himself at the news and swept from the room with three guards at his heels. He waited until he had reached the stair to fold his banyan tight and hold out his hand for a pistol. It was slipped into his hand and he looked down at its crudity of wood and steel. He had never felt anything colder.

He regretted his slippers that made his walk seem clumsy against the proficient stride of the guards at his side. He had never visited his study in the night, had never noticed how wide the passage was now that it was empty, how silent his court when the glory departed with the sun.

His white door was one he had seen a thousand times, but now it appeared with some disease upon its handle. He watched his hand reach out, then draw back to palm his pistol's cock. He nodded to one of his men to open the door instead, as if in his mind there was something treacherous in opening it himself. It pushed in, brightness bathing them all, and Philippe went through, his pistol raised.

His hand shielded his eyes to blank out the blinding white light from the laterna magica shining off the far wall. An image of three compromised couples shone from the white plaster wall. The guards at his back gaped at the scene and Philippe, his pistol forgotten, laughed riotously at the fumbling figure of Law adjusting himself hurriedly in a chair beside the machine.

Law stood and his breeches fell as he began to protest at the intrusion. Sparing him his shame, Philippe shooed the guards from the room with his laughter and handed one of them his pistol.

He turned back to face Law as he pulled up his breeches with Scottish curses that needed no translation. Philippe wiped tears from his eyes and steadied himself against a table.

'Oh, Lass!' he cried. 'And here I thought you almost dead!' He pushed a fist against his mouth as a choking belch caught his throat. 'What would your wife say, Lass?' he began to fold over, his guffaws bringing him back up. 'I thought you disapproved of my magic light!'

Law straightened himself and stood in front of the lantern's beam, where the men and women now rippled across his blouse. He coughed a hand to his mouth. 'My wife is away. A man grows lonely, Milord.'

Philippe could barely speak and his voice squeaked awkwardly. 'Oh, I know, Lass! I know! But have I not invited you upstairs enough?'

'I do not crave infidelity, Milord.'

Philippe staggered over to his friend, clapped his hands on his shoulders and shook him thankfully. 'No, Lass. No you do not. You are the better of us all. Especially those who thought ill of you.' Slowly he lowered the lever that doused the candle inside the machine and the room darkened again, hiding the relief on the regent's face.

Law checked his buttons once more. 'Well, with Milord's permission, I should like to retire back to my apartments. I have humiliated myself enough for one evening, I feel.'

Philippe lovingly patted Law's shoulder and wiped a tear from the corner of his eye. Then his eyes widened in horror at the sight of his chair, that had been pulled back from his desk. His back straightened instantly.

'One moment, Lass,' his tone reverted to the man who commanded France. 'One moment.' He went around his desk, his hands grasping the shoulders of the gold and green fauteuil chair.

Law turned. 'Milord?'

Philippe hesitated, stood like a statue beside the chair and his desk, his head lowered. 'You have forgotten one thing, Lass.'

Law resisted the pull of his feet toward the door. Another two feet and he would have been in the corridor and away to his rooms. But fortune had already blessed him twice: once when he had heard their approach in the hall without, and twice because it was only out of necessity on entering that he had decided to use the brightest light source in the room – the magic lantern. He held his breath as Philippe raised his head and silently prayed for a third stroke of luck.

'You forget your lamp.' Philippe indicated Law's lantern on the corner of the desk. 'It is dark out there, my friend.'

Law berated his foolishness too theatrically, with a slap to his forehead. He retrieved his lamp. 'Would you wish to accompany me, Milord?'

Philippe shook his head slowly. 'I have my guards. Goodnight, Lass.' He waited until Law had reached the door, watched his hand grip the handle then spoke slowly, painfully.

'Why, Lass?' his voice sounded regretful. He repeated the question when Law looked back. 'Why?'

'Milord?' Law raised his lamp as if peering into a mine, half his face illuminated.

Philippe said nothing and ran his hands beneath his chair. He experienced the strangest rush of blood to his head as he felt the bag still resting in its web. His fingers felt the familiar square shape but still he needed to see. He pulled the bag free and rose up with the diamond in his hand, no longer caring if Law saw it or not. Law gasped at the sight of the diamond as naturally as any man.

Philippe caressed the stone, his shame reflecting from its surface. 'Nothing, Lass. Nothing.' He ran the stone between his fingers, seeing deep within it as Devlin had done, as all had done; the diamond fed on the soul like a succubus if one looked at it for too long.

'I begin to feel that sometimes I judge every man by my own woes. Goodnight, my friend.'

The bag swallowed up the stone again and he buried the bag in his robe's pocket as Law left hurriedly, the guards brushing past him into the room.

'Leave me!' Philippe barked and they bowed out again to wait for his word.

The closed door and the absence of Law's lamp left him

alone in the darkened study. He went to a long window and slipped aside the curtain to let some of the lamplight of Paris fall in.

He should not be alone now. He had guests to attend to; the guards were waiting to escort him back. But the diamond and his misjudgement of Law had reminded him of his cursed life since its acquisition.

He pulled from his other pocket the small oil of her, the Duchesse de Berry, his Marie-Louise, Marie-Louise with the little mouth, and let her glow in the soft light.

Upstairs was the empty chair: a place for her always at his *fêtes*. It had been over a year since her death and that of the unborn child. He brushed a tear from the glass surface of the miniature with his cheek and whimpered for her forgiveness, so that it looked as if the crystal might break under his clumsy hands.

He had found the romance of the blood that surrounded the diamond amusing when Law had first told him the tale and had laughed at Pitt's hiding like a rat until it had been sold.

Those stories had bargained Pitt to a lower price but Philippe himself had found no price higher. The pitch of his sorrow now was unseemly for the Regent of France and the guards in the passage moved away from the door, dutifully refusing to hear the muffled lament. From above drifted down the sounds of squeals and laughter, the string quartet stimulating romance, and these distracted the soldiers enough from the sound of weeping.

Chapter Twenty-Four

Monday
The second week

*D*evlin made his way back to Law's office in the Rue de Quincampoix. He walked stiffly; the nights aboard the small ship had him rubbing his bones against each other. Like his men he was weary of it and had begun to long for his cot and cabin. He missed his stern windows that rolled the clouds up and down as he ate, whose glass he could touch and almost predict the next day's weather. If Law had succeeded, he would be back in his ship's embrace soon enough.

He had not continued the pretence of the baker and just wore the honest sailor slops. Nobody paid him any mind as he cut through the swathes of Parisians fighting for shares in the streets.

Some investors had worked out a perfect plan to access the plethora of agents. They would line up their carriages like stepping stones from one side to the other and walk between them without ever having to touch the ground, often doubling their money from seat to seat, trading with their acquaintances before the ink had dried.

Devlin kept his head low as he elbowed his way through. Law's door was invisible against the throng and he had to check the walls and shutters above for some plaque to confirm that he had reached the spot that had been so quiet yesterday.

Fortunate then that Law had been keeping watch for him from his open window and called down to the tanned face so distinctive amidst the white wigs. Devlin looked up, the two of them sharing a friendly recognition out of place with their conspiracy; then they became solemn again as they remembered.

Devlin bulled his way to the house, his attitude unchallenged as Italian princes shared blows with Dutch earls, and duchesses screeched and pulled at one another's earrings. Law's coachman lounged in the doorway, a blunderbuss nestling in his arms. His presence was enough to keep most of the crowd from Law's office but he jerked up straight as the sailor arrowed towards him.

He half-cocked the weapon with his palm and let the massive barrel-mouth casually stare out from over his crooked arm. The sailor came on, never even glanced at the weapon and tapped his forehead. 'John Law expects me.'

The bold English, the use of the Scottish name over the more familiar Monsieur Lass stuck a needle into the sentry. Without looking behind, his eye still on the crowd, he reached back and opened the door, letting the sailor slip past and close it himself.

Law was waiting for him at the top of the stairs. His arms welcoming him like family. Devlin declined the embrace.

'I take it all is to the good, John?' he walked ahead and into Law's chambers. Law trotted faithfully behind, sealing them from the world with the closing of his door.

'All goes well enough, Captain.' He went to his window and closed off the roar and bustle below. 'That's better.'

'Is it like that often?' Devlin indicated to the window. 'Those lunatics?'

'Regretfully,' Law said and scurried around to his desk. 'I feel they believe the fury of it means their dealings must be the saving grace of France. For surely only the most important things are violent.' He sat. 'I believe at the height of the madness in London some rogue made a fortune selling shares in a company that no-one was permitted to know what it did. Now, to our business. *Our* speculation.'

Devlin struck out his hand, his other curled into a white fist.

'Just give me the bloody thing if you have it! I've wasted enough time dancing to gentlemen's tunes! No flourish, no speeches! Just put it up and I'll be gone!'

'Captain!' Law squared his shoulders. 'I do not deserve such an outburst! Last night I committed a crime against my country! I took abjuration against my homeland for this regency. This is not something I take lightly! After my part, after what I have done last night, I think some measure of respect would—'

His words were cut short by Devlin's kick to his desk, pushing his chair to the wall. Law grabbed at his flying papers and inkwells.

'What *you* have done! You've picked a pocket! I'm weighing my men for a noose!' He kicked the wood again, less in anger, more just the frustration clamouring to be uncaged.

He liked Law, there was nothing of politics or scorn about him, but on the Monday past the pirate had been in Newgate. He could still smell it on his skin over the stench of fish and smoked wool.

Law slept in palaces, owned country estates and town-houses for the different aspects of the seasons; he belonged to a class that had dozens of pairs of shoes yet never trod the streets, had matching hats and coats but never knew rain or cold. All wolves at lambing time. Devlin still liked him, yet the fool needed to understand. When you steal something you run, run fast and far. Now was not the time to chink glasses and admire; that attitude to their failing business schemes over the summer had brought them to this act and, over all of them, over all their power and position, Devlin would be in charge of his own fate.

More gently he reached out his hand. 'Just give me the damned thing.'

Law pulled open a drawer. He dropped the diamond into the pirate's palm as if it were a coin begged.

Without a look Devlin buried the weight into a pocket, the blood of it passed, and he turned on his heels. He stopped by the door.

'You know the next hours of your life will depend on me getting this back to Walpole. If I fail there will be no urgency to grant you clemency in England. No escape when it all falls around you. Do you trust them?'

Law played at his necktie. 'I have always been running, Captain. The fate of the South Sea Company hangs – if you forgive the term – on you getting that stone back to London. It will be September in two days. On the eighth the company must declare its assets. Your country has put its faith in its banks and companies. Your country no longer wishes to make and produce when they can get rich on mystery and chance. If you can save the fortune of the largest company in England you will save the others.'

Devlin tipped him the grin that had been missing for almost a week now.

'Not my country, John. They forget that.' He vanished through the door, the last Law would ever see of him.

Law sat back, blew out a breath like a man reprieved, then looked to the blackboard that still wore Devlin's childish drawings. The fury in their scrapes and symbols was worth considering. He wished Walpole could consider their significance also.

Chapter Twenty-Five

Two days later. September.

'*There's* something wrong.' Devlin stood at the tartane's bow, his voice somehow carrying back to the others despite it being barely more than an inner thought.

They were out of the mouth of Le Havre, just part of the flotilla of fishermen and bale-laden ships trying not to run into each other in the early morning.

'What is wrong?' Dandon came up, ducking under the single lateen sail. He could see what purported to be the *Shadow* moored maybe only two miles from them. She sat, anchored fore and aft, in soundings deep enough for her three-hundred tons, a pool of other frigates and merchants around her, their boats all plying the waters and ferrying their goods to the harbour, or waiting for victuallers and customs officers to attend.

Devlin watched the play of activity, of innocent *cabotage*, of coastal trade. He looked between each of the ships not more than a cable away from their own girl. 'Nothing,' he said at last, but called Peter Sam up just the same.

Nothing suspicious in the *Shadow* waiting for them – her orders had been plain enough – but Peter confirmed as best he could without spyglass that the ship had some pain about her.

Her yards looked weak, her rigging limp yet no men tending

withal. The gunwale faced them and her starboard side was sheeted in sail-cloth.

'Just drying out new sail maybe,' Peter suggested.

'Or hiding damage.'

'Perhaps Bill had some trouble. Better to hide it.'

'Aye.' Devlin saw the blue-and-white merchant flag hanging from the backstay, the white flag on the main declaring a clean ship, a ship free from plague. All was well.

Half an hour would tell. Raise the sail. Come in slow. All the while Devlin and Peter Sam at the bow looking out for Black Bill's head. Hugh Harris, sensing his captain's unease, rifled pointlessly for some teeth amongst the *Junot*'s furniture. Marlin spikes, knives, wooden hammers. Toys. Fishermen's tools. Nothing with the heft of even a belaying pin.

He grimaced and tucked some of the pathetic rusty steel in his belt, then looked up at Albany and eyed his sword enviously as he passed him to confer with Devlin.

Albany came to Devlin's side furthest from Peter Sam and hung as heroically as he could from the nearest rope above his head, foot planted against the gunwale.

'So to the ship, Captain. We should drink deep tonight. Get out of these slops. Some proper food. I feel after these cod-bones the last few days I would relish even your "Poor-John". Is that the phrase?'

Devlin and Peter Sam looked him up and down. 'I'll get you drunk as a lord if it'll pipe you down, Albany.' His tone gave away nothing about his wariness of approaching his own ship. He waited for Albany to ask about the diamond, to indicate yet again that he should hold it if they were to return amid pirates, forgetting his own company. But Albany only breathed deep on the refreshing wind, forgiving the sting of it watering his eyes.

They closed on the *Shadow*. The waves grew higher and creamier as they reverberated off her bow. The small tartane pulled almost magnetically towards her now.

Peter Sam went aft to the tiller while Dandon held on to the gunwale as the sea grew more lively. Albany stayed beside his partner who had grown darkly silent.

'Are you not pleased, Captain? We have done it have we not?'

Devlin had been counting the masts amongst the pool of ships. At least two square-rigged and pocked with black. Tainted with battle. The glow of white coats, gleaming off the morning sun, running along their weatherboards. Too many tricornes. But then he heard Black Bill calling from the *Shadow*. Her freeboard stretched above them now, the final short distance slamming away quickly, the Jacob's ladder welcoming them home.

Bill stood at the bulwark nettings. He yelled for a belaying rope for the tartane. He grinned at the sight of Devlin's return and waved them in. He prayed that Devlin was shrewd enough to note that he smiled rarely, that he would find his exuberance a signal that something was amiss. He struggled to not look down at the French marines crouched beneath the bulwarks aiming their muskets at him and laughed Devlin in like a favoured son.

Trouin watched him carefully, his pistols drawn and primed. He was crouched low with several of his officers around the mizzen and nodded calmly to reassure the others that ringed the foremast.

Bide, bide. Time enough for glory.

Peter Sam took the rope and belayed it with his arms. The tartane pivoted to the *Shadow*'s hull, Devlin already stretching to the ladder. Bill watched him fight with the ropes like a boy with his first catch in a net. He moved closer to the bulwark, muskets prodding into his side. Trouin waved them down, checked the pans on his pistols once more.

Bill looked away from Devlin's scrambling and caught Peter Sam's eye.

Eight years he had known Peter Sam. Three years with Devlin, three with Seth Toombs, their captain late of Devlin's hand. Before that, two as Newfoundland lost souls, cold and dying together. Tens of thousands of miles. Four ships and hundreds of men, some still with them, most gone. Each day different and every tomorrow the same hempen end promised.

Peter Sam looked up at the red eyes above the tremendous black beard and held the belaying rope tighter across his leather bracers, his strength pulling them closer. After years of living within inches of each other he could identify a new look on Bill's face.

Devlin found his purchase and smiled up at Bill, who moved from Peter's worry to look down with the same strange cocked head as his father had done when he had left through the butcher's door four guineas richer.

Bill's mouth opened to speak, then forever opened as a shot from beneath the gunwale sprayed a red mist out of the side of his skull, almost a powder, almost silently, just a small crack that no-one would recall hearing and Black Bill fell like a beaten horse, his final sound in his ears the screaming of his name from Peter Sam.

'*Bill*!'

Trouin flew up. 'No firing! No firing!' The death of such a beloved man would cost dear. Already the pirates began to struggle in their ropes where they sat along the gangway, the click of their guards' muskets only angering them further.

'Up! Up!' Trouin shouted. 'To arms!'

Devlin looked up to the space where Bill's head had lifted away, now filled with musket mouths pointing down at him. A dozen more paraded along the gunwale, all with a ready eye along their sight, all marked at him, all grinning behind their triggers.

Numbers would normally be enough to still a single man's progress but more than one of them looked behind to Trouin when the pirate only ascended faster, as if an army were at his back – and then there was. The soldiers swung their aim to the giant climbing up behind Devlin and howling like a mad bear.

'Do not fire!' Trouin yelled. 'He is mine!'

Devlin dragged himself through the port by yanking down the nearest musket barrel, the bearer pulling his trigger as he held on to the gun, the shot disappearing into the sea. The next had his weapon slammed into his chin, sending him reeling back along the gunwale into his comrades. And now Devlin had space. His feet were back on his deck. His bound crew in the gangway were now trying to rise, their guards beating them back down.

Someone was shouting orders, French orders, orders not to shoot. Good enough a word for Devlin to stand with only his fists and feet and now the roar behind him, the heat of Peter Sam, always at his back, and any Frenchman who had dared to rush forward now found his head pounded against any convenient fixture or else was flung backwards to the sea where Hugh Harris climbing the ladder found the spirit to giggle as they fell past him.

Albany drew his sword and stared at the dancing on the ship and the men struggling in the water. Dandon calmly pushed his arm down.

'This is just a venting, Albany. It is over. Devlin's blood will cool momentarily. I have seen this before.'

'But the diamond!'

Dandon looked at him almost in awe. 'Ah, yes, for that's the concern.'

Trouin watched, even admired, as two men beat back his force like a scythe through a wheat field. They had plucked muskets as if offered – clamped hands over the locks and rammed the butts into faces of men not used to such a close, snarling fight. Then they swung the guns like clubs, the pair of them now standing protectively over the body of their fallen man.

But end it must, now, as a third pirate leapt to the deck and sliced blades across eyes and noses, and joined his brothers in guarding the dead body. And this one was laughing. That could not mean anything good, and with his knives, only real harm to his men.

Trouin signalled to the guards standing over the crew along the gangway. They fired over the heads of the boarding trio, the rattling fire at least enough to stall their blows and switch their anger in a new direction instead – easy pickings now that they faced empty guns. But Devlin blocked Peter and Hugh to a halt as Trouin waved a pistol for his men to race down from the quarterdeck and fo'c'sle. Suddenly thirty men corralled the three pirates around the mainmast. Pikes, muskets and cutlasses trembled over every inch of them.

The three dropped their stolen muskets and edged around their small territory, testing the courage of the souls hiding behind their steel and lead.

Hugh Harris ran his knife down one cheek then the other, drawing his own blood. He flashed his fearsome grin at the soldiers staring wide-eyed. Peter Sam spat on his hands then ground out his words to the nearest pale face.

'*Come on!*'

'*Enough!*' Trouin cried in English for his guests. He put his pistols to his sash. His men parted and raised a saluting avenue of muskets for him that led straight to Devlin.

Over his blood, his fists white, Devlin took in the man and somewhere, from a decade back, in another world, he recognised the man in white and red, though not as one who had taken his ship. The face was older of course, soft jowls where once had been a granite jaw-line, but him nonetheless; it could be no other.

'*Trouin*,' Devlin whispered and Trouin smiled and stopped at a sword's distance.

'You know me, pirate?'

'Enough. Enough to understand how my ship is lost.'

'You flatter me, Captain,' he began to affect a courteous wave of his hand then his eye fell to the corpse at Devlin's feet. 'I am most sorry for the loss of this man, Captain. I assure you I will punish severely the man responsible.'

Devlin looked around. 'So will I.'

Trouin affected not to hear and clicked his fingers to have Bill's corpse removed from where it unbalanced everything.

Peter Sam slapped them away like children and the muskets' barrels rattled to his chest. But Trouin knew the look.

'Let him be,' he said, and Devlin nodded to Peter Sam who went down on his knee and lifted Bill's head to his lap.

Bill weighed fifteen stone at least and the first sight that greeted the soaked marines clambering back up from the sea where Peter had flung them was the big man carrying Bill to the main hatch cover to gently lay him down.

He covered the face with his own kerchief to shield him from Bill's dead eyes looking up; Peter Sam knew well that dead eyes lingered open even if you tried to close them. Devlin turned away, rounding on Trouin. Then he looked down at himself, his sailor's slops and clogs.

I need my coat, he thought, my hat, my boots. I'm not the man I need to be. Trouin saw his shame. Gallantly ignored it.

'You and I should talk, Captain. I will have the last of your men brought up from the boat. Will you confess that you pirated the boat?'

'No man was harmed,' Devlin said.

'That is of little consequence. You will hang, but first I must discuss your parole if no more of your men are to die this day.' He held out his hand. 'Come: you should get changed. I will not take you seriously in this garb. It will degrade my table.'

Devlin looked over his men held along the gangway. Trouin had kept them above to run the ship and to keep as hostage meat. The others he supposed were either kept below or on Trouin's ship. He never thought them dead. His men looked back at him. A long expectant look. He walked behind Trouin to the cabin that had once been his castle. He threw one glance back to Peter Sam and Hugh Harris and they held his eye until the cabin door closed behind him.

Chapter Twenty-Six

*D*evlin, no qualms about dressing in front of Trouin and
two of his marines, strode across the cabin that had
once been his. From his broad locker seat he took a slow time
in changing from the poor sailor back to the bold pirate, a
quixotic knight donning his poor but trusted armour. Holland
shirt, Damask waistcoat, dark twill coat, all stolen, fitted for
other men. His ancient boots. The same he had worn since
taking them from a dying Frenchman on an African archipelago three years gone. He stamped them on, looking to the
luck in their soles. His favoured left-locked pistol lay patiently.
Devlin let her lie. He dumped his slops into the locker, the
diamond bundled within, and slammed the lid. He faced
Trouin. Devlin was the pirate again.

Trouin, sat in one of the only two chairs and looked disa-
greeably about the cabin.

'I notice comfort is something you pirates do not seem to
favour, Captain,' he indicated with a glove the empty room.

One table, two chairs, books and bottles in equal abundance, the bindings and glass the same green, reds and browns
as if they were chosen to match.

'It is quite touching. It is as if, in her sparseness, she is only
half-finished, fresh and new. A ship cut back to the bone.'

Devlin stepped forward. 'You wanted my parole,' he said.

'Indeed,' Trouin brushed some dust from Devlin's table.

'To look at you I'm sure I have it. To begin well I should like to know how it is that you know me. I am sure it is not from statues and paintings. I do not know myself from them.'

'Time ago I saw you paraded in Paris. During the war.'

'Ah,' Trouin sat back. 'And some time after you signed to the Marine Royale?'

Trouin's small revelation of his past was subtly given out to let Devlin know that any cards he might try to conceal would have backs made of glass.

'My belly inspired me. There were many Irishmen signed.'

'Yet you joined the English when it served to save your skin. You are a cuckoo with your loyalties.'

'I was captured. I helped save my officers' lives by translating for the English captain.' That had been John Coxon. The man had made post-captain on the Irishman's information.

'And no doubt offered as much treason as you could to preserve yourself.'

Devlin had heard enough of his past. That young man was but a distant cousin to him now. The same blood, some features similar, but uncomfortable to shake hands with.

'What now, Milord? You have my ship, my men. Where do I sign for your mercy for them?'

Trouin ran a thumbnail down his face as he studied the man before him. It had only been two days since he had captured the *Shadow* and that had not been too difficult. He had given Bill his hoop to jump through and Bill had done so and fallen against the rocks just as Trouin had planned.

There had been blood, but the *Shadow* was outmanned and outgunned and too wounded. Black Bill had sworn he was Devlin and that Trouin had done a great deed – one which the best English navy bloods could not. But sly Trouin knew he had stumbled on a larger game; he knew that he was not facing the pirate who had eluded the world.

The real pirate captain was gone; a French tartane's crew was present with only their ship missing, and their bellies fuller than they had ever been; on a promise that they would have their ship back in time, and the fact that they were taken near Le Havre. Black Bill had sweated enough for Trouin to suspect that all he had to do was return to Le Havre and wait.

Now he had the pirate: now he had the final page. Still missing was the first.

'You seem to accept your fate most willingly for one who has commanded so many and been free for so long. And you pirate in *my* waters when your own Caribbean is so rich and so much easier. Suppose you tell me, Captain, what is your real purpose on this little sea?'

Devlin looked at the guards. Soldiers, just soldiers. He could take them both in the same time it took to count them. He would have a gun, a shield in the old captain at his table, enough of his finest men to take back the ship.

Trouin watched the pendulum swinging across the pirate's thoughts and Devlin snapped back to the sound of a pistol cocking to his guts.

Trouin grinned. 'I insist, on your parole, to enlighten me.'

The cabin door opened and Trouin's gun stayed on the pirate as Albany Holmes was escorted in. The escort saluted, backed out and closed the door.

Trouin noted both the pale face, distinctive against the rest of the dark crew, and the narrowing of Devlin's eyes. This fellow was not one of them and Trouin knew a wedge when he saw one. And this man had been on the tartane. His presence could be entertained.

'Who are you to disturb me, sir?'

Albany brushed down his poor cloth and bowed with the faintest respect. He ignored Devlin and squared himself before Trouin, speaking loud and slow for the foreigner to understand.

'Your Honour, Captain. My name is Albany Holmes. I present myself to you as a representative of His Majesty's government. This ship is under privateering rules of the King, an ally of your own. I insist that this ship is released under my own cognisance and is allowed to continue on its way. Any manner of affront may be taken up with his Lordship Townshend at a later date when we return to England under my honour.' He straightened as best he could in his ill-fitting wool. 'I'm sure your admiral would prefer that you respect your own code of trade with regard to His Majesty's privateers.'

Trouin uncocked his weapon. 'Yes. Yes, I'm sure *my* admiral would concede such rights to your king. That is if I *had* an admiral. Or if I needed to make concessions. Unfortunately – for your plea – I am burdened with being in entire command of the waters beneath your feet, and the captain and I were about to discuss the day. He at least had the decency to be aware of the man he was addressing before he opened his mouth.'

Albany sniffed, looked sheepishly at Devlin's anger but held his ground, as all gentlemen do with regard to those who must work for their bread.

'I did not catch your name?'

Trouin smiled as he might at a capon presented as a hen for his supper. 'If you have privateering papers, let me see them. But I do not think that, however voluminous they may be, there will be any line in them that allows you to pirate a French vessel in her own waters.'

Albany haughtily agreed as if he were not at fault. 'Quite so. Nevertheless I insist that this vessel return to England. We are on a mission that will benefit the whole of Europe and for which you will only be rewarded for allowing us to continue.'

Devlin sprang forward. 'Albany! *Enough*!' He could have still won this day if the damned Englishman had not flapped his tongue. The guards put out their muskets and the pirate stopped.

Albany waved him away. This was his stage now. The Irish bog-trotter did not understand politics. The boldness of an English gentleman impressed lesser nationalities throughout the world, and his voice was his letter of introduction.

'The captain is ignorant of the larger purpose for which both our crowns are in jeopardy if we are not allowed to cruise on.' He stepped to the table.

'I only require enough men to take the ship in. You can take the pirate as reward. His captaincy is no longer needed and he has broken his orders in taking one of your ships. He would be disavowed and hung on his return at my insistence for such an act. You may have my assurance as a gentleman on that fact.'

Trouin dropped a glove to the table, the draught of which caused the single candle on the table to crackle and suffer. It grew again as his breath fanned it. 'Thank you, sir. It may have taken me hours to remove from the pirate that which you have given with such grace. But perhaps I need to know one thing more.'

He stood slowly but his pistol swiftly reversed so that the cap and butt became a bludgeon, and he scraped it against the overhead beam as he brought it down across Albany's temple just hard enough to crack him to his knees.

He gripped a spluttering Albany by his wool slops and

pulled him up face to face. 'What, *sir*, for your king, and *my* country are you doing in *my* waters!'

'*Trouin*!' Devlin yelled, and the chef d'escadre dropped Albany and span his pistol back to the pirate.

'He's just a long-coat fop! Sent to watch and note, that's all.' Devlin stabbed his finger at his own chest. 'I'm the one. I'll show you what we're doing if it'll give my men a month's trial. Breath to make their ends to a priest.'

He turned away to the locker-seats. The guards cocked their muskets at the sudden movement but Trouin put up his hand for them to hold back.

Devlin plucked the diamond from his rags and tossed it to the table where it bounced and chimed joyously. Trouin clapped a hand over the spinning gem and then slowly uncovered it.

Devlin saw all their eyes fall to the stone, saw it capture them all as it had always done since it had been wrenched from the mud of the Parteal mine's walls.

Distraction enough.

He flew at both guards, using their muskets as their weakest points. Their faith in their iron vanished in such a small space.

He pushed the long guns up into their faces, forcing their skulls against the bulkhead where their hats fell across their eyes, and then he swept their feet away with his leg. One of their muskets Devlin grasped upended in his fists and he cracked it down into their noses one by one, again and again as if shovelling a hole until they stopped trying to get up.

He knew Trouin would have his gun on him, would be crouching and aiming at his back, and he knew Albany would not take any advantage. He dropped against his cabin wall and rolled up one of the bodies to cover himself, flung the musket away and shouted for his life. English now, knowing Trouin would understand, gambling that his men would not.

'You and me, Trouin! Talk this out! Shoot that ponce, but that diamond is Philippe's stone! The King's stone for his crown. I've got it. I've taken it. That's what I'm doing here. You can take it back.' He breathed deep, let the sight of the diamond do its work. 'How would you like to be a hero again, Milord?'

Albany squealed from where he cowered on the floor. '*Devlin*! You betray your king! God damn you, sir!'

'Shut your hole! I'm trying to save your life! What'll it be, Milord? Will you hear me out or will we die slapping at each other in my cabin?'

Trouin's pistol swung first at Albany then towards Devlin crouched behind one of his semi-conscious guards.

'You have my ear, Captain. You have no weapon?'

'None.' He rolled the body aside leaving his head and belly exposed to Trouin's pistol and repeated his word distinctly. 'None.'

Trouin was ready to shoot the pirate now, more so than before when he came aboard and ploughed through his men. Why let him live? Devlin's only hand, although meaner than any of Trouin's cards, was that the death of Bill had stirred the pirates. If he gave them now the death of their captain the order he had gained would be lost. And then the diamond presented itself. Perhaps it was the missing page Trouin was looking for. Devlin had given Trouin a mystery, a question, the word 'hero' mentioned once and enough.

Trouin lowered the doghead of his pistol but kept it in his hand. 'Then we will talk. On this diamond and your word.' He turned to Albany. 'And you will be quiet until spoken to. King or no king, you will wait.'

He glared at his men wiping blood from their faces and retrieving their muskets. He nodded to the pirate. 'You and I will talk. Before you bleed any more of my men.'

Dandon stood with Peter Sam, under guard, and watched Albany stumble from the cabin dabbing at his head.

'That does not look promising, my Peter Sam,' Dandon breathed. He had given some warning to Albany that approaching the new master with demands might not go well. Trouin's blow had also bruised Albany's conceit and he fell in beside Dandon, checking his kerchief continuously for blood.

'We are doomed,' Albany attested. 'Devlin will give us up. He has given the frog the gem for his own hide. Our mission is lost and we will all hang for pirates.'

Dandon kept his eyes on the cabin door, thinking about the conversation going on behind it. 'So, Albany, you cracked your own head in frustration when Devlin bowed, no doubt?'

Albany said nothing but could feel the glare of Peter Sam, abreast of Dandon.

Inside, Devlin took a seat, the guards at his shoulders. Trouin had taken a pencil and paper from the baize-lined drawer within the table, speaking unaccented English as he wrote.

'I will give you a few minutes, Captain. As you have already broken the parole that I granted by further attacking my men you will lose your right to be treated as a gentleman. You will be chained as a prisoner along with the rest of your men.' His writing hand paused and spun the diamond. 'Now tell me how you acquired this gem, if it is the Regent as you say.'

Devlin looked up at the men at his shoulders.

Trouin tapped the table to bring his attention back to only

him. 'Do not worry. They do not understand. Speak of what you have done. Is it truly the Regent?'

'It is. The Pitt Diamond as it was.' He hung one arm over the back of his chair lazily. 'And there is some truth in Albany's speech. We are on a mission for the crown, or at least its government.'

'Jackals every one, I'm sure.' Trouin went back to his page, ready to take down the confession of the pirate.

'That's a given, but,' he pointed to the stone on the table, 'that diamond is worth a king's ransom; what say you on its worth to a pirate's ransom, Commodore?'

Trouin leant back. 'It is not yours to offer. It is mine. Along with everything you once thought you owned.'

'So what is to drive me to tell you all I know?'

Trouin flung the pencil down and sprang to his feet at Devlin's arrogance.

'It is over, Captain! You know that, surely? I will take this ship into Brest, with my two ships as escort. Your men will be tried and hung. *You* will be tried for piracy and treason, for you once deigned to be a part of my fleet! A special privilege for you! You will be broken on the wheel like a noble for such a crime!' He glowered down at the pirate.

'Three years you have been at the game, and perhaps in your conceit you expect that it has not ended yet! But you know me. You know in your heart that this is how it ends!'

Devlin looked up into the oddly kind brown eyes. 'You'd best give me back my ship. Take the diamond and I'll be on my way. I'll do you no harm.'

Trouin snorted and kicked away the legs of Devlin's chair. The pirate crashed backwards onto the boards, the guards' muskets' mouths pointing at his grinning face. He brushed them aside and dragged himself up. He was still talking.

'You've a day to get into Brest. A day with me and my men. That's a long day in the company of pirates.'

Trouin glared back. 'Then I kill you now, if it is so dangerous to keep you alive.'

'Ah, but where's the glory in bringing me in dead? You never beat me. We had no fight in your waters. You bested my old sailing master, that's all.' Demeaning Bill choked, but Devlin was flying now. He cocked a thumb to the guards. 'Your own men will let out that we argued. That there was a diamond. A fight. The whole ship will know. And then maybe you killed me out of fear. Or maybe you killed me for the diamond. You know how ships whisper. What would you prefer your men to say of you?' He picked himself up and took his seat under the watch of the muskets. 'But I could swear that I'll lay down. Go in under my honour. And my men will be good little boys.'

Trouin's anger turned to mirth. He sat down with the pirate. He had studied the history of the man. The grin opposite was not a mask covering a brag. There was mettle in his deeds. He glanced again at the fat square diamond.

'You have taken this diamond from the regent, I am to believe? If I judged you only on that you are a dead man. Your crimes pile up like firewood yet you speak to me of honour and bargaining when you have nothing to give. I must say, Captain, that you are one of the strangest men who thinks himself significant that I have ever met.'

Devlin leant forward. 'For four years I fished out of St Malo. I learnt of Breton men. Learnt *from* Breton men. Heard of you like a god. Your brothers have always sought a republic from the nobles. You were a corsair, as much a pirate as me, and stole Dutch and English ships like picking up pebbles. Not to defend *them* but to protect your own lands. I would honour you to say that the first man I became was born out of those years.'

Trouin leant in also. The pirate's knowledge of him was intriguing. There had been nothing of his Breton life in the official record.

Devlin went on. 'The second man I became was from shining shoes and brushing coats. I was a servant. But I never forgot those Breton men and their dignity, and when I saw you today I recalled your tales.'

Trouin looked at his marines. Young. Young men born of France, not his realm. All his men weighed less in courage than this pirate who had at least lived through his years.

'So? You know of me. And yes, I was pirate once it could be said. But now I have your ship and you. Your end has nothing to do with Trouin and his deeds these past thirty years. You are an enemy to my king.'

'No king. A man who *would* be king. And I have not heard your name for years. You do not belong in their world. Does Paris still sing your praises?' He noticed the pencil had written nothing.

'You can tickle the pup they sent to watch me, and I'm sure he will tell you all you wish to know. But I learnt my honour from Bretons. You would have to remove my head to make it talk. And your *king* would want my confession for I have names to give.'

Trouin stood. 'I am dry, Captain. Would you join me in a drink from your own store?'

'After this.' Devlin also stood, both of them leaning in over the table, the diamond palely lighting their faces as the afternoon sun came through the stern windows.

'I can give you my oath as a man once of Breton that you can take us, curtailed, into Brest. I'll make no bones against you and my men will follow. Or you can spend the next night and day wondering when I'll make my move; when my men will rise against your boys. These aren't men with wives and families like some of yours might be. They got nothing to lose and they'd rather die in the scuppers than at the end of a rope.'

'And then what? You take back your ship? The same ship that I took with my two vessels. The ships that are at our quarters even now?'

'You didn't take it from me, Milord.'

Trouin closed his eyes, as if finding the arrogance blinding. He went to the roped shelf of bottles, searched for a cup or glass then gave up and pulled a cork on the deepest bottle. There was something in the pirate's words. The ending seemed written. Take them to Brest, return the diamond, bow to the crowds. But a favoured man of theirs had been killed when he, Trouin, had promised otherwise on his honour. And after that just three of them had begun with some success to assail his crew. Devlin had a hundred pirates of that kidney. The shame of it if he rolled into Brest with nothing. No one would remember the past, only the present failure. His chance to return to glory would be lost, irretrievably.

So chain them all, mount a twenty-four hour guard, strip them of their clothes. He took a drink.

But the pirate had waltzed into Paris and taken the diamond from a palace. Trouin was sure that such an act would have been thought impossible yesterday. And a whole night and a day until Brest.

He turned back to the table. He needed the pirates to accept that they were beaten; for their captain that had returned to them to tell them so. He offered the bottle.

'From the stones in your words, Captain, I would suspect

that you have already had a long drink this morning. You may need a little more for the rest of your nonsense.'

He waited for Devlin to take a swig then took the bottle back and drank but just a sip, holding it longer to his lips as if drinking more. 'Now,' he pretended to belch. 'What is it you propose? For my honour?'

Hugh Harris had found Dan Teague among the pirates chained along the gangway. He knelt beside him and learnt what he could about the days when they had been separated. But for a few bruises Dan was fine and Devlin's two most dangerous cut-throats even chuckled and nudged each other at the prospect of their fate, all beneath the curious looks of the marines that watched over them.

Dandon, Peter Sam and Albany, like Hugh, were not restrained. After Devlin had been taken to the cabin, Dandon and Peter had carried Bill's corpse below to the cockpit. Now they stood at the mainmast, alone and together, surrounded by guns and boarding pikes; all the same, still alone together.

Then came action, and they lifted their heads. The door to the cabin opened and officers were called. Moments later sailors and soldiers cleared amidships. Peter Sam, Dandon and Albany were barged to the gunwale as tarpaulins were removed, the spare spars taken away and a hauling and yelling started up for the boats between the masts to be cast astern.

'What goes on, Peter?' Dandon asked.

'Clearing the decks,' he growled. 'Doubt it's to share prizes. A hanging most likely.'

Albany baulked. 'Indeed. All of us one by one I'll be sure. Your captain saving himself, no doubt.'

Peter Sam cared nothing for the muskets around him. He reached across Dandon and punched Albany lightly in the side of his head. A tap, a father's recrimination, but enough for Albany to falter sideways.

Albany rubbed his head. With Trouin's pistol-whip and Peter's thump his indignity was growing more painful. 'I am only saying what we are all thinking!'

'If you were,' Dandon stepped in front of him, blocking Peter. 'You'd throw yourself into the sea.'

Albany threw his kerchief to the deck. 'You fools do not understand what has been lost this day!' He sidled over to the French marines for protection. 'I wash my hands of all of you.'

They ignored him as the cabin door opened again and Trouin and Devlin strode out into the heat, shielding their eyes from the glare after the darkness of the coach. Both men were in shirt sleeves, a grim aspect between them, rolling their shoulders, tightening sashes, as if about to wrestle with the whole ship.

Dandon craned his neck. 'What is this, Peter Sam?'

Peter Sam shrugged and nervous muskets twitched as he smiled at his captain's approach. Devlin looked to the big man, whose eye was bright and assured, and moved on to Albany.

'Your sword, Albany.' Devlin held out his arm, his hand grasping. It was not a request.

'I think not,' Albany turned his sword-hip away. 'I will hear what has transpired first, traitor.'

Devlin's hand closed to a fist and hammered into Albany's paunch. The young noble gasped and fell to his knees.

'Pity,' Devlin said. ' You might have had an interest in me doing well.'

Peter Sam and Dandon had only heard for the asking of a sword. 'You're fighting?' Peter demanded.

Devlin turned away from the retching Albany. 'I've made a

deal. This is no ordinary man. He's a corsair of old. A legend. I can use that. I can challenge his greatness and he will take that bait.'

Dandon looked over the ship to the middle-aged man now whistling his sword through the air. 'A duel? For what odds?'

Albany struggled up to one knee. 'His hide, that's what. Your captain was French once. Did you not know? He conspires with frogs!'

The three closed together, Albany forgotten. Devlin lowered his voice. 'He's a man who lived on glory. If he could go into Brest with another tale to add . . . my death might be worth something.'

'Worth what?' Peter Sam stood taller.

Devlin called for Hugh, sent him to find him a good hanger, a face-cutter, a bone-breaker. Questioning nothing, Hugh span away as if Devlin had only asked for a glass of water. He brushed past Trouin's men with his sharp elbows. Devlin looked between his two closest brothers, as if memorising their faces for eternity.

'This is my fault. I'll settle it. I've given my word you'll all hold if I lose. Don't make me a liar.'

'*Lose?*' Peter Sam leant into Devlin's face. 'What cards have you cut? I'll not hold to watch you die!'

Devlin patted the slab of an arm. 'I'm good, Peter. Stand down.'

Albany burst into their group. 'This is madness! What have you promised to that frog?'

Devlin gave Albany his court, his due. Little mattered now. 'He has agreed that if I win, if he cries quarter, I'll surrender myself. The ship to sail on without me, the men free. If I lose, he takes all. My death is part of the bargain, either here and now by his hand or in Brest. And all of us to abide by this.

We'll all lay down. I brought us into this. I should be the only one to die because of it.'

'And the diamond?' Albany asked.

'Fuck the diamond and fuck you. Beg for your own hide if you wish. Your schemes are done. He has the diamond and its luck.' He turned in time for Hugh to plant the back-sword in his fist.

'Old,' Hugh said. 'But Welsh steel, Cap'n,' as if the pitted blade were Caledfwlch itself.

Devlin thanked him and joined every eye on the ship in watching Trouin cut his quarter, measuring his space in the world within the reach of a thirty-inch blade. His feet were learning the map of every coaming, every bitt and fairlead that might trip them; his blade-point every hanging sheet and halyard. Trouin was placing them all rigidly in a sixth-sense instinct that had taken him alive through a hundred boardings.

When he was captain of a squadron of ships he had commissioned aboard a fencing master to ensure that his officers would learn how to quart and tierce in a space shrunk to inches on a ship. Deck fights were *corps-a-corps*, body to body, fists and pummelling as much as assault with the sword itself.

He faced the butcher-boy standing awkwardly afore the mast with his inelegant sword limp at his side. Trouin flexed his cutlass between his fingers, appraised the strength of the tang in his fist. A glass of wine came from one of his officers. He snarled and slapped the glass from the young man's hand to the sea, splashing the deck with red spatters. The startled white-coat skipped back along the gangway.

Gentleman pups. Young nobles who knew nothing. He would show them. Show them how a Breton fights.

The butcher-boy, the poacher, the guttersnipe, stepped

away from his brothers, twitched his blade, measured nothing. Already Trouin's men began to climb the shrouds for a better view, to empty the deck. The chained pirates were forced to the fo'c'sle in silence and Trouin's officers to the quarterdeck; the *Shadow* was now displaying more oak than she ever had as the two men came closer.

A sword-fight falls down to a world of threes. The average contest lasts no more than thirty seconds using probably thirty inches of blade, of which only three inches are needed for a kill to the throat or chest, by one of three forms of assault: the strike, the cut and the thrust. And finally your fate depends on mastering the holy trinity of the blade – the point, the edge and the hilt, for that *will* overcome.

Trouin had known a sword longer than he had known women and now he held this one to his face in salute. Waiting now. Half a minute to glory.

The butcher's boy had first wielded a sword three years ago fighting off the men who now stood behind him, beating them from his master's cabin door. But he could fight, had fought all his life one way or another, and even if this combat were to be his last it was for something worth more than just a square of table in a tavern or for other men's gold.

Trouin stepped forward easily. The *salle d'armes* may have been no more than twelve feet of oak but there was an entire arena of confidence around him. 'Are you sure this is what you want, pirate?' He rapped his sword against his leg. 'You will die.'

Devlin followed his movements like a mirror. 'Then you will be a hero. As you should.'

Trouin bowed his chin. 'And your men? They will follow what you say?'

'Do you remember when men did that for you, René? The feel of it in your chest?'

Trouin cast no look at the young officers whose faith belonged to a new order, a regency of operas and lapsed virtues. But this could still be his world, still being of service to France. To bring back the diamond for the new king. To have Paris in his debt again.

'I do remember. And that will do for me.'

Devlin stopped circling and broke the false friendship as he swung and rang his sword off a chain hanging from the mizzen, the crash of it snapping the air.

'Come on then,' he beckoned with his sword. 'You swear before this deck. You surrender and my ship goes free. You have me and the diamond.'

'And all of you, and you dead when I beat you. An easy oath.' Trouin counted his steps. Seven. Seven feet. All recorded. All the space he would need and keep to, just as he had been taught as a boy. 'You will die and I take all. A page of my story.'

Devlin balanced his sword. 'Just know, René: this is a better end than I had ever hoped for.'

Chapter Twenty-Seven

*T*he first pass was a testing of forte, to hear the strength in the steel, to see how their thirty inches of death compared. And then another back again, to counter, to see if the first strike had shocked enough to slow down the other's hand, and determine if his mettle matched his steel.

Devlin felt the power of a forearm honed for decades sing up his arm and he jumped back, which only pulled the corsair at him, at his throat, shaving his neck, the steel palpable as the smell of it whisked back with its master.

The pirate appeared to be already on his back-foot, and Trouin's men began to cheer from the shrouds as the two passed across the stage. The pirates remained still, but had dark looks for the Frenchmen above them, each of them picking a man to chill with their solemn stares.

Watch the shoulder and the eyes, Devlin, not the sword. Dead amateurs and Shakespeare players clash at swords. Treat the sword as your fist in a brawl. Go for flesh.

Trouin saw Devlin's thought, his eyes giving him away, pointing to where he would strike.

Poor boy. And Trouin countered before Devlin moved.

Yet the body was not there when he came, and instead the pirate's edge sliced to his head.

Trouin weaved as if dodging an eye-level branch in a woodland stroll, the slice missing by a thumb's width.

Very good, pirate. But how is this?

A *passeta sotto*. Trouin's left side almost to the deck, the fulcrum of his body thrusting his tip to Devlin's guts. Twenty men had died in the first three seconds from such a touch. Years and years of them swept away – but again the body was no longer there and again the sword came for his head.

Trouin reeled back as the steel cut into empty air before his eyes. He saluted again to acknowledge to his opponent and to assure him he would not underestimate him again. That mistake had passed.

A bead of sweat formed on Trouin's lip, and he blinked rapidly to clear his vision of moisture. Devlin saw it. The deck was always a warm place but now it was scorching in the sun. They both took a breath. Almost twenty years lay between the two. Every second Devlin stayed alive those years would count more, would wear on the older man. His only chance. But the lion came on again.

Once, twice, across and past the younger man and a strike to his back without a glance. Peter Sam closed his eyes at the sight of the edge cutting across Devlin's spine and already Trouin had turned and lunged.

Devlin spun as the point came. He landed against the mizzen, its oak at his back, a cold stripe of blood running down his back, Death's scythe tasting blood.

Trouin would not thrust at a man with a tree to his back. Perhaps this was how the pirate had survived before? A witless officer diving forward only to find his blade stuck into oak. But a cut would not get so pig-stuck and he swept across the butcher-boy's side.

Not enough fat on him to hit. Devlin leapt aside, his blade still there and catching the forte of the cutlass like a vice with his own, the peal of it causing his men to jeer.

Trouin's forehead began truly to drip; a swift left hand to his brow as they gathered again. Devlin pushed him back through the last inch of blade and dared him on.

Trouin thrust forward again, knowing a coil of rope lay behind the butcher-boy's heels – he was well taught to use the area around him as a weapon.

But a pirate had no teacher, no rules. Devlin grabbed the arm as the thrust came by and whirled him away, and the chef d'escardre of the Marine Royale stumbled and fell to the deck.

Trouin had no recall of the last time he felt his back on any floor, never mind the deck of a ship he had taken. The pirates' laughter from the fo'c'sle reddened his face as he pushed himself to his feet, sword out, chest pumping beneath his shirt.

Devlin saw the shirt heave and Trouin tasted sweat. He sucked deep the close September afternoon but the fight still showed cool on the butcher-boy's face. But Trouin had drawn blood. That would count.

Pity the boy had not remained in the Marine Royale. Pity he did not have this man for his own. Double pity he must end him.

Now the old lessons. The ones the pirate did not know. *Prise de Fer*, bind, *croise*. Treat his blade with the contempt of a riverside reed, use it against him, show him how a Breton fights.

As he came on the pirates began to stamp their feet slowly, all of them, Albany looking around nervously as the marines cocked their muskets and the whole deck shook. Trouin's own men no longer cheering.

Trouin found the old count again, his feet stepping with the cut of his sword. One, two, three, four, five. Each count a step and a strike, trying to break the man backing away, break him with sheer power. Five strikes enough to weaken anybody.

Anybody, damn him! He will open, he will parry wrong, he does not know, he knows nothing.

I am René Duguay-Trouin. *Break*, damn you!

He beat Devlin to the gunwale, every blow blocked with the fine Welsh back-sword, the sound echoing the anvils and hammers of both their steels' births, the sword-smiths knowing that their hard work through the night would count for one man, for one day.

The gunwale bit into the wound across Devlin's spine and he reacted as the pirate he was. His fist slammed into Trouin's jaw, and felt sick for it as he saw the great man fly away once more to the deck.

The whole ship gasped as Trouin's sword jumped out of his hand. The pirates no longer thumped the deck, the French officers stared agape at the sword and their commodore scrabbling for his footing; the lesser of them lowered their heads.

Devlin had Trouin's back to him. His hide and all its glorious blood-letting organs were open to his point. His recalled a similar sight, of Valentim Mendes crawling ignominiously to his sword in that house in Charles Town two years ago. The nobleman whose hand he had taken, whose ship he had taken, whose life he had taken . . . Still a guilt unpaid for, a victory outweighed. He let Trouin find his sword and rise and wipe the wet from his head with a limp cuff.

Trouin's white shirt ran with perspiration but the pirate had not broken a sweat. Trouin had mistaken one thing only. He had judged the butcher-boy as a pirate. He had forgotten the one thing that the boy had given pride for:

He had been a Breton once.

'What is this worth?' he breathed across the deck. 'Our fighting?'

Devlin lowered his sword. 'A diamond. Saving nobles who

know how to feast and fornicate and have forgotten what a kingdom means.'

Trouin brushed white foam from the corner of his mouth. 'Is that worth dying for?'

Devlin brought up his sword. 'You tell me. I fight for my men.'

Trouin raised his blade, set his feet solid through aching thighs. 'Then you may be better than me.'

But his officers had seen enough.

One raised look and a nod to the shrouds was given as the combatants scraped their swords and backed off for perhaps one final assault. Devlin to die or Trouin to surrender according to their terms, although that thought did not exist within the heart of the old corsair. This would be a fine end; let someone else write his memoirs.

But a musket levelled down at the pirate from above and only Dandon saw the movement from the corner of his eye. He saw the butt to the shoulder and followed the path down to his friend. He still stood by the foremast with Peter Sam, Hugh Harris and Albany – but only Albany saw Dandon's head tilt upwards, only Albany heard him take a breath to yell out.

Albany's sword held one secret, a fine folly built hidden within it, not unusual for a gentleman when pistol swords and drinking vials in the hollowed hilt were talking points at gaming tables. The pommel of his sword unscrewed and out slipped a blue steel dagger.

Dandon's warning to his captain never came. Instead his eyes widened as the dagger plunged and ground sideways into the meat of his back, and then it was gone away into the sword again before he slumped to the deck. Albany's arms helped him down while he cursed the French soldiers all around.

'*Peter*!' he yelled. 'Dandon has been killed by these French dogs!'

Peter Sam looked down to Albany cradling Dandon and missed the shot.

Devlin never heard the crack that slammed a hot lead ball into his back and kicked him over. He was on his knees, his spine on fire, his eyes locked on Trouin soundlessly screaming at his men.

'Not this way!' Trouin bellowed at his officers. 'Not this way!' He swept his hand across all their protests and fell to his knee before Devlin and bowed as the pirate collapsed to the deck, a growing black stain across his shirt.

Peter Sam pushed Albany away from Dandon, the soldiers forming a circle of pointed muskets around them. He held Dandon and looked into his draining face.

Dandon coughed. 'No blood! That is to the good. The captain, Peter. He is shot.'

'I'll take care of that. You are hurt bad, popinjay.' Peter could feel the warmth spreading over the arm holding Dandon's body.

'True, Peter, but as Bartin has it: I am hurt but I am not slain. I'll lay me down and bleed awhile and then I'll rise and fight again. Have no fear.'

Peter Sam held him tighter as Dandon began to shake. 'Do you still not know when to shut up, ponce?'

Peter Sam laid Dandon down gently and looked at his fallen captain. And then Peter Sam looked across the deck at Trouin.

And then Peter Sam stood up.

Chapter Twenty-Eight

✗

*T*rouin could feel the heat of the big man's fury burning its way towards him. Officers drew pistols and the marines cocked their muskets and stayed Peter Sam's path with their bayonets, his scorn and anger rattling them as still he came on.

Control of the fo'c'sle shrunk as the pirates cursed and spat, pulled against their chains, the musketeers heaving them back with braced guns.

This was not how Trouin had seen the course of the day. He had hoped to gain the pirate's respect – at least, as much as the caged could respect their captors. Now their captain had been cheated. He had given up the ship and Trouin knew how that must have felt inside him.

And all this by his men, against his omnipotent word, when the pirate had only shown him dignity and approbation.

Peter Sam brushed the bayonets aside and Trouin waved them back further and looked up into the face of a man wronged and all the more dangerous for it.

'I am sorry,' he said. 'You would be right to strike me down but for now and for the best I would ask you allow me to help tend to these men. I *swear* to you that the guilty will be punished.' He dared to touch the huge bare arm and Peter looked down at the hand upon him. 'Help me to help them. I have a surgeon on my ship. I shall send for him.' His officers began to protest, their pistols still on the bulk of the man in leather. Before he could reprimand them a weak voice called from the deck behind.

'No need!' Dandon, leaning against Hugh, limped forward. 'There is no time. He *has* a doctor. He has . . . me.' He gulped, his throat dry and this simple action ached. 'An egregious barber-surgeon but . . .' he slumped and Hugh hoisted him up. 'But at least that title has the convenience that I can bandage the slips of my blade as I shave, Milord.'

They were before Peter and Trouin now. 'Let him help,' Dandon pleaded to Peter. 'Into the cabin with our boy.'

Trouin watched the young man sweat and fade before him, watched his eyes smart and blink. 'You will need a surgeon for yourself, sir.'

'I believe I heard you were to send for your own. That will do for me but first my friend is dying, and I would not wish to live if that matter goes further, sir.'

Trouin and Peter Sam carried the limp body of the pirate to the table in the cabin and fetched the shargreen etui of ivory-hilted probes and scissors that Dandon called for and even made way for the filthy Hugh Harris to slip into the cabin.

Trouin studied them. These pirates. Dandon, Peter Sam and Hugh. The gentleman, Albany, he observed, did not join them as water was fetched from the scuttlebutt and Devlin's shirt was cut away and his back sponged clean. Hugh helped Dandon's hand while Peter Sam held his captain fast.

Trouin backed away as if he had violated some ancient ritual and thought of his own past. The corsair at sea at sixteen, the brotherhood and adventure, the time when he had been loved; surely it was this memory that had led to taking his cutlass off the wall.

This should have all been a facile matter. Take a pirate

ship. An enemy of mankind. Nothing but good could come of it for him and his men. He watched Devlin flinch awake. For a moment, Trouin's eyes met the pirate's before they closed again. He looked anywhere else but at the tableau before him, unable as he was to hide the chagrin and envy he felt for these brothers.

Chapter Twenty-Nine

✗

*D*evlin awoke in the night, the cold cobalt light running through the stern windows of the cabin inched out the familiar room gradually like an oil-colour half finished. Still flat on the table he heaved painfully onto an elbow, a stabbing across his back warning him that that was as far as he would be able to move. A creak sounded from one corner as fingers pulled open the shutters on a lantern, allowing out a flood of amber light and revealing Trouin's seated form.

'You are alive and awake, Captain. I am pleased to see it.'

Devlin tentatively put his hand to his wound, felt the tight straps of linen wrapped around him – his shirt torn up. Defiantly he sat with clenched jaw. He would not show Trouin his agony. A snore erupted from nearby and he twisted to the familiar noise and reassuring lump of Peter Sam in repose.

'He has not left your side. It is only in the last hour that he has slept and only then when I feigned sleep myself.' Trouin stood and carried a crock jug of water to the table. 'You will be thirsty.'

Devlin took the jug, 'I'm starving, I know that much.'

'That is to the good. Your body wishes to live.' Trouin stepped back. 'However, Captain, I do not know how aware you were that it was your man Dandon who removed your bullet. He was severely wounded himself. Also by my men, I am ashamed to say.'

Devlin drank. His mind cleared. Dandon was absent from the room. 'Where is he?' His voice betrayed his worst fear.

Trouin lowered his eyes then jumped at the speed of the hand that grabbed him.

'Where is he?' Devlin snarled as Peter Sam snuffled awake at the sudden movement.

Trouin plucked his shirt free. 'He is below. He is bad but alive.' He related how he had witnessed Dandon stagger and faint but never pause until the lead ball was free and Hugh had stitched and bandaged the wound. At which point, in relief, Dandon fell to the floor in his own pool of blood.

'Your men stabbed him. Shot me. Is that the spirit of Bretons now?'

Trouin turned away. 'I know not what to say, Captain. No man has come forward to confess to either crime,' he spun back. 'And I cannot believe that I am speaking with a pirate about crimes committed against him.'

'Aye,' Devlin swung off the table, found he could stand and waved Peter away as he came forward to help. 'You've won anyways.'

Trouin watched him limp to the locker for a new shirt. That very morning he had seen the pirate change from one set of clothes to another. Now, somehow in a different world, it was as if watching him change from one man to another. A harder man, and not like the officers of his own: they were chiselled out of marble, yes, but their notions of honour were seemingly folded out of paper. Nobles, all of them. And Trouin despite the king's blessing was still not one of them.

On Louis's death they had taken away Trouin's sea and sequestered him in Calais's medieval fort. Year after year he had stood before archbishops and the court and they had steepled their fingers across their chests and shaken their heads at granting their most successful captain a uniform.

'It cannot be done, Your Majesty. He is not of the blood. It would be an offence to God.'

He watched the new shirt's back already begin to stick to Devlin's wound through his dressings. Trouin had also bled time and again for other men. He had been a corsair, a privateer for his country, a pirate to their enemies. This young man was too similar. He had pictured a fat, rolling, toothless drunkard chancing his way across the sea. Instead he had met a man who offered a duel to save the lives of his men and offer up himself win or lose.

Peter Sam disappeared to find food. The room did not need his words on the matter. His captain lived for now and that would do. Tomorrow they may well want for today. But tomorrow mattered less and these men needed to talk.

Trouin picked up the papers that referred to the pirate. There was a pile but he had seen nothing in them that told him of the man and his men. He wondered how his own name yellowed in the tomes of his enemies and what history would make of his final acts. An old flabby fool embarrassing his country. His men of the new regime deciding above him to end his duel of honour with a bullet to the back of a mere pirate no less, to save his dignity. He dropped the papers onto the blood-stained table.

'You know we have not shaped a course? We are still anchored near my shores, near your shores. You are still only a day away from your goal as it was.'

Something of the pirate returned to Devlin. He stood straighter. The world began to turn again.

Trouin saw the change. 'This diamond, this "Regent", it cost my country greatly at a time when she could ill-afford it. You stole it under arms?'

'I replaced it with its likeness. The same copy used to barter its sale in the first place. It is hoped that no-one will notice.'

'So if I return that which is not missed to a man who is not my king and knows me only as the guardian of an old citadel. What rewards can I expect?'

'If you take me in, take my story as true, reveal the diamond as replaced, you'll be a hero. You'd have captured me when no-else has laid a hand.'

'That may well be a great thing.' Trouin spoke with the conviction of a man justifying his taxes. 'You wish to see your friend. I can see it.' He held out his hand. 'I will help you to him.'

Devlin took the hand, and two men who had fought and clashed hours before linked arms and inched from the cabin to the deck below. Peter Sam returned, his bowl of stew covered with a muslin cloth. He watched Trouin half carry Devlin down the companion stair, cradling him with every painful step. He put the bowl on the table and followed faithfully.

It was an hour or so before dawn. Half the ship lay asleep. A blue crack between the sea and the sky heralded the sun, heralded the end of the pirates' last day of freedom. After seeing Dandon alive and sleeping Trouin walked Devlin to the expanse between the shrouds along the gangway, away from any curious ears of those stationed over the companions fore and aft.

The September night's dew on the tarred ropes and wood gave their world a sheen that it rarely possessed. A silver edge, crisp and new, unnatural as a dream. The pirate thought that at any minute he would be woken by Dog-Leg with a cup of pea-berry coffee and be back in the warmth of the Caribbean. Wished it so.

'You will die if I bring you into Brest.' Trouin snapped Devlin from his slumber. Devlin was unfocused; his wound needed rest and willed him to lie down. He leant on the gunwale barely listening to Trouin and looked only at the dawn.

'If you make it to Paris you will be broken on the wheel.' The pirate showed no concern. Trouin shivered at the morning. He came closer. 'Pirate? If you had the diamond in your grasp, why did you not sail off and damn them all? Why risk any of this? You do not seem to be afraid of any of us in this world.'

Trouin thought he had seen a prodigal grin slant across the lowered face, but the light was dim and it might have only been the pain.

Devlin thought of Valentim Mendes, the governor of the Verdes whose ship he had stolen, whose hand he had exploded from his body, who had died beside him when they stood together – the guilt still unassuaged, a guilt that did not belong in a pirate's slender conscience.

'Maybe I wanted to do something right. Maybe I wanted to fail.' He looked at the commodore. 'I believed you would kill me. And from you that would have been a grand death. I never thought in my life I would have traded words with a man such as you. And now I feel no gratitude in being alive.'

Around them the dark receded, little by little the mile around the *Shadow* again showed the pool of ships around them, Trouin's two at their stern. Devlin lay anchored between failure and success. A day away from England. He had almost made it.

Trouin took a deep breath, held it, tasting the sea as other men might savour the perfume of their infant's hair.

'I have made a decision, pirate. It is not the right decision, but it will do. If you want we could make an agreement like the peasants that they regard us as. For we are not gentlemen as they measure them.'

Devlin straightened. 'Go on.'

'Our countries do not need diamonds to save them. They need their people. My final glory should not be the tale of how my men shot my foe in the back to save my skin from a duel *I* had granted. Nor that I killed unarmed men who had given their acquiescence and parole. And have ungrateful lieutenants pleasure themselves on the consequences.'

'Agreed.'

'I cannot find peace with such an end. Nor can I give a false king satisfaction who has made it his ambition to bring down my own countrymen with contrived conspiracies. He has executed many Bretons to keep his nobles and his own back safe from questioning. In wronging you I have wronged myself and yet there is not one man in my command who would understand this.'

'*I* understand.' Devlin's heart beat hard. 'Suppose I offer that none will profit from this diamond? My word on the bodies of my dead.'

'You could hurt them?'

'I could take the diamond from them. They only hurt in their purses.'

'And how do I know that you will keep your word? I could take this diamond myself, throw it to the sea, that would end them all just as surely.'

'Aye, but where would be the glory in that? Better to see their faces through me. I'll send it back to the earth in front of them. When it falls even Philippe will hear the crash of it. I promise you that.' He watched the sun flash its first light over the horizon. 'And I promise you I will see it in their eyes. And you will hear it fall.'

Trouin watched the rising sun along with him. 'I should like to hear that sound.' He laid a finger to the pirate's chest. 'But we will agree many things first if I am to give you back your ship.'

Devlin took Trouin's arm, too pained to stand on his own. 'You were to show me Albany's sword.'

Two of his officers watched their commodore hobble the pirate along the gangway and exchanged a look. They would need orders soon but needed first to decide who should stay and breakfast on the pirate's offal and who should row back to their own hams and coops. Their commodore obviously had chosen the biscuits and rancid gravy of his youth.

Chapter Thirty

✖

Albany was tied to the others below. He had slept awkwardly and now shifted awake to find that his situation had not improved. Their guards rested against their muskets or sat on barrels and grumbled back and forth about how they would be the last to eat.

The morning light came through the main hatch and already the heat began to ferment. Albany's haunches were asleep and he shuffled against the pirate body beside him. Dan Teague elbowed him off.

Albany elbowed back. Dan's patience was at an end. He had seen Hugh Harris and Peter Sam ascend and itched to be with them. He could smell the powder from the magazine's hemp curtain, knew that only feet away were pistols and steel. He could taste it, and these men that dared to lord it over him were already dead. Dead for what they had done to Bill. His cold thoughts were turned aside by Albany still wriggling.

'Will you stop, ponce!'

'I cannot! My arse is numb from a night of this. I shall be grateful when we move off for a properly appointed gaol!'

Dan noticed then that the ship had not yet begun to stir. They were still anchored and that was for the good. For days he had been tied with his brothers. They had been led to the head in groups of six, fed in groups of six, and had quickly surmised that their guards had little grasp of English let alone the almost gypsy language that the pirates shared.

A plan of sorts had been made and been made easier once the guards believed that the men had accepted their fate. The soldiers had checked their bonds less often as one day tumbled dully into another and their charges only yelled for food and drink and cursed their mothers more mildly than before.

Dan Teague and the others had only to wait, to bide time until their clever captain and Peter Sam returned. And now that had happened, and Hugh Harris when he had come back aboard had sidled close to his mate Dan Teague and slipped a gully into his shirt.

Dan showed his yellow teeth to one of the moustached guards who returned the grin before remembering his duty and put on his sullen look again. But both of them started as the crack of a gun echoed over the ship and the guards jumped and snapped at their muskets.

'Oh, and what is this now?' howled Albany.

'About *fucking* time!' Dan threw his loosened bonds free along with six of the others and went for his knife. 'I'm dying for a piss!'

'Back!' Devlin loosed a pistol shot over the heads of the white-coats who had leapt forward as he blazed from the cabin. He held Albany's sword tight across Trouin's throat. He dropped the smoking pistol and before it hit the deck his own left-locked brute replaced it. 'Back, or I'll slit his throat and shoot you for looking!'

Peter Sam and Hugh Harris were at the foremast. They needed no word. They cracked the noses of the nearest marines and covered the rest with their snatched muskets before anyone could move and even before the bodies had fallen. This was their trade, the thing they did well, and the marines had heard enough bloodstained stories to look aft for more responsible men.

Trouin's officers cocked pistols and dragged out rapiers, and Trouin saw in their wide eyes that they had decided that the pirate's desperation would be short-lived. There were only three of them left aboard now. He had advised Devlin as they conspired in the cabin that the others would leave to breakfast with their own men, so that now would be the time to take the ship.

Trouin relieved them of their oaths. 'Leave him be! He will kill me and his men will kill you!' They followed his eye-line to Peter Sam and Hugh, their muskets trained across the deck.

Devlin had told Trouin that they would act so but even he did not expect the shouts of a fight coming up from below until the aft companion hatch flew up and Dan Teague appeared with someone else's blood on him. But he had promised Trouin no blood and he needed to gain control fast – Hugh and Dan would need to be muzzled.

'To me, Peter Sam!' he called, knowing the others would follow their quartermaster. Devlin edged along the gangway, keeping Trouin's body facing the white coats. The marines' control was vanishing fast as the other pirates came after Dan up the ladder. They had opened the weapon lockers and had their braces of pistols tucked about them or back around their necks on slings and found two men each to push to their knees and freed them of the terrible duty that their muskets gave them. It had taken less than a minute to change their world.

From *La Françoise*, Trouin's sister ship, Captain Cassard patted away the traces of his fish sauce from the corners of his mouth and thought carefully on the word just given that boats were coming across from the pirate ship. The man standing in his cabin door waited for a more appropriate reaction other than Cassard's re-examination of his breakfast plate.

'Is the commodore with them?' he asked at last.

'No, Captain.'

'Then perhaps it is an escort for me. I am ordered back.' He stood and took up his hat reluctantly. 'My abeyance is ended.'

He came out of the cabin to where his valet held out his coat. He shook it on, plucked his shirt cuffs free from the sleeves and squinted at the pair of boats slapping urgently through the water. He would castigate them for not maintaining a proper order.

'*Captain!*' The marine who had interrupted Cassard's breakfast waved his arm toward the pirate ship. 'She is underway!'

'About time,' Cassard sniffed, buttoning up half of his plate buttons. There were pirates aloft readying to drop sail. Supper in Brest he consoled himself. He ordered for similar action to be taken and stepped to the entry port to receive his men.

The men in the boats shouted now as they closed under the shade of the ship, some dropping oars to gesture frantically back to the pirate vessel. Only then did Cassard notice the absence of muskets that usually pointed skyward from those not rowing. That was certainly odd and out of sorts, but these had been strange days; nevertheless he called for his officers to attend.

He looked over the noisy boats to the ship beyond. The main and forecourse shimmied free. Could he hear the capstan from here? Not over the pleading of the boats below, every other word a confusing scrap of cursing and terror from excited peasants – but his breakfast shifted upwards as he saw the flash of an axe cut the pirate's cable free and the hawser fall into the sea with a crash of white water.

And then the *Shadow* began to move, moved like a waking giant, and her gun ports heaved open and the black eyes stared along their freeboard and Cassard felt the touch of his father's ghost on the back of his neck.

He did not watch the gallants fall or see the jibs run out, he was too busy yelling for stations, for powder and shot. Cassard prayed that *La Patiente* far off their stern quarter had also seen what had just occurred.

The marines clambered aboard. A salute. A piece of paper thrust into Cassard's hand. He read once, twice, the concise and calm hand of René Duguay-Trouin, and then his own hands began to tremble and the paper to rip within his white grip.

Chapter Thirty-One

C assard.

The pirate has taken back his ship. I and the remainder of officers to be held against reprisal from La Françoise *and* La Patiente. *We are to be set free at the first fetter for Godwin sands. The captain and men from the captured tartane have returned to their ship and I order to escort them into Brest and report. We are unharmed.*

I order to refrain from chase that will instigate our execution. I have given my word that you will obey. I will take any other action as mutiny.

Report to Brest then take us up tomorrow and know that I take the pirate captain's word of honour as strongly as I measure my own. Do not allow me the occasion to measure it against yours, Cassard.

Duguay Trouin. Chef d'Escardre Marine Royale. September 2nd, 1720.

Trouin looked up from the deck of the tartane to the frigate birds that had swung off the departing *Shadow* and now preened themselves on his spars; their allegiance only to comfort, a trait shared with the peacocks of the new France that he did not fully understand.

And so Trouin had agreed with the pirate that he and his

officers would descend to the tartane, and that there would be no rescue from the treacherous, shifting Godwin sands for the pirate was not sailing to the Kent coast.

Trouin would sail into Brest with the Breton fishermen and not have any wrong word presumptuously set against him. Meanwhile, the pirate would head north to Falmouth for his rendezvous. Any hunt east would miss him. The diamond was on the way to its destination and fate.

They had parted on a brief accord.

'You will not fire on my men,' Trouin had insisted before climbing down to the tartane. 'And especially you will never return to my waters as long as you live.' He held the pirate's eyes with his own. 'I will kill you if I hear of you again on my sea.'

Devlin steadied the man's arm as he descended. 'I would deserve it.'

Trouin held onto the forearm and Devlin felt the vice of thirty years of battle. 'You promise that you will break them? That I will hear the sound?'

Devlin lowered him down. 'With my last breath, Milord.'

Trouin watched the *Shadow* shrink into the sun. Behind him the sailors of the tartane had already begun to return to their normal routine, the ship getting underway. Soon Cassard would be able to discern him and his men amongst them. *La Françoise* was already beginning to swing and come about.

If a pirate captain kept his word perhaps some of the worst of the nobles that had extracted the marrow of his country would feel the diamond cut them. Perhaps men would put faith in their own country again and not the whims of a golden handful.

When countries fall, the rich run but the poor must stay where they are, stay and make do. When the rich fall? He could only imagine and smile at the thought of the terror in their hearts.

'If I have committed a crime, a treachery, it is not at the loss of my countrymen or my honour. *That* I have regained.' The thought carried him down to the shoulders of his men. The boldest of them cleared his throat and removed his hat. Trouin nodded for him to speak.

'We are to rejoin *La Françoise*, Commodore? Give chase again?'

Trouin waved a glove to the sailors of the tartane.

'You see these men? The pirates harmed none of them. Each of them has a story to tell that will buy them wine for the rest of their days. We killed men who had surrendered.'

'But our honour?' he protested. 'Our duty to France?'

Trouin patted the strong shoulder fondly. 'Do you know Despreaux, young man? He says honour is like an island, rugged and without shores. Once we have left it, we can never return.'

It was Dandon's turn to wake in the night and find a consort by his side.

'How you doing?' Devlin asked.

Dandon rolled his head to the voice. 'I am alive?'

'You may wish not to be. When you can stand we'll take you to the cabin.'

Dandon tried to rise but the table seemed to pull him back. 'Perhaps a small drink would encourage, Captain?'

Devlin shook his head. 'No drink tonight. In honour of Bill.' The body of their sailing master lay beyond the curtain, wrapped in the tarpaulin and bound with the cordage that he had looked after half his life. Tomorrow he would be back to the sea.

'Just a huckleberry's worth, Captain? Some laudanum

then?' He winced and pleaded. 'Babes in arms take laudanum, I entreat you, Patrick!'

Devlin stood. 'You are better than I thought. You will take broth.'

'Broth? You are endeavouring to murder me!'

Dandon noticed then the swing of the lamp, the rattling of bottles. 'We are moving?' His sallow face fell with realisation of what that meant. 'Perhaps I would be better to remain dead.'

'We are free.'

Dandon coughed, his stitches forgotten, and lifted himself up. 'In truth?'

'Trouin found himself again. He remembered what he once was.'

Dandon sighed himself back down again. 'I do not know what you mean but am soothed to hear it.' Then his voice lowered as if talking only to himself. 'I had a dream, Patrick. You were in Newgate gaol again. I was in desperate want of a silver key to free you for you had grown too big for your cell. This caused you great . . . pain.'

Devlin turned to leave, pulled the curtain aside and looked at the crowd around Bill's wrapped body. 'The body sweats bad dreams when it's dying. Pay it no mind.'

'I shan't now I know we are free and slept through the danger and making of it. Your wound fares well, my swollen liver will not let me die, and we are back to the Caribbee.'

'No. To England. We have the diamond still. A date to keep. I'll get your broth.' He closed the curtain. Dandon was suddenly afflicted with more than pain.

'*England*!' he hissed. 'Bloody England? How many times shall I die for a drink!' He called to the lank curtain hoping his captain could still hear. 'At least I can pick up the damn new coat I have paid for!'

Chapter Thirty-Two

✗

If ever there was a nation that had been twenty-three
years ruining itself and recovered in a moment
This is the time.
If ever a government paid its debts without money and
exchanged all the cash in the kingdom for bits of paper
which had neither any body to pay them for or any
intrinsic fund to pay themselves
This is the time.
If ever a credit was raised without a foundation and
built up to a height that not only was likely to fall but
indeed was impossible to stand
This is the time.

From 'The Original Journal'. Author unknown.
Dec 1719.

L ondon is a turbulent city both in noise and humour. Apart from the general populace, who seem to intermingle amiably enough, with silk and sackcloth brushing shoulders, there are the hawkers, the costers and tradesmen on the streets competing alongside the shopkeepers – competing with everything from sticks of lashed rabbits to 'marking stones' of red and black chalk for householders to mark their linen against thieves. Then there are the chairmen with their sedans dodging the wooden- and iron-wheeled carriages clattering along the granite setts and flat cobbles, forcing the new visitor to stand stock still until his sense returns after being knocked by the din. Meanwhile, the observant pickpocket takes advantage of the dumbstruck statue and the commotion all around.

None of this cacophony, however, could compete with the urgency and lustiness that emanated from Jonathan's and the other dozen coffee houses and taverns that cramped Change Alley. Here the stock-jobbers met and teased out purses by more discrete means, and all within pleasing earshot of the Bank in Walbrook, South Sea House in Threadneedle and the East India offices in Leadenhall.

Walpole had been in Garraway's until two, observing and lunching before taking a cab at Cornhill to his appointment with the prince at Leicester House. It was now Friday, September sixth. The midsummer madness had seen subscribers to the Company rise to over fourteen million, each one confident in the promise of a dividend come the end of the year. At the opening of their books in August the Company had declared its stock at over eight-hundred percent of its original value and so released yet more stock to meet the demand – backed by the Bank of England, naturally.

But those who knew that the ships were empty, who knew that America would sink beneath the waves if she carried the load expected of her, had sent a pirate on a task and that was now almost overdue. Already Walpole had noted that the stock had fallen over two hundred percent in the time since Devlin's departure.

September eighth almost upon them. A Sunday. The prince would need to be reassured that all was still well. At least conspiracy had been easier with the king's extended absence in Hanover, and Walpole smiled at the thought that he had at least one good word for the prince.

'So where is he, Walpole?' The prince stared out from his window over the throng in the square below. He was not formally dressed and anyone who was able to look up and discern him through the leaden windows would see a dishev-elled man in a torn purple banyan and cap, with two days' growth of beard, sinking wine and smoking like a poet.

Walpole sat in the same chair as he had in January, when the plan had been formed and when the pirate's name had been first spoken – when it was clear that the company that had existed for barely a decade had careered out of control.

'He is not late, Your Highness. My man in Falmouth will be expected by the end of the day. With or without him.'

The prince turned. 'Without him?'

'It was always more probable that he would fail. The conse-quence is what we should talk of now. I would expect to hear from Law as to our success or otherwise and I have heard no rumours of a calamity in Paris. But, as Sunday will fall before, I have arranged for what shall occur.'

'Occur? *Occur?*' The prince filled his glass. 'Bankruptcy is what shall occur, so!'

Walpole nodded. 'We should take the attitudes of the Danes and Dutch who say that bankruptcy has no shame but is a necessity to good business.'

'It will be a shame to me!'

'Quite. Although I hope Your Highness will remember that it was I who divested him of his shares and his own director-ship of the Welch company's bubble which is now set to burst. The king, however, still remains as appointed head of the South Sea. Your Highness's own involvement has been absent for five years. No-one will remember that you were its honorary governor. But they will remember the patronage of the one who was when it fell.'

The prince cocked his head, his voice intrigued. 'Explain, so?'

Walpole stretched, a beef luncheon beginning to sit heavily on him. 'Your father agreed to accept the Company's offer to take up the national debt, well aware that this would absolve his own debt along with it. As governor of the Company for the last two years it may be suggested that he may have had some culpability in that agreement.'

'Did not your ministers also accept interests in the assurance of that act?'

Walpole snorted past the accusations. 'They were not *my* ministers. They were Tories lining their coats like gypsies!'

The prince grinned as he poured more wine and Walpole, declining a glass continued. 'My thoughts are that the king's popularity will not benefit greatly if we are forced to drag him back from his beloved homeland to account for the actions leading to the ruination of his people.' He shifted in his seat. 'Whereas His Highness's ascension will only flourish.'

The prince held his glass still, halfway to his lips. 'And the pirate? If he brings us the diamond?'

'That is all to the good. I have an affirmation that, once cut, over one hundred further pieces can be made worth ten-thousand apiece; and worth more once the diamond price rises when it is known that these diamonds are an asset of the South Sea and more set to come.'

'More?'

'We will attest that the diamonds are a product of the colonies, a sample even, a taste of promise.'

'A lie?'

'A canard. And I have recruited several ministers, from both sides, to attend the assembly on the eighth to wax lyrical about the success of the directors in their management.'

'And why would they offer such praise?'

'Enough of them would not wish it to be annotated, if the Company collapses, how much stock they have accepted in the past in order to ensure that the Company's petitions were granted.'

The prince's command of English did not stretch to the expression of sarcasm and Walpole missed the innuendo as he saluted with his glass. 'Then all will be right with the world.'

A scream from the square below brought them both to the window. A Germanic curse escaped the prince's lips as he spilt his wine down his front, but he soon forgot his annoyance as they squeezed together at the window to watch as a black coach bowled rattling over the cobblestones towards the house from the top of the square.

People dove aside at the thunder and roar of the horses and wheels, honest carriages pulling up sharply as the runaway tore along the side of the avenue.

'The man's mad!' the prince laughed. The coachman, cloaked in black, whipped his path through the crowds, pulling back the snorting white-eyed horses only as he came to the wall of the house. It was then that the prince and Walpole noticed the kerchief hiding his face but not his distinctive bald dome of a head.

The two soldiers at the gates ducked back from the hooves and the homicidal wheels, then remembered their muskets and raised them to their shoulders. The coach did not halt, slowed only enough for a door to fly open and two bodies to hit the road at the soldiers' feet, booted out by an unseen occupant.

With the crack of whip and a bellow from the masked

driver the coach ripped away, almost keeling over as it took the corner in a grating whine, the sentries finally shooting uselessly through thick dust into its disappearing back. From the floor above, the watchers saw past the dust to the black and white cloth nailed to the rear.

Walpole gripped the prince's wrist at the sight of the grinning skull with two pistols crossed beneath, set in a compass rose, laughing its way out of the square.

'What the devil?' the prince exclaimed.

'The devil is right,' Walpole studied the bound men below, thankfully alive. 'And that apparition, Your Highness, was my coach from Falmouth.'

There would be nothing to fear, no sweat to bead on a banker's brow, if the South Seas investment had been, pound for pound, coin for its paper's worth. But in order for the stock to be made available for all, the Company had granted concessions and changed the rules of purchase. Firstly, and simply enough, women were allowed to buy stock. This single amendment changed the Company's fortunes almost overnight, for the natural secrecy of women and the gambling tendencies of their husbands ensured that the Company now received income from both sides of the household. Secondly – the thread which spun the fate that the country now hung by – were the unheard-of terms that the Company offered.

For the first time the government and the Bank of England sanctioned a private company to extend credit to the purchase of shares. Just a ten-percent deposit could secure a hundred pounds' worth of South Sea stock, and the phrase 'nothing to pay for the first year' entered the public consciousness.

Public credit grew to an unparalleled summit as even the East India Company, whose worth certainly at least existed in material things, followed suit. Credit became a byword for wealth instead of debt and a man's balance sheet was set to be worth only the amount of credit he could muster, regardless of the weight of coin in his pockets. And if the Company failed? A company that owned the national debt, a company guaranteed by government act and the Bank of England? The corrupt triumvirate of council, finance and business would forever be linked in the public mind, and the palace of Westminster regarded as no more than a gentlemen's gambling den. Where could the people's faith lie if the gentry with all their education and experience had failed them?

But it would not fail. The coach was a sign, a bold one, bold as the red sash the pirate wore, and as dramatic as the final act of one of Charles Johnson's melodramas.

And it meant the diamond was in London. Somewhere.

Excusing himself from the prince, Walpole ran to the gate of the house, dragging footmen with him to escort his men inside. Already a crowd had gathered to see the bound and gagged men flapping and wide-eyed as landed trout. He yelled for the soldiers to shut the gate and bid the footmen carry them to the servants' side of the house.

Descending to the scullery, Walpole ordered the bound men to be carried to chairs and then pushed the footmen from the room, wiping the sweat from his face at the uncommon exertion. He waited for his pulse to return to normal and looked between the struggling forms of the coachman and his man, Dashwood, whom he had set to wait for the pirate at the inn in Falmouth.

Walpole's chest rose and fell, and he felt a strong temptation to leave the men gagged, dreading what might spill out of their mouths. The men squirmed and complained through their linen gags and when Walpole went for perhaps too large a knife to cut their bonds they squealed louder. Walpole marvelled at the insanity of him cutting men free; his wildest dreams had never envisaged stranger. He felt his dignity to be no more elevated than the scullery he stood in.

Once free and gasping, both men begged for a drink. Walpole was only able to find some warm milk, which they drank joyfully. He took a chair opposite and waited for them to calm down. The crock jug slammed to the table. Then Dashwood took a deep breath and rubbed his wrists.

Dashwood was a scrivener, a trusted clerk who carried sealing wax in his pockets and whose hands were ingrained with blue ink. He had enjoyed the pleasure of the sea air and the hospitality of the inn at his master's expense but he had not expected bruises and terror from the pirates as reward for his service.

His eyes were red and his cheeks flushed in the aftermath of tears.

The other man was a hired coachman and not of Walpole's staff. He was rougher, with a bony face and hunched shoulders. His face showed the harder marks of defiance but less shame. He sat as if waiting for recompense, where Dashwood waited for sympathy.

'Now,' Walpole kept his tone gentle, with the same brevity as when asking a new maid where his silver spoons had gone. 'What do you have to tell me, Dashwood?'

The coachman opened his mouth, Walpole raised his hand to silence him. 'I will hear Dashwood.'

Dashwood exhaled, brought out a fold of paper from his coat and slapped it down on Walpole's side of the table. 'That is for you, Your Honour. From him.'

Walpole took the paper but did not read it. 'What happened?' he asked.

Dashwood shrivelled. He was twenty-four and engaged, had slept with one woman in his life, had fought with his father over his choice of trade, come to London from Lincoln and found the patronage of great men. He had three men working under him and had his eye on a small-holding in Hertfordshire. But he had almost forgotten his own name when the pirate had woken him with a pistol to his face. He began to cry again now and Walpole sighed and turned to the coachman instead.

Now came a tale by a man used to the games of hard men.

Night had brought the pirates in. Dashwood was dragged from his bed and a gold coin thrown to the landlord. A big bald bastard with a hand-cannon to match had punched the coachman from his slumber in the stable. They rode through the night, the big man at the reins, the Irish one and another keeping Dashwood and himself bound to the floor of the coach, iron at their heads. The other, the one not Irish, the one not calm, had scars on his face and blood on his grinning teeth, his hair matted with filth, his swivelling eye moving hungrily from knife, to pistol, to both of them on the floor of the carriage. The Irish one sat back in the corner, catching sleep or looking out of the window like he was to the theatre.

'The mad one sang of ghosts. Told us the colour of rich men's livers. Whistled a tune of his own. Begged us to go for him when his captain slept.'

Dashwood found his voice. 'He cut a button from both our coats! He swallowed them and laughed!' His head sank in misery. 'He licked my face! Said he would cut my lips off if I pissed myself!'

'But he didn't though, did he?' the coachman sneered.

Walpole thanked them both and peeled open the folded letter. His surprise at the quality of the hand was soon lost in the measure of the words and each line punctuated by Dashwood's sobs from across the table.

Walpole rose with a scrape of his chair across the stone floor. 'Stop your blubbering, Dashwood. Be thankful you are alive.' He tossed some gold to the coachman who slammed his hand upon it as soon as it fell. '*You* may go. I thank you for your discretion in this matter. And if you give me cause to not thank you, know that I am aware of where I may find you, sir.'

He left through the kitchen to the servants' stair and barked orders for food to be taken to the two before he climbed upstairs to show the letter to the prince. A long, dark night lay ahead for London, of that he was certain.

Chapter Thirty-Three

W.

I have the stone. I have lost men because of it, the cost of which you cannot count. But I shall measure it and for more than we have bargained. I do not trust to come to the house and I am sure Newgate has not forgotten me.

I will take your amnesty and your coin but the manner of its getting will be mine.

I will be on the river east of the bridge, two o'clock on the night you receive this. I keep your man Albany as surety. You can have the diamond and your man. Do not look for me. I will find you.

Bring who you may, any gun you feel, but you especially will be there. I will put the diamond only into your hand.

D.

'He is insane!' The prince let the letter fall to his desk. 'His Majesty's first minister meeting a pirate on the Thames? The arrogance of the man! It is inconceivable, Walpole.' But still Walpole could see the amusement on the prince's face.

Walpole needed a seat and took one without invitation. And rarely for him, he needed a drink, yet for the first time in their acquaintance he found the prince's rooms dry.

'Surprising he has allowed that I may have the company of arms. And I shall take that offer.'

The prince puffed his chest. 'I will come, should he dare anything else.'

Walpole forgot his dry mouth and shifted forward in his chair. 'His Highness will not be there. *That* I must insist on.' The prince put his fists to his hips and glared at him.

'That is to say it is my council that His Highness's presence would cause undue danger to his own personage. His Highness's kingdom will have need for him to be unharmed and unsullied by soiling his hands in such a manner. His Highness has already been too generous in his patronage in this matter.'

But the prince had adventure in his eye and Walpole swallowed a sigh, for the prince's mind was made up.

'Nonsense. I am sure the pirate was fond. He will have no wish to harm me. We are both men of action. We hire a wherry do we not?'

Walpole pushed himself from the seat wearily. 'I will see to the arrangements. I have my own vessel. We can but accept. We have no means of contacting Devlin to suggest otherwise.' He pinched his nose and reached for his hat. 'Besides, we need the gem.' Then solemnly, he added, 'And perhaps the river is just the place to lose a body.' He did not pause for the prince to interject. 'I will supply a keen guard, but I beg Your Highness to arm himself.' He bowed and began to back from the room, showing the prince the top of his head as he padded backwards.

'You expect danger?'

Walpole lifted his head at the door. 'I expect nothing else. He says he will measure the cost for more than we have bargained but he fails to allude to the price. He also talks of Albany, yet he was not in the coach with them according to my man whose story I have just heard. That concerns me. I suggest His Highness get some rest. I will return after midnight.'

He left the prince to deliberate on his parting words and pulled out his watch in order to avoid the eye of Secretary Timms in the corridor. Timms would know everything soon enough and Walpole had only hours to inform Townshend and Stanhope that tomorrow they may need a new paymaster general. The heaviness of his hand upon the balustrade as he descended the stairway was greater than he realised.

'Ho, Edwin! Remember me?' Edwin Tinkerman, he of the red Doggett coat, fastest wherryman on the Thames, looked up to the top of the steps and the man in the black coat beaming down at him. Edwin's passenger also looked – but only once and then looked away, for the Irish-sounding fellow looked like he hung around the wharf taverns too much and had a worn cutlass to prove it. Edwin landed, and also avoided the second look, mainly due to the sound instinct that if a fellow asked if you remembered him the next moment would reveal a bill or knife in his hand.

He doffed his velvet cap to his passenger and took the fare hurriedly pushed into his hand. The gentleman dashed up the stairs, his hat lowered as he fled past the tall stranger.

The man stepped down. 'I remember your red coat, my lad. Do you recall my shilling?' It was almost dusk now, September dusk, the end of summer and the granite setts were already damp and slippery. The fog of peat and sea-coal fires smudged the gabled roofs of the Surrey side of London and people had begun already to pull their shawls and scarves tighter around them.

'I've come for my change,' he said, but he smiled all the same and Edwin looked down at the brown bucket-top boots that were older than both of them.

'Aye, Cap'n!' he said. 'Let you off at Execution didn't I? Leicester House, Cap'n, Monday last!'

Was it only then? Twelve days? It had been warm. The weather was changing as swiftly as events. Men dead, good men. Dandon still unable to stand and Devlin's own biting injury slowing his every move, a taut pain forcing a limp to not stretch it further.

Edwin saw the face distracted and pained; he hoped the remark about the shilling was as jocose as it sounded. 'Are you all well, Cap'n?'

And then the pain and the thoughts were gone. 'I want your boat, Edwin. I want you and your boat. One hour but a long one. What say you?'

Edwin could see in the face that his options would be slight if any, so he blustered like any Londoner. 'I don't know, Cap'n. I could make a lot of money in an hour.'

'Can you make gold?' And Devlin showed him the face of King Louis and paid it into his hand.

Edwin closed his fist around two months' wages. 'Well,' he pulled down the peak of his cap, for this was secrecy. 'If you put it like that, Cap'n . . .'

Albany Holmes was not tied, nor deprived of the sword he so treasured. He was free to move around the upstairs room of the Plough, the inn that had favoured the pirate's gold, the landlord swallowing his fear of refusal by bolstering his pride with coin. Besides, there was no need to restrain Albany when Hugh Harris and his twin turnover pistols guarded him: restraining Albany would have been a folly akin to tying up chickens to protect the foxes.

Albany paraded around the room, and had already rubbed clean a circle of the bottle glass window to look out on the street below. Occasionally he swung a hateful glance at Hugh who only grinned back with a pistol crooked in his arm, swinging his leg like an imbecile to a tune whistling inside his head, counting the holes he would place in Albany if he moved wrong but once, planning to tell Devlin that he moved wrong twice. Still, Hugh was set aback and stopped his swinging leg when Albany ceased his pacing and looked warmly at him.

'Hugh is it not?' Albany asked. He had spent almost the last fortnight with the pirate, close enough to smell him on the tartane to Paris, and had even sailed from Madagascar with the rogue during their last encounter. The name was still a guess, however.

'Aye.' It was the first word Hugh had ever spoken to the long-coat, who was a fop once again now he had returned to his London clothes.

'You know I am a man of means? That has not escaped you?'

Hugh had about two thousand pounds to his own account but did not own a horse or a Buckinghamshire estate, so nodded accordingly.

Albany took a step closer, mindful of the sheen of sweat on the brute's face as being either nervousness or a dry liver.

'We could both leave this place,' he held out his arms, both to remove them from his sword and to highlight the damp, shoddy room. 'I have a patron in George Lee. Soon to be *Sir* George Lee. We are both founding members of the Hellfire Club here in London at the Greyhound inn. There are many pleasures we could indoctrinate you in that you have only dreamt of. We could make Oxford by tomorrow and George would reward you greatly for my freedom . . . as would I.' He took another step. 'It is only one door we have to walk through.'

Hugh leant forward, rubbing his chin, and Albany relaxed and raised his own chin for Hugh's word.

Hugh spoke slowly and clearly. 'You do know that I would

take pleasure in shooting you in the face? We are accorded on this? I would count it as supper – you understand?'

Albany grumbled something and went back to pacing at the window. He watched the lamp-lighters at their work.

There came a knock at the door, softly, more to not startle Hugh than ask for entrance. Devlin and Peter Sam walked in. They had abandoned the coach in Southwark after finding Edwin and watched human vultures instantly strip it to a carcass. He pitied the horses for their fate as cackling widows dragged them away; he at least hoped that some children might get some meat, or that the sale of the leather bridles would help someone walk and talk for another week. Even the velvet seats seemed to have a price as a fight ensued over their ownership. The pirates walked away as the teeth and nails of women bit and scraped, and aproned men went about the wheels with care and skilled hammers and nodded to the two for their gift.

Peter Sam held their flag in his arms, bundled like a newborn, and they turned their backs; the Caribbean seemed civilised in comparison but they the last to judge. The coach was just a point scored against Walpole, a possession credited on the pirates' side to the loss of Black Bill. Hurt rich men in their purse. Eight hundred pounds' worth of coach. Bill's body sent to the sea yesterday. Weigh that if you can.

'Albany,' Devlin stated the name. 'You are with me tonight.' He took his pistol off his belt. A time ago he had adapted a hanger to its stock as he had seen gentlemen carry pistols. It made for more comfortable wear but could jump if you moved fast. Devlin lately was not moving so fast as to worry about it.

He checked the load and made sure that Albany saw its bore and its master's confidence. 'I'll take one of your Dolep's as well, Hugh.' He held out his hand and Hugh slapped the weapon in his fist without question. The Dolep pistol, two barrels, under and over. Three shots for Devlin that his bad back would not slow. As he was he could not rely on his cutlass: every strike would be agony.

'And what, pray, are we to do?' Albany scoffed. 'The opera? A bagnio house? Find some arse over quim for your ape?'

The floor shook as Peter Sam exploded from the door; he grabbed a chair and Albany went for his sword.

Albany was not fast enough and Peter nailed him to the plaster with the chair legs and dust flew from the walls with the impact. Albany, winded and pinned, struggled then grinned as Devlin dragged the bald man back.

He still had worth, obviously; the pirate had need of him. He smiled more broadly as Peter Sam crushed the chair in his hands like kindling and stormed from the room.

Albany brushed down his coat. 'Hah! I think he has a fancy for me! He protests too much!'

Devlin dismissed Hugh to calm Peter Sam. He shook his head at Albany and went for the door.

Albany jeered at his back. 'I tire of you all! Bring me some supper and I'll forget the apology. But know that Walpole will hear all of this.'

Devlin's hand was on the doorknob as Albany went on: 'You are dismissed.'

The pirate checked that the corridor was empty, then Albany watched him close and lock the door, the key poking out of his fist as he turned and slowly crossed the room. Something like a grin was slashed across the pirate's face.

Chapter Thirty-Four

✗

Walpole did not wait for the sleepy servant to get up from his stool. He pushed open the double doors of the prince's chambers and framed himself dramatically in the doorway like a bloodied soldier announcing the death of a king.

Timms and the prince looked up unimpressed. Walpole was dressed like a clergyman after mass. Dull black coat and scarf, round hat, no imperious wig, the same half-gaiters since the afternoon. Walpole's reaction to what met his eyes was very different: he stared wide-eyed at the prince, who had apparently gone through his dressing-up box for his finest pirate gear. Or at least a prince's version of it.

Deerskin breeches and ruddy deerskin coat to match. A red silk sash that trailed to his calves and, discordantly, a black jockey's cap bouncing in his hands. Boots were clearly unsuitable for any evening so whale-skin buckled shoes and black stockings would suffice.

The prince slapped his thigh as he rested his foot on the window seat. 'We three are well met!' he cheered, as innocents do before they die.

Walpole walked in, found a glass this time and helped himself. 'We shall leave shortly, Your Highness.' He glanced at Timms in his funeral cloth. 'You will accompany, Timms?'

Timms was dry and coughed that he would. 'But no arms, Minister. I will observe only.'

Walpole snorted. 'We will all observe, I hope. I will carry no arms.'

The prince went to his desk. 'But I shall. As befits.'

He opened a maplewood box and stuffed about his sash two silver and ebony Acquafresca pistols: Italian genius with Parisian styling. They had been a gift from the Duke of Tuscany but never fired. Now they were at last being loaded, by candlelight, by a grinning prince.

'This will be a fine night! What is our plan, Walpole?'

Plan? Walpole thought. This was no plan, this was an aberration run up a mast for an idiot's salute.

'His Highness will appreciate that his safety is foremost in my mind. To that end I will take precautions. We will not be alone on the water.' He sank his wine, and secretary Timms felt braver at his words. 'We will meet the pirate on the river. We have our bag of gold,' he slapped the pocket of his coat and a soft jangle rang out. 'He has our diamond. If he has some notion to cheat us I will cut him down.'

The prince placed his cap rakishly over one brow. 'And once we have the gem? We let him go with our gold?'

Walpole walked back to the wine, poured just enough to steady his hand and dared to speak to the prince with his back still turned. 'That depends on how grateful he is for our allowing him to assist us.'

Timms cleared his throat. 'And what of Albany Holmes?'

Walpole's neck clicked as his head went back to swallow his glass whole. 'He would understand I'm sure,' he wiped his scarlet lips. 'And do not underestimate Albany Holmes, Mister Timms. The pirate and he have a history that I would dread wished upon even you. I chose him for that very reason. They will not part with the shaking of hands.'

The hoot of an owl drew all their pale faces to the night outside.

The prince slapped his thigh again. 'An owl in Leicester square! Bless my soul what an omen, no?'

Walpole spoke kindly to the Prince of Wales. 'A group of owls is called a parliament. That may be fitting.'

'Did not the Romans perceive owls as the warning of death?' Timms touched the nearest wood to him.

Walpole slammed down his glass. 'Depends if you read Latin or Greek, Mister Timms.'

The prince cocked his ear to the haunting sound as it bounced off the walls of the square again. His education was superior to both of theirs.

'*Deep night, dark night, the silent of the night. The time when screech-owls cry, and ban-dogs howl, and spirits walk and ghosts break up their graves.*'

Walpole sniffed and tightened his scarf about him. 'I have always found Shakespeare to be nonsense.' He noticed the letter of the pirate lying near the wine.

There should be no trace. Nooses could be fashioned from paper.

He snatched it up. Three steps and he had thrown it to the great fireplace; he poked it as the letter crackled.

'Come. His Highness will permit me to lead. We will meet the pirate.'

Timms blew out the lights in the room, and their footsteps echoed through the house as they descended the winding stairs in silence, the sconces on the walls casting dancing shadows before them until Walpole opened the door and the night snatched them away.

* * *

Devlin studied the diamond in his hand then closed his fist around its sparkle, still apparent even in the dark. He had heard only of the death concerning the diamond's origin, and did not believe in curses; but he knew nothing of the regent's loss of his beloved daughter. And then Bill had died and men had been wounded although compensated in silver for their pain, as was the pirate's way. And others – himself – scarred forever, still bleeding through their shirts. This night he would be rid of it. He buried the stone in his pocket, paid it no more mind.

He offered Albany a chew of his tobacco, affecting to forget that Albany's hands were tied, his mouth gagged. Then Devlin went back to his watch of the river.

They waited by the wet waterman stairs off Cherry Gardens on the Surrey side where there was no lamplight to cast a glow on them.

Devlin lounged against the slimy stair wall and sliced tobacco with his ebony-hilted dagger, its blade just as black. Once he had neglected to pack it about him and had been as lost as a carpenter without a nail, almost dying at the hands of Hib Gow in a garden in Charles Town two years before. Never again.

A noise drifted over the river, that of water screwing away from the sweep of a pole, the pleasant sound of London still at work, and out of place for Devlin's work to come.

He whistled low and the oar pushed again bringing the bow of Edwin's wherry into view; it bumped against the steps a second later. Devlin saw that Edwin had turned his red jacket inside out, as soldiers do when they desert and become 'turn-coats'. Wise man, he thought, but he was amused at Edwin's crude attempt at a mask made of sackcloth: two holes poked through a nose-bag, as if hiding a disfigured head. His wife had probably insisted on such now her husband was a man of means with a gold coin buried in a pat of butter. He made a ghoulish form emerging from out of the cold fog rising off the river. Perfect, Devlin thought. Good man. Walpole will shit when he sees us. I'm escorted by Charon himself across the River Styx.

He stowed his dagger at his back where it sat against his stitches and held out his arm to Albany, pulling him by his cuff down the steps.

'It's time, Albany,' he said, and they went to the boat. 'This is when you leave me.'

They entered the ethereal world of the Thames at night, with the stroke of the damp fog curling along the strakes of Edwin's wherry, the flip and gold-green sheen of scales as sturgeon hunted safely now that the fishermen had retired for the night. Birds drifted half-asleep on the water, one cautious eye open as the boat rolled by. The giant ships were anchored three or four abreast, chained together – the sound of the gaol as the chains bobbed with the tide, their lights winking at them as they passed. And the bridge.

Progress now: a false horizon of amber light and sea-coal smog, the sound of the water churning through the nineteen arches growing louder as they approached the Tower and Devlin leaning forward to pick out his quarry.

The streets and bustle of London were far away, the river unreal as a dream, the foul smell and its snickering tide raising every hair on Devlin's nape as he listened for company upon her surface.

Walpole eased open the front shutter of his lamp and at the bow fish splashed and leapt away. High tide; their man's oar sank deep as he rowed. They had joined the river at the Tower stairs, and at the sighting of the lamp two other punts began to move away from the walls of Traitor's Gate just ahead of them; but deliberately slower, as if wading through molasses, with the soldiers keeping low in the boats.

The prince checked his silver guns. No moon. Pity. The guns would have looked splendid in the moonlight. He tried to pierce the fog with his gaze but it danced and teased and only the cross-trees and sidelights of the dozens of sleeping ships arose clearly from it.

'Where is he, Walpole?' he hissed to the man straining himself over the bow. Walpole heard but said nothing. He thought of his bed, where he should be. This intrigue demeaned him but he had once been a prisoner of the Tower they now passed and he knew feuds and hate because of it. He would not be debased by a pirate. He would take the diamond, save the Company, raise a king and become the First Minister and the most powerful man in the kingdom, under the noses of those who had thought him beaten. He could forego a little damp for that reward.

Timms was the first to hear it, for the edge of his fear had sharpened his senses. He grabbed the ferryman's hand to still his oar as the sound of wood in the water plied closer.

Chapter Thirty-Five

*D*evlin unbound Albany and tossed away the moist rag that had stopped his mouth. 'You be a good boy, now.' Devlin patted his shoulder and Albany winced where the bruises Devlin had dealt him smarted beneath his silk.

Devlin had punched him with the key poking from his fist. It was with the aim to hurt, to weaken his arms and legs so if Albany suddenly became heroic he would first have to fight over that.

On the tartane, before Paris, he had spoken to Albany about life, about suffering, the waiting for the sword to fall. If lucky, it was only the small things. A small beating would count sure enough.

Albany did not give Devlin the pleasure of seeing him grateful for his freedom. He had his sword, for Devlin had no fear to keep it from him and was well aware that he would return his baggage as he found it.

He had his sword. A small thing, but one that would count sure enough. And the dagger within that the pirate did not know of.

'Do you see them?' Albany asked. He was at the stern. Edwin, in his mask and Devlin in his stillness, were leaning over the bow. Devlin did not reply – there was no need as the fog parted and the figures appeared, as if floating on top of it, Walpole's light spreading wide over the brume.

'No closer!' Devlin called and waved Edwin to stop. Edwin braked as if he had hit a wall and Devlin held fast as he lurched forward. 'Stay where you are!' he called to the boat ahead.

Walpole signalled for their man to halt and the boat bucked as the man with lesser skill grunted and struggled, the prince muttering a German curse as the cold filth of the water splashed his silver pistols.

They could see Devlin and Edwin now as the tide rocked them and belched against the wood and echoed back from the moored ships along the shore. Walpole could not hear the soldiers' boats and prayed that Devlin was denied the same. Engaging him in conversation might assure that continued.

'What now? I have come as requested!' He held up his lamp, stood clumsily, one hand to the gunwale. 'I have your money!' Surely the pirate's only concern.

'I have your man!' Devlin called back, his voice seeming to create a wave that rolled under their keel and heeled them back like a wind, their pilot battling against it.

Walpole swept his lamp to the voice and Timms gasped at the grotesque image of Edwin in his mask, the pirate beside him less fearsome. 'And the . . .' Walpole thought on his choice of words. '*Issue*? You have the conclusion?'

Devlin stood, held his hand over his eyes against Walpole's beam. 'I have what you need!' Something in the tone of his words was mocking but Walpole took it only as conceit. Another wave rolled beneath them, larger, and Walpole staggered, his lamp swaying madly, and the soldier's boats began to speed towards them.

Walpole gathered himself again, their man pushing them closer where they had lost ground. He opened another shutter on his lamp and Devlin glowed before him, a strange viridian smoke now mingling with the fog behind. Walpole was enchanted by the mystery of the river at night. Perhaps he was after all in his bed? But dreams are not cold.

'Shall I come closer? Pass our goods between us?' A friendly voice.

Devlin cupped his hand to his mouth. 'Can you see me?'

Another wave surged beneath them. The prince cursed and Timms gripped the gunwale for mercy. Walpole was sure now that he could hear the creak of the soldiers' boats, the rattle of their brass, the river distorting the sounds to appear all around, the creaking of wood and cordage getting closer and larger. Perhaps this was the way of the river, its nature to magnify sound; and so he called louder.

'I can see you.'

The prince appeared at Walpole's shoulder, his voice lower than Walpole had ever heard it, a lover's query.

'I can hear music ahead?'

Walpole dismissed the question, its utterance pointless – did the fool have no mind as to what was occurring?

'The river is banked with countless taverns, Your Highness,' he whispered kindly. 'The river is carrying the sound.'

'At this hour?' the prince looked about him. The fog was now impenetrable, but Walpole could feel some massive presence in the air in front of them, as if another bridge had suddenly sprung across the river ahead.

'No,' he said. 'They would be shut up, no?' He caught the whimsical music now. A fiddle in front of them and far away, behind the pirate.

The notes formed a question on the night like a blank tombstone, but his craning after the noise was broken by the pirate's shout.

'If you can see me that is good enough! Now see this!'

Devlin's hand rose above his head, Walpole's lantern-light

bounced off the unmistakeable diamond balanced on his fingers.

Walpole did not know what else to scream.

'*Devlin!*'

The pirate thrust an accusing fist at the horrified face. 'To hell with your schemes!'

For Bill, for Trouin, for Dandon.

For the blood.

He brought his arm back, the point of the diamond biting into his fist as he leaned to throw it over all their heads, but he froze at the scrape of a scabbard and Edwin's panicked warning from behind him.

'*Cap'n!*'

Devlin gripped the stone and turned. Albany's sword was coming on.

'You will *not*!' Albany whistled the blade. 'You will *not*!' Its point raised high. 'Give that to me, *dog*!'

Devlin planted his feet, ran the stone through his palm. He could toss it still, but they might find it if they saw it fall. He wanted to plant it deep. Deep where it hurt. High and far through the fog where mudlarks would dream of it forever as their lucky day.

He drew his antler-hilted hanger, but kept the diamond in his hand so there was no dagger poniard for his other fist. His pistols he thought of for the moment after he killed Albany, for there was no chance Walpole travelled alone. His kind even hunted foxes in packs and *they* had only teeth. He could pull his pistols now . . . but where would be the game, the punishment, in that?

'Come on then,' he called Albany on with his beckoning blade. 'Come on, *Eton*. Come on, *Oxford*.' He grinned him in. 'Let's see it.'

Albany stayed back just enough to unscrew the dagger

from his sword's hilt and pulled its black blade free, holy joy at the look on Devlin's face as realisation dawned.

Dandon.

Dandon on the *Shadow* trying to warn Devlin of the shot. Dandon stabbed. Peter Sam swearing that Albany's sword never moved. Albany challenging Trouin's marines over their guilt.

Albany circled both his blades. 'I got him good, didn't I?' He yelled to the boat. 'Walpole! I have him! But they—' His breath was cut dead as Devlin's hanger slammed down against the eighty-five guinea blade – his own rule to always go for flesh blinded by the need to destroy.

Go for meat. The regret of the dead to clash at swords.

Edwin moved quickly. Perhaps it was the boats with the chink of muskets coming out of the gloom; perhaps it was his wife's arms enfolding him close when he had left for the night drawing him back home; perhaps it was the madness rocking his wherry as blade counted against blade – but he began to show the mettle that won him his prize Doggett coat.

The fastest man on the Thames he was, and there was no coin that Walpole could throw that would find a better, worthier man.

The wherry moved like a whip, a magical withdrawal, and Walpole grabbed for it foolishly as Devlin and Albany pitched like drunkards.

'*Get them*!' Walpole roared to the black shapes now raising their muskets, even the swift waterman not faster than lead; but the soldiers took their time to aim at the blur whispering off into the thick fog.

The prince sank back to the soft form of Timms beneath him, scolding the secretary's cowardice and ordering their waterman to the chase. He could hear the clash of steel on the boat that arrowed away, men fighting aboard it, and wished himself upon it too. At least the music was heroic, growing louder and bolder all the time. The stench of brimstone was surely not in his imagination but somehow linked to the green glow looming heavier every moment.

Devlin and Albany. No room for honour. No knights across a battlefield. On his first day back in London Devlin had seen dogs fighting over a horse's pizzle. Themselves now. Heads rutting, kicks and punches, brows clashing. First the hilts and guards of their swords and now their fists and Devlin's stitches were rent open. Albany had his dagger stabbing; Devlin swept it away every time but it would find its mark.

Devlin's fist was still wrapped around the cursed diamond. *Drop it. Release your hand and pull your own dagger. End it now.*

The diamond had only ever known blood. But if he died and the stone became theirs? Nothing gained. The dead wasted. If he took it with his dying body to the water they might lose it still.

Hold on. Keep standing. You've fought in gutters with less space.

Blood trickled down his back. Why does a man's body betray him when he needs it most? As if it is always seeking death? The blood ran warm, then cold in an instant.

When men fight to kill they fight like children. That with Trouin had been a fight of honour. It had rules that made sense even to those who watched it. This struggle was children brawling, and children fight for hate. But children do not fight with blades and they live to fight again. Devlin and Albany's breath clouded on each other's necks like lovers, the only sound they could hear.

Hold on, Devlin thought. Hold on to make Bill smile. For Trouin to hear the sound of the diamond falling.

'*Cap'n*!' Edwin ducked as he heard the slow firing of muskets muffled by the fog, but too high from the clumsy lobsters on the pitching water. But Albany stiffened at the whistling of lead over his head and Devlin needed nothing more than that.

He dropped the diamond at his feet and grabbed Albany's wrist and held him close where their swords would not matter.

Albany felt his wrist and dagger turned towards his waist-coat. Another hand controlled his will.

The last sound Albany heard was the musket volley chipping into the oak of the monster that had ploughed out of the fog behind him and then the small hiss of his liver bursting as his dagger was twisted against him, Devlin's fist driving deep and grinding as Albany had done to Dandon.

Albany clasped him like a brother, held his last breath wide-mouthed and stared pleadingly into Devlin's eyes. Devlin shoved him to the Thames. Gone. Gone as easily as the rest of them. Bags of bones and flesh like the sacks he dumped in the river for the butcher when he was a boy. Not one day had passed when those bags weighed less than him and he hated them still. The sweat was the same and he wiped his face and the moment had gone. But still work to do yet.

He stooped to pick up his glistening burden with a fist running with another's blood, covering it like a glove.

Then he looked up to his girl come to meet him.

The green smoke pouring off the cauldron on deck, the jigging scrape of Hugh Harris's fiddle, the beat of an army of cutlasses pounding the gunwale – a thousand throats it seemed to those who heard, the jeers daring even the Tower to try them.

Devlin turned to see where Walpole was, then nodded that all was well to Edwin now there was an empty space where Albany had sat.

The soldiers gaped at the ship that had broken out of the luminescent fog. The noise, the fury, the potential of swivel guns swinging to bear at them from the black ship, all proved too much to stand. A handful of men faced cannon and cannibals. The darkness would cover the treachery and shame of whichever one of them broke first, and Walpole heard their urgent retreat.

The prince rose. 'Good *God*!' but he could not help a grin as he looked up at the bow, veiled like a phantom but with just enough of her prow and bowsprit rising and falling over Devlin's shoulder to show them who she was; the eerie green cloud curling up the masts and clinging to the skeletal crosstrees.

The prince called to Walpole, who could not hear him above the crowing from the pirate ship. Ships began to awake at the clamour and the shots, different languages darting questions back and forth about the drum beats of fists of steel, the bells, the strange emerald smoke rising and mingling with the fog. But some whispered to their mates that they had seen and heard those 'vapours' before, and scuttled back to their hammocks.

Devlin stepped to Edwin who was shivering beneath his mask, his hands white on his oar. In front of them in the other boat stood three men, the one with the lamp shouting and cursing, begging the next. A shriek escaped from Timms as Albany's body bumped gruesomely against their boat.

'The diamond!' Walpole screamed, forgetting all propriety. 'I will double your money! I have your pardon! The boat rocked with his fury but steadied when Devlin raised his fist again and the ship suddenly ceased its drumming on the gunwales.

Silence. Only Edwin noticed the steady gentle tap by his feet and looked down at the spreading slick of black around the pirate's boots. He looked up at the face which showed no pain save for a single train of sweat running from Devlin's hair down his face.

Walpole remembered the prince and his pistols. 'Your Highness! Shoot him down!'

George flopped down next to Timms, put away his pistols and stared Walpole down. The minister had overplayed his cards. Walpole twisted back to the grinning pirate and did the only thing he could to snuff the man from his sight: he hurled his lantern at him with a grunt.

A splash and hiss in the water, a roar of laughter from the darkness of the ship, and Walpole sank back and waited. There would be a speech. If pirates delivered speeches at the gallows there would surely be one now.

Devlin's wound had torn. He was weakening but would not let them see him fall. He swept his arm back, looking once to see all their eyes upon him.

'I brought you your stone.'

He threw it arcing over their heads, as if trying to send it back to the stars, and the first great diamond of the world dissolved into the fog forever. Walpole's gaze followed it hopelessly, and he did not see Edwin pull Devlin up from where he had collapsed. No-one would ever be able to swear that they heard the Regent hit the water.

At almost three in the morning, Saturday September seventh 1720, London – the financial and governmental centre of the entire kingdom – suddenly was nothing more than a house of straw. Its faith had been placed not in its people but in paper, in ephemeral 'things'. Things that even the ignorant fish of the Thames nibbled at once, twice, then discarded as just a stone.

The soldiers rowed to the minister's boat once the pirate

ship slowly began to turn. Two of them dragged up Albany's corpse into their boat, if only because he prevented them getting in closer as he bobbed and buffeted between. An eighty-five guinea Dutch sword was still clasped in his fist, but only for a moment, as his rescuers winked at each other.

The captain vowed to Walpole that they would hunt down the waterman who had aided the pirate and had disappeared into the fog once the pirate had left. Walpole did not listen. The pirate ship was being warped round by her boats. She moved reluctantly, as if she still had unfinished business and her seams groaned in her unwillingness to turn away.

Walpole sat back with the prince. Not a word was worth uttering. The music lilted once more from the ship, jollier now and further galling the ministerial blood. He lowered his head until the chortle of the prince lifted it back up.

George whistled. 'My! What bones that man has about him, so!'

The *Shadow* had come about, her escutcheon proudly showing her name in green and gold; no shame, no disguise. There was none here to frighten them.

Her side and mast lights were lit, bright halos burning away the shroud of fog. The twin stern lanterns had gasped into life and the black flag from the fluttering ensign-staff was busy shooing the moths away from their glass. The prince exclaimed in delight at the sight of a white skull set in a compass rose, two crossed pistols beneath.

And a pirate ship sailed down the Thames.

Hungry children do not sleep well and an excuse to wake need only be the merest sound, for there may be food when you wake from a straw bed four floors up in the eaves of a house of six families, where a square of glass does for a window that does not open, and the draught all about is more than enough to carry the sound of a distant fiddle.

The grime, moistened by spit, was quickly rubbed away from the pane of glass. A ship passes Limehouse down below, a square rigger you are sure despite the early morning fog and the ghostly green emanation trailing behind her.

With your ear closer you can hear men singing but the words are too far away to make out. Fist against fist to your eyes and you make your own spyglass to stare down at the ship and bring it closer. And your heart stops, and your eyes widen in the dark night.

You have seen them hung, your mother covering your eyes at the gibbets of tar and flesh in the streets; you have seen their bodies staked out against the tide, and you can even draw the word from the lurid headlines of discarded broadsheets if you try hard enough.

But this must be a dream and those stories belong to the wide blue sea and not your voyages of wooden swords; not to your squelching through the mud and stones of low tide and swearing that the green and white bits of glass you find there are really emeralds and diamonds. You have a paper box full of them beside your bed, guarded by a terrier pup.

But she might really be there. That black flag is real and bold, as large and fearless as you ever imagined it to be. And surely no dream could conjure the only words your ear, pressed to the glass, could hear before the ship sailed on forever from your small view onto another world. It was the line you sang all day long until a piece of bread came to finally shut your trap – but still you murmured it through your full mouth, and beat your feet against the table leg.

'*. . . and most wickedly I did, as I sailed.*'

Chapter Thirty-Six

A South Sea Ballad, 1720. Author unknown.

'Five hundred millions, notes and bonds, our stocks are
worth in value;
But neither lie in goods or lands or money let me tell ye.
Yet though our foreign trade is lost of mighty wealth
we vapour,
When all the riches that we boast consist in scraps
of paper.'

*D*awn, and Dandon awoke in less of a sweat. He was in
the Great Cabin, stretched on a locker beneath the
stern windows, clothed in shirt and breeches. He lifted his
head to the glass and thankfully saw open sea, although the
sky seemed just as wet and met it with a graveyard drabness.
Devlin watched him and used the scratch of his striker spark-
ing flame for his pipe to draw his friend's attention.

'We're coursing north,' he said when Dandon turned his
head. 'Taking the long way round. Around the coast and
Scotland. Respect to Trouin. I'm sure he'd kill me else.' He sat
bare-chested, his midriff wrapped in linen to hold tight his
wound. Someone had bandaged him and laudanum mellowed
his pain. Dandon saw how lean he was without hat and coat,
how ordinary; unclothed, the captain was somewhere else.

Devlin was just a man sunk in a chair enjoying a Sunday pipe, his black hair about his shoulders, only his scars glistening with exhaustion detailing his harder lot in life.

'Where are we going?' Dandon swung his feet to the floor – no small talk or greeting from either of them. The last week had exhausted everyone's breath, had even throttled Dandon's verbosity.

'Winter, so the Caribbee. Away from these men. Be free again.'

Dandon tried to remember how it had ended and realised he had not been a part of it. 'And the diamond?'

Devlin shifted in his seat, just to move his wound that burned if kept still. 'That's all gone.' He drew long on his pipe. 'It was Albany who did for you.' The cold look on him that Dandon feared would become permanent crept in. 'That's all done as well.'

Dandon wiped his forehead. 'Did many . . . die?'

Devlin blew out a wraith of smoke. 'Only those who needed.' He saw the concern. 'What ails, Dandon?'

'Nothing, my friend. It is only that of late – for lack of a confessor – I have worried about your soul. I concern myself that it would be a pitiful fate for the world if you became as black of heart as some of your peers.' He checked the face for recrimination or for the rakish grin that at least belonged to a hero in one of Cervantes' romances; for that was who he imagined his friend to be.

Devlin dragged on his pipe. 'I'll take the world as it finds me. Treat men as they treat me. That's all I need. And what do you want, Dandon?'

Dandon tried to stand but his own wound held him down. 'I want to sleep peacefully. I want to owe no man and I want to drink and eat what I want. Take love where I will and laugh more than I should be expected to weep.'

'No hearth?' Devlin asked. 'No home and children?'

Dandon swayed himself slowly upright, his eye on the hitches of rope that held the amber and brown bottles. Their pull was stronger than his pain. 'Oh, I'm sure the Lord has his hands full with those souls. The Devil has us and appreciates us more I'm sure. And now – in light of what we have done – where do we stand?'

Devlin stood to join him, and picked a spiced rum for noon. 'No pardon. No letter. The whole of the Earth against us.' He picked up a clay cup for each of them and poured deep. Both men placed a palm to their wounds and grimaced like arthritic old men.

Dandon tapped his cup against his captain's. 'Aye, as ever it shall be! None to stop us, all to fear us!'

'But never back to England,' Devlin tapped the cups again. 'I've known whores care less about coin.'

Leicester House, the evening of Sunday eighth. A circle of men around a table, the same table as before when first the pirate and the diamond were tasked, and only two absent: the aforementioned rogue and Albany Holmes, the one sent to chaperone the devil.

James Stanhope, Charles Townshend, Robert Walpole. Secretaries of State, Chief Ministers, Lords of the Treasury, muttered into their chests and wine like the husbands of unfaithful wives. Bitter and hurt, angered and embarrassed, all the more motive to sink a whole case of Medoc.

Only the prince, dressed for the opera and not the funeral that his companions seemed late returned from, showed any signs of *c'est la vie*. He smoked contentedly and watched each man's vehemence flush his cheeks like a slap. Donating his wine was a small price for such amusement.

'And what now, Robert?' Stanhope hissed. 'The Company is lost. It is only days before the share falls further!'

'The meeting was good enough, James,' Walpole filled his glass. 'Forestalled. We must convene the Commons. Have the Bank promise to shore up the Company's shortfalls.'

Townshend slammed the table. '*Again*? Brother, the people are not that naïve, the Bank is not that naïve!'

Walpole snarled back. 'The people will do what I say is best for them! They would have the directors' heads if we do not assure something! We will make promise to secure funds from those who have profited and run! That will quiet them!'

Townshend huffed and crossed his arms. 'The whole country owes! I have coachmen who dreamed to have their own coachman! The Company gave credit to those who could not afford and who will still be paying in their graves for a debt that has a negative value! It does not take a doctor to detect the madness!'

Walpole softened his voice, as if bribing children with honey. 'Gentlemen. We are removing ourselves from the point with wasteful extremes. What is done is done. We should be grateful that those of us privy enough to the Company's fate sold our stock at its highest.'

The prince interrupted with a haze of blue smoke. 'Ah! Sold to some poor wretch who is now blowing his brains out no doubt!'

Walpole bowed, smiling all the way to his canines. 'I hope not, Your Highness. Nevertheless, we will swear to extract every dishonest farthing from every stock-jobber and gold-smith. I will not have their bodies swinging in the streets.'

'Oh, no,' The prince leaned back. 'You Englishmen, we say, are like starlings around a barn. You shoot at them and they fly away only to return to the same spot a moment later. You will find that the public will rely on you to save them, only to shoot at them later on, never going for the farmer and his gun or for a different spot.'

Walpole did not smile this time. 'Your Highness has a most eloquent mind.'

Townshend took off his wig, threw it to the table like a dead rabbit, grabbed the carafe and poured only for himself.

'Enough of this!' He almost ate his glass. 'It is the pirate who has damned us! The diamond could have shown the Company had promise! He has cost all! Where is *his* head? The goldsmiths can wait!'

Walpole hated him from across the table; his sister's choice of husband still baffled him. 'Do not suppose, brother, that any thought will distract me from that particular personage.'

The prince crossed his legs and breathed out another cloud of Brazilian smoke. 'And what, pray, will you do about the beast? He is gone like a Jew with the philosopher's stone. His task immaculately completed, even if the ending is sour.' He leaned forward. 'He beat you all. Robbed you like infants. It would be a splendid anecdote should I be vain to use it and able to remove my own complicity.'

Walpole pushed himself up in his chair. 'The man in question is already an enemy to all mankind, as His Majesty declared of them all. Those pirates that did not take the amnesty afforded to them by Act have almost been wiped from the earth.' He reached to drag back the carafe from Townshend, poured to the brim of his glass and looked deep into the blood-like liquid.

'There will be no satisfaction in the course of the coming months. We will find some solace if we can tar the corpse of . . .' his throat caught on the name, stifling a chill that would take a good bed and hot lemon to dispel his hour on the river.

'I will tar the corpse of that man. I will give it one hour of every day to find him and bring him to me.'

Townshend scoffed with a snort. '*Find him*? For we will have his address!'

'I may not have that, brother, but I know men.'

The prince's nose sniffed a fox. 'You know where he is?'

'When incarcerated the pirate gave a name. Not his own. Secretary Timms thought it merely prudent but I supposed it to be much more. It meant something to the man. A name more than just a name. It took only one afternoon to find what it meant.'

Townshend dropped his air of parody. 'What name? He has an enemy? A man who will betray him?'

Walpole drummed his fingers on the table. 'An ex-officer of His Majesty's navy who may own more culpability than even he supposes. He found Devlin twice before and I'm sure hides an immeasurable desire to do so again. The pirate was once his servant. He now hides his shame in the colonies but he was most able in his day. He had a good record, too – at least until his servant turned against the world.'

The prince giggled at the conspiracy and held his fingers to his mouth to cover his delight. 'Oh, say you have something against this man! That he will charge across oceans to have his revenge! That he will die for his honour!'

Walpole blushed. 'Something in that manner, Your Highness. It will cost us naught at least save a ship and some men I am sure.'

Townshend sat straighter. 'How long will this take? It took months to find the pirate before?'

'Not so long, brother, I assure you. Their world shrinks every day. And, once I have the right man, it will no longer exist at all.'

Epilogue

Boston. The Province of Massachusetts Bay.
January 1721.

From Long Wharf, where the countless brimful ships laden with oxen, wood, fish and furs titled Boston as the trading capital of New England, it is a stroll along King Street to Merchant's Row where the finest importers and chandlers sell from proper shop-fronts to the citizens of God's own city on the hill.

Dominating the row at its end is the wooden triangular warehouse where the Dutch India Company smuggles and sells tea for a third less than the British India and furnishes parcels of fine negroes in the summer.

Initially starting in trade as a sea chandler for rope and instruments to pick oakum or chart the stars, John Coxon had now passed into the purveying of general goods as the needs of his customers demanded. So it was that on a freezing January morning, former Post-Captain John Coxon RN helped Mrs Keyne decide between a blue or green toile roll for a spring dress.

'I don't know, Mr Coxon. I think I should prefer something in Madder Red if that was available?'

Coxon shoved back the green roll to its rack. 'I have nothing in Madder, Mrs Keyne. I have what I have.'

Mrs Keyne was no matriarch with extravagant silk and

bustle. She was of puritan stock through and through. A bonnet for modesty; black wool dress and Irish linen. A spring fancy was an important determination. She smiled gently. She liked John Coxon. He had good parson manners. A former sea-captain by rumour and gait but kept himself to himself – more's the pity, for those families seeking a match that a striking lean gentleman in his forties would make for a good daughter. After all, there was certainly something of a lonely aspect about a man who spent his walks by the wharves, wistfully staring out to sea. Perhaps a tragedy there, a lost love. How wonderful that would be.

Mrs Keyne lowered her chin coyly. John Coxon was no simple shopkeeper. No apron, always smartly pressed in sombre cloth, but a man of means and guile she was sure, an experienced intelligence behind his eyes. 'What about some other fabric, Mr Coxon? Something that might have only just come in and you haven't had time to put out yet?'

Coxon pushed back the blue roll as well. 'Madam?'

Mrs Keyne looked over her shoulder at the empty shop. 'Maybe some "pirate" cotton, Mr Coxon? Just a few yards?'

Coxon's lips thinned. 'Indian cotton is illegal, Mrs Keyne. The crown wishes we support domestic textiles.'

'Oh, I know, but I hear it shall be grown here soon enough and I have heard that there is trade of it along the post-road aways. Pirates do so love the Carolinas, don't you know? And I'm sure I have seen some ladies hereabout with a dress or two, haven't I?'

The bell rang above the door. Two gentlemen, heads low, shut back the door quietly and began to browse: they wore long black coats and white perukes under sharp dark tricornes. Coxon checked them once then looked back to the diminutive lady who wished to trade with pirates.

'Not from my stock, Mrs Keyne. I'll have no truck with pirates.' He looked up as across the room one of the gentlemen began to toy with his brass scales. He picked up a price-list and handed it to Mrs Keyne. 'If you'll observe I have a fair bill for silk and calico if the toile is not of service. I'll allow you a few moments to peruse whilst I serve these two gentlemen.' He bowed and moved his way around the counter, his approach not turning the backs of the two black stripes of men.

'Can I assist, Gentlemen?'

They swivelled round. 'Captain Coxon?' the taller of them questioned, his face expecting no denial. Mrs Keyne looked back at them demurely over her shoulder.

'I am,' Coxon did not even blink. 'Who might you be to know me?'

A chin dipped respectfully. 'We are from the Navy Board. Mr Duke and Mr King. We should like a private word.' A smiling eye to Mrs Keyne.

Coxon spun on his heel but Mrs Keyne was already leaving, excusing herself with the list which she promised to return tomorrow once she had made up her mind and told everybody she knew of what she had just seen. Coxon locked the door behind her.

'Mr *Duke* and Mr *King*? Is that what passes for imagination at the Board these days?'

The taller, Mr King, walked to the rear as he spoke, appraising the store, nodding in admiration. 'You have done well, Captain Coxon. A fine business I'm sure. Impressive for a pension of say . . . thirty, forty pounds a year?'

Mr Duke agreed. 'Started cheap no doubt. Worked your way up. Like the old days.'

Coxon looked from one to the other. King's Letter boys. Officers at no more than sixteen, volunteered from families of better quality. Earls' and knights' offspring not a rector's son like himself, shipped with an apple and a bible. Their kind was always envious of those who had earned their captaincy the hard way and, despite their purse, they would have to wait for men like him to die.

So, then, they should remember their place and not waste a captain's time, however it was he had begun and ended.

'Your business, Gentlemen? For any longer of your talk will start to impede on mine.'

'You left New Providence almost two years ago now, Captain. Gave up your commission.'

'I have papers to prove, if that is what you query.'

Mr King tapped at some crock jars, then left his study of the shelves. 'No, no. That is all well. But your king would like for you to consider a few months' service again.'

Coxon felt himself relax, unaware that he had been tense. 'I am retired, sirs. I was well convinced I was never to make admiral I assure you.' He went back behind his counter where his raised stage put him above them both. 'You may thank His Majesty for me but I should like to decline.'

Mr King smiled sympathetically. 'Tell me, John, how much coin does it take to purchase and set up such a shop? Where would you suppose a fellow gets enough gold . . . French gold perhaps, to buy a building outright as even the most briefest enquiries can discover?'

Coxon blinked.

In 1717 the pirate Devlin had stolen a chest of King Louis's gold. Snatched it from French and English guard – from Coxon's guard. Stolen from an unnamed island. *The* Island, as it had come to be known in his memory. A year later and the chest had turned up on New Providence, a pirate Bahama island where Devlin had left what remained, the dregs of the chest, with a young whore who died before he could return to collect it. She had bequeathed it to Coxon, the only one on Providence who had been on The Island, who had been there at its taking. He had buried it with her, knowing the pirate would be back, and would find Coxon waiting. That had been a long story and Devlin had bested them all. But he did not get the chest. Coxon was not a dishonest man and was well versed in his father's scripture:

'*For nothing is secret that shall not be made manifest; neither any thing hid that shall not be known and come abroad.*'

He knew when he dug up the gold and gave up his commission to Governor Woodes Rogers that this day would come. But he had deserved some reward. He felt so little guilt that he hadn't even changed his name. He absently picked up a green coffee bean from its sack, rubbing it between calloused fingers.

'I always thought of a store in Boston . . .'

Mr Duke stepped forward and removed his hat in a flurry of powder. 'Understand, Captain, that our visit is not paid out of any intention to discredit you. Or to mark such an illustrious career with scandal.' That was a sneer. Coxon's ass of a dance at Devlin's craic had made him a laughing stock over port and cards, he was certain.

'We sincerely need your help. Your king has need of you. There is no crime other than your refusal, for which you will be judged. But should you refuse . . .'

Mr King sniffed the cinnamon and paper air of the shop, the smell of rope and brass. 'It is such a pretty store. You must be very happy here, John. It would be a pity to—'.

Coxon threw the coffee bean to King's buckled shoes and rushed down from his stage. 'Do not threaten me, *sir*! I fought French and Spanish gods-of-men before you scuffed your first knee! Your implication belittles us both!' He pointed to the black lines about his eyes. 'That is powder, sir! Earned and paid for! Do not suppose—'

'The pirate *Devlin*, Captain!' Mr Duke shouted down Coxon's tirade and Coxon stopped.

'You say what now?' A terrible recollection on his face.

'Oh, you know the name?' Duke put back on his hat. 'That is the matter that brings us here. Whatever else you may fear, I pray it is not him.'

Coxon stepped back. 'What of Devlin?'

King wiped a spot of Coxon's spittle from his lip. 'Patrick Devlin. Your former servant for several years. Irish traitor and once a sailor in the Marine Royale before you rescued him. Now a pirate captain. At least twice ducked away from you.'

'The second time he had a white flag. He gave the king the secret of porcelain.'

'Ah, yes. The price of which has dropped dramatically since. Thank you for that. I had several pieces that lost their value.'

Faces appeared at Coxon's door, tried to push their way in. Coxon gave the empathetic look of the shopkeeper when it is time for him to close for dinner and drew the curtain across their indignation. He turned back to the black coats. Always black coats. The pawns of government standing in front of bishops, kings, queens and knights.

'What about Devlin?'

Mr King seemed suddenly to age before his eyes. He crushed the bean beneath his heel. 'He has committed his last deceit against his country. You could not conceive the harm he has done.'

Coxon sniffed. 'I can imagine. If you were fool enough to trust him.'

King put his hands behind his back, spaced apart his feet.

Mr Duke stifled his amusement at the pose of a ham upon the stage.

'He must die, Captain. He will have no quarter, no card to pull from his sleeve, no purchase to buy his way out. Not even a noose. We are not interested. Just any death will satisfy, I promise. From the highest order, the *very* highest order, and you will have *carte blanche* to do whatever you deem necessary.'

Coxon too put his hands behind his back. The king himself was now standing on Coxon's quarterdeck. 'Are you sure? I take it that by your words you have already underestimated him once?'

'We were wrong not to engage those who knew him best. But I have not travelled for more than a month to indulge your vanity, John. Your presence I'm sure will intrigue him, draw him out. You know him best. Knew him first. I'm sure you would like to know him last.'

Coxon looked about his small world full of Mrs Keyneses and streets that never moved and horizons that never changed. He contemplated both men and they looked back at him like birds of prey. A strong dislike was already in the air about them. The small fire in the shop spat embers from its weak sea-coal and January crept in at every window, under every gap of wood. Coxon stamped on the glowing ashes dancing on his floor.

So cold. The Caribbean so warm. He waited one minute to stoke the fire and flick at its ash then turned and tossed the poker away without a care. The violent clang and peal of it as it bounced and danced across the wooden floor made the two young officers flinch like surprised deer.

Coxon grinned. 'If that can startle you, lads, we may have to rethink your passage into this.' He brushed the smut off his hands. 'I will need a week to set my affairs in order.'

Author's Note

✕

*D*iamonds. Whether a ring on your finger or the tool itself used to cut more of them from the earth, diamonds represent a portable power and wealth that has made the financial world turn since one man begged the ear of another and showed him these shining scrapings of the earth.

In the British Museum, after you've taken a breath at the beauty of the building outside and dropped a few pounds into those massive perspex drums, you must choose which of the hundreds of rooms to enter and survey the wonders of the world bequeathed to you.

In the 'Enlightenment' room, in a most inauspicious glass and wood case, you can see the replica of the Pitt diamond which features in this story and did indeed cost five thousand eighteenth-century pounds to create (approximate to £400,000 today). It is made of paste, which may make a modern reader scoff, although at the time paste diamonds were an artisan's craft almost of equal intricateness and value to the lapidary's art in cutting the 'real thing' – hence the price-tag. Interestingly enough, the diamond in the Louvre with the remaining French crown jewels is also a paste replica, as much as the one displayed beside it in the royal crown. The real diamond is locked safely away, mainly because the visitor may stand next to the display case, as opposed to straining for a distant glimpse of the Mona Lisa.

And it would be unwise to openly exhibit a diamond valued at between £40–50 million.

Today the Regent diamond is largely a forgotten wonder, except to aficionados. Diamonds like everything else have their fashions, and coloured diamonds have been the favour in the collector of the twentieth century – a trend that appears to be continuing into the twenty-first.

But there is something intrinsically romantic about these gems and I do not know a single one of the great diamonds of the world that does not have a string of tales attached to it that are so full of sorrow and drama that one couldn't imagine them more so.

But I did try.

As for the Pitt-Regent, it was indeed the 'First Diamond of the World' for almost two hundred years, when India was the place to find such stones and before the empires of the world began to exploit the African continent for raw materials instead of slaves.

The story of the Indian slave who gouged a hole in his leg to smuggle the diamond from the mine and buy his freedom is most likely true, as is the part in it of the sea-captain who hung himself in remorse. Also true is that Pitt never slept in the same bed twice and took to disguising himself until he was rid of the diamond; but after our story ends the diamond's adventures continued.

Without the modern connotations of the emotive phrase 'Blood Diamond', its archaic reference is to the death and bad luck that often seemed to plague the owners of great gems. In addition to the death of the slave who originally took the Regent from the mine, and the death of the captain who murdered him, the luck of some of the principal characters of the diamond's story was not good, either.

John Law, himself almost a victim of smallpox as a youth, watched his favourite son contract the disease shortly after negotiating the sale of the diamond to the French. His decision to remove his wife and family to one of his country estates at least saved his life. His luck, however, took a plunge after the fall of the French Bank Royale and the collapse of his American companies.

John Law died in poverty and alone (the worst word in any language) from pneumonia in a Venice hotel in 1729. Curiously, he had in his possession a brilliant cushion diamond which he had carried with him from France when he had fled the financial collapse. He had pawned the diamond many times but always redeemed it thanks to his skill in gambling, which floated him for his remaining years. Why he never sold the diamond is matter for his own unwritten memoirs. I had hoped that I might wrangle into my story that Law's diamond was the original Regent, but that seemed just a little too far-fetched. I recall from my researches that Law's smaller diamond turned up first in the Austrian crown jewels and later the Russian, Tzarist ones, where it remains today and has blood enough for its own story.

Law was pardoned for the crime of murder under the grace of Robert Walpole and after the collapse – and after our story ends – he initially ran to England. There he stayed for nine months until disgrace and shame forced him to hide in the more forgiving realms of Europe.

Philippe, the French regent, suffered his own tragedies once he had taken possession of the diamond. He lost his beloved daughter and unborn grandson, as recorded in my story, but also almost lost France. As for the hints in the story that he may have had an incestuous affair with his daughter and was thus the father of her unborn child – this is, horribly, almost considered true by contemporary accounts. We do not have the Duchess of Berry's or Philippe's confession, but the supposition among both courtiers and commoners was widespread enough.

Philippe died in the arms of his eighteen-year-old mistress – an exemplary demise for a libertine – shortly after the ascension to the throne of the boy king in 1723, after which the diamond officially became part of the crown jewels. Half a century later, Marie Antoinette wore it in the crown of a black velvet hat; and Napoleon carried it in the pommel of his imperial sword from 1812 until 1814 and his exile to Elba. I doubt anyone would disagree that those years did not bring him much luck. In short, seven of the owners of the gem before Napoleon met their deaths on the guillotine.

At first glance it would seem that Thomas 'Diamond' Pitt himself escaped any unusually bad luck concerning the diamond, unless of course one considers financial and social ruin after the 'South Sea Bubble' burst in London.

In the months after the South Sea collapse his son-in-law Lord Stanhope died, followed by his daughter Lucy, Stanhope's widow, in childbirth. His eldest son Robert, who smuggled the diamond from Madras to England in a hidden compartment in the heel of his shoe, passed in 1727. 'Diamond' Pitt himself died the year before.

His son Lord Londonderry, who features briefly in the story and who, with John Law, was a protagonist in selling the diamond, worked with Law consistently afterwards in trying to restore his family's fortune. He died in 1729, in the same month as John Law.

As for the South Sea Bubble, I had intended this financial cataclysm to hover in the background of the story and not to make it a linchpin. There have been many novels which have used the disaster as a catalyst and I didn't want it to be anything more than a minor 'character'. But I have to say that it was part of my intention to show how our present, disastrous financial circumstances have occurred again and again and will continue to do so (almost inevitably every hundred years) for as long as a few hundred men are in control of the world's finances.

Fortunately, as history also attests, such financial disasters often bring about a more stable political age of reason and constraint. Certainly Robert Walpole's rise to become Britain's first prime minister after the bubble led Britain into a new era when the country rose in prominence to dominate both France and Spain on the world stage, and where she developed her American colonies – if only to the point where independence became inevitable.

Today we are coming into an age of new governments throughout the world, with new outlooks and new ideals, as older ones are discredited and die out. Contradictorily, it is a dark age of enlightenment.

One of the most enjoyable aspects of my research was the escape from Newgate prison. Yes, there actually was a tunnel that led from the church to the prison, as inconceivable as that seems. It is now sealed off, although the door to it can still be seen in the church, as can the bell that used to be rung outside the condemned cells at Sunday midnight. I suppose the possibility of a tunnel beneath the Old Bailey would even today inspire escapes or terrorist notions – so just whisper about it if you can.

For those who may be further interested there is a pub on the corner opposite where the prison used to stand called the Viaduct Tavern. If it is quiet, and if you ask nicely, the Australian barman will take you down to the cells that still remain below. He might mistakenly inform you that they are a sample of Newgate's oldest. In the story Dandon catches his breath and looks up at the Giltspur Compter. These cells are in fact part of that gaol and not, as is often reported, Newgate. Still, if you can spend more than two minutes down there you're better than I am.

René Duguay-Trouin. There isn't a pirate fan in the world who does not know this name and I would hope that maritime enthusiasts of all nations hold him in equal regard. But the British tend to have a one-sided view when it comes to naval history so I'll assume most readers may be unaware of Trouin. You will correct that as soon as you close this book.

He is actually mentioned in both the previous Devlin books, but only in passing in order to lay stepping stones so that he could eventually make a personal appearance. I have only touched upon the man but I couldn't have let Devlin go across the channel without meeting him. I also wanted Trouin to illustrate the injustice of how, after the death of Louis XIV, the French regime returned to giving positions of power to those of high birth rather than ability.

Unable to revoke Trouin's royally-bestowed title, Philippe buried him under paperwork in Calais and even planned to ship him to the Indies as 'Council for Marines', thus removing Trouin entirely from his beloved France. Fortunately, Philippe died before he could commit such a crime against the admiral who had captured Rio de Janeiro – and over three hundred and twenty English and Dutch ships during the wars – for his king. Although he ended his life penniless, subjugated by nobles who did not acknowledge him or recognise their debt to the boy from St Malo, his legacy is that his name has graced more French warships than any other man in history, kings included.

Jonathan Wild, self-proclaimed Thief-Taker General. I've

just always wanted to give that bloke a hiding. By bringing Devlin into London when Wild was at the pinnacle of his career I managed to reach down the centuries and do just that. I couldn't kill him because I just can't seem to cross that line with actual characters, but as Devlin says, 'I think this one's time will come soon enough.'

There's one more thing.

I hope you may not even have noticed, but this book takes place mostly on land; there's not a palm tree or Caribbean island in sight. This was always my plan. Pirates can go anywhere, their world free to roam. And if the end of this book is anything to go by that world's about to get a lot bigger.

And you're invited.

Mark Keating, August 2011.